BLACKBERRY PIE

A HAP-PIE-LY EVER AFTER STORY

Katelyn Brawn

The Omnibus Publishing
Baltimore, MD

Interior Book Layout ©2015 BookDesignTemplates.com

Edited by and Cover Design by Wendy Dean, MAE, The Omnibus Publishing.

Blackberry Pie / Katelyn Brawn. -- 1st ed.

ISBN 978-0-0000000-0-0 / Library of Congress number

Contents

*To the woman who taught me to love myself
again and helped me save my own life.*

Thank you, Gina. This one's for you.

"You alone are enough. You have nothing to prove to anybody."

—Maya Angelou

The greatest gift my mother ever gave me was a sewing machine. She never cared much for material things, and it wasn't because she couldn't afford them. She used to tell me that experiences were worth more than physical objects could ever be. I spent the majority of my formative years staring at the stars on our backyard camping trips, making up funny names for each one. We'd often raid the lost and found at the YMCA and put on a fashion show in the locker room only for us. She spawned my love of fashion. I'm glad I have those memories from before I knew how bad things were.

"Rosie-Rose, we are not the kind of people who live inside their little boxes," she'd say after losing another job. Money was always on the tight side. She taught me how to mend and create my own clothes to make them last longer. From then on, my fingers stayed glued to the sewing machine. I lose myself and all sense of time in the clicking sound of the needle moving back and forth through fabrics. I

Click. Click. Click. The sound keeps pace with the bray of my heart.

Whether baking pies at Hap-PIE-ly Ever After Pie Shop or stitching together my clothes and sketching designs for them, it's easier to drown myself in hobbies than face the real world.

Harpersgrove has one place to buy fabrics, and it's not a great selection because it's such a small town. But Mrs. Mullaney, the lovely owner of Sew Cute, always does an impressive job of accommodating what I need. She provided once more when I walked in yesterday to buy fabric for a new, albeit unfortunate, dress I needed to make for myself. The stiff chill from the early morning air outside did nothing to touch the feeling indoors. It was as if the joy evaporated out of every room I entered.

The jingle bells, which Mrs. Mullaney wouldn't take down until at least the summer, sang their merry song inside the shop. I resented their happiness. Mrs. Mullaney shuffled from the back in her custom orthotic tennis shoes and slightly hunched stature. Her glasses hung around her neck by a pearl chain, and wisps of white hair levitated in curls off her head as if by magic. When she saw me, the immediate head tilt that stalked me at every personal interaction since I found out what happened painted her face. News travels too fast in a small town.

"Hello, sweet girl, how are you holding up?" she asked as she hurried forward to grasp my arm. It's an impulse I don't understand, this need to touch someone in moments of sadness. I wanted a bubble.

I'm not in a chatty mood, but I forced a smile to my lips. "I'm fine, Mrs. M. I need to make a dress."

She placed her hand under my arm like her frail little body was somehow going to brace me. "Of course, dear, right this way," she said as we shuffled toward my usual wall of black cloth. I was a one-trick pony for the most part. Slutty Sandy from the end of *Grease* was my motif. Lots of black-on-black with a side of black. But that's not what caught my eye. Today wasn't a day for normal. Finally wiggling my way out of Mrs. Mullaney's hands, I spotted a dark purple satin. I scooped it up and let my fingers wander the slippery fabric.

"What color is this?" I mumbled absently, losing myself in the violet hue. Mrs. Mullaney scrambled for her clipboard.

"Ah, here it is," she began, her unpolished nail running down the lines on her paper. "It's called Blackberry."

A scoff rippled through me as I hugged the material against my chest. How fitting. The fruit of Mom's favorite dessert and mine. And it's not black. She'd like that. It made sense to wear something outside of what I usually wear. It's a dress for an event that is so alien that it doesn't make sense. My mother's funeral was something I always knew I'd attend earlier than any of my friends. But that didn't prepare me for how soon it would come.

I don't sleep much. It's not a secret, and everyone knows that about me. My brain can't turn off, and I get restless. It's always been like that, but it got a lot worse after my mom left me with my three great-aunts six years ago. Now, I can't even stay in bed when the insomnia hits. I have to get up and move—do things. There are rare occasions, though, where human biology takes over, and I sleep through the night. It's like the Loch Ness monster; you hear it exists, but no one believes it. I had one of those sleeps the night she died. It's like she knew. In my dream, I was drifting on top of black water. My ears were submerged, and the *glug, glug, glug* of the ripples worked its hypnotic dance and lulled me deeper and deeper until the sound turned to a scream.

I awoke to Meredith's hand on my shoulder, gently shaking me. "No," I groaned, fuzzy from sleep. I squish my face back into my pillow. The remains of my black mascara and red lipstick smearing everywhere. In my haze, I couldn't wholly process that Aunts Meredith, Norah, and Shawna were standing around my bed like the witches from *Macbeth*.

Something wicked this way comes, indeed.

After her parents died in a car accident, my mom came to live with her aunts, two divorced and one widowed, when she was thirteen, She left me with them when I was eleven after she decided to run away and ruin her own life—a freaking Peters tradition of abandonment. I squinted against the nonexistent light as I sat up in my bed. Meredith, with her single long sleeping braid, sat on my mattress while Shawna paced uncomfortably in the corner. Norah, by far the least warm and fuzzy of the sisters, kept the door frame up, ready for a quick escape. My fingernails scratch against my scalp, and I yawn.

"You people know how little I sleep. Someone better be dead."

Norah flips the light switch on, and my eyes burn from the harsh light. "Sit up and listen," she mutters, her voice flat as she fiddles with the pedometer on her wrist.

I turn my attention to Meredith, who is openly my favorite of the aunts. Norah is in my business too much, and often, I need a reminder that Shawna even exists. Meredith is the perfect balance.

"Mere," I begin, the moniker of "Aunt" before their names never did anything for me. "What's going on?" The acidic feeling of dread rises in my throat as I wonder if I really want to know.

Meredith braces her hand on the other side of my outstretched legs, and I know this is the closest she'll come to holding me without my permission. "Rose, I'm sorry to have to tell you this—," she trails off into nothing, and somewhere deep down, I know.

"Is she hurt? In the hospital? Did she get arrested? What is it this time?" I ask. It's getting near impossible to swallow against that feeling in my throat. I need her to come out with it. The only thing I can think of is that my mother got herself into some kind of trouble that my aunts were going to have to bail her out of—again.

Meredith looks back to her sisters for help. Shawna, quiet, non-confrontational, meek Shawna, steps forward to take over.

"Honey, I'm sorry, but your mother overdosed early this evening. They couldn't bring her back this time."

A high-pitched hum zaps between my ears as the gears in my head grind to a piercing halt. "I don't understand," I hear myself say, although I don't recall giving my brain the command to form the words.

"Yes, you do," I hear Norah murmur, but she makes no move away from the door.

My heart started to pound against my ribs as I tried to find the trick. I wait for them to start laughing and tell me it's a sick joke, but they don't. I realize how stupid I'm being. This news is not a surprise.

My mom started using drugs when I was still in diapers. I knew she was going to die. It's incredible, though, how knowing something will happen does nothing to dampen the effects when it does. I know that her substance use disorder started with alcohol and somehow it evolved into heroin.

The details were not ones anyone shared with a child. We lived with my aunts, and it's not like there were a lot of opportunities for direct exposure. It wasn't until I was eleven that I saw her do it. The memory burned itself on my brain like a scar. It was before I completely gave up on sleep. The aunts were out that night. We were the only two in the house, which almost never occurred. They didn't trust her enough for that to happen often. I wandered out of the bedroom I shared with her, sleepy-eyed and wondering where she was.

She was sitting on the scratchy couch, her feet tucked under her, clad only in a white tank top and black underwear. Her messy blonde hair was pulled up on her head, and she didn't look like herself. A dizzy haze swam in her eyes, her breathing labored. I would think she was about to fall over. Then I noticed the belt strapped tight around her upper arm. It was a weird fashion choice, especially when she wasn't wearing any other clothes, but my mom was the coolest. I thought that she must have been on the cutting edge of something new.

Then, she centered on me. I watched her pupils grow and shrink like her eyes couldn't quite make me out. "There's my beauty," she murmured, her teeth never separating as she spoke.

Her little pink tongue jutted out of her mouth to lick across her dry, chapped lips. She opened her arm, the one without the belt, to me. Cautiously, I approached her, winding a long tendril of my blonde hair through my fingers. I curled up into her side, laying my hand flat against her thigh. My skin is much darker than hers, almost coppery, always sun-kissed, while Mama was as white as snow. I sometimes wonder if I wear powder-white makeup because of her complexion. I wanted to look more like her.

"Can't sleep, baby?" she asked, reaching for something on the coffee table. I shook my head against her chest, my eyes already feeling heavier against her body. It always amazed me how she could be so skinny yet warm. She took a deep breath, and my eyes settled on what she'd picked up. It was a needle, like the kind you'd get at the doctor. I sank back into the couch as far as I could. I hated shots. Mama wasn't a doctor. Why did she have the needle? The thick brown liquid inside looked like some kind of potion out of *Harry Potter*. Something was wrong.

She kept me tucked into her, my arms wrapped around her tiny waist like she was my last and only lifeline. She pulled the belt tighter around her arm, securing the leather between her teeth to keep it tight. Angry blue and purple veins screamed against her translucent skin. I swore they would pop out at any moment.

For a second, I thought she forgot about me. Her arm holding the needle was still wrapped tightly around my shoulders, hugging me to her side. I squeezed my eyes shut when the needle went in, like when I got my shots. I could never look. When it was over, her whole body relaxed. She practically oozed into the seat. A breath released from her lips like she'd been underwater for too long.

"Rosie girl," she said absently, the words hissing from her lips. "I can't sleep either." She held up the used syringe, and I gulped against the angry acid feeling at the back of my throat.

"One stick of the needle, and you sleep a hundred years."

Then, her body got stiff, and I forgot how to breathe. Her eyes panned down to me, shame flooding them as she drank me in. Her eyes widened as we stared at each other for moments too long. She uncurled me from her arms, leaning forward, elbows on her knees, and mumbled, "Go to bed, Rosaline."

That was the moment—the moment it all changed.

CHAPTER TWO

Now I sit at my seafoam sewing machine, foot pressing back and forth against the pedal on the floor. I only had black thread, and it didn't precisely match the deep purple of this fabric. No one could see the difference unless they stuck their face directly in the seams, but that didn't stop me from muttering unhappily. I should rip it all out, find the purple thread, and start over. This dress has to be perfect. I can't accept anything less.

As I swivel the project to turn under the arm of the machine, the needle catches the pad of my thumb. "Biscuits!" I screech, my thumb flying into my mouth, sucking away the pain. I pull my hand away and watch the little bubble of blood pucker up over the surface of my angry pink skin. My mother's voice drifts through my brain, "One stick of the needle, and you sleep a hundred years."

Rage bubbles up from the pit of my stomach and sits heavy like a stone where my heart should be. My mom may have lost her battle to the needle, but I'm not her. I'll stay awake instead.

"That's a pretty color," I hear from behind me, and I don't have to turn to find out it's Meredith.

Of my three aunts, she is the only one who doesn't cause the hairs on my neck to stand on end when she speaks. When Norah talks, I know I'm bound to get yelled at or lectured. With Shawna, tears are always on the way. But Meredith talks to me.

The bleeding on my thumb stops before I start sewing again. I prefer the sound of silence. The squeaking of the sewing machine pedal lends itself well to that.

"Thanks," I murmur as I stitch. Usually, I don't mind talking to Meredith. But right now, I can't take another person asking if I'm okay. That word has lost all meaning anyway.

"I like that you're not going with black. I think she would have liked that," she says, and I can tell she has made no move to enter my room without my permission. Meredith has always been good with boundaries.

"You stalking the doorway all night, or are you coming in?"

My sewing machine sits in the corner of my bedroom, facing a window so I can always see outside. The floor shifts and creaks under her weight when she walks to sit on my bed, across from me. I can see her out of the far corner of my eye. Her dark hair twists on top of her head like a giant cinnamon bun, frizzy curls popping up around her face. She pulls her black cardigan tight around her plump little body and rubs her eyes with her free hand. The dark circles betray how fatigued she is. I keep sewing.

"Okay," she says, letting out a long breath.

Oh, please, Mere, please don't check in with me.

We don't have that kind of guardian/dependent relationship. I stop pedaling, but can't bring myself to look over at her. My finger runs along the edge of the blackberry fabric and the lacy trim I've sewn to the bottom of the material.

Meredith continues, not waiting for my full attention. "We decided it's best to have one service tomorrow, only a funeral. We don't want to give this community's less than gracious members any opportunity to gawk at Holly like she's a sideshow attraction."

My eyes close, and a flutter rushes through my body at the sound of my mother's first name. I prefer to think of her in a more abstract sense. "My mom" can be a memory, like a book or movie character. Holly is a person—was a person.

"We bought a plot in the cemetery near your grandparents. Gets a lot of sun."

The awkwardness pools thickly in the air to the point that it's suffocating. I go back to sewing. I need to do something with my hands, but Meredith keeps talking.

"We'd like you to say something at the service."

That stops me dead in my tracks. I push the dress onto my sewing table and swivel in my black desk chair to face Meredith. My blonde eyebrows arch up to my hairline as I balance my elbows on my knees. I feel like a football player ready to hit the person across from me.

"You'd like me to say something about what?" I squeak, ready for a fight. I don't belong among the people. There's a reason why they stuck me in the kitchen at my job: to make things instead of serving customers. I'm short, curt, and sometimes rude. I live in a small town where my mom was a teen parent with no father for her child.

On top of that, she was a drug addict. On top of that, she gave me up to her aunts before disappearing. Meredith only wants the funeral and no viewing to keep my mom from being the center of anyone's cruel attention. News flash: I don't want that for me either.

Meredith's head cocks to the side, and that look of pity that I've wanted to avoid crosses her face. I don't need that look from anyone, least of all from someone in this situation with me. "Rosie," she begins, settling forward with her hands on her knees. Our faces are only a few inches apart. I feel like I should pull away, but I don't. I will not fall for her game of chicken. "Rosie, she's your mom."

"That's debatable," I murmur back through a clenched jaw. The woman did surrender me, signing over all her parental rights. Legally, she's not my mom; she's someone I'm biologically related to. That's it. It's not like I've seen her or spoken to her in the last six years. I wouldn't have anything to say.

Meredith's expression never changes. "It's not, actually," she says, her fingers drumming against her knees. "Holly had many problems, Rose, but she loved you."

"Can you stop calling her that?" I snap, my eyes fixating on a point in the carpet where I'd melted a crayon with Norah's lighter when I was a kid. There's still a faint shade of purple that remains.

"Your mother had a lot of problems. I will not deny that for one second, but she's your mother. You're her only child; besides the three of us, she's your only family. It would be best for you to be the one to say something."

My eyes bug wide as a metallic taste swims through my mouth, and panic floods my body. "I'm sorry, did you say that you want me to give the eulogy? Have we met?"

She softly smiles as she pushes to her feet, then leans forward and kisses me on the head. She doesn't pull away immediately, her warm lips lingering in my hair.

"Whatever you say will be the right thing. Think it over. You'll figure it out." She leaves the room casually, like she didn't ruin my life.

Public speaking is not a part of what makes me Rosaline May Peters. I loathe speaking in front of large groups of people. Especially when those people will be gross and crying over a woman I'm supposed to know better than anyone but don't know at all. My mom chose not to be part of my life, and now I'm supposed to pretend like she was the center of it. How do I even do that?

My steps on the pedal become hurried as I rush through, finishing my dress. I want to be done with it and burn it as soon as the funeral is over. I hold the garment out in front of me, silky fabric running through my fingers. A simple scoop neckline with an A-line skirt, each lined with black lace against the dark purple, looks back at me. It's one of the better dresses I've made lately. I simultaneously love and hate it.

My brain wants to crumble it up, throw it in my trash can, then light it on fire. Luckily, my body opts to hang it up in my closet instead.

I flip off my light and lie flat on my back on the narrow twin bed. When my mom left, Shawna told me I could buy whatever color sheets and the bedspread I wanted. She took me to the store and picked up every pink and purple combination of flowers and butterflies, hoping for my approval. I remember moving past her, grabbing a plain black comforter and black sheet set, and throwing them in the cart. I've never seen her this defeated. I flex my fingers against the familiar softness, grayed by countless washes. I wish I could fold myself up and drift into a dreamless sleep. I wish I could drift, but I know I won't, and I can't. Sleep always eludes me, and tonight will be no different.

I sit up and huff, throwing my fists into the bed, the sound absorbed by the fluff. I pulled on a pair of black leggings and an oversized Brown sweatshirt that Bella gave me. She's going there in the fall. This genuine moment made me realize we were all only months from moving on. I've placed all my eggs in one school basket. The basket still hasn't sent me a reply. I throw my hair into a messy ponytail and shove my feet in red flats. Some part of me needs to remain. I catch a glimpse of myself in the mirror as I pass by before slowly doubling back, drinking myself in.

It looks like I have two black eyes the way my black eyeliner smudges under my lashes. My red lipstick smears onto my cheek, like after a vigorous round of kissing. I grab a makeup wipe from my little vanity and wipe away my mask. My skin is darker than the pale makeup I wear. It takes a lot of work to blend it to look natural against my bronzed complexion, but I don't care about hiding it now. With my face fresh and clean, I don't recognize the girl looking back at me. I could sit here and stare at this stranger until the sun rises, but I never spend time in the mirror outside of getting my makeup on. I swing my purse over my head and open my bedroom window.

I started sneaking out when I was twelve, after the insomnia took over. We live in a ranch-style home, making sneaking out easy. I felt like a badass preteen for leaving the house without the aunts' permission. Last year, I started using the front entrance because, really, who were we kidding? They knew I left the house often, and I knew they knew. But tonight, I'm aware that they're watching me. Everyone's eyes are on me, and I don't want to deal.

I consider hopping in the car to drive the two minutes to my destination, but the crispness of the air settles well in my lungs. It reminds me that I'm alive. Finally, I crest the top of the hill in the middle of town, and Hap-PIE-ly Ever After comes into view. I slide my key into the door of my true home and immediately feel the tension release between my shoulders. I'm fed up of pinched, uncomfortable faces and people tiptoeing around me. Inside the peace of the pie shop, I find silence and everything I need. Life comes to me and the restaurant when the lights come on. I take in the checkered floor, neon counter stools, ancient cash register, and displays ready for beautiful pies.

In the far corner of the room sits our owner's jukebox. She'd bought it for the first shop she'd opened and decided to leave it here. I fish around in my purse for as many quarters as I can find and load them into the slot. The other girls I work with groan when Beattie allows me to put an album on, knowing I'll go with something in the Broadway genre. Of course, they're right. The opening song of *Dear Evan Hansen* flows through the empty restaurant as I return to my kitchen.

The smell of flour, butter, and sugar wraps around me like a comforting hug once I'm inside. Two stainless steel work tables form an "L" at the corner to my right, lined with mismatched ceramic pie dishes and three large stand mixers. I make crust dough at an absurdly high level. To the left are my three rows of ovens. I can smell the baked goodness even in my mind. In the back are my two industrial refrigerators, and next to them is my walk-in pantry.

I recall when I arrived for my interview last year. The aunts insisted I needed a job. Norah said it wasn't healthy for a girl my age to hold up in her room all day making clothes. She seemed to think it was a road to serial killing—a logical connection for sure.

I considered applying for a job at Rust's Drugstore. It wouldn't be a problem since my friend Goldie's family owned it. When I approached Goldie about it, she said, "I can ask my grandfather if you want, but what about that new place across the street?" The week before, there was a grand unveiling only worthy of a small town like Harpersgrove. "I'm thinking about applying over there."

I remember how my face scrunched up at the idea of working in food service. That involved people, and I didn't do well with people. Stocking shelves under the cover of darkness seemed much more my style. But I let Goldie convince me to go in for an interview anyway. When I sat down with Beattie, the fearless leader of our small shop, all knowledge of anything related to food and being human seemed to fall from my brain. People who looked like Beattie didn't live in Harpersgrove. From her unkempt red curls to her nose ring and casual clothes on a workday, I had never seen anyone like her. At least not since my mother left town. I wanted to be around her more than I wanted my next breath.

She crossed her legs at the knee and swiveled on her neon-colored stool toward me, tapping her pen on my application. "All right, Rosaline," she began. I bit my tongue hard enough to draw blood to stop my face from contorting into twisted disgust. My name is stupid. "Tell me about yourself."

I hadn't expected it to start with such a loaded question. I pushed and pulled on the sleeves of my sweater, fidgety and anything but cool.

"Well, I'm Rosie. I, um, I make clothes." It was like being an alien incapable of forming thoughts.

Beattie, even then, was completely level-headed and kind. She didn't look at me like I was stupid or slow; she simply nodded. "Okay, and you want to be a waitress here?"

"Oh, God no!" My knee-jerk reaction came out before I could catch the words. My skin blanched under my white makeup—no time to backpedal.

A smirk crept to the corners of her mouth as her glasses fell down the bridge of her nose, her eyes peering over their rims. She laid the pen down and squared her shoulders to me. "Well, that is what you're here to interview for, right?"

From my silence and blank stare, I assumed she realized the core of the problem: I do not do people well. She pushed her glasses up into her hair, drumming the fingers of her other hand against her chin.

"Hmm," she hummed as I became all too aware of the makeup beading in sweat on my upper lip. "Do you have baking experience?"

Steeped in my lies about knowing how to bake, I stood over an assortment of sugars, flour, fruits, and sweets with a cold chill hovering over my body. How did one make a pie crust? I knew I could pull out the computer in my pocket and look up a recipe, but my brain was slower that day.

I searched my memories for any baking-related information, but my mom was not known for her cooking skills, except for one thing. It wasn't a pie, but rather a pie adjacent. Hopefully, it would do.

My mom had this thing about blackberries. She said they were harder to bake into desserts because of the seeds, but that didn't mean we should ignore them. "Blueberries and cherries can't get all the attention, Rosie Rose," she used to say to me. "The difficult ones deserve the spotlight, too." Together, we would make one, and only one, dessert—blackberry cobbler.

It took me longer than it should. An experienced baker would whip it out in minutes, but I second-guessed every measurement I made. I melted things and stirred others. I added sugar, flour, and butter to various bowls and dishes. I guessed the oven temperature, threw my concoction into the heat, and hoped for the best.

It ended up being a complete and total disaster. It was somehow burned and undercooked, too sweet and too salty, and contained more flour than needed in seven cobblers. It was such a mess that I assumed Beattie would chase me out with a torch or pitchfork, but she didn't. She told me to arrive promptly back at eight o'clock that evening to start training me. It was the first example of Beattie knowing what I needed before I had any clue. She gave me the basics, and I figured out the rest along the way.

Now, I stand in the truest home I have ever had, staring at scattered ingredients, more lost than ever. I didn't want to make a pie for the first time since starting here. Another thing my mother could steal from me.

I take a deep breath and decide to do what I always do when I have a block. Whether baking, sewing, or anything else, I dance it out. I imagine I'm on the Broadway stage. I pick up a broom to use as a microphone as I jive to the crooning stylings of Ben Platt. I spin around on my heels and jump on the counter, stepping back and forth, swaying with the music.

I'd only do this because it's two o'clock in the morning, and I know no one can see me. I fell off the counter in shock and pure terror. When I flipped around to see a man standing outside the storefront window staring at me.

I jumped up as quickly as my legs would allow. I peek from behind the counter, thinking maybe I imagined it. No one in this town, other than me, is out past nine o'clock. Ever. But when my eyes crest the top of the counter, the guy is still outside, staring at me. For some reason, that enraged me.

"What the hell?!" I shouted, storming toward the window. "I could've broken my neck!"

I allow myself to take a comprehensive look at him. Tall and blonde, his hair curly and falling into his dark eyes. He wore jeans, a gray shirt, and a brown leather jacket. Very simple, a little rebellious, like me.

His brow furrows as he stares, amusement playing on his face.

"What are you doing?"

"What am I doing?" I shout. "What are you doing, stalking about in the middle of the night!"

A slight smile appears in the corner of his mouth. "Stalking about?"

I storm off back toward the kitchen and slide behind the wall that divides me from the rest of the shop. After a few moments, I check to see if the stranger is still there.

He is.

"What are you doing?" he asks again.

"Who are you?"

He shrugs and says, "I don't know if I want to divulge that information."

I stand up straight to see through the window.

"Why not?"

He smiles a little brighter. "Well, I'm not sure I want someone who jumps around psychotically to know my name or anything. Or was that supposed to be dancing?" He's making fun of me. I don't like it.

I narrow my eyes in his direction. "Go away," I say, slipping back down the other side to hide. It's an ostrich defense. Out of sight, out of mind.

I hear him laugh as he responds, "Good night, crazy girl."

I wait a few minutes before I stand back up, confident that he's gone. I rest my chin on the lip of the window and stare out into the outside darkness that he's abandoned. I don't know why, but a smile touches my face. It's nice, for once in these last few days, to have some-one look at me without seeing my mother.

It's nice to be *me*—Rosie.

The following day, I woke up with my arms at my sides, still dressed in yesterday's clothes. For the first time in many years, I want to return to sleep and stay in bed indefinitely. Today is a day I could miss, but I am okay with it. I can already hear the aunts down the hall in the kitchen getting ready. Norah will rush in any second and force me out of bed if I don't do it myself.

I drag my sad, heavy body into the shower and rinse the pain of yesterday away. The heat seeps deep into my bones, but I can't shake the chill. After I blow-dry my hair and pin it back in a low bun, I plop myself down at the vanity Norah made for my fifteenth birthday. She claimed she did it to stop me from scattering my makeup around the house, but I think she might like me.

My natural skin tone is eternally tan, the tan most women would kill for, yet I always hide it under my pale makeup. Dark circles surround my soft, brown eyes from my lack of sleep. My lips are pale pink, and my eyelashes are translucent against my lids. I lift my foundation brush to my cheek, but pause before it touches. I look back at my reflection, a naked face I never take the time to know. If Lifetime movies have taught me anything, today will be full of tears. I'm pretty sure my tear ducts welded shut when I was eleven, but better safe than sorry. No one likes to see a girl with streaming, streaky makeup down her face.

I pull on my black tights and new dark purple dress. The fit is perfect, of course. I've made enough dresses for myself that I don't need to try them on beforehand. I always hit my mark. It covers the purple rose tattoo on the inside of my left shoulder. I'll get plenty of stares and whispers already. I don't intend to add any extra fuel to the fire. The final cherry on the sundae is my red dance heels in a Mary Jane style. If there's one principle my mother stood for that I've carried over into my life, it's that a woman is not complete without a red pair of shoes.

I take one look back in the mirror before joining my family. Returning my gaze is a girl, equal parts friend and stranger. It makes sense considering how disjointed I feel. I grab a red rose barrette and stick it into my bun, relief running through me at the slightest familiar comfort.

My heels click down the hall while my brain registers far more voices than the three of my aunts in the kitchen. Voices I know well.

Lined up against the counter, sipping coffee and munching on pastries, stood Elle, Blanche, Nixie, Bella, Goldie, and Beattie. My Hap-PIE-ly Ever After family, the people that matter most. And on each of their feet, a pair of red shoes. From Elle's bow-tied red heels, Goldie's ballerina flats, and Blanche's bright red tennis shoes. Her cheeks pink up when she sees me. "I'm sorry. They're the only red shoes I own."

I shake my head, an unabashed grin stretching across my face. "Don't apologize," I begin, crossing the room to wrap my arms around her tall and slender frame. "It's perfect."

Beside us, I hear Nixie, in her classic sappy style, sniffling away, trying and failing to hold back tears. I uncurl myself from Blanche and pull the frizzy redhead I love. "Now, now," I begin, squeezing her to me. "We'll have none of that."

"I'm sorry, Rosie," Nixie whimpers as Goldie flashes her a death glare from across the group. Nixie tends to be overly emotional, but today, I envy it. I should be a puddle of tears, but I feel more like laughing than crying.

"I'm surprised you're all here. I assumed we'd see you at the church." The Peters family never had religious leanings. But in a small town, there aren't many other places to host a funeral.

Goldie, my greatest and oldest friend in all the world, shrugs her shoulders up to her ears. "We figured it was best to go in with you. People are assholes."

"Preach!" Norah exclaims, raising her mug in a toast. Norah may be going a little Irish with her coffee this morning. Not that I can blame her. I'd do it if I could get away with it.

It was easy to know what Goldie meant. My mother was the town's black sheep. It started when both her parents died, but at least then, people were on her side. That all changed when she had me. Even though she wasn't the only teen mom in town, Goldie's mom included, she was the one crucified. Her boyfriend's family moved him away as soon as she got pregnant, leaving her and the aunts all alone with me. It didn't take long after I was born for my mom to crack under the pressure. I don't think she ever got over her boyfriend leaving, and a daily reminder of me made it worse She did the only thing she could in her mind to forget. She slipped into a severe substance use disorder. It's not an excuse, and it doesn't make it okay.

That's why pulling information from the aunts was more complicated than pulling teeth. I could piece enough together to figure out something of the picture. Meredith always tells me that no one wakes up one day and decides to be an addict. That sticks with me. When I was little, I remember my mom holding on tightly to my hand as eyes cast our way and whispers began on all sides. I knew we were different, but I never thought different was bad until someone told me it was. I don't want them to whisper and stare at her now. She's suffered enough.

I sit next to Goldie's boyfriend, Dubuque, dressed in a black suit with a white shirt and no tie. His curly black hair pushed back from his eyes with an elastic band. He's talking across the table to Elle's boyfriend, Finn, in a dark gray suit with a red tie. The perfect part in his brown hair makes him look like he's ready to do my taxes as he taps away on his phone screen. On the other two sides of the rectangular table are Bella's brother, Jonah, and her boyfriend, Conrad. It still takes me a few moments to ad to Conrad's appearance. Burns from a car accident covered an entire side of his body, and Bella took a job in New York to tutor him. Ever since she's been back, he's visited as much as possible. Jonah and Conrad exchange awkward, slow sign language across the table to one another. The expression on Jonah's face was pained as Conrad struggled to form the words in sign language. Bella's brother has no chill.

I should be the grateful host and talk to them, but I've spent my life almost exclusively with all women. Boys make me uncomfortable. The blonde from the shop last night pops into the front of my mind, and my eyes blink haphazardly to clear him from it.

When it's time to go, the girls pair off with their boyfriends, and my aunts pull on their jackets. The sheer amount of black mixed with small pops of red looks so uniform that I'm glad I'm wearing purple. Blanche lays her hand on my shoulder. "Want to ride with me?"

I was hoping to walk. Maybe I could run away into the pie shop and avoid this altogether, but that's less than realistic. They'd find me. I follow Blanche to her family van, wondering why all the girls aren't coming with us. Blanche, her dad, and her seven brothers all fit in here. It seems like a better use of fossil fuels to me.

Blanche starts the car, and children's music blares through the speakers. A giggle escapes me, and her hands fly to the power button. She takes a deep breath, settling her head against the rest and motioning to the car seat in the back with her thumb. "My little brothers have particular musical tastes."

I scrunch in my seat to stare at the poor dead trees out the window. Still lost to the bite of winter, the leaves haven't returned yet. It would feel strange for the world to be green and full of life today. Everything should reflect outward how it is inward.

Blanche is too quiet, and I brace myself for the "Sorry, your mom's dead" sympathy that continuously hits me like a wave. Today will be absolute torture. How long do they do that? A day? Two? A thousand? I can't keep this up for more than five without imploding. But Blanche, in her ever-so-Blanche way, completely surprises me. I turn in my seat to face her, taking in the pale dusting of freckles that spread across her nose and wrap behind her ear. Not an ounce of pity flows from her lips when she rambles, "Listen, I'm only going to say this once, and if you ever want to bring it up again, you can, but I won't. I never wanted anyone else to join the Dead Moms Club, but you did, and I'm sorry."

I realize how in my head I've been. Of course, I'm allowed, especially today, but it never occurred to me that I wasn't alone. Blanche's mom died a few years ago. The difference, of course, was that her mom was around; mine wasn't. She gets to feel broken up, and I don't.

"No one else will get it. They'll try, but they won't understand, and you'll be glad that they don't, but it sucks." The car falls eerily silent, and I'm unsure if I'm supposed to speak. Luckily, Blanche fills it for me. "I want you to know that I do get it."

I don't know what to say. I can be serious and complimentary towards anyone when the situation calls for it. But if others try to be that way with me, I become a vampire melting in the sunshine, hissing all the way down to hell. Instead of adding something sweet and sentimental, I say, "Dead Moms Club, huh? Are there hats or a membership card or something?"

Blanche is a lot like me. She never takes anything too seriously. Laughter sputters from her when she says, "I'll be sure to get you an official T-shirt." We both fall into an incredibly inappropriate puddle of giggles.

A block from the church, she swipes the undersides of her eyes and says, "We should probably get it together. I don't think anyone would understand us laughing."

The church comes into view like a scary apparition you see before death. It lies on a side street behind the elementary school, a location big enough for a large parking lot. My stomach flips at the line upon line of cars. I know people in my town are curious and gossipy, but I didn't want them to be snoopy with my mom. Piling out of their vehicles, I spot Elle's mother and sisters. There are a couple of Blanche's brothers, and I spy Goldie's mom and grandparents. Then I see Nixie's sisters, Dixie, Pixie, Trixie, and Dot, as well as Bella's parents.

But it's not only the relatives of my friends. In all his waddling old man glory, Mayor Byron shuffles out of his Lincoln, his wife close behind. There's Mr. Cooper, my art teacher, wearing his hipster glasses pushed into his curly brown hair. His black tie sat flat against his flannel button-up. Finally, my only other friend at Harpersgrove Senior High School emerges from his car.

I met Beau Lawson in the sixth grade when his family moved here from California. It seemed like a weird switch to me, movie stars to the middle of nowhere, but Beau seemed to fit into a small town better than I ever have. He rocks his afro, horn-rimmed glasses, and *Lord of the Rings* shirts, of which he must have a hundred. We bonded over our shared love of art class. For me, it's mainly sketching people for clothes, but Beau—he has a gift. What he can create with watercolors comes from the mind of a genius. He's known for sitting out by the football field, earbuds firmly in place as he ignores the snickers and jokes from jocks half his size. Beau could crush anyone with his bare hands, but he's much more the gentle giant.

After he rounds Mr. Cooper's car, he quickly gets to me. He closes the space in about four steps, dressed in his father's button-up shirt and khakis. He wraps his arms around my shoulders, lifting my feet. "Sorry, Friend," he whispers against my head.

I pat his back awkwardly, my arms pinned at my sides. "Thank you, Friend." And I mean it, he doesn't have to be here, but he came anyway. That means something when you're seventeen. Mr. Cooper offers a wave, still leaning against his car, and Beau walks back to join him. It's okay. I think most people might be afraid to be around me like grief is contagious or something.

Other random people from my school that I doubt I've ever spoken to litter the lot. I wish I could bar them from the entrance. They aren't here for me or to pay their respects to my mom. They're here for the day off school and maybe to have a story to remember when they think their parents are the worst. At least they're not like Rosie's. One such girl is the demonic Lucy Wilcox. I glimpse her standing alongside her father and little sister, Kathren. Lucy has made it her life's mission to make everyone who doesn't fit into her perfect bubble miserable. Goldie, my eternal bodyguard, places her hand on my elbow, saying, "I will happily punch her out for you. I've been looking for an excuse for years. You'd be helping me out."

I shake my head, turning my back on Satan and every other lookie-loo here to gawk at the Peters family. I begin to make my way towards the church. Meredith waits in the doorway for me, her hand stretched out.

"I want to get this over with," I murmur to her.

Shawna goes to church every Sunday. She tells me God provides answers that the world doesn't give. I went with her a few times after my mom left. I liked the pretty painted windows and fancy dresses everyone wore, but the music was sad, and I never really understood what was going on. I haven't been inside this building in more than five years. I never had any intention of coming back.

Pastor Richard, who's been ninety for the last forty years, shuffles slowly, cane in hand, in our general direction, serpentining down the center aisle. It wouldn't surprise me if he sat in one of the pews to take a break. The aunts flank me on all sides, Norah behind, Meredith and Shawna to my left and right, respectively. I'm pretty sure they're trying to keep me from running out the door screaming at the top of my lungs. I've never felt this lit aflame from the inside. My skin is about to burst. After I feel like I've aged twenty years, the reverend finally reaches us and extends his hand to Shawna.

Each of my aunts plays a role, and Shawna's is to channel the God connection. She envelops one of his hands in both of hers as he says, "I am profoundly sorry for your loss," he says, his beady gaze locks on me. "I hope you and your family can take comfort in Holly's soul being with our Lord. She can now be redeemed."

For a woman who I'm sure had little to no effect on my life, I feel incredibly defensive of how other people view my mother. I want to punch him in the middle of his absurd, egg-shaped little head. The idea that people like my mom were nothing until they died and God decided they were worthy made me want to scream. As screwed up as she was, for the first decade of my life, she was everything. She created me, and no one gets to say otherwise as far as I'm concerned.

"Rosalie," Pastor Richard said to me with a tip of his head.

I feel Meredith's hand squeeze on my wrist, trying to numb my rage. I grit my teeth, the pressure ready to shatter them. "It's Rosaline," I utter, forcing myself to swallow the scream. I hate using my full name. The fact that he got it wrong, probably on purpose, makes me want to shout it from the rooftops as my one and only identity.

He waves me off like a ridiculous little girl as he takes Shawna's arm and leads us to the front of the room. Meredith's fingers move to intertwine with my own. Norah's hand falls on my opposite shoulder and squeezes. I'm unsure if they're trying to comfort or keep me from a criminal act. Either way, it's suffocating.

We sit in the front pew on the aisle: Shawna, Norah, me, and Meredith. I've never sat in the front row at a funeral. There's something much sadder about the view from here. I keep my focus trained forward, ignoring the sounds of people filtering into the church behind us. It's not like I could look back even if I wanted to. I'm fixed on the simple wooden box on the altar. The simple wooden box with a single rose on top, and the simple wooden box with my mom inside. My soul drops as my feet push hard against the floor like I'm trying to glue myself here. My insides are fighting to push out in every direction. The lid remained closed, and the only solace is that no one will ever stare at her again. My fingers white knuckle on the seat beneath me. Am I trying to keep myself grounded or stop myself from running to her?

I know the girls are in the row behind me. Their boyfriends will have moved on to sit with their families. There's an unspoken bond in the world of female friendship, at least with ours. We come first; everyone else is secondary.

Meredith slides a folded piece of paper onto my lap. On the cover is a picture of my mother when she was about my age, maybe a little younger. Her long blonde hair sat back in a tight ponytail. Her face is clear of makeup, and her cheeks flushed from laughing. She stands on top of a rock in the middle of the woods behind the high school in shorts and a t-shirt, her hands proudly on her hips. The smile stretched across her lips is one I can't remember. It's effortlessly happy. Nothing about my mother was effortless from the time that I knew her. It was probably one of the last good pictures ever taken of her.

Meredith rests her chin on my shoulder and whispers, "I took that picture. I think you might be in there. I'm sure she told us about you a few days later."

And that's the change, the switch. Before me, my mother was happy; after me, she was a mess. Her life could be distinctly divided into two factions: BR (Before Rosie) and AR (After Rosie). It didn't take much imagination to figure out which one was better. My mother's soft brown eyes hold me in a warmth I can't understand, and I feel like I should cry. I'm supposed to cry. The backs of my eyes sting, but no tears form. I flip the paper over in my lap.

Pastor Richard hobbles his way up to the pulpit to begin the service about a woman he didn't like and knew even less. It takes the feeling of Goldie's reassuring hand on my shoulder from behind to keep me in my seat. My mother is too exposed here. This day can't end fast enough.

"Good morning," he begins—a soft rumble of similar responses replies. I say nothing. "Today, we celebrate the life of Holly Peters while we mourn her passing. Holly was born and raised in our great town and gave us the gift of a single daughter, sweet Rosalie."

At least two more hands grasp my shoulders to keep me seated. The fury bubbles up inside me. He did it on purpose. I know he did. Meredith hurries up the aisle and steps to whisper something in his ear. Her hand brushes my mother's casket when she passes, all the contact she can muster.

Pastor Richard bobs his head a few times before he says, "Her daughter *Rosaline*, I apologize." Another murmur sounds, and people tell him it isn't important, which is fitting. I've never felt important.

Before I knew it, Old Richard was repeating my name.

"Rosaline," he says, apparently not for the first time, as I can feel the attention shift. I look panicked at Meredith, who squeezes my arm and urges me forward. "Say what you feel," she encourages as she lets me enter the aisle. My ankles quake in my heels. I place one foot directly in front of the other like a tightrope walker until I reach the pulpit.

The pastor moves slowly to the side, eyeing me like a venomous predator. He's probably worried the ceiling will fall on my heathen head. I grip the sides of the old wooden podium and try to balance. I should have written something down. I let my scrutiny roam the congregation—rookie mistake. The room isn't full; it's standing-room-only. Damn vultures, these people don't know her. They shouldn't be here. I try to focus on the good people. My friends' families scatter the room. I know they're here for their daughters and, in essence, me. I wish that were enough to keep me from seeing everyone else. Low snickers and too many whispers deafen me as I clutch the wood like a lifeline. When I open my mouth to tell them what I think of them, one face grabs me at the far back of the church.

The feeling of nauseating deja vu settles low in my abdomen. Standing against the back wall is a man I can't with any certainty say I've ever met, yet I'm overwhelmed with familiarity. Something about him makes me eerily calm and terrified all at once.

Panic rises through my body as I realize I've been standing here too long without saying anything. Everyone probably thinks I'm broken. How wrong would that be? I turn to the aunts for rescue. I notice that Meredith locks on the same point as me, and Norah is already bee-lining it down the side aisle toward the man.

"Good morning," I croak out before I lose the entire room in awkward silence. Norah slows and turns to look at me instead. It's clear they don't want him here, and I will demand more information later. My brain is completely blank. I have nothing to say. I laser in on my friends. Elle grips Blanche's arm. Bella watches me through her fingers—Nixie's crying. But Goldie nods, reassuring me, pushing me on. She knows I can do this even if I don't.

"Thank you all for coming. My family and I appreciate it."

That's it. That's all I got. I wish Goldie would come up and do the damn thing for me. I search my brain, and the only thing I find brings me back to Broadway, more importantly, Broadway with pie involved.

Pie is everything. The lyrics to a song from *Waitress* dance across my consciousness. I can't help but mold them to sound like some endearing speech about my mom.

"My mom was imperfect," I begin, blatantly plagiarizing lines from a Broadway show to make a point that I couldn't in my own words. I press my lips together, hoping no one's the wiser when I see several people wiping the undersides of their eyes. It must have been okay.

My knees are still shaking when I abandon the pulpit and pass the casket. I pause for a second, but don't reach out like Meredith did. I wouldn't know what to do with my mother in the flesh. How on earth am I supposed to handle her now?

I sit back next to Meredith; Norah still hovers by the entrance. I don't know if he's still there, and I'm too afraid to look. Meredith lightly pinches my arm, her version of holding my hand, and says, "I knew you could do it." All thanks to a show about pie.

Pie saves the day once again.

The rest of the service passes in a blur, as does the time at the burial plot. Four sad little chairs lined up in front of a deep hole in the ground—only us and the pastor there as they lowered her down. And then there's one single moment, when the casket sits cold at the bottom of the grave. The straps pull away, and Pastor Richard steps aside when a wave of crippling finality settles over us. All three of the aunts burst into sobs. Shawna wails, Meredith weeps, and Norah shakes.

But me? I feel nothing. There is nothing but a cold stone in the pit of my stomach as I stare at the hole where they dropped my mother. Am I sad? Am I hurting? Am I relieved? Am I glad? Or am I simply nothing?

There's only the hollow shell of who I'm supposed to be.

CHAPTER FOUR

I insist upon walking myself over to the pie shop alone. Shawna's full-body sobs make me so uneasy that I have to fight the urge to push her over and run away. My breath releases in frosty gusts as I cross my arms over my chest to keep warm. Of course, I know the chill has nothing to do with the weather. It's in my bones, and no amount of layers or body heat can touch it.

Beattie refused to take no for an answer when it came to having the reception at the shop. She told me it's what family does. That word is strange to me. What is a family anyway? I guess the aunts are mine. Then I look at people like my friends. They have moms, dads, brothers, and sisters, and that's what a family should be. A family has to have at least one parent. I have a hodgepodge from the Island of Misfit Toys

I stand in the middle of the street and stare into the shop's windows at the people moving back and forth inside. The sea of black sweaters and suits seems suffocating even from here. How on earth am I supposed to handle this? "You know, you are the only person people will notice is missing," Mr. Cooper remarks, walking up beside me. I push a stray hair away from my face and turn to him. "Where's Beau?" I ask, unable to face any conversation.

"Oh, he went in already. Said he was dying for pie," Mr. Cooper laughs. I get it, though. I make a good pie. "How about I walk in with you? I'll be a human shield if you need one." I know he's joking, but that sounds like a fantastic idea. His hipster handsomeness might keep the folks off of me.

"We could always leave," I counter, my interest in going to my safe haven decreasing every second. I want to be in the comfort of my pies, not those who come with them today.

He shakes his head. "Come on, kid, it won't be that bad."

The inside is worse than I imagined. I don't know what would have upset me more: people sobbing, crying, and telling fake stories like they knew her, or what was occurring. Everyone laughed and talked like no one died while they shoved their faces full of free pie. I can feel the fury burning inside me like a ready and willing volcano. I leave the security of Mr. Cooper to jump headfirst into the abyss of people. The girls, my girls, all diligently work the counter, aprons over the fronts of their black dresses as they slice and serve all my hard work away. I consider looking for the aunts and demanding all this shuts down pronto, and for the vultures to either start paying or get the hell out.

I think about looking for Beattie to do the same. Then, I do what I always do instead. I avoid. I swivel past the counter to the kitchen, the only place I feel safe. I will have to make up the inventory we're losing anyway. I may as well start now. I distantly hear Goldie's voice attempting to slow me down, but she can't deter me. I sputter to a stop inside the doors at the sight of an alien stranger in my holy kitchen. Her long black hair is pulled back in a ponytail against her golden skin while she pours flour into my mixing bowl. One of my white aprons spreads across the waist of her black jumpsuit. It looks like she's right at home in the kitchen—my kitchen.

"What the hell?" I hear from my lips before my brain can catch up. Her round brown eyes widen like a startled baby farm animal. "Oh!

Hi Rosie!" She fumbles while trying to place the flour back on the counter, sending it cascading in a cloud through the air like a crop duster. My whole soul heats into a blind rage. I'm about to unleash the anger I've been suppressing onto this one, poor person who has nothing to do with it. Then, like she always does,

Goldie saves me from myself. She coughs through the cloud as she walks into the kitchen. She waves her hand back and forth to try to clear the haze when she notices the buggy look in my eyes.

"Rose," she starts slowly, circling me like a trainer on a hungry caged lion. "You know Allisin," she says matter-of-factly, as though that name should mean anything. "Dubuque's sister and," the twitching in my eye amplifies, "my boyfriend?"

Of course, I know who Dubuque is and his relationship with Goldie. That doesn't explain what she's doing here in my kitchen.

"Why is she in here?" I manage through a clenched jaw. Allisin's on her hands and knees, trying to sweep the sea of white into a pile, her black pants coated in it.

Goldie's eyes narrow. Today is not a day for anyone to get cross with me. "She's a baker, and I figured you could use the help today. She was happy to step in." Instead of seeming like a kindness, it feels like a betrayal.

"Dude," I snap at the girl on the floor. "Get up." She scrambles to her feet like I'm some kind of drill sergeant, then mumbles something about the bathroom as she flees the kitchen.

"Listen," Goldie clips, her voice calm and even, "today is an incredibly shitty day for you. It's levels of shitty I won't pretend to understand. But if you could kindly not be a bitch to everyone that's trying to help you, that would be great." She's attempting to be cute, but it's not working.

Everything about her, from her freakishly long blonde hair to her perfect body, perfect boyfriend, supportive mom, and wonderful grandparents, makes me want to punch her in her perfect face. Her mother was a teen mom, too, yet she stuck around for Goldie.

"I'm not being a bitch!" I snap back, trying to put things in order after the stranger invasion. Truth is, nothing is out of place, but that doesn't mean I don't feel the need to act otherwise. "I don't understand why you'd let someone into my personal space without asking me if it was okay."

"Because you would have said it wasn't. You want to be back here where you can hide from everyone out there, and most of the time, we let you do that, but you can't today. I'm sorry."

"And you already bring in my replacement?" I've had extreme anxiety at the notion that in a few short months, we'll all be scattering off to different parts of the country for college. That is, if the college ever gets back to me. "Who knows, I may not even be leaving."

Her eyes roll so far back into her head that her retinas must detach. "Jesus, you're insecure." She places her hands on my shoulders and squeezes enough that my muscles release. "Parsons is going to accept you. You're going to make beautiful, amazing, world-changing fashion for the rest of time."

Parsons School of Design is the dream. It's the only place I have ever cared about. The only thing that ever felt anywhere close to right. I had always been afraid to want anything because wanting leads to disappointment. But I want Parsons.

"You don't know that," I murmur, putting my forehead against her sternum. I am the itty-bitty of our friend group, spending my life amongst the trees.

She kisses my head through my mass of hair. "Yes, I do. I'm sure of very few things, but I'm certain about you." I smile despite myself. Our moment breaks at the sound of Norah's angry voice on the other side of the door.

"Kyle, you need to go. Now is not the time." As a human being, Norah is a bit gruff and abrasive, but there's an extra level of urgency to her tone that pulls my focus. I hop up to my knees on the counter by the kitchen window and peer through the other side to see. My tongue slips down my throat at the sight of the man from the church standing toe to toe with my aunt.

"I want to see her in person once, that's all," he says, his voice deeper than I expected. Norah's eyes snap up to mine in the window as if she could sense me. She doesn't say anything, but her tense body language speaks volumes, and for once, I listen. I flip around to sit on the cool stainless steel table and focus on the feeling of air entering and leaving my lungs.

Gold is at my side as always. "What's up?" she asks, placing her hands on my raised knees. I point my thumb in the direction of the dining area. "I think my father's out there."

On my walk to the pie shop, the memory came to me, and seeing him again reinforced it. I've only ever seen one picture of him, hidden in my mother's underwear drawer when I was a little girl. He was younger then, but his eyes are hard to deny. I see them every day when I look in the mirror. I knew the picture was of my father from the way my mom reacted when she saw me with it. In the photo, he was about my age, in a blue and yellow Harpersgrove High football uniform, with his arm around my mom's shoulders. His tight copper curls clung to his head, tipped against my mother's while she laughed hard enough that her eyes disappeared.

When my mom caught me with the picture, she practically leaped across the room to snatch it from me. "Stay out of my shit!" She screamed, sending me fleeing from the room. She may have told me to stay away, but I snuck back in to look at it as many times as I could before she left with it. The image is tattooed on my memory.

And now, he stands here in my pie shop on the day of my mother's funeral. In a three-piece suit, no less. Who is he trying to impress? He's cut his curls down to the skin, only a whisper of hair left on the top of his head. A faint beard lines his jaw, and glasses cover his eyes, but there's no denying it now that I'm up close. He is the man from my mother's picture, and even though I have no proof of it and can't be sure, I know that's who he is.

Goldie's double takes like I've slapped her. "He's who?!" She scrambles to peer out of the foggy glass circle in the middle of the door. Her brow crinkles as she rocks her weight back and forth between her feet.

"Is it the guy talking to Norah?"

"Yep," I mutter, counting the tiles in the ceiling. The last time I felt this panicky, it took counting to eighty-seven before I calmed down.

"I didn't think you knew who he was," her voice sounds hurt like I've kept some major secret about myself from her.

"I don't, not really. My mom had a picture of her and this guy when I was little. I always had a feeling it was him. Then I saw him at the service and felt pretty certain it was the same guy. He was in the back of the room and looked broken."

It was the only word for it. Broken, lost, and devastated for everything missed. You couldn't fake what I saw in that picture. My parents loved each other. I guess I would look a little broken, too, if, after almost eighteen years, I'd never reached out to the woman I loved, the mother of my child. He deserved to look shattered.

"And he chooses your mom's funeral to show up for the first time?" she asks, hurrying up beside me onto the counter. The back of my head bounces against the wall.

"I guess he ran out of time. Haven't you ever done that—said that you should make plans with someone then put it off and put it off? Maybe he put it off too long."

Goldie mulls it over in her mind a few times, her feet tapping to their unknown rhythm on the table. "I live in Harpersgrove," she says finally, her eyebrows pulled close together. "I can't avoid anyone, let alone my own family."

"What about your dad?" I ask, unsure if this is a safe place to tread. Goldie is notoriously open about everything in her life. She has no secrets, especially not from me, and has never seemed to care what people think of her. I like to think I'm that way, but I know it's untrue. I'm the queen of "fake it till I make it."

She shrugs, inspecting the ends of her impossibly long blonde ponytail. "We have our monthly dinners. They're as uncomfortable today as they were when I was little. I promise, if my dad could avoid me, he would do it."

To call that relationship complicated would be an understatement. Unlike my father, Goldie's dad stayed in Harpersgrove after her mom got pregnant. He returned after college and formed a new life with his new wife and kids—a replacement family. Goldie, in her classic fashion, likes to act unaffected. I've never bought it for a second.

"Of course, I do get to play the 'we don't know each other, but we're related' game with my father and grandparents when I run into them out and about town. So there's that." We share a giggle because silence seems too loud.

"Since I'm already in here," I begin, switching the sails to go another way. "I may as well stay and make some pies or clean up. Allisin can go home."

"Oh no, you don't," she says, hopping off the counter and pulling me down. "You're going back out there, and you're going to be a most gracious host and talk to every single person." She can tell I'd rather gouge out my eyes because she grabs my hand and says, "Don't worry, I'll stick with you the whole time."

As she promised, Goldie stayed by me, holding my hand almost the entire day. I felt like a little girl sticking to her mother's skirt as Goldie spoke for me to most people. I had nothing to say anyway.
I wanted to stay and help clean up, but the aunts weren't hearing it. Norah's ironclad arm circled my shoulders and led me away as my friends set to work, undoing the day around my mother.

I wanted to be a part of getting things back to normal. The aunts wanted us to be together. I don't know how to be together.

We stayed in our funeral clothes, sitting around the dining room table, nibbling on one of the six boxes of leftovers that Beattie had sent home with us. The quiet house seemed much louder.

I excused myself after forcing down a piece of blackberry pie. It tasted ashy in my mouth. I needed the peace, craved it, and I'd earned it. I fall onto my bed in what feels like a thousand hours later, more physically and emotionally exhausted than ever. Fake smiles and sad faces make me tired. I am no actress. But now I lie wide awake and staring at the glow-in-the-dark stars and moons I'd stuck to the ceiling when I was thirteen. Since sleeping was always a problem, I appreciated having something to stare at when the insomnia won. Their illuminated green color has faded over the years, and it's been a while since I took the time to appreciate the shapes I made. My thoughts drift to my mom and our made-up names for constellations.

I roll to a sitting position, my feet dangling a few inches off the floor over the side of my bed. Even after this exhausting day, sleep eludes me. When I was a little girl, I had no choice but to stare, wide awake, up at those fake stars. Now, I can leave, run, and escape my feelings. And I know where to go—the only place, of course.

I like the walk to the pie shop, especially in the middle of the night. Harpersgrove is most peaceful without all the people. I have a feeling most towns are like that. I like listening to the birds in the trees, and tonight, I hear the hoot of owls. I miss the rustling of the leaves on the trees, which makes me feel less alone. When I turn the corner, I swear I spot another person's silhouette off in the distance. It's probably my brain trying to fix the loneliness.

It's after midnight when I unlock the door of the shop. I can feel the tension rush from my tight shoulders and back. My feet cross onto the black and white checkered floor. The seasonally inappropriate flip-flps on them slapping against the linoleum. I could get used to this dressing-down thing. I fled my house in shorts and an oversized T-shirt from a local band.

Everything's all right inside Hap-PIE-ly Ever After.

In the kitchen, I tie one of my aprons around my waist, ready for the distraction of baking to pull me out of my head. After the number of people here today, I'm sure supplies are low without me picking up

the slack, and I'm grateful. I need to lose myself in butter, flour, fruit , and sugar. But when I open the fridge to assess the required work, my jaw drops at line upon line of pies. That Allisin girl is better than I anticipated. There's not a spare inch of space in the fridge for even one of my creations. I've been made obsolete. It puts a significant damper on my evening plans for distraction from my real life.

Back in the dining room, I grab the sketch pad under the register. When the creative gods of baking won't speak to me, I like to have another avenue available. I am always thinking of the next dress to make. The current project was a big one. All the girls agreed to let me make their prom dresses as long as I agreed to go. That was a hard compromise, but I couldn't resist the opportunity to create multiple gowns for such a fancy occasion. I had already finished the designs for Bella and Elle, but I found myself stuck on Blanche. Her long, lean figure with arms and legs that carry on for days, paired with a general lack of boobs, should have been ideal.

The girl looked like a runway model, but that wasn't my usual type. I made clothes for girls like me, curvy and short, or Goldie, curvy and tall, but curvy is always in the picture. My fingers covered in the graphite color of my pencil, I lose myself in drawing. I lean against the aching in my spine, my head falling back to see the world upside down. The guy from the night before is standing across the street watching. I fall off my stool and smack onto the tile. Grace is not one of my finer skills.

I pop up, trying to shake it off like nothing happened, watching him cross the street toward me. He's standing there with his arms crossed over his chest, his blonde hair brushing across his pretty eyes. He's cute.

Stomping up to the locked door, I try to look as pissed off as I feel, but if the smirk in the corner of his mouth is any indication, he's rather amused.

"What the hell is your problem?" I demand. "Do you have nothing better to do than stalk young girls?" His continued stare ticks me off more. "What?!" I scream.

"Are you mentally ill?" he asks, knocking me once again off my feet, only this time metaphorically.

"What?"

He rocks back on his heels, hands deep in his pockets. "Well, last night, you were standing on the counter, thrashing around like a shark out of water. And tonight, you're sitting calmly at the counter, doodling. So, are you insane?"

My mouth hangs open, but I can't seem to close it. The insensitivity in his question is the perfect example of why I don't talk to people. They're too stupid or rude to function correctly.

"Good night, you jerk," I mutter as I reach for the handle of the blinds on the door.

He laughs, "Oh, come on, don't be so sensitive. It's hard to find someone who's a night owl like me."

I turn back on my heel, crossing my arms over my chest. "And what does that make us? Best friends or something."

He smiles at me, and my stomach flips.

"Why don't you let me in, and we'll talk about it."

I shake my head and say, "Didn't your mother teach you to never talk to strangers?"

He shrugs. "Didn't your mother ever teach you to be kind to your neighbors?"

"My mother never taught me a thing," I say with a smile, but he doesn't know that it's the truth.

He looks past me into the store. "You know I'm pretty hungry, and a small town like this doesn't have many places open this late. That's some mighty good-looking pie."

I narrow my eyes. "I don't know you. I'm not letting you in here."

He presses his hand up to the glass. "I'm doing this because I can't shake your hand through the door. I'm Joshua McDonald."

I feel stupid doing it, but I place my hand over his like some weird prayer. "I'm Rosie Peters."

He flashes me his pearly whites. "Nice to meet you. Now that we're not strangers, can I come in?"

I drop my hand from the glass. "No, you could be an axe murderer, Joshua McDonald."

He sighs. "What if I promise that I'm not? Come on, I know you want some company."

"I will need a little more convincing." My aunts didn't raise a fool. I sit in front of the door and motion for him to do the same.

"Seriously?" he asks with a cocked eyebrow.

"If you want entry and pie, you have to earn it."

After a series of benign questions, I've learned that Joshua is a senior at New Shiloh High School, has two sisters, flosses every day, and doesn't eat asparagus. None of these is proof that he is not a serial murderer. Every reasonable bone in my body tells me not to. But perhaps I'm crazier than I realize because I find myself on my feet, flipping the lock and opening the door.

"Come on in," I said. "Dazzle me some more."

"Okay, Joshua McDonald of New Shiloh, what brings you to Harpersgrove at this late hour?" I ask him while sharing a piece of strawberry and rhubarb pie. It was the only one I made with my hands left in the entire shop. I still feel uneasy about the invasion of my territory.

He shrugs, finishing our third piece, and I cut another. "I don't know. I've already done everything there is to do after midnight in New Shiloh, so I decided to try somewhere new. Spread my wings."

His long fingers flit through the sky like he might sprout feathers and fly away.

"There's stuff to do after midnight in your town?" Everything closes here by nine, and that's pushing it.

"Yeah, there's a bunch of things." Joshua looks at me like some kind of cute and pathetic animated creature. Why should that be so obvious? New Shiloh isn't New York. I know there are things to do in big cities all night long. Cities don't sleep. Small towns do, and while Harspergrove is teeny tiny, New Shiloh is no NYC.

"Like what?" I ask, wondering if it's out of curiosity or some smug need to prove him wrong.

He grins as he fills his mouth with an obscene bite of pie. Boys have crazy appetites.

"How about I show you?"

I pull the plate back and take a bite. No one will outdo me. I jab my fork into a far too large piece and wedge it in my mouth.

"Is this where I finally find out you're a serial killer?"

"Sweetheart, I couldn't possibly show you all my cards," he laughs, his eyes sparkling with something I can't pin down. "But you could let me show you one or two."

It sends a thrill through me, which I find borderline frightening, considering I'm semi-turned on by a guy I don't know and who could very well be a lunatic. Oh well, one more thing to add to the list of topics featured in my memoirs one day.

I narrow my eyes at him, sizing him up. I shake my head. "No. No way am I going gallivanting with some guy I don't know in the wee hours of the morning in a town that isn't mine. Not going to happen."

Joshua stared at me like I had strawberry seeds in my teeth. I thump my fork against the counter and demand, "What?"

"Gallivanting? Wee hours of the morning? What Rodgers and Hammerstein musical did you escape from?" he comments, taking another massive bite of pie. At least he likes it.

"Don't insult the masters," I mumble through a full mouth. My friends would die if they saw me. Well, they'd die because I'm talking to a guy at all, but it would push them over the edge to see how unladylike I'm being. I could practically hear Goldie screaming.

"Oklahoma, where the wind comes sweeping down the plains!" he sings with his arms stretched out before him like Hugh Jackman at the Tony Awards.

A giggle escapes me as I cover my mouth with my hand. It feels strange to laugh, like it's for the first time. "A man who knows his musicals."

He rolls his eyes and dramatically flops onto the counter, narrowly missing the rest of the pie. I fight the urge to wrap my arms around the ceramic dish and protect my baby.

"I know, I know," he groans, rolling his head to the side to let me see those piercing eyes. A girl could get used to that view. "My mom has been dragging me as her date to the big theater in Baltimore every time a new show premieres for as long as I can remember."

"Color me jealous," I respond, lowering my chin to the counter, bringing us to eye level.

He describes going to the theater as a punishment. I can't get my head around that. I had never been and probably never would. I'd happily be his mom's date.

"You're a fan?" he asks, propping his head on his elbow.

"You could say that." My shoulders shrug up to my ears as I feel my cheeks begin to pink. What a weird thing to be embarrassed by. His pinky finger runs a line up the side of my hand. It tickles in a way that I feel down in my toes, making it hard to swallow.

"Come on," he croons, his finger still touching my hand. "Let me show you some things."

After a moment too long of silence, he pulls his hand away, and I miss the touch. "Unless you're chicken." I know I'm playing right into what he wants, but I'll be damned if anyone's going to call me chicken.

I narrow my eyes and whisper, "Game on, buddy."

Then he laughs; a full-on belly laugh that brings color to his cheeks and tears to his eyes. Every attempt to be my usual cool self falls hard at my feet, like a lead balloon filled with disappointment. When his ability to breathe returns, he asks, "Are you lost? Do you mean to be in a cheesy eighties action movie? I'm sure I could get you directions if that's the case."

I pout. I try not to, but my lip will not stay in. I grabbed Joshua's plate. "No more for you," I mumble, throwing his dish into the busing bin behind the counter. He gapes at me. You'd think I had slapped him instead of taking his plate.

"What was that for?"

I roll my eyes. "Don't get snippy, princess. You've had enough."

"It's not bourbon, Peters. You don't have to be snatchy about it." I slide my plate to him. "Happy?" His head of blonde hair bobs up and down, mouth full as he mumbles,

"Very, thank you."

He dabs the corners of his mouth with a napkin like a classic gentleman.

"Where do you guys get these from?"

"Pardon?" I ask.

"The pies dummy," he begins, licking his thumb to nab all the crumbs. "Where do you guys get all the pies?"

Is he kidding? Where does he think?

"I make them," I say, digging my fork directly into the pie tin, the tines scraping the bottom with a shrill screech.

"No way! You did not make this."

"I sure did. I make everything we sell here." I point back towards my laboratory and say, "My kitchen."

"Nope, don't buy it." He casts me a little lopsided grin, and my heart skips a beat. I shake it off. Maybe it's heart palpitations. I may need a doctor.

"I only speak the truth."

He shrugs, saying, "I don't believe you. You're going to have to prove it to me."

I couldn't help but smirk. "You want me to make you a pie?" He nods enthusiastically like a little boy. "But you just ate a whole one."

"Come on now, don't make it sound like I ate it alone. You had plenty."

I smirk, tightening the hold of my arms around my chest. "You want me to show you how to bake?"

He leans back on the stool and shakes his head. "No, I want to watch you do it." His gray eyes darken as he stares at me. My knees turn to jelly, and I have to grasp the counter to keep from falling over.

"That's weird," I say, trying to keep the composure in my voice, but hating myself at the crack in it I hear.

"What's odd about it? I find it fascinating," he says with a devilish grin. What I need is to get a grip.

"What's fascinating about my baking exactly?"

He chews on his cheek as his eyes trail up and down my body. *Oh my God, is he checking me out?*

I suddenly feel naked, and not in a good way. He waves his finger up and down in my direction. "Seeing you do it? Yeah, that's pretty fascinating without explanation."

"I have no idea what you mean." There was nothing sexy about me. I could only imagine what my makeup-less face looked like.

"Come on, Rosie, you've got this whole, laid back 'don't-give-a shit' look about you. It's hot that you don't care what you look like." Hearing him say my name covers the backhanded compliment he served up.

I pick up the empty pie tin and carry it back through the kitchen doors. I need a second to breathe, and I can't do that while Joshua is sitting there looking the way he does. That floppy blonde hair that lies over his eyes in a way that looks effortless, but I know better. I'm a queen of hair products, and his hair probably took longer to put together than mine ever has. His stormy eyes lock in and follow me like a freaking heat-seeking missile. The only time I've ever noticed a guy staring at me, it usually came with a snicker or an older man leering.

Neither is ideal.

Joshua looks at me like he's trying to figure me out. Like I'm a puzzle without a solution. After a breath and a deep scrub of the ceramic pie dish, I collect myself enough to walk back into the dining room with at least a semblance of my usual chill. I plaster on a smile and push through the door, only to realize there's no one on the other side. *Where did he go?*

Maybe I'm going crazy. Perhaps Josh was never there. But under the lip of a metal napkin dispenser, I see scribbles on a discarded napkin. My fingers tremble as I pull it free. In black block letters, it reads,

"Thanks for the pie, Peters. I'll meet you here tomorrow night at eleven. Wear comfortable shoes."

I press the napkin against my chest.

He's coming back.

CHAPTER FIVE

I crawl into my bed at four fifteen in the morning. I pull the sweat-shirt over my head, leaving me in my bra and shorts. My hair falls out of its ponytail like a platinum wave across my faded black sheets. The ceiling fan moves slowly, whipping in circles over my head. My eyes blink shut in slow succession as sleep, in its rarest form, takes me over.

I'm floating on the sea of dark water, but now I'm on my face, holding my breath for fear of drowning. My eyes blink against the darkness, hoping I'll ad, but I don't. And then the screaming is back.

When I wake, the ceiling fan is still spinning. I haven't moved an inch. Orange and pink rays of the sun filter through the slats in my shades and settle on my face. I stretch back to glimpse the clock on the edge of my nightstand. 6:04. I slept for less than two hours. Most people would consider that a decent nap. For me, it's a typical night. I consider crashing back onto my mattress even though I know I won't fall back asleep.

It's a school day, and I could probably milk this thing for another week or two if I wanted. Everyone's aware that school is not my favorite place to be. Of course, I know what staying home means. The aunts would hover. They would bombard me with questions, concerns, and demands to eat. Shawna especially loves to shove food in my face when she thinks I'm sad. I might as well go to a place where I can zone everyone out. At least my friends are there.

Groaning, I force myself to stand, pushing forward and into my little bathroom. While I'm waiting for the shower to warm, I catch sight of my body in the mirror. Permanently bronzed skin disturbed only by the purple rose tattoo on my left shoulder that I'd gotten at fourteen years old. I don't know why I did it. I'm not sure whether it was to piss off the aunts or my mother, even though she wasn't around to see it. The guy who did it was an old friend of my mom's who had no hang-ups about tattooing a child. I should have known better, but I never knew better. He asked me what I wanted, and I told him a rose. The purple was an afterthought. I'm far from original. My first tattoo represents my first name, but I love it all the same. The aunts flipped the first time they saw it, which didn't take long considering how low-cut most of my clothes were, but I didn't care. The following year, I got my lip pierced, and that didn't go over well either. It felt good to do those things. The pain and the rebellion made me feel alive.

The shower practically melts my skin, and it's still not hot enough. I scrub with every ounce of passion my body possesses, like I'm trying to burst through my pores. I rake a wide-toothed comb through the conditioner in my hair. I'm shocked that I don't take out clumps the way I'm ripping them. I feel like I should be crying and sobbing. Isn't a shower, alone, the right place to do that? But not a single tear arrives. What kind of monster doesn't cry over the death of their mother?

I rub my eyes like a sleepy little girl when I return to my bedroom after drying my hair. I plop onto my vanity seat and cringe at the fluffy white-blonde ball staring back at me. I pick up my brush and pull it through over and over until it finally calms down in the waves I'm used to. This would be the usual point in my day where I'd assault my scalp and the ozone with hair spray, pulling it all back in my sig-nature bun. Today my hands have no desire to reach for the can. I dig around in one of the drawers until I find a toothed headband and slide it into my hair. I can't recall the last time I wore it down.

On the right side of my vanity is where I keep my makeup. It's an undertaking that can take me upwards of an hour to transform me into the pale creature I know all too well. I turn my face from left to right in the mirror, taking in the person staring back. Blonde eyelashes rim my lids under dark blonde brows. Nothing on my face goes together. I chew on the inside of the labret, pierced through my lip, and swapped it out with a simple silver hoop. It doesn't stand out as much, and I want to blend in for the first time in my life. I rub my hands with moisturizer, but can't bring myself to cover up. Instead, I opt for a few mascara brushes and a pale lip gloss. The person looking back is a stranger; maybe that's who I need to be right now.

Opening my closet, I'm bombarded by a sea of black and pleather. My skin itches at the sameness. Nothing is normal anymore, and I can't pretend to wear something that is. I dive in, pushing through article upon article of clothing I've made myself that are all the same. I'm half tempted to wear my damn funeral dress when I find a bag of clothes in the back. Shawna tries her hardest to buy me things that a "respectable young lady" would wear. They end up in their bags, sadly collecting a musty smell in the bottom of my closet.

I rip open the plastic of the knotted bag and pull out a white, cable-knit sweater and a pair of high-waisted jeans. I run my fingers along the warm, stiff yarn. It's not something anyone my age would wear. It's something a middle-aged mom would pick out. It's perfect.

I layered a light gray tank top under the sweater to minimize the itching and finished the look with a pair of spotless white Keds. I tuck the front of my sweater into the high waist of the pants. I'm a hippy and proud and refuse to lose sight of that under a shapeless top, even in my disguise. I twirl in front of my full-length mirror and take in the "mom from a nineties movie" look. Hopefully, no one would realize it's me. That's my intention, anyway.

I scoop my backpack off the floor and head toward the kitchen to grab a cup of coffee before going to school. Usually, I'd call Goldie to get me or guilt Meredith into letting me use her car. I'll walk almost anywhere but to school. Today, however, I think the crisp stroll in new shoes might be the self-flagellation I need.

In the dining room, Shawna sits eating a bowl of oatmeal and reading the morning paper. Her thin, rectangular glasses balance on the edge of her nose as she scans the paper at an alarming speed. Those same eyes switch to me when I enter the kitchen.

"Well, look who's up early," she says, as high and light as I've ever heard. I'm sure Shawna was a fairy in a past life. Norah and Meredith wear sweatpants and a t-shirt to bed. Shawna prefers the look of an older time, in a classic nightgown, usually made of silk. Her dark burgundy dressing gown ties around her slender waist, and I can see the matching slippers under the dining room table.

"What are you doing?" she says while she pushes her glasses up into her pale blonde curls, streaked with white.

I take solace in the bubbling sound of coffee filling my travel mug. God bless Shawna and her early-bird tendencies. I survive purely on caffeine and spite. "I'm going to school."

Shawna rounds the counter and leans against the wall. "You know no one expects you to go back this soon, right?" she asks, forcing herself to keep her distance. Shawna is a hugger and a touchy-feely type. It's taken many years to get her to understand that I am not.

My shoulders shrug up to my ears. I focus on pouring the half and half into my mug rather than on the intense stare from my overly concerned aunt. "I know, but he best thing I can do right now is return to a sense of normal."

It's not a lie. The last thing I want to do is mope around here with people who are grieving, and school is where I'm supposed to be today anyway. That sounds normal enough to me.

"Normal?" she questions. The silence thickens until I see it like opaque paint.

"Rosaline, what are you wearing?"

I secured the top on my mug and put the half and half away without looking back at her. My resolve is fragile, and I don't want her to break it.

"What? You bought them for me."

"Oh, I'm aware of that, but I believe your exact words upon receiving them were, 'You'll never catch me dead in those old lady clothes.'"

I cringe as the memory floods back to me. Shawna is the most maternal of the aunts. I did everything I could, especially when my mom first left, to let her nurturing ways slide off me like Teflon.

"I thought change was good."

"Change is good," she repeats, taking a daring step toward me. I wonder how much it would hurt to jump through the glass of the kitchen window. If she touches me, I don't know what will happen. "The timing is a little worrisome."

"I want to go to school, Shawna, that's all. I don't want to dwell on it and sit around being sad. I want to go to school."

I'm not sure if it's my pleading or the drained look on my face that softened her, but she retreated the step she'd taken. "Well, do you want to take my car? I'm not going to work today."

I shake my head, scooping up my book bag off the floor. I kiss her soft cheek hard as I pass her and feel her smile. It doesn't take much.

"No, I'll walk. It will be good for me."

Before I can get too far, she wraps her slender fingers around my wrist and squeezes with enough pressure that I feel it. "I love you, Rosie girl," she murmurs, her eyes shiny. I know the waterworks are about to begin, and I have to get out of here, or I'll never get to leave.

This time, I kiss her on the temple and say, "I love you too, Shawna."

And it's the truth.

Foregoing a jacket may have been a mistake on my brisk walk to school. The cold wind whips through the yarn gaps in my sweater, and I hug myself for warmth. I almost put my earbuds in and let music float me away, but I can't bring myself to do it. The sounds of Harpersgrove in the early morning have a musical beauty that's too hard to miss out on. Even in the dead of winter, unless there's snow on the ground, my elderly neighbor, Mr. Porter, will mow his lawn. At seven in the morning he's at it wearing only underwear, a terry cloth bathrobe with black socks in sandals while singing Frank Sinatra at the top of his lungs. All this is much to the chagrin of his duplex partner, Mrs. Marcozzi, who screams at him in rapid-fire Italian while he sings louder.

At the end of my road, I turn left onto Bleeker Street, where a happy little Yorkie meets me with yappy barks and a pink bow in her hair. She hops up and down through the chain link fence, making me wonder if I could get the aunts to get me a dog. Who can be sad when they're looking at a dog?

I detour and walk down Main Street through the center of town. I pass Tilly's Flower Shop and wave to Julio through the window as he sorts orders for the day's deliveries. The old weather vane on the roof of the building squeaks as it spins in circles with the changing wind. And then I pass the shop, my shop, and glance inside at the few patrons eating breakfast. Beattie and Flo, a woman we rarely see as she works while the rest of us are in school, serve the people sitting at the counter. I wish I were in there with them. Beattie spots me staring and furrows her brow when she sees me. She moves around the counter toward me, and I sprint away like I stole something. I'll pay for it with a long talk later, but I can't take a motherly, disapproving speech right now.

The school's parking lot is slowly filling with the cars of my classmates and teachers by the time I arrive. Walking by, I'm not oblivious to more than one double-take. Harpsergrove isn't known for many new students, and I look different enough to be a new person. I loop my thumbs through the straps of my bag and pull hard against my back, my eyes cast down, and start to pick up speed. It takes everything in me not to hiss at them. I'm already the daughter of the dead heroin-addicted teen mom. Why not add complete psychopath to the list of gossip?

I'm about to break for it and sprint through the lot when a long train of golden hair steps in my way. "Ro, what are you doing here?" Goldie asks, placing her hand on my arm. Over her shoulder, I notice her boyfriend, Dub, bouncing uncomfortably between his feet. His friends stand a few cars back, and I'm sure he wants to go to them, but doesn't want to leave Goldie.

"I go to school here."

I try to step around her again, but she blocks my path. Behind her, Dub is slowly taking steps toward his friends. Support has limits on how far it can go.

"Dude," she begins, holding up her hands to prove she isn't going to touch me again. "I'm trying hard not to focus on your nervous breakdown outfit. Could you talk to me for a second?"

The clothes could have been a better idea. "I'm already exhausted, Goldie. I want to get back to normal."

"*Normal*" is a word that has lost every bit of meaning. I cross my arms over my chest and brush past her, desperate to get inside.

"What about this is normal?" she calls after me, and my cheeks flush red—first Shawna, now my best friend. Goldie may be the perfect popular girl who doesn't mind stares, but I'm not. I tuck my chin down to my chest and walk as fast as I can without running.

I find refuge in burying my face in my open locker, something I hardly ever use. It took three tries to get the combination right.

"Rosie," I hear softly from the other side of the open door. I groan and let it swing shut, revealing a concerned Elle on the other side, her soft brown hair pulled back from her face in a tight ponytail. Like all my friends, I must tilt my head up to look her in the eye. Why am I so short?

"Yes?" I say, echoing her questioning tone. I try to look calm, leaning my shoulder into the line of lockers, but I'm sure I resemble a kid from a catalog ad selling back-to-school gear.

"I didn't think I'd see you here," she responds, her voice a few octaves too high, but her real attention is on the sweater. I know I only wear black, but the sheer amount of people looking at me like my wearing anything else is a sign of mental illness is starting to tick me off.

I decided the only decent response was to force a smile, a tactic I hadn't tried yet. The alarmed look on Elle's face tells me it's the wrong choice. I'm exhausted to the point I can barely stand.

"I'm not a delicate little flower, Michelle. I've got this."

Before I can scurry away, she puts her arms around my shoulders, pulling me hard against her, my face flush with her flat chest. In every place I curve, Elle willows. She rests her chin on my head, and I resist the urge to snuggle with her and take what she's offering. Weakness is a flaw that I refuse to show.

"You may not be delicate and fragile, but you are our flower, Rosie Rose," she murmurs into my hair. Usually, I'd follow her and hang out in the room with her and Nixie until their teacher kicked me out. But not today.

I turn on my heel and fight the urge to run again, mainly because I don't know if I'd be running away or toward something. Elle's words float on the surface of the black water that has become my brain. At the same time, she got it both right and wrong. I am fragile, incredibly fragile, but not like a flower. I'm fragile like a bomb.

The day drifts away from me in a cloud of whispers and people walking on eggshells. I hid in the bathroom all morning and through lunch. I can't take the girls pitying me with their side glances and hushed tones. I want things to be how they were again, whatever that means.

I linger outside my last class of the day. I don't know how I would take it if my art room weren't how I remembered it. Mr. Cooper looks up from his desk and squints behind his Buddy Holly glasses. The corner of his mouth twitches up as he says, "It's good to see you, Rosie." He's my favorite person at the moment.

The genuine smile that spreads across my face fills my whole body with a warmth I haven't felt in days. Leave it to Mr. Cooper to bring it to light. I take my seat on a stool next to Beau. He peers at me over the lip of his Lord of the Rings sketchbook, his eyebrows pulling close together. "Friend," he starts cautiously in his customary greeting. He scans me from behind his thick glasses. "What are you wearing?" At least he wasn't saying I shouldn't be here.

I pushed my fluff of marshmallow hair behind my shoulder and pulled my sketch pad out of my bag. "I needed to be different today."

Beau's attention turns to the yellow duck he's drawing with fancy colored pencils. He holds up his fist for me to bump, which I do, and says, "Right on." Of all the people in the world, I'm glad I have Beau not to judge me. My other friends are like parents; they do it because they genuinely care about me. Having one person who can let me breathe is a nice thing.

My favorite thing about this art class in my senior year is that we're largely left to our own devices. The six of us have dedicated ourselves to art for most of our school careers. I welcome the silence and the fact that every person remains in their little bubbles. At the end of class, I'm left with a lovely sketch in charcoal of three lean and long girls with arms around each other. Their faces are blank, like those of Amish dolls, but their clothes are intricately detailed. That's my way.

As I pack my bag to leave, Mr. Cooper approaches my desk with a cautious smile and says, "Hang back for a minute, okay?" Dread rushes through my bloodstream. I may be a rebel, but I don't like to get into trouble.

"I feel like this is either the best or the worst time to bring this up." My breath catches. It can't be anything too wrong, can it? Mr. Cooper has been the one teacher who looked out for me throughout high school. The level to which he believes in me is uncomfortable and borderline disturbing. In matters of fight or flight, I am the queen of flying! He reaches inside his jacket and pulls out a large, fat, white envelope. I forget, for the first time since it happened, that my mother has died. For only this moment, the sole thing that exists is that envelope.

"Is that—is that?" I stammer because my ability to form language has been completely lost.

Mr. Cooper turns the envelope over, and I catch the name Parsons in big bold letters. My tongue swells three times its size. They don't send the big envelope for rejections, do they? His index finger taps the corner as he watches me skeptically from behind his glasses.

"You know, most people check this stuff online nowadays. I even checked mine online," he laughs, trying to sound older than he is. "More intriguing, though, is why you had them send it to me at the school?"

"Honestly?" I take his silence as confirmation. I lean against the desk across from his and cross my arms over my chest, forming every protective barrier I can. "I didn't want my aunts to see it. They would try to make me feel better if things went sour, which would only make it worse. Same thing with the pie shop and my friends. I can't take disappointing them."

The envelope invades my field of vision. This moment is real. He nudges the envelope in my ribs, and I take it without my brain creating the command. I feel out of control and hyper-focused at the same time. "Well," he begins, a warm smile spreading across his mouth and crinkles forming in the corners of his eyes. "No matter what, you can't disappoint me. I'm proud of you for trying."

His words make me want to cry. How messed up is that? Not the death of my mother, but a single moment with a teacher could bring me to tears. He lets go of the envelope and gives me full responsibility. I hope he doesn't try to hug me if it's bad. I'd probably panic and punch him. Or worse, be unable to let go.

My heartbeat thumps in my ears, and the room falls to a distant hum when my finger runs across the sealed white edge. My hand trembles as I pull the contents out from inside. Against my effort, my left eye closes and refuses to open, as if rejection would be less harsh if seen through only one eye. I scanned the date and my name at the top of the paper, then finally read the body of the letter. One word and one word only grabs me. "Congratulations!"

A breath releases like air from a balloon as I deflate into a puddle against the desk, all my weight against it. I turn the packet around, my hands still shaking, to show Mr. Cooper. My mouth couldn't form the words, and my brain could create the thought. Ever so slowly, a face-splitting grin spreads across Mr. Cooper's face before he pushes off the desk and lets out a resounding, "Yee-haw, girl!" Before I know it, he's pulled me into a congratulatory hug. "I knew you could do it!"

I wait for the lump of anxiety to go down in my throat or for some kind of joy or warmth to comfort me, but nothing happens. Not a thing changed. Shouldn't the news of getting into the only school I wanted effect me in some way? Shouldn't I be happy or at least relieved? Why is the plaguing threat of dread coursing through my body instead? Too many questions. Too many mixed emotions. There is too much of Mr. Cooper standing too close and smelling too good. I clear my throat and step back to find my teacher still beaming.

My cheeks flush, and I remember not wearing makeup that would help hide my embarrassment. I reach up and tuck my hair behind my ears before cradling the packet against my chest. "Thank you, Mr.

Cooper," my hushed voice whispers. "I couldn't have done this without you." And it's the truth. I never would have applied if he hadn't made me.

Of course, I drove him to the edge of his sanity when I refused to apply anywhere else. *"Jesus, Rose,"* I remember him saying when I informed him of my choice. *"Is it the application fees? Because I swear, I will help you pay for them if it means you give yourself a better shot."* I didn't know how to tell him then that it wouldn't work. I was a Peters, my mother's daughter, and all-or-nothing was kind of the way we did things. If it couldn't be Parsons, it would be nothing, but I didn't know what to feel even now that I had it. I lift my bag from the floor and shove the packet inside, out of my face, and out of my mind for at least a moment.

"I have to get to work." I try to wrestle up a smile, but I'm sure it comes across as a pained grimace. It's not the truth either. Beattie has no plans to see me today or have me show up at the shop. We have enough pie, supplied by Allisin, to get us through a minor apocalypse. They don't need me, but I don't have to remind them.

The concern etched on Mr. Cooper's face is palpable and suffocating. I have to get out of this room. The papers burn a hole through my bag and into my back, and I feel my feet running away, but from what, I can't be sure. Typically, after school, I wait for one of the girls to walk or ride to work with, but I'd rather chew off my arm than do that today. I want the peace of my kitchen and absolutely nothing else. I'll find a way to bolt myself inside if I have to.

The small, gold bell dings when I push into the pie shop, and I feel my joints relax and pop like I've been holding the tension of the world this whole time. Bella's leaning over the counter, her boyfriend sitting across from her, both engrossed in the book between them. Conrad had lost some time in school due to his injuries, and Bella was doing her best to help him catch up and graduate. He spends a decent amount of time away from his home in New York and down here with her. A frown forms on her lovely face as I approach. "What are you doing here?" she asks, and I lose it.

I throw my arms up and stomp in a small circle around myself like a disgruntled toddler. I'm exhausted, frustrated, and emotional, and have no outlet. I don't need it here. "Please, please, I've gotten it all day from everyone at school. Please don't do it here."

Bella stares, face frozen. I might implode, explode, or freak out more than I already have. "Okay. Got it. Won't even mention the sweater."

An inhuman sound rumbles from my throat as I pound past her and into the kitchen. I'm rude and don't acknowledge Conrad, but he strikes me as one of the few people unaffected by such an action. He's already back to reading. The rest of the negativity flees my body when I cross the threshold into the kitchen. This little windowless room, which always smells like heat and flour, settles something in me.

I open one of the refrigerators and let my muscle memory take over as I pull out the necessary ingredients without thinking. A great deal can change in a matter of a year. I went from painstakingly checking and rechecking every recipe detail on my phone to letting my body disconnect from my brain and trust my instincts. I grab a pint of blackberries and a pint of raspberries from the second fridge and set them in front of me. I pull out a mixing bowl and throw the berries in, then grab a potato masher to go to town on the poor, innocent fruits. I am incredibly aware of my bag sitting by the door, and the papers I know are inside it. It makes my pulse race. I squish harder against the berries, taking out my undefinable emotions there. When they're sufficiently macerated, I realize I have no real plan for them. My brain goes blank on how to make a fruit pie. The seeds from the blackberries float at the top of the mix, and my mom flashes through my brain. She thought blackberries deserved to be special, even though they were different. She was wrong.

The seeds get stuck in teeth and crunch too loud, disturbing the general joy of dessert. Blackberries aren't notable because they're different. They're a nuisance because they're different. I want to throw the whole thing against the wall, shatter it, break it. Break something. Break everything. I want to make inanimate objects feel and take the pain and anger I'm feeling. Get it out of my body. I slam my fists on either side of the bowl into the stainless steel work table, and the sound echoes through the room. I could throw it away or change it and make it into something better. Change it into something everyone would enjoy.

I return to the fridge for more supplies—cream in a pot on the stove. Sugar gets dumped into a mixer with eggs beside it, and I'll separate the yolks in a minute. Occasionally, Bella yells back through the little window that they need something out front. I warmed a couple of Allisin's creations in the oven, then take another bowl and anchor a strainer to remove the seeds from the fruit. I slice the two vanilla beans down the center and toss them into the pot with the cream. Using a wooden spoon, I stir the white liquid in slow, circular motions until bubbles form. I turn off the heat, scrape the vanilla bean seeds, add some gelatin, and set it aside.

Picking up an egg to crack it into a bowl, it smashes in my hand, shells floating in the goo. "Damn it," I mumble under my breath as I grab another—same result. I white-knuckle grip the counter and force myself to take a few deep breaths. Cracking eggs takes finesse.

"Settle down," I demand of myself. The third egg is the charm as I swish the contents back and forth to ensure that the egg white falls into the bowl, leaving only the nice yellow yolk in the shell before dropping the goopy goodness into the mixer with the sugar. Repeat four more times. Gelatin is a kitchen wonder. Need a substitute for eggs? Use gelatin. Need to make plastic-looking edible flowers? Use gelatin. Want to make a DIY blackhead pore strip? GELATIN. It's also fantastic at thickening a Bavarian cream like I'm making.

When things are properly whisked, I slowly mix in the syrupy, strained fruits, turning the cream into a lovely swirl of purple and pink. I pour the whole thing into two refrigerated graham cracker crusts I prepared a few days ago and stick them in the fridge. It'll be hours before they set. That can be the hard thing with pies. Waiting.

I surveyed the damage left from my rampage. I may have used every bowl and utensil in the kitchen. I bet Allisin doesn't make a mess like this. My head shakes from side to side. I need to stop. I still have my job, and no one is replacing me. Besides, Beattie will need someone new when I'm off at college in the fall. If I go, that is. That thought hits me like a brick through my stomach, and I'm all too aware of the papers in my bag again. I should run through the shop screaming at the top of my lungs, "I got in! I got in!" and then run home to the aunts, but I won't. I can't even comprehend it. Instead, I slap my hand on the swinging door.

There's a pleasant buzz of conversation and the clinking and scraping of plates that fills the shop in its regular orchestra of sounds. Bella bumps her hip against me, carrying two pieces of blueberry pie in her hands to a pair of customers at the counter. "You okay?" She reads me well.

I take a deep breath and give myself a second to respond, knowing she'll be one of the few not to be critical of my answer. "Yeah," I say finally, and it's a lie, but it's one I can live with. My friends don't need to hold my shit on their shoulders. It's a weight I can carry alone. Besides, if I talk too much, I will blurt out everything about my acceptance into Parsons. Considering I have no idea how to feel about it, that would be a mistake with this crowd. They'd demand a celebration, which might be the final thing to break me.

Blanche is the only other person working this afternoon with Bella and me, and subtly, this is not something she's known for.

"What the hell are you wearing?" she shrieks as she rounds the counter. As always, she's dressed for a run in a pair of blue shorts and a New Shiloh Track red t-shirt. Her sleek black bob is pushed away from her freckled face with a yellow elastic headband. Blanche never has anything to hide.

I can tell it's taking everything in her for Bella not to fling the pie in her hands at Blanche's face. Feeling the need to fend off a possible food fight, I take a step forward and grab Blanche by the arms, pulling her down to plant a kiss on her cheek. Remembering that I won't be leaving a red smear behind it takes a second. Blanche inspects me from the side like I'm some kind of predator ready to snap. I pat my hand on her cheek and turn back to the kitchen. That's enough human interaction for now.

Bella and Blanche whisper in a harsh, anxious hush as I go back through the swinging door. I pine for the day that the world balances itself out, and I return to being Rosie on the sidelines instead of Rosie in the spotlight.

I deep clean the kitchen like I haven't in over a month. The room sparkles by the time the sun sets, and the last of the girls has left. Bella lingers the longest. At a quarter after nine, she stands in the doorway of the kitchen, her ring of keys spinning on her finger. "Maybe call it a night?" she asks, but I know it's more of a plea. Everyone worries too much about me.

Stacking and restacking the pie dishes in an order that makes no sense or difference, I turn my back to her to avoid eye contact.

"I'm going to do a little more, and then I'll head home. Promise."

If I sleep, I'll probably crash on the couch in Beattie's office. The aunts will be hovering at home, and I need some peace. Bella knows me well enough to see through me, but also loves me enough to let it go.

"Get some sleep," she says in parting as she walks toward the door. I don't breathe again until I hear the dead bolt turn.

Alone at last.

CHAPTER SIX

At eleven thirty, I'm six pints of strawberries into a tower when a knock sounds from the front of the shop. My entire body freezes before tilting to the side to see what ax-murderer has come to finish me off. Looking as delectable and dangerous as the first time I saw him, Joshua McDonald lingers outside the entrance, leering at me with a mischievous grin.

I pause on my side of the glass before letting him in. His brown leather jacket over a white t-shirt, faded denim jeans, and boots make him look like some modern-day James Dean.

"You know," he begins, his voice muffled by the door. "It's colder out here than it looks." He sports a face-splitting grin, and I feel balanced for the first time all day.

I flip the lock and open the door for him. He shoves his hands in his jacket pockets and flicks a loose lock of hair away from his forehead. He smells like sandalwood and maple syrup. I want to snuggle into him like a hug. It's clear from the half smile on his face that he knows how pretty he is. I would think the cocky, pretty boy thing would be a major turn-off for me, but that was because I'd never seen it on Joshua McDonald. This boy could make anything look good.

A husky chuckle rumbles in his throat as he motions to my tower of strawberries. "You are a weird girl, Rosie Peters."

"Hey, now, that's modern art!" I exclaim with false outrage. "You better be nice to me, or I won't share my millions with you."

He leans down to my level, eyes hooded as he murmurs, "And how would you suggest I be nice?"

I forget how to function. I never want him to stop looking at me.

"Take me somewhere," I'm able to croak out. To me, it felt like I was screaming in his face. The underside of the counter looks like an excellent place to curl up and die. He grins wider, watching me like I'm a fascinating animal in the zoo. Maybe a panda.

"Take you where?" he asks, giving nothing away. I'm the only one affected.

"Yeah, you know, yesterday you told me you'd show me the late-night offerings of New Shiloh."

He sits on one of the neon stools, a playful smile ever present. "I did say something like that, didn't I? Let's go then."

He reaches out to me, and even his hands are beautiful. Long fingers, trimmed nails, no visible scars. Beautiful. He encircles my wrist like he's afraid I'll try to run away. My breath catches at the warmth that spreads through my skin and up my arm. My pulse sped under Joshua's thumb. The corner of his mouth twitches, and I wonder if he feels it, too.

"Where's your coat?" he asks as I throw my purse over my head. I pull on the hem of my sweater. It might be brisk, but it's not dead-of-winter cold anymore. He shakes his head, shrugs out of his jacket, and then extends it to me. I open my mouth to argue, but he stares me into silence.

"Trust me, you're gonna need it."

"What about you?" I ask, sliding my arms into the sleeves, overcome by the warm, smoky smell of boy. I wasn't sure I could return it even if he asked.

He takes my hand and tugs me along. "I'll be fine."

I lock the door before pulling the lapels of his jacket closer to me. When I turn around, Joshua's leaning against a deathtrap on two wheels. My heart aches like I'm dying because this is always how I imagined it, how my mom left.

The image changes slightly every time, but one thing remains the same. Mom is on the back of a guy's motorcycle in my dreams. Of course, I have no idea how it happened. She left me sitting on the coin-operated rusted horse outside the drug store, something an eleven-year-old was too grown-up to ride on. But I would have done anything my mom asked me. She handed me a stack of quarters I'd stuck in my jeans pocket and told me she had to see someone, but she'd be right back. The minutes turned to hours as I lost myself in the whining of the spring in the horse's base until my legs were numb. The sun had set, but I kept bouncing and swinging. If my mother said she'd be right back, she would be right back. Pop, Goldie's grandfather, came to get me off the horse. It was after eight o'clock, five hours after I'd watched her walk away. He said nothing, placing his sweater over my head and taking me by the hand. I've always loved that about him, the strong, silent type. He took me to the aunts.

I remember walking in and heading straight for Norah. She may be the least warm and fuzzy, but she's the strongest. She placed her hand on my head, and we didn't speak again that night. Mom was already gone. And now Joshua seems to think I'll be getting on a deathtrap like the one I was certain took my mother away.

"What's that?" I ask, motioning to the bike like I'd never seen one before.

A throaty chuckle flows through his body as he picks up the helmets off the back. He hands one to me, a giant contraption to cushion my entire skull. It doesn't seem like it would help much if we blew up in a giant fireball of death.

"You're not scared, are you?" he asks, a challenge in his stormy gaze.

The rational side of my brain wants to politely hand the helmet back and then run screaming for my safety down the street toward home. As it usually is, the rational side of my brain doesn't win. My brow furrows, and I shimmy the helmet over my ears. The compression is intense, but my brain feels secure. "Nope!" I exclaim with all the conviction of a deflating balloon, but if Joshua notices, he's enough of a gentleman not to register it.

He snaps his helmet into place. One big enough to protect the top of his head. It would be fitting to offer him the one I'm wearing. The mini helmet is his backup, but I'm terrified enough without risking anything more.

His leg swings over the bike, and the image of him straddling it, even with the absurd helmet, is the most hyper-masculine thing I've ever seen, and it makes my soul zing in the best way possible. His white shirt stretches against honed muscles that are too tan for the end of winter in Maryland. His corn-colored hair curls up in wisps around the edge of the mini helmet, and I have to fight the urge to run my fingers across them. He put his sunglasses in place, which is puzzling, considering it's the middle of the night. Then, he looks toward me. That beautiful smile is ever present on his face.

"You coming? Or are you going to stand there?" he asks, balancing his fingers on the handlebars, one foot propped up off the ground. Oh, so cool. While I'm here, I'm simply trying not to fall over.

I zip the jacket to my chin and force my feet to move. How is my ungraceful self supposed to get on this thing without killing both of us or making a fool out of me? A snicker escapes him like he can hear my internal thoughts. "Swing your right leg over. Don't worry. I'll catch you if you start falling."

Easy for him to say. I pick up my foot and somehow don't end up on the ground, but rather with my legs on either side of a hot guy's butt. The realization rushes every ounce of blood to my cheeks, and I'm grateful for the face guard. Without turning his head, he reaches back and grabs my wrists, pulling my arms around his body.

"You need to hold on tight," he explains, securing my hands at his stomach, my fingers entwining. "You hold on. I've got everything else." And I believe him.

I only screamed twice. I deserve a damn medal for only screaming twice. The first time we pulled onto a main road, I would have sworn we were going ninety miles an hour. The first time we took a turn with a bit of speed, I was sure we were tipping over. A part of me hoped that Joshua would never stop driving because then I wouldn't have to face his horror at my reactions, but alas, we had to stop.

He gently pats my hands, locked at his waist, and I hesitantly let him go. "You okay back there?"

My fingers may have dislodged, but my body is still molded to his back. I can't move.

"Okay, okay," he coos, kindness warming his deep voice. His hands encircle mine, and the first deep breath since we started floods my lungs. "I can't get off until you do, so let's go ahead and dismount?" I miss his warmth as soon as I pull away. I plead with my body not to fall when I swing my leg over. My luck with gracefulness has to run out eventually, but my feet both make it into the crunchy gravel of the parking lot where we've landed. Joshua was standing in front of me less than a second later.

His hands go to either side of my head to help me pull off the helmet, which releases with a pop. The heat returns to my cheeks as his fingers trace under my chin.

"You're cute," he states before tousling my blonde hair. Internally, I'm screaming. My hair is in its natural state with no hairspray in sight.

"Where are we exactly?" I ask, fluffing my locks back into place. The parking lot was vacant, with one lone blinking light barely illuminating a four-foot radius around us. Behind is a single brick building with a window lined with neon lights. Zero clues.

The corner of his mouth turns up as he reaches down and pulls his t-shirt over his head, a white undershirt left behind.

What is happening?

"Are you wearing anything under your sweater?" Horror must flash across my eyes by the way he shakes his head. "We're going to need it."

I don't understand, but I don't question either, slipping his jacket off my arms to whip my sweater over my head. My skin bursts into goosebumps. I toss the sweater at him and put the jacket back on.

An unnatural, honking laugh, far removed from his aloof persona, comes from his mouth. "Cold?" he exclaims when he's reclaimed his breath.

I hug his jacket close, caught up in the smell of him. "You're the one who took my sweater. Want to tell me why?"

He extends his hand to me, and I forget all about the temperature. "I'll show you," he says in that deep, gravelly way that turns my insides to mush.

He tugs me toward the anonymous brick building with the neon light windows. I've seen enough horror movies to know that as a blonde girl who can't run, I have no business going into this place. If one of my friends had been with me, I would've locked myself in the car and demanded to go home, but not with Joshua. With zero evidence or reason, I trust this guy. Insanity, since he could be the psycho, good-looking, Ted Bundy-esque serial killer that's walking me into my doom. But I don't care. I'll at least have something pretty to look at while I die.

We enter to a jingle on the other side, much like what we have at the pie shop. To the right is an entire wall of front-loading washers and dryers, silent at this time of night. "Are we in a laundromat?" I ask, gaping at the incredibly unromantic setting.

Did I read this completely wrong? He squeezes my hand, a silent reprimand in pressure. "Patience, Grasshopper," he whispers before calling into the room, "Hey Leon! You here?"

"That you, Josh?" I hear from behind a thick curtain at the back of the room. It pushes aside, and a bowlegged older man hobbles from behind it, relying heavily on the cane on his right side. Joshua releases my hand to take the old man's, who chuckles at the firm shake. "Never do sleep, do you, Bub?"

"Too much to see, sir," Joshua responds, in a light, high pitch. It reminds me of how Bella speaks to her mom. A lot of love there.

Leon ducks around my escort to offer me a winning smile as if the two remembered I was here with them.

"Well, this is a first," he says as he hobbles in my direction. "Nice to meet you, young lady. I'm Leon Chance."

I'm confused. What is happening? I reach past Joshua and take Leon's hand, which is rough from seemingly years of work. "Rosie Peters."

He responds with a sharp nod, turning his attention back to Joshua. "Well, young man, you know the rules." Joshua lifts his hand with my sweater and his shirt.

"Then I'll leave you to it. It's a pleasure to have met you, Rosie Peters."

He shuffles away through another door, and I peek at the office behind it. Clean and orderly, it reminds me of a loan shark's desk from a mobster movie. All it needs is the swinging fluorescent light.

"Can I have even a small clue about what's happening? Is this a fight club?" I ask, a mix of horror and excitement. I've always thought I could throw some serious punches. Unfortunately, I cry at the sight of a paper cut, so it's a toss-up.

He tugs me toward the washers, opens one, and throws our clothes inside.

"Well, if it were a fight club, we couldn't talk about it, could we?" He has a point. The grin stretches back to life as he adds fabric softener and detergent.

"And besides, what if this is all there is? It could be an artistic display, watching the clothes swish back and forth in the water. You could add it to your art show with your cartons of strawberries."

Mocking, but there is something hypnotic about a washing machine. I'd watched more than one in my time, but I would never tell Joshua that.

He smiles a little brighter after he starts the washer and throws his arm over my shoulders, squeezing me to his side, and my insides turn into jello. I don't care what we're doing as long as he holds onto me.

"Okay, okay, I guess you've been patient enough."

He heads toward the curtain where Leon had initially emerged. A million possibilities rush through my brain. Leatherface's den full of human skin lampshades? Meth lab? A sweatshop full of small children making shoes? The options are endless and could be better. Joshua pushes the curtain aside. It takes a solid second to process what I see.

"Is this a bowling alley?"

Two short lanes end with a line of tiny pins set up in a pyramid. A small automatic ball return separates the two, and the continuous hum of the ancient machinery fills the air. He grins beside me like a little boy with a treasure he's decided to share.

"That it is. Leon lets the late-night customers bowl while they wash, but you have to wash to do it."

"Hence why you took my sweater."

"Hence indeed."

I shrug off the jacket and place it on one of the two plastic chairs by the scoreboard. Joshua takes a step toward me, entering my personal bubble, but for once, I don't care. One long, perfect finger reaches up to trace the tattoo's outline on my shoulder. His brow furrows as the corners of his mouth turn down.

"This is—interesting," he says, tracing the black outline on the purple flower.

It's like my throat fills with pebbles that I can't swallow.

"Interesting, bad?" I squeak.

He lets an exasperated breath through his nose before settling away from me. I sense the cold from the space between our bodies instantly.

"Interesting," he says flatly.

Why do I feel like I've been scolded?

"You ever bowled duckpin?" he asks, switching gears.

"I've never bowled at all."

His eyes quadruple in size as his head snaps around to me fast enough to spin like Linda Blair's.

"How is that possible?"

"Could you make it sound a little less like I grew up feral?" My fingers skim the row of brightly colored balls lined up between the two lanes.

"It's kind of like you did," he mumbles, scooping up one of the balls and tossing it between his hands. He grabs me with his free hand and pulls me in front of him. Every hair on my body stands on edge as the bare skin of my arms brushes against his torso. He molds his body around my back, and my limbs forget how to move at the intimate nature of our position. He puts a small orange ball in the palm of my hand as his lips brush over my ear, whispering, "Relax."

I take a deep breath when his fingers trail down my sides, and I focus every ounce of energy to keep myself from giggling. His hands settle on my hips, and it's all too much. Too intimate. And quickly, he pulls back.

"On second thought," he says, backing away to sit in one of the orange plastic chairs. "I'd rather see what you think you're supposed to do."

I can feel the heat radiate up my shoulders and to my neck. Being put on display makes me squirrely, and the idea of a hot guy doing the staring is even worse. But I am a mighty Amazonian woman. I got this. I walk up to the line, testing the weight of the heavy ball in my hands. I remember watching *The Big Lebowski* and *Kingpin* with Goldie at our local movie theater, the Representative. She has an obsession with old movies, and I mainly use them for rare occasions when I need to take a nap. My toes brush the edge of the black line at the end of my lane, and I've got nothing. I can feel Joshua's ogling back, and I choose to stop thinking so hard and do whatever my body commands.

Why on earth does my stupid body decide to split my legs and bend forward to throw the ball from between my thighs? I flashed Joshua with a less-than-flattering view of my butt. I should totally burst through the wall and keep running toward Harpersgrove and the closet in my bedroom. No one would find me there. Worse than that, the ball only makes it halfway down the lane before sadly rolling to the gutter. The ten arrogant pins still standing and mocking me from across the way are unnecessarily cruel.

He tugs his lower lip between his teeth to try and hide a smile or a laugh. I can appreciate the effort. He leans back, his elbows balanced on the back of the chair, relaxed and effortless, while I find it awkward to be wearing skin. "Well, that was interesting."

"Don't leave me to my own devices," I mutter while I fiddle with the hem of my tank top.

He pushes off the chair smoothly, taking three solid and confident strides toward me. He stands close enough to me that I can feel the heat radiating from his skin. His eyelids fall heavy as he stares down at me, his gaze searching for something in my own.

"You need my help then?"

Whoa. What happened? Did I give up some super sexy vibe that I wasn't aware I possessed? My weight shifts as I try to make myself taller. Joshua has the upper hand in the realm of physical intimidation.

I may be small, but I'm mighty. I square my shoulders to him and tuck my hands in the back pockets of my jeans. "Maybe I do," I murmur, fully aware that I'm pushing my boobs out in a shameless way that I do not apologize for.

My breath catches when he pushes his thumbs through my belt loops and tugs me toward him, my body flush against his. Every ounce of serenity flees my being. My hands leave my pockets and circle his forearms to keep from falling over, and his hands settle to my lower back above my butt. The sensation of his skin against mine is scorching as his relaxed gaze scans my face. He's going to kiss me. I can feel it. But he doesn't make a single movement. I start to lose myself in the dizzying scent of boy's body spray and clean sweat, shockingly male. His fingers flex against my back, my one reminder that this is not a dream. The air moves through my lungs in shaky breaths as he brings a finger under my chin to tilt my face up toward his. It's happening. This is precisely what I need. I need someone to pull me completely out of my head, and the current chaos is my life. Kissing Joshua is the perfect thing to do. My body relaxes into him, giving myself over. And then he pulls away.

Unable to perform any human function, like moving or breathing, I find myself cemented in my place, my arms up and eyes closed. What happened? After what feels like an agonizing lifetime, I come back to the room. I'm pretty sure I must have had a psychotic episode and imagined the entire thing. Utter and complete bafflement is all I feel as I watch him casually bowl.

What the literal hell?! I realize I have limited experience with boys, but there's no way I read this situation that wrong. He glances back at me over his shoulder and flashes me that winning grin. "Are you gonna bowl, or are you gonna stand there?" Message received. I'm a dumb dumb who can't read a boy's intentions.

When our clothes are clean and dry, and I've lost two games of bowling, we slip back into our shirts. It's like a warm and comforting hug. Considering how tight every muscle of my body has been for the last hour, I take the release happily. We bid our goodbyes to Leon as he shuffles back to the alley side of the laundromat with a grumble of farewell. Joshua picks up my helmet and balances it on his hip, but doesn't hand it over. I let out a frustrated breath. I'm ready to be home, back in my bed or hiding under the counter in the shop. I don't want to feel this flutter in my chest when I look at him and know it's only in my head.

His head cocks to the side, and his focus narrows like he's trying to read my mind. I'm too on display, too exposed, as he stares. I've had enough of people looking at me. "What?!" I finally exclaim when I can't take it anymore.

He balances the helmet back on the bike, closing the distance between us in two strong strides. One of his hands grips my hip, pulling me against him, and the other reaches behind my head, holding me at the nape of my neck. I can feel and smell his breath on my skin, minty and warm. My hands stay pinned between our chests, and I'm not sure if I'm even breathing. Before another synapse can fire in my brain, he tugs my face closer, his mouth sealing over mine. My eyes fly open. I'm unsure if it's out of surprise or the fear of missing something. It's only when the tip of his tongue runs across the edge of my lower lip that I soften.

I relax no sooner than he's pulling away, snapping me back to reality. His mood swings are giving me whiplash. His hands remain firmly in place, his skin scorching against me. A flicker of something I can't define—playful, or funny—flashes through his eyes as he tugs on my hair. "Don't be stupid," he mumbles before kissing the tip of my nose and letting me go.

What—

Just—

Happened?

My entire body freezes like a computer glitch as he turns back to the motorcycle to grab my helmet, securing it over my head when it's clear that my arms and legs no longer work. I spent the entire ride back to Harpersgrove trying to process it. The whipping sound of air and the lack of need to make conversation allow me to fall deeper into the spiral of my thoughts. It reminds me of the black water from my dreams. Does he like me? Is he messing with me? What's his angle? What the hell is going on? I decided to ask him all these questions the second I got off this bike.

He drives me back to the pie shop as the soft beginnings of pink sky rise over the horizon. It'll be time to wake up before I know it—our combined weight shifts to the side as he urges me off behind him. I face away from him and toward the pie shop to take off my helmet. I'm ready to retreat to normalcy and away from this imbalance. I start to slide off his jacket, missing its warmth immediately, when he grips my upper arms from behind. His breath is warm on my ear as he pushes the leather back over my shoulders.

"Why don't you hold onto that for next time? I have others," he says before pressing his lips into the crook of my neck, his tongue darting out to taste my skin, sending a pulse of heat through my entire body.

I forget every ounce of doubt that only a moment before filled me. I twist around to kiss him full-on, lose myself in him, but he's already getting back on the bike. It's like being seasick the way he pulls me around. He offers me a wink before he drives away. I don't have his phone number, and we didn't make plans, but he said there would be a next time. I focused on the good, and those kisses were good, instead of the uneasiness of sitting like a heavy rock in my stomach.

CHAPTER SEVEN

The tumble through my bedroom window at four-thirty in the morning is less than graceful and only leaves me an hour or so to sleep. A decent night. I hit the floor no sooner than the light beside my bed turned on. Every ninja skill and jungle training moment that past selves must have gone through kicks into gear as I pounce in the direction of my bed.

"What the hell are you doing?" Norah asks from her spot on my mattress.

"What the hell am *I* doing?" I shriek, fighting off the impulse to beat her senseless with my shoe. "What the hell are *you* doing?"

My aunt sits up and motions for me to join her on the bed. No, no, no, I've seen this horror movie before. One never goes toward the witch. When I don't move, she pats the bed hard, sending home the message that this is not a request. With a begrudging sigh, I drop my purse by the window and settle on the floor across from her.

"I thought we'd stopped with the sneaking through the window thing?"

Picking at the pilled fabric on my faded black sheets, I shrug my shoulders to my ears. "Seemed like good nostalgia," I offer up in lieu of the truth, but my aunt is no dummy.

"Couldn't possibly be that you're avoiding us?" she asks, nudging me with her foot. Norah has zero interest in letting me hide in myself. The aunts have hovered more in the last two days than in the previous two years. Avoidance is a better option than dealing.

"Norah, I have to get up in an hour for school. Can we talk about this later?" I huff, flexing against the groaning protest in my joints. My body passed exhaustion hours ago.

"Will we, though?"

I don't need this. I don't need people to suddenly show interest in how I'm doing only because my mother died.

"Are we going to talk about the guy at the funeral?" One of them has to answer me eventually. Either that or it will be the perfect shut-down to any conversation I don't want to be a part of for the rest of my life. It sounds like a win either way.

She chews on the inside of her cheek as she shakes her head. "That's irrelevant to what we're discussing, and you know it."

I squelch the rage boiling inside at being treated like a stupid child. "You want information? Me too! You guys are keeping things about my life from me."

She doesn't miss a beat and retorts, "He's not a part of your life. He made that choice."

"But I didn't!" I shriek, the top of the fury pot blowing off, steam pouring from my ears like a cartoon character.

Norah pushes to her feet and towers over me as she chastises, "Keep your voice down. No matter what you think, you are not the only person in this house."

She couldn't have shocked me more if she'd slapped me. I pride my-self on leaving the smallest footprint possible in this place. I never get in anyone's way and never ask anyone for anything. Not even Norah gets to make me feel otherwise.

"He's my father, isn't he? Why don't I have the right to know who he is?"

"I don't want you to bring this up anymore, Rosie. It's not good for any of us."

"It's not good for me to know who my father is?" I demand, my octave too high.

"You don't have a father!" she snaps back, her fists balling at her sides. My knees let go, and I fall back onto my bed—the freaking roller coaster of emotion. "I probably shouldn't have said that," she murmurs, her gaze focused on her hands. The fatigue sweeps over me like a heavy blanket. I want answers, but for once, I want to sleep more.

"I know I don't have parents, but two people did make me, and I'm pretty sure only one of them is dead."

She noticeably winces, like it's not true, which of course it is. Even when my mom was around, she was more of a big sister than a mother. Norah lays back, stretching herself out on my little mattress. She opens her arms to me and waves me to her, to settle in like I did when I was younger and unaware of how mean she was. I want to resist, but my muscle memory reminds me of how warm and squishy she is, and I give in to the comfort. I put my cheek on the flat part of her chest under her collarbone. My arms curled against my torso. We lay like that in uncomfortable silence for a few long moments, my body relaxing into the rhythm of her breathing and begging for sleep before I heard her again.

"Kyle Roosevelt," she whispers. That's his name."

Something about him being an intangible figure was easier to grasp. I expect to cry, faced with information my brain isn't ready for, but I don't. A chill runs through my body, waiting for more facts I know aren't coming. It was hard enough for Norah to give up what she did. I know that, but Norah doesn't move, and neither do I. There's comfort in the childlike familiarity of how she embraces me, allowing me to sink away. Sleep takes me before my eyes even fully close.

I'm back in the black water, facing down and holding my breath. The screaming surrounds me in all directions. It only subsides when I breathe deep, so deep that the water should flood my lungs and kill me.

It doesn't. I breathe when I should be dead.

Norah's gone by the time I wake up. We'll never speak of the moment again. This I know. Norah's even less warm and fuzzy than I am. I open my closet, rubbing my makeup-less face as I survey my options. I flip through my regular clothes, black on black on black. They seem wrong. I rip open another forgotten plastic bag of clothes from Shawna and pull out a long-sleeved olive and hunter-green plaid dress and a pair of brown tights. It reminds me of something a World War II-era German governess with a hairy mole would wear. It's not me—it's perfect. I slip it over my head and pull my hair back into a severe ponytail, leaving my face on full display. I swap out the thick black ring I usually wear around my lip for a clear plastic stud that blends into my skin. Chapstick is my only makeup. I feel myself falling in love with the stranger in the mirror.

In the kitchen, all three aunts sit around the table, watching me like predators as I pour a cup of life-saving coffee into a travel mug.

"What?"

Meredith narrows her glare before saying, "I'm going to ask you this once. Do you need to go see someone?" she asks, her fingers gripping the table's edge. I can't tell if she's trying to hold herself back from running to comfort me or throttle me.

Color flushes my cheeks. I don't need anyone telling me I'm crazy. I know that already. "Don't be dramatic, Mere. It doesn't suit you."

Her chair screeches against the floor when she pushes to stand. Shawna cracks the knuckles in her hands in a repeated rhythm to soothe her discomfort at the coming argument. She can sense a fight like a pig finds truffles. Norah remains surprisingly quiet—not at all her style. Maybe she's still reeling from earlier that morning. Perhaps she already told the others about it.

"Go walk yourself back to your room, look in the mirror, and then tell me I'm being dramatic," Meredith replies, closing the space between the dining room and the kitchen.

I could bang my head against the wall right now. Why does everyone care about my damn clothes? "Seriously? I'm not allowed to try out a different style?"

"The timing is concerning, sweetheart," Shawna tries to explain, the sound of her cracking joints momentarily pausing before starting back up again.

Meredith's eyes narrow further as she approaches me and reaches out to grab my chin. She barely touches me, but her fingers bruise my skin.

"Where's your normal lip ring?"

I whip my head back, leaving her hand suspended in mid-air. "Jesus, Mere, weren't you the one who chewed me out for days over getting it done in the first place?" I shouted, searching for my backpack. I need out of this house.

She plants her hands on her round hips and comes eye-to-eye with me. I may be short, but Meredith is shorter. Of course, I'm pretty sure she's the girl Shakespeare was writing about when he said, "Though she is but little, she is fierce."

My aunt is full of fire. "First of all," she begins, bringing her finger up to my face. "You were fourteen years old and came home with a piece of metal through your face. Excuse the hell out of me for having a problem with that. Secondly, you and I both know that this is no coincidence. You haven't worn a color since you were six years old."

"Black is a color," I mumble, but she never pauses.

"And the fact that someone," her voice carries over into the dining room to Norah, who sinks further into her seat, "decided to tell you about Kyle without consulting the rest of us also doesn't seem like a coincidence."

"I already apologized," Norah calls back, but it's clear that this is a moment between me and Meredith alone.

She grips my upper arms, forcing our gazes to meet. Except for her dark hair, she looks like the pictures of my grandfather. "Look at me, kid," Meredith says, her expression softening enough that it doesn't hurt to hold her gaze. "I'm worried about you. Talk to me."

For a second, I imagine it. I imagine collapsing into Meredith's arms and letting emotion finally take over. I imagine demanding more information about my father, the information I have the right to possess. I imagine telling them about Joshua and Parsons. I imagine crying for my mother and everything. I don't know how to feel about her. But I don't, I can't, I won't. I roll my shoulders and shrug out of her grip, but she doesn't fight me.

"Stop watching me under a microscope. I'm fine." That word is starting to lose all meaning.

No part of Meredith's demeanor or stance changes, but I can feel the hint of sadness radiating off her skin. I don't need her to feel sorry for me. "The fact that you're saying that," she begins as the air thickens and crackles between us. "Shows how not fine you are."

The defiant side of my brain wants to yell, "Do something!" An even smaller part of me wishes she would. I wish Meredith would force me to talk to her and get it all out in the open, but the louder part of me, engulfed in black water, can't take it. Instead, I throw my bag over my shoulder and scurry away from the kitchen and my wardens. School has to be better than this.

Instead, school is still as weird as any *Twilight Zone* episode could ever hope to be. People smile at me. I have gone through the Harpersgrove educational system for nearly thirteen years with these people, and they have never smiled. Yesterday was about averted glances and whispers. Today seems to be all catlike grins and saccharine sweetness.

One of the heaviest books falls to the floor while getting them out of my locker. A groan moves through my soul, turning it into a much bigger deal than what it is. That's the way of things. When big things are going wrong, every single little hiccup amplifies. I'm about to pick it up when Lucy Wilcox, the resident mean girl, reaches down and gets it for me. We trade a long and intense stare, her holding the book out to me all the while before I yelp, "Drop it!"

You'd think I'd asked her for her kidney. Her face contorted into a twisted Picasso-level mess before responding, "*What?*"

"You heard me," I snap, smacking the book out of her hands, and it plummets to the ground with a loud thump. Lucy Wilcox being nice to me is a level of weirdness I cannot handle. If she's trying to make me feel better after a lifetime of cruelty, this might be worse than I'm ready to admit.

She pans back up from the book to me, and she stares, but her sense of pity is gone. Fire burns in her there instead before she pivots away. She throws a passing "Freak!" back over her shoulder, and my body feels at peace again. That will teach her to try and be nice!

Too many people hold doors open for me or ask if I need a pen, even when I have one in my hand. I prefer my invisibility. It doesn't even stop when I get to art class, and Beau dares to pull my chair out for me. "Don't you dare," I hiss, jabbing a finger into his round face.

He sports the same twisted look that Lucy had as I push my seat back in and pull it out for myself. "Having a bad day, Friend?" he asks, returning his attention to his work, his massive poof of fluffy hair creating its wind as he goes. I hated his stupid hair and his stupid Hobbit t-shirt.

NO ONE NEEDS A THOUSAND GOLLUM SHIRTS!

I'm mad that I even know who Gollum is, and that's all Beau's fault. "I'm fine."

Ahh, there's that word again. I tug at the uncomfortable neckline of my dress and slap my sketchbook onto the work table, the sound echoing through the room.

"You're dressed like you're ready to beat small school children. I doubt you're fine, Rosie." Beau never calls me by my first name. I'm not sure where our moniker of "Friend" came from, but one day, it was there and stuck. I don't like the way my name fits in his mouth. It feels wrong, but I guess that's appropriate. Everything's wrong.

I let the rest of the class pass in a blur of too much sugary sweetness before ducking by home on my way to the pie shop. I can't imagine getting through a work shift in this awful dress. It was an experiment gone wrong. I traded it for a plain white shirt and the high-waisted jeans I'd worn yesterday. The cut of the shirt puts my purple rose tattoo on display, and for the first time, I'm embarrassed by it. I hurry out my window to the shop. I can't handle the aunts right now.

My shoes are full of lead on my walk down the most familiar streets of my life. I walk the center, single, faded white line on the warped asphalt like a tightrope. Heel to toe. Heel to toe. One of the glories of living in a town as small as Harpersgrove is that I'll never need to look up from my feet. No cars are coming at me. There are some things to adore about a small-town life; there are plenty of things you don't. I know I would fit in better in a place like New York or Los Angeles, a place too big for the past to follow me. But I live here, where people have long memories.

The front door jingles when I push into the everyday bustle of the pie shop. A quick swivel of heads turn to see who's entered as always, but, of course, since it's me, the stares linger. Having had enough attention for one lifetime, I take a deep curtsey to ensure everyone knows I've seen them stare. They turn back so fast to their pie that one might think someone is taking it from them.

Elle glides past, tray balanced up on her shoulder. "Damn," she murmurs with a smile, handing the folks at the closest table their cherry pie. "I was looking forward to seeing you work in that horrid dress you wore today." Her long brown ponytail swishes between her shoulder blades, and she tucks the empty tray under her arm. I know she's making fun of me, but a fluttering relief rushes through my stomach at the fact that one person is treating me normally again.

I follow her back to the kitchen, where she drops the tray onto the pile of empty ones and hops up to sit on my counter. From somewhere else in the restaurant, Bella is internally screaming. She hates it when we sit on top of the work tables.

"So," Elle begins, her hips shifting back and forth as she tries to find a comfortable position. "I have news."

I tie my apron behind my back and try to ignore the anxiety lump forming at the back of my throat. It's been a week of too much news. I doubt my poor little brain can take anymore. "Rose," Elle begins, pulling me out of my head with her laugh. "It's nothing bad, I promise. It's a good thing."

I lower my weight against the table beside her. "Sorry, news hasn't been my friend lately." For only a second, Elle gives me the head tilt, the look of pity I don't want. I can't lose the one person who's started to treat me regularly again. "What's your news?"

She lifts her palms forward, bracing me for the thrill. "I, Michelle Antoinette Conner, got into UCLA!" The school's name comes out at an octave only dogs can hear.

I'm pulled from my glumness and sadness and sucked thoroughly into Elle's rainbow of joy. She jumps off the table and wraps her arms around my shoulders, pressing me into her.

"Congratulations, Elle," I mumble into her chest, the sentiment muffled by her body.

"Have you heard from Parsons yet?" she asks, her bright eyes making me hopeful. I decide I'll feel more secure if I start telling people.

"Yeah, I got the letter yesterday."

If a human being could take on the form of an exploding firecracker, it would look a lot like Elle does right now. Her skin starts to vibrate noticeably as her weight bounces back and forth between her feet in rapid succession.

"Omigod! Omigod! Omigod!!!" Her voice hits at that same ear-piercing level that shatters glass. I place my hand over my favorite pie dish on the counter to protect it from the sound. "How are you not jumping out of your skin right now, girl?"

Everything I had hoped to feel in telling her, some extra semblance of excitement, has not been realized. I still feel as blasé and off about the whole thing as when Mr. Cooper handed me the letter.

"I don't know. I'm not even sure I'm gonna go." I roll my shoulders to shrug myself out of her grip.

"Excuse me?" she says, her eyebrows pushing in together giving off a Frida Khalo vibe. "You've only been talking about going to that school for as long as I've known you."

I start pulling random things down from the shelves I have no particular use for, but I hope if I look busy enough, she'll disappear. I'm sure she'll believe I need cornstarch, salt, and bananas for a pie, right?

"I'm not saying it isn't, but I've had some other big things on my mind recently."

She follows me around the kitchen like a baby duck, hot on my heels. The claustrophobia is setting in. "Rosie, other than pies, you're all about fashion. You've spent weeks stressed out, waiting for the acceptance letter. How can you act like this is no big deal?" She's getting squeaky again. It's giving me a headache.

"It doesn't seem like as big of a deal anymore. What do you want from me, Elle?" Even my friends have become overbearing. It's enough already.

She's quiet for a moment too long, forcing me to look up to her. All six feet of judgment stare back at me with a slack-jawed "duh" expression.

"What do I want from you?" she asks, her voice low and breathy.

Tears form, and jealousy and anger pool in my stomach. She can cry for me, but why can't I shed one tear for my mother?

"Rosie, I'm worried about you."

That old irrational anger that bubbled inside with Meredith this morning lights up again. "I don't need you to worry about me, Elle," I growl, stepping toward her in deliberate strides that narrow the space left for her in my kitchen. "What I need is for you to leave me alone."

Her eyes widen when her back hits the door. I push it open for her with the flat of my hand. "Go," I hiss. Not even a moment of hesitation crosses her before she's gone, the swinging, squeaky hinge the only indication she was there at all.

I'm an asshole and a righteous one. It's a lethal combination.

Figuring I need to take on some form of self-flagellation for this, I force myself to make a pie that actually tastes good from my weird and random ingredients. I ditch the cornstarch but use the salt in a caramel, brown the bananas, and ta-da! Bananas Foster Pie, or as I intend to call it, "Elle, Sorry I'm a Jerk, Here's Some Sugar" Pie. The title needs some work.

I cut the first slice through the caramelized top of the dessert, and I'm acutely aware that I'm not alone. Three people peer back at me in the little window that separates the kitchen from the rest of the shop. Elle, Bella, and Nixie stare unblinking, unnerving back at me.

"Are you sharing?" Nixie asks, her head nodding toward the pie.

Usually, the girls have to wait until our once-a-month tasting night to try anything new, but since it's an apology pie, I should share it. I nod, and Nixie's head is the first to disappear, followed quickly by the other two. The kitchen door swings back and forth, and my friends pile into the room.

"Tattle tail," I mutter as Elle enters last. She dares to stick her tongue out at me before taking a place on the counter against the wall. Nixie cuts herself a piece of pie and digs in, most likely to keep herself from crying, and Bella, dearest Bella, takes it upon herself to talk some sense into me.

"Okay," she begins, folding her hands behind her back and rocking back on her heels. "Want to tell me about Parsons?" Since returning from New York, she's ditched her wardrobe of never-ending black leggings and oversized sweaters for jeans and fitted tops. Yet no one seems to drag her over the coals for her new fashion choices!

All the remorse and kindness I'd baked into the pie has fled my body. Baking works in both directions sometimes. "Nope," I mumble, throwing on the water in the sink, ignoring the way Elle flinches against the splash.

Elle leans over and turns the water back off. Avoidance is not going to work.

"We're concerned, okay," she says, reaching for my hand, but the heat radiating off her skin hurts. "You've been talking about this forever. We can't believe you suddenly don't want it."

"I'm not saying I don't want it," I snap back, pushing my hands over my hair. "But I'm not saying I do either."

"Listen," Bella begins again, stepping up to the plate, incapable of backing down. "I expected more from you."

The head of our fearless leader, Beattie, pops through the little window. "Do I still have a staff?" she barks, and I've never been more grateful to her. "Rosie, can you please heat a cherry pie for me? I served the last piece out here."

Bella's disappointment still hangs heavy in the air. Only one line from one book enters my mind. "If you expect nothing from somebody, you are never disappointed." *The Bell Jar* is the one book I've connected with throughout my school career. Perhaps that's concerning.

Before I can even reach it, Bella throws herself at the double ovens.

"What are you doing?!" I demand, annoyed and worried she might burn herself.

Her expression never falters as she proclaims, "When you start empathizing with Sylvia Plath, it's time to step away from the oven."

Of all people, I should have known that Bella would get the reference—annoying little bookworm. Elle taps Nixie on the shoulder and the actual plan takes form: leave me alone with the disappointed mom-faced Bella. When we're left with only each other, Bella leans back against the oven again.

"Can you move, please," I quietly demand. I expect disobedience; everyone seems to feel the need to be difficult, but Bella simply moves away. I'm grateful. I shovel the cherry, blueberry, and peach pie into the oven and set it to warm.

"I haven't known you as long as some of the other girls have, but one thing I know for sure is the look on your face when you talk about making clothes."

"This has nothing to do with that," I grumble, wishing I could take a page from Sylvia Plath—or a step further and go full-on *Hansel and Gretel*, climbing all the way into the oven. It would at least get me away. I don't need another voice of reason.

Bella's warm hands press against either of my cheeks. "Can you take a step back for two seconds and realize how bananas this is for the people who love you?"

Damn voice of reason.

I don't wretch myself away with the fury boiling inside me, but I do pull away from her hands. "Bells, I need to figure some things out. Why isn't that okay?" I snap, sending my friend a mile away, pulled into herself. I feel bad for that, but refuse to linger on it.

"It is okay," she says, trying to regain her ground. She's the ship, and I'm the storm. I'm a hurricane with a freaking heartbeat. I destroy everyone in my wake. "But I won't stop worrying about you in the meantime." She moves back through the swinging door. I don't blame her. I probably wouldn't hang around to hear my response, either.

The evening falls in a hushed silence as everyone seems poised to leave me alone. I know I should feel bad, and I'm sure that Bella has directed them to avoid the dragon, but I'm more grateful than remorseful. Everyone has to know by now that I got into Parsons. I thought Elle could keep a secret.

My friends don't get it. This decision isn't about my mother. How am I, your basic orphan, supposed to afford college, let alone one that means I'd have to live in New York? It was reckless and irresponsible to only apply to one school. What was I thinking? I can check if New Shiloh Community College has some fashion design classes I can enroll in. Then I can keep working here, making pies and responsibly paying for school. Isn't that the adult thing to do? Shouldn't that be the right thing? Maybe I need to propose that to them to show that I have thought about this. Of course, I must get the nerve up to talk to the aunts first. That needs to come from a level of bravery that I am not sure I possess.

At closing time, the girls waved to me through the window, like children leaving animals at the zoo; no one came too close. I'm glad to see them go. Even with the distance, their presence was stifling. It's strange because I don't know him well, but Joshua is the only person I want to see right now. Something about him calms me. I settle in at the counter and wait, certain he'll come.

CHAPTER EIGHT

But Joshua doesn't show up. In fact, it would be a whole week before I'd see him again. I fall into a deep, never-ending void of pointlessly checking my phone for a text that isn't going to come. You're a big dummy, Rosie Rose. You never gave the boy your phone number. It shouldn't affect me. It's not like we made plans that he ignored, but I still expected him to show up that first night. Instead, I spend my week moping and avoiding all the people who love me. I have no interest in talking about college ever again as I become more resolved in my plan to blow off New York. I've almost acquired enough nerve to tell the aunts my choice. Almost.

I fill my days with school, making pies, and spend my evenings torturing myself, staring out the shop window, waiting for him to appear magically. Occasionally, I scribble out notes and designs for the prom dresses I've promised to make, but I am uninspired and not much comes from it. When he finally does come to see me, my stomach fills with those annoying fluttering butterflies at the sight of that blonde head and leather jacket.

Tripping over my feet to get to him as fast as possible, I abandon every scrap of dignity I've ever possessed. It might as well go out the window with all the hurt I had felt over not seeing Joshua for seven solid days. The grin that spreads across my face takes me from cute to insane in an instant. I'm so happy to see him that it could have been a month, and I would have forgotten the time that lapsed.

In a swift moment, faster than a blink, his hands burrow in my hair, and his mouth seals over mine. Having no time to catch my breath, I go weak in the knees and grab his waist to keep me on my feet. We linger there, the forgotten space between the warmth of the shop and the crispness of the air outside. It sends my senses into overdrive. Only when I'm settling into a groove does he pull away, tousling my hair with one of his hands.

"Hi," he says as he brushes past me into the shop. My weight falls back, my chest rising and falling like I'd run a marathon.

He heads to the counter and sits, his back to me, already searching for pie. I run my hands over my red and black plaid shirt, lifted from Shawna's closet, and try to bring some levity to the room. He swivels in his seat, squeaks resonating through the quiet.

"Hey, stranger," I say.

"What do you mean?" he asks, staring back at me like I've spoken in German.

This is why I should never try to be coy. It never comes out right. "Oh," I begin, my fingers knotting together at my waist. "I was making a joke because I haven't seen you in, like, a week."

He cocks an eyebrow up into his hairline as his elbows balance back against the counter. The edge of his shirt pulls up slightly to reveal unnaturally tanned skin. "Don't be stupid," he chuckles, pulling the cover off a cellophane-wrapped apple pie. I guess that's the end of the conversation.

Once I'm behind the counter again, I hand him a plate, but he seems more interested in chowing down half of a pie with a fork. I put the plates away. I wait for him to say something to break up the silence, but he keeps eating.

"How was your week?" I ask with a smile, trying to get something resembling a dialogue moving. He watches from under impossibly long lashes, and scoffs before returning to eating.

What?

I return to his side, sitting on the neon stool beside him. A nervous lump has formed at the back of my throat, and I'm fighting the urge to either cry or throw up.

"Is everything okay?" Even as the words come out of my mouth, I wish I could swallow them. Nothing good can come from this.

His eyes roll over with such force that I'm sure his retinas must detach. "Jesus, I'm fine."

My body curls back in on itself, like I might implode. Joshua sighs loud enough for me to feel it in my toes before his arm wraps around my shoulders. "It's been a long couple of days. Can we focus on the fact that I'm here now?"

I fall further into my body, like slipping deeper into that black water. Joshua hypnotizes me with that smile, and I don't even realize it. He swivels in his seat and pulls me toward him between his legs while sliding his hands into the back pockets of my jeans. It's such an intimate gesture that any ice on my heart has melted into a puddle. I am goo. He rests his forehead against mine, and I'm overwhelmed by his warmth and scent. Why do people do drugs? They need a whiff of Joshua McDonald instead.

"Hey," he mumbles. He tilts his chin forward to kiss me, and I forget my name, let alone any black water. "I'm happy to be here with you. Can that be what you care about?"

I'm about to answer when I hear knocking behind me. A quick peek at the clock tells me it's after ten o'clock. Harpersgrovians don't even know that this time of day exists! It shouldn't surprise me when I turn to see another New Shiloh resident at the door. Blanche's face pinches together as she stands stiff like a pole outside.

Clad only in running shorts and a long-sleeved t-shirt, she has to be cold. Joshua turns with me, and the two lock eyes. It makes sense that they know each other; they go to the same school, but something in my chest hurts knowing he exists to others outside me.

"Are you going to let me in, or are you gonna leave me out here?" she calls through the glass, her stare never leaving Joshua. He's settled back into his laid back stance, ankles crossed, elbows balanced on the counter, but the way he's watching Blanche is almost predatory.

I hustle to relieve my friend from the cold. I open it, but she makes no quick move to come inside. She stays glued on Joshua.

"It's pretty cold out there. You coming in?" I joke, trying to break up some of the palpable tension thick in the air between them.

Her hand brushes mine as she moves past me into the shop. "Josh," she says. She is six feet, two inches of sass, like an Asian supermodel. My ordinarily chatty friend seems to have very few words.

A different smile, meaner than I've seen, crosses Joshua's face as he stares back at her. "Blanche," he offers up in an over-the-top southern drawl. More malice drips from it than one word should be able to hold.

"What's up, Blanche?" I ask curtly. I am not a fan of conflict, and a flare of fear rises in me at the idea that Joshua might bolt because of her. It makes me hate her, and the realization sends an unpleasant chill up my spine.

She looks at me for the first time. The scatter of freckles across her nose squish up near her eyes as she sneers. "I have a history paper to finish, and Bella said she had a book here she thought I could use."

"A book?"

"Trust me, I know," she says when she sees my face. "I thought the internet existed to keep me from driving all the way to the Harpersgrove this late at night." She looks back to Joshua. "But it looks like it's good that I did."

"Well," he begins pushing to his feet. Panic stampedes through my body. He's finally here after a week without seeing him! "That's my cue." I could punch Blanche right now. He reaches out and grabs my hand as he passes. "I'll see you later, Rosaline," it's the first time my whole first name doesn't make me recoil, and I can't help the way I smile. Before he leaves, he scribbles a series of digits on my hand with a Sharpie, and it's the only saving grace of this crappy moment that I finally have his number.

He and Blanche share a final death glare before he heads back outside like a mirage I can't hold onto. The moment the door bangs shut, Blanche is on me like a lion on a zebra carcass. "What the literal hell, Rose?!" she shrieks. That's the Blanche I know and love.

"You're trying to 'literal hell' me?" I throw it right back, "The literal hell, Blanche!" I'm sure every inch of my skin flushed crimson if the heat pulsing through my limbs is any indicator.

She follows me around the counter; even though it should be obvious, I'm trying to escape her. "Do you know who that was?" she demands, taking everything out of my hand that I pick up to try and distract myself from looking at her.

I take a deep breath through my nose and imagine I'm a balloon inflating to the point of bursting. "That was Joshua McDonald," I say with a confidence that doesn't quite meet my heart. Not only physically but in all ways, I feel small around Blanche. She is a presence.

Her hands plant on her narrow hips as she blocks any escape from around the counter. Damn it, I'm the girl in the horror movie that runs into the basement instead of outside to the running car. "And do you know who he is?" she asks again. I'll let silence be my answer. I know what I need to know. A groan sounds low in her throat and erupts out of her mouth like a volcano. "Do you remember that girl that Elle's boyfriend Finn used to date?" she asks.

She's grabbed my attention. Damn it. "Yeah, I remember that girl. She was here the day Elle dropped all the pie on Finn."

I start to deflate as I'm forced to consider for the first time that Joshua might have a girlfriend. It would make sense, I guess. He is beautiful and composed, but that girl is a monster.

"That would be Mallory McDonald," she says, overemphasizing the last name. Huzzah! Unless this is a lead-up to some backwoods, swamp people stuff, the two are definitely not dating. "They're twins, and let me say, Mal is a rotten apple, and they come from the same freakin' tree. I know bad apples, Rose, trust me."

She's expecting some extreme reaction from me, but what has she even said? Yeah, maybe he has a crappy sister, but I have—had—a crappy mom, and that doesn't mean I'm a terrible person.

"And?" I say, my tone is snarky. I don't like snap judgments without evidence. I've encountered far too many of those in my life.

"He's not a good guy, Rosie," she continues, following me as I duck under her arm and head back to my kitchen. This kitchen is my calm place, but everyone seems damned determined to do it.

"Why?" I ask defiantly. "You have to give me a reason. You can't make baseless accusations about a person. You're better than that."

If I'd spit in her face, I don't think I would have shocked her more. I am not being irrational or crazy, and I don't appreciate her speaking to me like I am.

"Oh, okay," she says. "I'm telling you, I know this guy, and you don't. I've gone to school with him my whole life. Unfortunately for me, we run in a similar crowd. He doesn't treat people well, and he comes from a toxic family. Why can't you let me look out for you?"

"Why can't you let me make my own decisions?"

She takes a long pause like I've seen Meredith do when I know she's trying not to yell. "Look," Blanche begins, holding me steady. "Everyone has been patient at letting you make your own decisions since your mom died. You think everyone hasn't had more than a few words for you and your weird wardrobe change?"

I want to throw myself on the floor and going full toddler. "If one more person brings up my damn clothes—"

"Rosaline, we're not talking about me here, fashion is your damn life, and you're dressed like a frumpy lumberjack, and it's not even ironic!" I glance down at my outfit of oversized red plaid and awkward-length black jeans. There's a part of my brain screaming for intervention, but the sad, slow, sloth part of me punches her in the face to shut her up.

"Oh," Blanche chirps, her hands flying out from her sides like she's about to take flight. "And don't even get me started on school." Every drop of blood in my body suddenly chills to the point that it feels frozen in my veins. "You think Elle didn't tell me? Do you know how hard it's been to not pound you for being stupid?"

"It's time for you to go," I hiss, fingernails cutting into the palms of my hands from the pressure building up like a boiling tea kettle inside me.

"Rosie, what is wrong with you?!" she shrieks, the sound piercing my ears like shattering glass. There's basically nothing of me left standing, and I'm not ready to send anything else tumbling to the ground.

The damn tea kettle explodes.

"My mother is dead, Blanche! A little consideration from my friends while I figure out my life would be nice. Or maybe you guys aren't actually my friends." I can feel my blood pounding through my temples, and I'm not sure if I'm ready to finally start crying or punch a few holes through the walls.

Angry tears well up in Blanche's eyes, and I'm unsure if I've ever seen her cry. It gives me that feeling of sitting on a chair with uneven legs.

"Really?" she hisses. Her pale skin flushes a deep pink. "You have the audacity to pull the dead mom card with me?" I open my mouth to counter, but she doesn't give me the chance.

"Stop!" she yelps with an outstretched hand to silence me. "You get latitude, but you know what you don't get to do?" Her body shakes with her rage, and I find myself powerless to do anything but stand there eerily motionless and take it. "You don't get to ruin your future while you deal. If you don't go to Parsons, you will hate yourself, Rosie. I know that, and you do, too. I refuse to believe that Rosie from before wouldn't be beating the literal shit out of you over this, and I'm going to stand here in her place and fight her fight until your ass wakes up!"

If there was ever a time to break down, to lean on another human being, this is it. But a blackness seeps through my limbs and into my heart like ink. You can't get it off your skin, and I know I won't be grasping that olive branch. I reach under the counter and practically throw the history book at Blanche.

"Our situations are not the same and you know it," I bark back at her, wishing I had things to throw and break, but nothing is mine. "You had a family to lean on when your mom died. Your dad and seven brothers. I have no one! I am all alone."

Blanche tosses the book on the counter as if it burned her. "Are you on glue?" she screams, her hands flying wildly. For a moment, I worry she might swing back and hit me. "You seriously think you're alone? That's insulting, Rosie!"

"It's not the same, and you know it. You're my friends, and yes, you're great friends. But as far as my family goes, I'm alone. I don't have parents, I don't have anyone! I. Am. Alone."

Using her thumbs, she wipes away a few tears I hadn't noticed spilling away from her cheeks and retrieves her book. Her head bobs up and down a few times as she composes herself, sucking a few deep breaths through her nose.

"If that's really what you think, Rosie," she begins, eerily calm and even, "then that's exactly what you deserve to be. Alone."

The cold that rushes in as she barges out seeps down to my bones, sending a violent shiver through me. The strong pedestal of my stance that I had been standing on moments before begins to wobble the longer I stand there. Exhaustion weighs heavily through every inch of my body. I fight hard to stay awake under the weight. I press the heels of my hands into the sockets, reveling in the pressure.

Blood rushes to my legs, propelling me to run—run far away. Leave the problems behind and never stop running in the opposite direction. My mom had it right. This wretched town and its people are a toxic poison; running away is the only way to survive. Of course, she didn't survive it, but the lesson stands. Who knows how much faster she would have declined and left the world if she'd stayed here?

Or was it was me?

It's the kind of thing no one ever wants to think, but what if you have to? *If it wasn't the drugs—*. My mind spirals. She kept me for eleven years. She stuck it out, being a parent for that long before she bailed without a goodbye. She cut the strings and ran away. She couldn't even bother to say goodbye. What if it was the only way to get away? What if it was the only way she could escape me? Cut and run and never look back. Why wasn't I worth sticking around for? Why wasn't I worth staying alive for?

That anger festering inside me explodes out through my skin like the destruction of a comic book villain via telekinetic powers. Running full force, I hit the front door with enough speed to knock the jingle bells off the handle. Before I know it, I'm standing in the middle of Main Street, hands buried deep in my hair that I haven't washed in three days, prepared to scream at the top of my lungs. If I'm not sleeping, no one in this damned town should sleep. I want to destroy everything in my path. Hurricane Rosie will be unlike anything this town has ever seen.

That's when I see it. That godforsaken, quarter-stealing, shaking, back-breaking, mechanical metal horse in front of the drug store. Its copper mane and chipped white body mock me up to its soulless black orbs. It knows and remembers that day that my mom left me there, and I had two welts on my behind for a week because I refused to get off it all day.

I stutter to a stop when I am finally in front of my nemesis, and I realize I have no idea what I'm planning to do. My teeth grit together, nearly shattering as I smack at the stupid metal horse. An act even less effective than I thought it would be. The jerk dares to snap on his spring back up at me. *Stay down, you equine bastard!*

My fists pound over and over onto the cold metal, bruising my skin, but I can't stop. My punches are as ineffectual as they would be against a brick wall, but I can't stop. My skin flushes as my breathing rushes out in sluggish puffs. The horse looks the same as when I got here—the jerk.

"Roz," I hear from over my shoulder, causing me to leave my skin behind in a puddle as my insides flee my body. It's surprising to find only Goldie's grandfather and proprietor of the establishment I'm currently vandalizing. Pop is the only person in the world authorized to call me Roz. Having no grandparents, I clung onto Goldie's Pop and Nana, and they've had no problem with it. Their other grandchildren live on the opposite side of the country. They like having someone else to share their love with.

Pop takes a final drag on the glowing cigarette between his teeth before tossing it to the ground and squashing it under his shoe. Smoke billows from his mouth like a puffy white cloud before he exits the shadows toward me. His dark tan, leathery skin is that of a man who spent his adult life working outside, not in a store, but I've never known him any other way. When Goldie and I were small, Pop had given up on saving what was left of his hair, shaving his head religiously every day like other people brush their teeth. I remember him taking the blades out of two razors and letting Goldie and I lather up with him and "shave" our faces alongside him. If I remember correctly, it ended in nothing more than a shaving cream battle between the three of us, with one very ticked-off Nana at its conclusion.

Pop tugs on the lapels of his denim jacket, which is older than time. "How ya doing, Roz?" he asks cautiously, like he's circling a wild animal.

"Not great, Pop," I mutter through a clenched jaw, attempting to hold in the extremity of my understatement. I haven't been great in a long time.

He takes the spot beside me, the top of my head coming to his shoulder. "Yeah, I had a feeling as much was true," he says as we gaze upon my mechanical nemesis.

"What are you doing out here, Pop? It's after midnight." My surrogate grandfather remains unfazed. Somehow, that only makes the beast inside me scream louder. "Easier to do the inventory when no one's in the store. Plus, you know I'm not much of a sleeper myself." It's true. There were days I used to sleep at Goldie's house as a child, and Pop would bring me to the shop with him after finding me lying on the front lawn in the middle of the night counting the stars. He used to let me take the lead in organizing the cosmetics. The rainbow theme I'd set across the nail polish still stands strong today.

Pop isn't big on physical affection. He's more the type to punch you in the arm than hug you to express his love. That doesn't stop him from placing his hand on my shoulder. The pressure of his fingers squeezing my skin is the most grounding sensation I've ever felt. My knees are weak. I'm exhausted.

"You know," Pop begins again, clearing his throat as he goes. "Your hands and feet aren't going to do much to that old horse." He reaches around the wooden post at the top of the steps leading up to the store and pulls back a crowbar. "This might do a little more damage."

I stare at the metal pole in his hand like a venomous snake poised to bite me. "People would hear," I murmur, crossing my arms in a protective hug over my body. Lining Main Street is shop upon shop, but the top floors of those buildings are primarily apartments. People would wake up.

Pop shrugs, the corners of his mouth turning down as he does, the moonlight reflecting off his cue ball of a head as it cocks to the side. "They would. I guess you have to decide how much it means to you." And then the crowbar is sitting heavy in my hand. The weight pulls my arm down as I stare at the horse's gleaming and challenging eyes. He's daring me to do it.

All the fight leaves my body in a rush as the crowbar clatters against the pavement at our feet. The weight of my body settles into Pop's side. His arm immediately encircles my shoulders, squeezing my arm for reassurance. He's there.

"Wanna work your magic on the lipstick display?" he asks, nudging me toward the front steps. Color coordination is exactly what I need right now.

My alarm awakens me with its normal roar to get ready for school. The groan that vibrates through my body shakes my bed. It's not that I want to go back to sleep. I don't want to go to school. By now, I'm sure that news of my scuffle with Blanche has reached the other girls, and no outcome is favorable if that's the case. The girls will either walk on eggshells around me or confront me, and I'm not in the mood for either.

I raise my hands to scrub my face into a state of semi-consciousness when a streak of black on my palm catches my attention, and I snap up straight in bed. Joshua wrote his phone number on my hand last night. I hadn't imagined it.

I reach for my phone and start typing a message. My brain throws on the brakes hard enough that I swear I can hear the squeal. It was less than ten hours ago that I saw Joshua. Would it seem too desperate to text him this early? Of course, I am desperate. I decided to give in to my impulses and type out a quick message to make sure he'd have my number, too. Put the ball back in his court.

I opt to dress in my usual style, but I am too weary to try and reinvent myself. I slip a long-sleeved black shirt over my head and pull on a pair of black jeans. My blonde hair twists on top of my head in a giant bun, and I plop down at my vanity to stare. My face hasn't gone this long without makeup since I started wearing it at age thirteen. No concealer under my eyes leaves the ever-present bruising from a consistent lack of sleep. My blonde eyelashes and eyebrows blend into my skin, almost to the degree they disappear. The staining that has lasted for years on my lips from my red lipstick has finally faded to reveal the ashen color of my mouth that also blends into my skin. I find myself missing the color.

Pulling open the middle drawer of makeup in my vanity, it squeals in protest from its lack of use over the last weeks. My arms are heavy and tired at the thought of doing all of it, and I don't think I want to, but a little bit might help. I grab a mascara tube and pink lip gloss and smear them both into place. The person staring back at me in the mirror reminds me of a much younger Rosie. I don't know her anymore. I am a very fluid concept at the moment.

In the kitchen, all three aunts pour over the newspaper in various segments at the table. "Morning, Sunshine," Meredith calls over to me as I fill a travel coffee cup to its brim. I offer a smile in return and see her light up as she nudges her sisters, who all promptly look up at me. There's nothing like being the newest monkey in the zoo. "You look nice today."

Fantastic. It'll be round two of "What are you wearing?" and I'm already spent.

"Thanks," I offer flatly, screwing the lid on my dark purple mug.

"Back to black?" Norah asks, her eyes never leaving the obits in her hand—morbid woman.

"All Johnny Cash, all day," I mutter, strongly considering grabbing something white or even baby blue to cover up the black, words I thought I'd never say.

Somehow, Norah crosses the space between us to be beside me in less than two seconds. "We need to talk, kiddo," she whispers, and a chill runs down my spine.

Grabbing my bag off the floor, I do my best to make my way around her while avoiding eye contact, but the freaking Amazon blocks me like a wall. "Nor, I need to get to school," I whine when she won't budge.

"I told you your father's name, and you haven't asked a single follow-up question," she whispers, as though the other aunts don't know. I thought she'd be happy about that. I didn't think she'd want me to bring it up again, and I kind of pushed it from my mind. The Google search may be sitting open in its tab on my phone, but I can't bring myself to look into a single result. I guess, to a point, I like the idea of pretending that he's not real. Like my mom, my father is this abstract idea, like Santa Claus. Kyle Roosevelt is a person.

I throw my arms down at my side. "Norah, I'm going to be late. Do you really want to contribute to delinquency?"

"I want you to come home right after school. We are having this conversation." She should know better after all these years that I don't respond well to commands. The aunts are not my parents.

"Whatever," I grumble as I brush past, throwing my hood over my head like some deeply tortured comic book character. Drama is a beautiful tool.

I need to pick a single aesthetic and stick with it because my classmates do not take change well. "Back to black" has caused a new round of points and stares. "Is she ever not begging for attention?" one very ballsy sophomore has the audacity to say all too loudly in the hallway.

I'm about to turn around and break my lifetime ban on violence when Goldie's arm encircles my shoulders.

"Relax, Killer," she mumbles as she kisses the top of my head through my cinnamon bun hair.

"Every single person in this town royally sucks. I can't do anything right." I kick the row of lower lockers one at a time as we walk down the slowly emptying hallway. After a long day of too much attention, I'm ready to disappear into the safety of art class.

"Every person, huh?" Goldie says with a laugh as she squeezes my shoulders.

"You're not people," I mumble, wrapping my arms around her middle. We end up walking in our own three-legged race.

"Hang in there, my dude," she says when we reach my classroom door. "You're going to be off in New York before you know it and forget all about this little town and all the little people in it."

My stomach drops at the idea. I interlock my fingers around her waist preventing her from walking away. "How about I stay here with you?"

She pulls me back to arm's length and examines my face with at a glacial pace. It feels like she's trying to memorize it. "Not for nothing, because I appreciate the sentiment," she begins, squeezing my arms to keep me from disappearing. "But if come the fall, you're still here working at the pie shop with me and not in New York living your dream, I will straight up kick your ass." With that and nothing else, she plants a firm kiss against my forehead before shoving me into the classroom away from her.

I stumble past Mr. Cooper, avoiding his attention as I find my seat. It might finally break me if he asks me about school. I can let down my friends and aunts, and it'll roll off my back, but there's something about Mr. Cooper and his blind faith in me that holds a little too much weight.

At our work table, Beau, as always, is already in his seat, working away on his latest project, but those are the only things that are the same. Beau has always famously sported an afro large enough to have a gravitational pull. That's why it's difficult to process what I'm seeing or not seeing as the case is. He cut his hair down nearly to his skin, faded and manicured to a degree that it's difficult to resist the urge to touch it. His beard, normally Unibomber in style, is clean-cut and crisp, framing his jaw to reveal a square shape I hadn't realized was there.

He dares to look at me like he hasn't turned the world upside down. Is this how people saw me the first day I came back after my mom's funeral? If so, I totally get the reaction now.

"Hi, Friend," he mumbles, his attention too focused on the watercolor ducks in front of him to pay me much attention. He's on a duck kick lately. His slightly stained fingertips trace the outline of the mama duck with such delicate care that I'd expect it to be soft to the touch.

"You got a haircut," I blurt out. I bite on the insides of my cheeks as soon as the words pass my lips.

"Look at you all observant," he says, pushing away from the desk and facing me. Dear god! He has new glasses, too. Since I've known him, Beau has always worn these grandpa glasses that remind me of Benjamin Franklin. Today, he has these sleek black frames that look like they're from this century. When I don't respond after a few beats too many, Beau starts to laugh, deep in his chest, his whole body shaking.

"Relax, Rosie, it was time for change. My mother said I could cut my hair on my own, or she would do it while I was sleeping. I decided to take the reins."

I pull out my sketch pad, feeling guilty that everyone else seems to be working, and even though I'm sure he doesn't care, it feels wrong to let down Mr. Cooper by slacking.

"You've had the hair ever since you could grow it, and now she says something?"

He shrugs, paying particular attention to the puddle in which one of the baby ducks is splashing. "Well, my last interview with RISD is this weekend, and my mom said it might be best if I looked less like a homeless man in the park screaming to the pigeons about the apocalypse." He laughs before adding, "No hyperbole; those were her exact words." The mention of college is like a punch in the stomach. I knew Beau was applying to almost every art school within a thousand-mile radius, but his heart is set on RISD.

"You're gonna nail it and grow up to be the next Van Gogh," he eyes me quizzically over the top of his glasses. "Or someone a little less disturbed… Of course, I can't place one at the moment."

He clasps his bear paw onto my shoulder, the heat from his palm radiating down the entire side of my body. "And one day you'll be making clothes like Gianni Versace, or someone less problematic." His grin stretches broad and white across the pumpkin that is his head. He reminds me of the Incredible Hulk, but that gentle, nice one from *Endgame*. Something about it coming from Beau makes the constant unease of my stomach around the idea of fashion steady a bit. Again, Sensitive Hulk.

Mr. Cooper stops by our desk, crouching down to our level, shoes squeaking against the floor as he does. "You two aren't checking out on me already, are you? Mr. Lawson's off to Rhode Island." Before Beau can protest and say that he hasn't received an acceptance letter yet, Mr. Cooper continues, "Project positivity, youngling." He turns to me, a smile stretching across imperfect teeth that prove he's human, before he says, "And Ms. Peters is going to be rocking it in the Big Apple!"

I can feel the energy crackle around me as Beau catches up to what Mr. Cooper has said. His chair slides out from under him before my body levitates off my stool. "You got in?! How could you not tell me that?" he shrieks while jostling me.

"I'm going to be sick if you don't put me down!" I squeal as my breathing starts to speed up. I might vomit anyway.

"Or you could join me in my freak out, nerd!" Beau shouts as my feet find their way back to the floor. "How are you not skipping down the halls?"

The sheer pressure of their judgment and expectation weighs heavy on my shoulders. My insides start to feel the crush. "I don't know if I'm going," I mumble under my breath, ashamed at the smallness of my voice.

Mr. Cooper and Beau trade a look of shock before all their attention falls back on my shoulders. My teacher takes his usual stance—crouched in front of me so he's actually staring up.

"I don't understand, Rosie, you've worked your butt off for this."

The space in my throat is suddenly too small. "I'm weighing all my options."

"You only applied to one school! What options?" Beau booms from behind me. I can't understand how anyone thinks they have the right to react stronger to this than I am. I'm approaching it like a level-headed adult. People my age plunge themselves into crippling debt for degrees that may come to nothing. And I want to go into fashion. I'm a white trash girl from a nowhere town in Maryland. Models in Milan won't be rocking the runways in a Rosie Peters design. The best I can hope for is a Wal-Mart line, and that's only if I'm lucky. Dreaming is for rich people.

Mr. Cooper lifts his hand in an attempt to settle Beau, turning his attention back to me.

"Rosie, I'm surprised to hear this. You were gung-ho about this application. What do your aunts think about this?"

I start chewing on the skin inside my cheek in a rhythmic fashion. "I haven't told them yet," I murmur as Beau throws his hands up and turns in a circle, muttering nonsensically to himself. To their credit, the other five students in the room try their best to stay focused on their projects, but it's no secret that our spectacle is worth watching.

Mr. Cooper's hand reaches up to lay warm on my shoulder. "Come out in the hallway with me for a second." Beau walks in our direction, too, but Mr. Cooper raises a hand to stop him. "You stay here, big guy. Give us a minute."

The hallway's silence is deafening, and there is no release from the booming pressure in my head. It reminds me of treading open water, the constant threat of drowning all around until exhaustion wins. The idea of letting go feels good right now.

"Okay," Mr. Cooper begins. "Can you tell me what *Twilight Zone* episode we've wandered into here?"

"I'm tired, Coop." I state matter-of-factly that the world's weight on my shoulders is starting to make it difficult to stand. "I don't want to talk about this anymore."

"We haven't talked about it at all, Rosie." He pushes his glasses up into his thick, dark hair, forcing me to look directly into the depths of his blue eyes. He's the kind of guy they make movies about, a classically handsome man who has no business being a teacher. He belongs on billboards in Times Square. "Can you understand why this is concerning to me?"

I swallow hard. The word "concern" has lost all meaning these days. I may be back in my regular clothes, but I've never felt less comfortable in my skin. "I guess," I mumble, squishing my toes into the floor, refusing to look up like a petulant child.

He ducks down to the level of my gaze, and I can't help the giggle that spills from seeing him upside down. "Talk to me, kid," he insists.

"You're like five years older than me, Coop," I say, straightening up to my full height. The blood instantly rushes to make my world sway.

His shoulders shrug up near his ears. "It's more like seven," he says with a smile. "And as your elder, I should be able to express some concern."

"I'm figuring it out, Coop," I groan for the seven thousandth time today.

"Okay," he interrupts before I can go further. "Lay them on me." The gaping, empty look I offer back must show that I need further explanation. All I hear is buzzing. "What are the alternatives?"

My brain struggles to find the answers it seeks. "Well, I could take a gap year to save money and find a more practical major."

His arms switch over his chest, pulling his shirt sleeves up his forearms. He's more freckly than I've ever noticed. "Define a 'practical major' for me."

"Come on, Coop," I whine, turning myself in a circle to change perspective. "What was I thinking? Fashion design?! That's what rich kids go to school for before their trust funds kick in. I need to do something like medical assistant training or data entry. Something there is work for."

Coop's brow furrows like he's looking at a stranger. "I'm sorry, Rosie, this feels like it's coming out of left field. We talked about the risks. You aren't some starry-eyed dreamer. You have talent, and yes, an artistic major presents some challenges, but you have the chops to do it."

"Nobody makes it, Coop!" I shriek, no longer caring that we're in the hallway of my school where people with their small minds and long memories could hear. "I am a God damn orphan from this piece of crap, middle-of-nowhere town, and I'm going to drown myself in debt going to school in freakin' New York City. And for what? For the minute possibility that I could be the underdog from a Lifetime movie that makes it? My life is not a fairy tale, Mr. Cooper! This is stupid reality where my mom is dead, and I'm going to die making pies. It's not great, it's not terrible, it's real."

I can feel the tears prick and threaten to reveal themselves, but I know they won't form. It doesn't stop me from turning away and stalking off in strong steps down the hall. I'm not be crying, but I know he can see it all the same on my face.

"Rosie," he calls out after me, but he never gets closer. I know he's not following. It's not time to leave, but it's the last period, and I can't imagine trying to stay in this building for even five more minutes. Mr. Cooper won't rat me out, but I don't think I care right now if he does. Let them give me detention, let them expel me, let them do something to shock my system. Maybe it's what I need.

CHAPTER NINE

Solace comes in crushing bananas. Mixing the remnant mush with sugar and a tiny pinch of salt in a metal bowl, my body quivers when my potato masher scrapes the sides of the bowl, sending a shock up my arm.

"Yo," Bella calls back through the little window. "I'm out of cherry. Can you heat one?"

I nod without looking up and am grateful there's some normalcy here. I know Bella could sense something was off when I arrived early, but to her credit, she didn't push. The only other person working with us this afternoon is Blanche, and we aren't exactly on speaking terms at the moment, so it's shaping up to be a quiet afternoon.

After sliding one and a half cherry pies into the oven, I return to the dressed-up baby food in my mixing bowl. It's not a pie yet, but that's the golden space. I love turning nothing into something. Tasting day, the one time a month when the girls get to try new concoctions, is later this week, but inspiration has been hard to find under the current weight of my life. Bring on the heavy cream and egg yolks. I'll make a banana cream pie. I'll think of something to make it fancy and unique, like kiwis.

The eerie sensation of someone watching settles over me as I crack eggs into my mixer. Bella's form fills the entry way, blocking all the light from the shop that her body can. "Hey," she begins, full of an emotion I can't quite place.

"You need more pie?" my voice cracks from disuse.

She scratches at the back of her head, eyes baring too intensely into me. "No—" she starts again, her voice trailing into a sea of nothingness.

"Spit it out, Southland. I'm trying to create genius back here." I mean for it to be funny, but her lower lip worries between her teeth, betraying an edge I'm not used to from her. "What's up, Bells?"

She closes the door behind her as she moves closer to me, her voice hushed when she speaks. "There's someone here to see you. I saw him during the wake when he was talking to Norah."

"He's out there?"

Bella places her hands on my upper arms and squeezes with firm enough pressure for it to register. "I can tell him to get lost if you want."

I'd be lying if I didn't say it had appeal. Was Kyle Roosevelt something I could handle with everything else on my plate? But the curiosity was too much to bear. I brush past Bella and out of the kitchen door to the shop. I almost fall over my feet at the infuriating normality of the man across from me. Trading out his funeral suit for a faded t-shirt, well-worn jeans, and a black pea coat, he looks like any man on the street. But he's not. He's my father. I pull the stool out from under the register Bella uses to do her homework and sit across from him. I'm grateful for the physical barrier of the counter. I'm not sure if I want to strangle him or hug him. He leans his weight back and forth on the neon stool upon which he sits, fidgets with his thin wire glasses, and pulls on the lapels of his coat. Incapable of sitting still.

In desperate need of something to do with my hands, I reach for the covered dish beside me and slice into the fresh cherry pie. I put a piece on a plate and slid it over to him. He looks at it like it's a bomb about to go off. I chew on my cheek and slap a fork next to his hand.

"Eat it," I command, and he jumps to the task at a speed that he must stab the roof of his mouth with the tines.

"I didn't think you'd come out," he says smoother than a lemon meringue pie. It throws my heart into my throat. I may have heard him speak to Norah through all the noise after the funeral, but it's very different when directed at me.

Chewing on the sensitive skin inside my cheek, I wrap my arms protectively around my middle. "I didn't think I would either."

He never lets go of his fork as his head bounces up and down a few times. Then his eyes locked with mine, and I forgot how to breathe. I see that same soft brown color every time I look in the mirror. Shawna says that the eyes are the window to the soul. Does this mean that we share the same one? Looking at him, I see only myself, and it scares me.

"I'm assuming you know who I am," he says after a beat. His chest rises and falls under a Campbell University t-shirt. Where is Campbell? I don't think I've heard of it. More pieces are falling together that make Kyle Roosevelt a person, and I don't think I like it.

"You're Kyle Roosevelt," I respond, refusing to make this any easier for him. Hurt feelings lead to petty responses.

He sits tall, and man is he tall, and he folds his hands on top of the counter. It takes everything in me not to slap them off. "That's my name, but do you know who I am?"

My teeth clench to a point where it feels like they may break. How do you hate a perfect stranger? "You're the guy who knocked up my mother and then abandoned her."

His jaw works back and forth under the stubbled skin of his cheek. My mother would be thirty-four, and he has to be the same age, give or take a year, yet the shadow of gray dusting the skin on his face and head betrays him to be older.

"I deserve that," he says softly, more to the pie than me.

"What do you want, Kyle?" I demand, tasting the metallic flavor of blood from biting on my cheek. "What could you want from me?"

He holds my gaze with a bravery I can't help but admire. I couldn't look the child I abandoned in the eye like that. "It's selfish," he begins, taking another bite of pie. "I know it's selfish to want to see you up close. I don't deserve it. I know that."

"Is that it?" I growl, anger bubbling in my stomach, ready to explode out the top of my head. "You wanted to look at me?"

"I wasn't planning on it. I know I don't have the right to talk to you, but," Kyle trails off as he swallows a few times. I swear to God, if he starts crying, I'm throwing punches. "Then you got up at the funeral, and I couldn't breathe. It was like Holly was up there, and I should have assumed that you would be there, but I swear to God, Rosaline, it hit me like a truck."

"My name is Rosie," I mutter when the shiver of hearing my name from my father's mouth settles in my ears.

He presses the heels of his hands into his forehead after folding his glasses on the counter in front of him. A smirk that I'd like to slap off his face appears.

"You go by Rosie?" Unable to form verbal words, I offer only a sharp nod. A humorless laugh rumbles deep in his chest. "Me too, when I was a kid."

"Wha—what?" I breathe. The world shifts into an old black-and-white episode of television. This man and I are the lone spots of Technicolor.

"My last name is Roosevelt, and because there were a bunch of other Kyle's, someone nicknamed me Rosie," he explains, that stupid smile lingering on his lips.

The top blew off the pressure cooker inside me.

"You abandoned her, and that bitch dared to name me after you?! Are you kidding?!" I scream, my skin alive with vibrating fury. I can't catch my breath, the oxygen sucks right into the fire burning inside.

Kyle pushes away from the counter to stand as I do, he visibly panics. He wasn't expecting this reaction. Neither was I. Even more unexpected than my response, was finding out that I am named after the man who left me.

"I am an orphan. I never had a father, and I only had a mother until I was eleven, and now she's dead. And you show up here now, after I'm seventeen, practically grown, and tell me she named me after you? And you have the nerve to smile about that?! It's not sweet. It's a God damn Greek tragedy!"

I pick up the plate he'd been eating off of and slam it down onto the counter, shattering the dish and sending cherries flying in all directions. The woman at the end of the counter gasps, even though the remnants of my fit don't come close to her. I'm about to turn my head and tell her as much when Blanche enters, dominates really, my field of vision.

"Go in the back," she demands, her body turned fully toward me. Behind her, I watch Kyle hand something to Bella before he finally leaves. *Good, go. You don't belong here.* But he doesn't leave. He stands there frozen, staring at me with tears rimming his eyes. Screw him. He doesn't get to cry.

"Go. In. The. Back." Blanche says again, overly enunciating every word. I'm mad at her, but it's not worth the fight.

The kitchen door barely closes behind me before I hear her start in on Kyle. "You need to get out of here." I don't hear his response, but she's quick to speak again. "There's a time and place for this crap, and here and now is neither. Leave her alone. She doesn't need this." The next thing I hear is the bell jingling on the front door, and I can breathe again.

The swinging door creaks open beside me, but I can't take it upon myself to look. I have to count the tiles in the ceiling to keep myself together. Breathe in. Breathe out. Blanche does not attempt to approach me, the light from the shop hitting the side of my face.

"You okay?" Blanche asks curtly. I nod a few times to acknowledge I've heard her, but I don't have it in me to speak. "Okay," she says. Although we are in a fight, she doesn't hate me.

"What did he give you?" I ask.

She still refuses to come into the kitchen with me but extends her hand. It's a business card; on the back, Kyle wrote his home address: New Shiloh. He lives twenty minutes away.

The silence deafens for the rest of the night as everyone avoids me. They don't ask for pies, dishes, or anything else. In part, I'm relieved, but the rest of me wishes they'd comfort me like a wounded baby bird.

At closing, Bella pops her head into the window above me. "We're headed out," she murmurs, trying not to spook the caged animal. "Do you need anything?"

I drop the dish in my hands into the sink's soapy water. The suds splash back onto my black shirt, and I let them fizzle there. I stare at the faucet, shaking my head back and forth. "No, I'm good, Bells," I whisper. My fingers grip the edge of the sink, terrified she'll pry further and panicked that she won't ask anything.

Her fingers tap the side of the window before she says, "I love you, Rosie Rose." I can't respond. I'm choking on the black water that seeps in at all my edges. I want to tell her I love her too, but I don't have it in me, and much to her credit, Bella doesn't wait for a response.

I can't go home. Maybe ever again. The looks on my aunts' faces as they try to figure me out are becoming too much. I may have to go to New York to get away. I opt instead to stay and make random things that might end up being pies. The bananas were a disaster, so I switched gears: magic with strawberry and chocolate. I don't think anything wrong can come from those.

It's deep into my third nearly-failed experiment when I hear a knock. I yelp, leaping away from the counter like a cat near a bathtub.

Whipping around, trying to control the pounding of my heart, clutching at my chest like it might run away, I search for the culprit. Standing outside is the only person I'm interested in seeing right now. Joshua's hands planted firmly on his hips, brushing back his black leather jacket from his white shirt. I scan up to his beautiful face, his beautiful, scowling, angry face. His lips pressed together in a thin line that makes them almost disappear.

Damn. He's pissed.

My feet shuffle in little cautious steps toward the door. After flipping the lock and pulling it open, Joshua makes no move toward me. No move at all. "Are you okay?" I ask, my voice meek and small.

He puffs like a slowly deflating balloon, his weight settling into the door frame. "Yeah, I'm fine," he groans, pushing past me into the shop. "I'm a little surprised, is all."

"By what?" I ask, flipping the lock before I turn back to him. Shoving his hands into his jacket pockets, he walks around me in slow circles, like I'm some kind of zoo attraction or prey.

"Do you have to ask?" he mumbles, rubbing his chin. He's close enough to me that I can hear the scratch of the blonde stubble on his skin. My stunned silence must be answer enough because he barely stops talking.

"What the hell are you wearing?" At that moment, I realized that Joshua had never encountered my usual Rosie costume. He met me in pajamas and has only seen me in my alternate clothes since. I glance down at my outfit. Is it that bad? The scoop neck of my black shirt does dip down a little low, and my pants are a little tight but pretty modest based on my dress history. I didn't cake on my makeup. I didn't even put a flower in my hair.

He stops dead before me, placing his hand under my chin to lift my gaze. His eyes sparkle as his thumb rubs across my lower lip. "You don't have to do this, you know," he says, smearing the pale pink lipstick back and forth. His palms move to either side of my face, and I can't help but rest my hands over his wrists to hold him in place. "You look more beautiful without a mask."

His eyes betray a disappointment that I'm not prepared to deal with. "I've had a bad day," I squeak, emotion choking my voice.

His eyes never leave mine as he shrugs out of his jacket and wraps it around my shoulders, zipping it under my chin. It smells like him. "Tell me about it."

After an hour and two pieces of pie each, Joshua sets his fork down amongst the crumbs. "Damn, this has all happened recently?" he asks.

Once I started talking, I couldn't stop. I couldn't bring up Parsons. I don't have it in me to discuss that with anyone else today, but the people who gave me life are more than enough cannon fodder for anyone to handle.

"Yeah, it's been a little nuts." That is an understatement of the century.

"I'm sorry about your mom," he says, taking my hand. "And your dad sounds like an asshole."

"I can't even call him my dad," I admit, hugging Joshua's jacket closer. I'd love to have a whole closet full of them. One for every season. "I don't know anything about him."

"I mean, there are plenty of days I wish I didn't know my dad. Ever consider you're lucky?" That's not a word many people associate with me. A modicum of panic swims in his eyes. "Obviously, the situation with your mom doesn't make you lucky. I didn't mean that. I hope you know I didn't mean that." Babbling has an adorable look on him.

"I understand what you mean. I don't know how much thought I ever put into it. I didn't miss my dad because I couldn't miss what was never there. I never thought of, 'Well, what about my dad?' I should have, but family was never my epicenter because I never had one. And there were times in the last few years when I missed my mom, but she was kind of strung out. I don't know how well I even knew her."

His ears perk up at the words "strung out," and I realize that I may have told him that she died, but not necessarily how.

"I live with three grandparent-aged ladies who do the best they can, but they're not parents. I don't know how to have parents."

"Does anyone know how to have parents?" he asks.

"I guess not."

He takes my hand and rubs his thumb across my knuckles.

"Want to take a walk?"

One of the nicest things about a small town like mine in the middle of the night is the soundtrack, simply nature's noises. No sirens or car horns or people yelling. The crickets and frogs are the orchestras here. Joshua and I walk down the middle of the street, the solid yellow lines between us. I am physically drawn to him, but I'm glad he's not touching me. I'd drown in him right now.

"Now you know all this stuff about me," I begin. "I don't know much about you. Outside of your mom practically forcing you to see musical theater."

"Well, that's because you're much more interesting than me," he says with a finality that I can't let stand. I need something.

"I know you're a twin. Your sister is Mallory, right?" I ask, forcing the door open with a crowbar, it seems.

He stops dead and turns to face me. Even with the fast-approaching spring, his breath escapes him in frosty puffs. "Did Blanche tell you that?"

"Um, no? I met her a few months ago. She came into the pie shop," I explain.

His mouth twitches with amusement. "Mallory McDonald? My sister came into your shop?"

My defenses rise to protect my happy place. "You make it sound like some seedy biker bar. It's a nice place with good food, and we're good people."

He grabs me by the lapels of my jacket and pulls me into him. Oh God, he smells amazing.

"Don't be stupid and get upset." He kisses the tip of my nose, and I momentarily forget my name. "I know all those things. I also know it's not the kind of place she'd normally go." And then he's kissing me, and my brain fizzles out into all its gray matter goodness.

When he finally lets me break for air, I scramble for thoughts because I have questions.

"Why don't you like Blanche?"

He groans and lets me go, taking substantial strides from me back down the street. I have to jog to catch up. "You should be asking why Blanche doesn't like me?"

"Why doesn't she like you?"

He shrugs, looking off in the distance like there's something more interesting to see. "I don't know. Blanche made a pass at me in tenth grade that I shot down. I guess she never got over it."

That didn't sound like Blanche.

"Really?"

"You think I'm lying to you?" he snaps, sharp enough to make me step back. The fierceness in his face relaxes into mush when he reaches out and grabs me again, pulling me in to kiss him. I resist at first, but it feels too good; before I know it, I'm on my tiptoes with my arms wrapped around his neck. He pulls back, smoothing my hair away from my face.

"Baby, I care about you. I don't want some jealous girl to make you think I don't."

"Blanche doesn't strike me like that kind of person," I say meekly, my head swimming over the endearment of "baby."

His index finger runs across the bottom hem of my shirt, and I barely remember who Blanche is anymore. "You're right. It's not my intention to attack your friend. I don't understand what else she could have against me."

Daringly, I pull him by his belt toward me. I can't seem to get him close enough. "Well, what if we go out with Blanche or my other friends? I'd like for you to get to know them."

His entire face contorts as though in pain. He groans before lifting me off the pavement. "Is it wrong that I like having you to myself?"

My short circuits when his nose grazes the shell of my ear. "Yeah, I guess I can't complain about that," I breathe, unable to form coherent thoughts.

He puts me down and takes my hand, and we start to walk again. "Tell me about Mayberry," he says, motioning around the town's center. He's not the first person to mention the Utopian town from a fifties TV show. I doubt Aunt Bea was anything like my aunts, and I'm no Opie.

"Well," I begin, taking in my childhood surroundings. "You've seen the pie shop, of course. Over there is the drugstore," with its metal horse still mocking me. "My best friend's family owns it. Her grandfather tends to let me go a little crazy rearranging the store when I can't sleep. Drives the old women batty when they can't find things the next day."

We pass the flower shop, fabric store, and salon, and I regale him with every story I can think of, some of which aren't even mine, but I can't stop talking. I don't want my time with him to end, and the silence around him makes me queasy. We pause in front of The Representative movie theater. Home to one big screen, a balcony, and an eighty-year-old popcorn machine.

"This looks like something out of World War II," Joshua remarks.

"Not far back enough. The movie theater dates back the nineteen-thirties. My aunts said their parents used to talk about watching the newsreels on the big screen and feeling like celebrities because of it."

I can feel him studying my face. It's the most important I've ever felt in my life, the direct center of another person's attention without a hint of mocking or repulsion. It's intoxicating.

"And what about you?" he asks, prompting me to turn and face him. "Do you feel like a celebrity when you're in there?"

It's hard to picture it in the dead of night when the lights are out on the marquee and no one is operating the ticket booth, but I often feel pulled back to another time when I came here. The theater doesn't show anything current, and people still, for the most part, dress up a bit to come.

"I guess I do when it's at its full glory. There is a Marilyn Monroe marathon showing next Friday. Would you'd like to come?" Beau usually sneaks Goldie and me in through the back door on the nights he's working, and I'm sure he'd do the same for Joshua and me.

"Marilyn Monroe, huh? Is that where this style change came from?"

I look down at my outfit, incredibly tame to my usual standards. "It's more Sandy from the end of *Grease*. It's the way I usually dress."

"Hmm," he muses, mulling it over as our bodies rock back and forth in a rhythmic dance. "I always preferred Sandy from the beginning."

"Yeah, she's good too."

"Better, much better," he insists, and I don't see the point in arguing.

"So, next weekend?" I ask, not wanting to get too far away.

He groans, taking a few long strides from me down the street. It takes my brain a few beats too long to realize I'm supposed to be following. He's tucked his hands into the pockets of his jeans. I guess we're not holding them anymore.

"Fine," he says after we've walked in silence. "I will come with you, but you're gonna owe me."

A giddy schoolgirl smile pinches my cheeks. "Thank you, it'll be fun."

His hands snake around my waist. "I guess I could think of worse ways to spend a Friday night than being alone with you in the dark."

Oh, me too, definitely me too.

"We could get dinner with my friend, Goldie, beforehand. Let me text her," I say, pulling my phone from my pocket.

He places his hand over mine, easing my phone down. "How about I meet you here. What time does this thing start?" The silence that hovers between us thickens. "I like our little bit of mystery," he says, answering my unspoken question. "I like you. I like the way we are. Can you give me this?"

He tucks my hair behind my ear, his fingers linger on my neck, and nothing matters anymore. I want Joshua to swallow me up and how he makes me feel. He's the one thing in my life right now that doesn't force me to think about my parents or college, and I need it like a drug.

"I guess it's not a big deal," I say, nestling my cheek into the palm of his hand.

The left side of his mouth turns up in a grin as he pulls my face towards his. "I'm falling for you, Rosie Peters," he says before kissed me.

That's good to hear because I know I'm already lost in him.

The following week falls into a numbing rhythm of a new normal. No one mentions my barrage of beige and brown tones, and I start to blend into the scenery. I should have done this years ago. I always thought my need for attention was a big "F-you" to people in this town who demonized my mom. Invisibility is better. Joshua is right; Sandy is the best at the beginning of the movie.

I miss the general peace I've always found in art class. To say that things between Beau and me feel strained would be an understatement.

He even switched seats with someone to sit further away from me. By Friday, I've had enough. I pull up a stool and sit across from him at his new spot. "Are you talking to me yet?"

"Depends," he says, his attention never moving from his mallard painting. "You ready to stop being an idiot?"

"That's a little harsh, Beau," I mutter, laying my chin on the table across from his watercolor ducks. If I quack, I wonder if he'll look at me.

"Tough love is my style with you, Friend," he says, dunking his brush in the water and leaving it there. "You're too talented to be this dumb. I'm performing my own intervention and will withhold my friendship until you're ready to do the right thing."

"That sounds a bit like blackmail."

"Desperate times, girly," he says, returning to the duck.

I can feel Mr. Cooper's eyes burning holes into my back well before I return to my seat. I make a pit stop at his desk. "I haven't made any decisions yet, Cooper. Stop staring."

"I didn't say anything!" he yelps, burying his face in his book.

"Yeah, you're both not saying a lot these days."

"Rosie, my dear," Mr. Cooper begins, removing his glasses. "You can't always have it both ways. Do you want space to figure out what you're doing without anyone else's input? That's fine; that's what you're getting, but that doesn't mean we have to like it. I can't imagine how hard this time is for you, but I also can't imagine that your mother would want you to throw away a promising future as you have."

"You didn't know my mom," I hiss, fingernails digging into the palms of my hands. Cooper is only a few years my senior. I don't need his sage wisdom. "Don't speak for her. She didn't think of me at all."

"I'm sure that's not true."

Before I can take it back, my fist slams into the table. A hush falls around the room, and I can feel the stares of my classmates shift to my direction.

"Do not use my mother as a weapon to guilt me into doing what you want. You didn't know her. Nobody did."

The feeling of a warm bear paw of a hand on my shoulder should soothe me, but all I want is to knock him away. "You need to check yourself, Friend," Beau murmurs close to my ear, his tongue clicking in his all-knowing, chastising way that makes me want to punch him.

I shimmy out from under his hold, ignoring the stares and whispers from the other people in my class, people I have always known the way you know heads of state or countries on a map. Picture and name recognition alone. I have no friends here. I grab my bag off my work table, knowing full well there's still a half-hour left to class.

"Whatever, none of this matters anyway," I announce to the class, becoming the spectacle I've always tried to avoid. "If the goal in life is to surpass our parents—I'm not a drug addict, and I don't have a baby I've abandoned—then I'm already leaps and bounds ahead of the rest of you."

"Rosie!" Beau booms through the air after me, but I'm already gone.

When Goldie and her boyfriend, Dub, show up at the pie shop, my anger has dissipated into nonthreatening steam. I've taken to the kitchen floor with a toothbrush, and vigorous scrubbing like that will take the fight out of anyone.

"Hey, love bug," Goldie says, lingering in the doorway to avoid my clean floor. "You about ready to go?"

I get up to my feet and toss the toothbrush in the sink to deal with another time. "Yeah, let me grab my bag."

"Is your fella meeting us there?" she asks, an edge to her voice. Part of me thinks Goldie's decided that Joshua is my imaginary friend. I can't blame her. It wouldn't be too off-brand if he were.

"That's the plan," I say, swiveling past her and through the door. Dub sits at one of the counter stools, scrolling through his phone, continuously flipping his curly black hair. The movement makes me twitchy. Why doesn't he pull it back?

"Hey, Rosie," he says, never glancing away from his screen.

"We should probably head over then. Marilyn waits for no man!" Goldie proclaims, hustling herself back toward the door.

"That's historically inaccurate, but I appreciate the energy," I add, following her, Dub somewhere behind me. "We're going to have to pay this time, by the way."

That stops my friend dead in her tracks. Dub and I both nearly fall over her. "What?!" she demands. "Why?! Is Beau-Beau not working? We never have to pay."

"Beau-Beau and I are in a bit of a standoff. I don't think he will be too inclined to give me four free passes into the theater."

"Well, that shouldn't be a problem for me. He likes me more than you."

That's true. Most people like Goldie more than me.

When we reach the theater, I immediately start scanning the small crowd for Joshua—a nervous thrill and energy course through my body at the idea of not only seeing him. Going on a date where other people will be around and see and interact with us will make it all the more real—much of the time I've spent with Joshua seemed like a dream to me.

"Describe him to me in vivid detail. I want to see if I can find him first," Goldie says, digging through her purse like Mary Poppins seeking a treasure.

"He's tall and blonde," I respond, trying to ignore her.

"He's me—you're dating me?"

I swat her away like the stubborn fly that she is. "Fine!" she huffs. "I'll go talk to Beau about getting us in." And with that, she's gone, and I have a moment of peace. Apprehension sits heavy like a stone in the pit of my stomach, and I know it won't go away until I see him. I fight the urge to pull out my phone and call him to see where he is. The minutes pass, and more and more people filter into the theater until it is only Dub, Goldie, and myself.

"Ro, are you sure he's coming? You should call him." Goldie offers. I have. Four times. Anything would be better than this embarrassment. Dub seems increasingly uncomfortable, and I'm unsure if it's for me or himself.

I have to admit to Goldie that he isn't answering my calls. She grabs my hand and turns to her boyfriend. "Babe, you are off the hook. Rosie and I are turning this into a girl's night."

He narrows his eyes at her. "Are you sure? I don't mind hanging." But the joy radiating off of him tells a very different story. He's practically skipping away by the time Goldie reassures him.

My human Barbie doll wraps her arm around my shoulders and leads me into the theater. "Come on, darlin'! Only us is better anyway."

Usually, old movie marathons at the theater are my happy space, a safe destination for me to go to when things suck, and right now, everything sucks. I can't even bring myself to enjoy Marilyn in all her glory, dancing and skipping across the screen with her beautiful, breathy voice because I'm too focused on Joshua. My hand has a vice-grip on my phone, and I am waiting for him to respond.

Where is he?

He told me he would be here. Goldie is sweet, but she will probe me for information later. God forbid any of this gets back to Blanche, and I must suffer through a long line of "I told you so's". And what if something's wrong? What if he got hurt on the trip from New Shiloh to Harpersgrove? He does ride that death trap. And here I am, judging and thinking the worst of him. I suck.

When the final film rolls its credits, Goldie and I hoot and applaud with our fellow theatergoers because that is tradition, and no one messes with a small-town tradition.

"You want to talk about it?" Goldie asks, slurping obnoxiously against the slushy ice in her cup large enough to drown a toddler.

"I don't know what there is to talk about," I mumble, tossing the sad trash of my four packs of candy into the bin.

"I'm worried about you, Rosaline," she says, keeping an arm's length away.

"You don't need to be Gwendelon. I'm fine. This whole thing is shitty, and I'd prefer not getting sucked in any deeper into my shame around it if that's okay with you." As we pass the threshold of the entrance way, I make eye contact with Beau as he sweeps up popcorn from the concession stand. Everyone is either mad or disappointed with me.

"Thanks for hanging out with me, Goldie," I mumble, pulling the hood of my sweater over my face.

"Rosie!" Goldie shouts after me as I hurry away, but I'm already on my way to the shop and away from anyone else I must think about.

I keep cleaning like the health inspector might show up any minute and go back to scrubbing with my trusty toothbrush. Baking is my comfort and reward, but it doesn't feel like I deserve that right now. Cleaning is a punishment, and that's what I get. I feel stupid and silly, like a little girl with hurt feelings. I take it all out on the grout of the kitchen floor.

"Rosie!" I hear from the front sometime later. I'm waist-deep into the industrial freezer and have to shimmy out like I'm on an Arctic cave dive.

When I round the corner out of the kitchen, Joshua is standing with his hands on his hips, his weight bouncing back and forth between his feet outside the entrance. All my hurt bubbles to the surface as I stomp toward him.

"What the hell?!" I demand, refusing to open the door. A physical barrier seems like a good idea.

"Woah, what is wrong with you?" he barks back, throwing his hands up in defense.

"Do you have any idea how humiliating that was? My best friend and her boyfriend stood there staring at 'Poor Pitiful Rosie' as I waited for you to show up."

"Rosie! What are you talking about? I'm supposed to get together with you and your friends tomorrow night. That's what you said!"

My entire body stalls as my brain turns to old TV static. "What are you talking about? I remember the conversation, Joshua. You knew it was tonight. Friday! Today is Friday!"

"Don't be stupid, Rosie. The conversation you had with me was definitely about tomorrow night. Or were you're thinking about another guy!" he snaps back at me.

"What? There's no other guy!"

He shakes his head and stares at the pavement. "You know what? I wanted to come and spend some time with you, but if all you want to do is attack me, then this is a mistake."

When he turns away and walks back toward his bike, a familiar panic rises in my throat. How certain could I be that I said Friday and not Saturday? Was it worth a fight with the one person who seemed unconditionally in my corner right now? I flip the dead bolt and hurry out after him.

"Wait, Joshua." I touch his arm, and he freezes like a statue. "I'm sorry."

He never breaks the connection he's holding with the inky black sky, but at least he's stopped moving. "Maybe I did say Saturday," I mumble, soft and broken. I'm glad he stopped moving.

"You know it kills me to have you attack me like that when I care about you as much as I do," he laments, ripping his fingers through his hair.

"You do?"

He stops dead and turns back to me, pulling me into his arms. "Of course I do, Rosie. I fall for you a little more every time I see you, but you have to stop hurting me like this." He cups my cheek in the palm of his hand, and I forget my name.

"I'm sorry," I whisper, snuggling into his hand. It's my favorite place.

"I forgive you," he says softly, kissing my forehead. "You should have my phone number, that we can avoid things like this in the future." But I have his number. He gave it to me. He extended his hand for my phone, and I gave it to him. Didn't we do this already? He wrote his number on my hand. I've been calling it all night. Oh well, it could be that I'm remembering that wrong, too.

"There," he says when he gives my phone back. For added dramatic flair, he boops me on the tip of my nose like a puppy.

He pulls me back into him, smoothing his hands out over my lower back before interlacing his fingers there. "You are such a mystery to me, Rosie Peters," he says, leaning in to kiss me at the corner of my mouth. Cue the brain jelly.

"What do you mean?" I ask.

"I see a beautiful, amazing girl in front of me, and I'm in awe of her."

He can't be talking about me.

"It's no wonder I'm falling in love with you, is it?"

And it comes out of nowhere, but my spirit warms as if every birthday wish I've made came true. "What did you say?" I breathlessly ask.

"I said I love you. It can't be that surprising, can it? Look at you. You're everything anyone could ever want."

My heart hurts. My heart aches as if he stabbed me. Everyone should know unequivocal love, but I have never felt that. He puts both hands on my cheeks and gently shushes me when I start to protest because there's no way he can mean it. He places his lips hard against mine and keeps me there.

"Shh, let me be in love with you. Let it be."

After that, I started to hear and see more from Joshua. It's like a switch flipped inside his brain; everything is fine now. I don't know what happened, but I like it. He starts showing up at the shop more often, always after hours, but that's okay. It's our time. After a few nights of his close and considerate attention, I bite the bullet and finally tell him about Parsons. I need to tell someone because my friends won't get it. They'll try to make decisions for me or criticize me for my hesitation, but Joshua loves me without the weight of previous expectations. I need that.

"What's your plan for next year?" I ask, chickening out only slightly in my entry. I'll tell him, but I want his side first.

He looks up from his second piece of apple pie, mouth still full of food, when he starts to speak, "I'm thinking University of Maryland, keep it close to home." Only then does he pick up on what I'm putting down. "What about you?"

My mouth goes dry enough that I'm sure puffs of dust will explode out. "Well," I croak, willing the saliva back where it belongs. "I got word that I got into Parsons in New York."

His brow furrows only briefly before he shovels another bite into his mouth. "What's that exactly?" Everything about him has darkened, making my body stand on edge.

Back to the Sahara. "It's uh- the uh- the Parsons School of Design. I have a real knack for fashion and making clothes. My art teacher seems to think I could have a real go of it."

He pushes the plate away from him, focusing his full attention on me. "That's awesome that you got in there, but doesn't it worry you to put all your eggs in a basket that you have a ninety-nine percent chance of failing at? How many people have become famous fashion designers, Rosie? What would you fall back on if it didn't work?"

Growing up with my mom and her chaotic lifestyle made me crave security, but I try to remember everything Mr. Cooper told me when he convinced me to apply.

"Well, there are many things you can do with a fashion degree other than being a big-time designer. You're right. Expecting that would be unrealistic. I could work for fashion brands, be a buyer for a retailer, a costumer, or a teacher. There are a lot of things I could do."

He mulls it over for a long moment. "It seems like a considerable risk to me with a very limited payoff," he says, taking a long drink of water. "And doesn't that kind of school cost a lot? I'm sure you didn't get much scholarship money."

"Why would you think that?" Not that it's a false statement, but the assumption stings a little.

"Oh, I don't mean you're not smart, sweetie. You're plenty smart, I'm sure, but I know how competitive those schools are. It seems like you're taking on too much."

"What do you suggest I do then?" I ask.

"What about going to community college for a couple of years and finding a real career option? You would still be close to your family and friends; you could keep working here, and I'd only be about an hour away." He adds the last bit as if it's the most significant selling point. It is an enticing cherry on top of the sundae he presented.

"I'll think about it," I say, taking everything back to the kitchen.

"It would be great. We'd be able to get a place off campus after freshman year. Start building something that's ours without my parents or your aunts. I don't see how we could do that if you're in New York and I'm here."

"That's something you'd want?" I breathe, emotion catching in my throat.

He looks at me like I'm the whole world, and I let myself believe it for a moment. "You're everything that I want."

It's the answer to all the questions in one statement. All the things I've wanted in a single package. The desire to be irresistibly desired. "We can make that work," I say after a tear escapes the brim of my lid. When Joshua's lips seal over mine, I can feel his joy, relief, and every bit of happiness one can hold radiating off of him and into me. I can do this. I can do it this way.

I know now that I need to start telling people. Half the folks in my life don't even know I got into school. I decided that it was best to start with the one person that gave my decision pause. He was the one to convince me to apply in the first place, and I'd be lying if I said I didn't feel a little guilty about where he was concerned.

"Hey, Mr. Cooper," I call him after the last bell rings, and my classmates start shuffling from the room. "Can I talk to you for a second?"

He pushes his glasses up the bridge of his nose, peering at me over the top of them from his desk. There's a happiness in them that makes me feel all the worse. "Sure, stranger, I was starting to think you'd forgotten how to talk to me." I guess I have been relatively quiet recently.

Gripping tight to the strap of my bag like the emergency ripcord of a parachute, I sit on the stool opposite him, feeling far too fidgety to stand. Beau's colossal frame takes up the doorway, creeping in that way he does best before Mr. Cooper waves him off. It must be clear I don't want an audience.

"What's up, Rosie?" my teacher asks when we're finally alone.

I fold my hands on the black work desk and try to stop my leg from bouncing beneath it. Out with it, Peters. "I wanted you to know I decided on school." His eyebrows stretch up to his hairline, and he waits. Squeezing my eyes shut, I blurt it out before I lose my nerve, "I'm not going to go to Parsons. I appreciate all your work getting me in, but I don't think it's a smart or practical choice for me."

He's quiet for a long time, and I'm afraid to even peek at the room again. When I finally do, I see his glasses pushed up into his hair, mouth gaping, and his jaw slack. He's staring at me like he's never seen me before. "I am waiting for you to tell me you're kidding," he mumbles, rubbing his hand over his weathered face.

"I'm not," I respond, sounding smaller than I'd like.

"Rosie, I need you to listen to me and listen carefully," he says, "I try not to force college on anybody. I know it isn't for everyone, but you need to do this." My defenses shoot up, and my walls hurry into place. He doesn't know what I need. "What are you going to do instead?"

I sit tall and resist picking the skin around my cuticles. "I'm going to keep working at the pie shop and then go to the community college and figure out what I want to do. Something that makes sense."

He's going to cry. Tears are brimming. Human emotion makes me uncomfortable, but especially with guys. I don't mean that in some toxic masculinity way. I didn't grow up with any men outside of Goldie's grandfather, a man who is the human embodiment of a Wild West tumbleweed. I don't know what to do when men cry.

"Rosie, we talked about this. You can do a ton of things with a degree from that school. You're good at what you do, outstanding in fact. Do you think I haven't noticed that you make all your clothes? Because I do notice. You're too good to do this to yourself. Is this about your mom? I'm here to talk if you need someone to hear you."

It always comes back to her.

I swat his hand away, and he recoils like I punched him. "Not everything has to be some kind of grief response. I don't want to go to the school because I don't want to go to the school." I opt to leave out that there's a boy involved, but it might knock me down a few pegs, and I'm not willing to sacrifice. "I appreciate all your work, and I'm sorry if I'm letting you down, but I've made my decision."

I feel like crap the rest of the night. Even the pies can't bring me joy. I'm snippy and mean to the girls, even smacking Bella's hand with a spatula, but it was her fault for touching my things. Joshua had already texted that he wouldn't make it out to see me tonight, and part of me was glad. I'm exhausted. A whole night of sleep would do me good.

When I cross the threshold of my house, the overwhelming urge to run in the opposite direction engulfs me, but my stupid human anatomy demands sleep. No sooner do I shut the door behind me than Meredith calls out, "Rosie, can you come here a minute, please?"

I find her in the living room, where the prickle of fear and panic mixes with the fire of rage. My three aunts and Mr. Cooper are sitting in a circle.

"What are you doing here?" I hiss through my teeth.

"Nah," Norah snaps definitively. "You most certainly don't get to do that right now. Have a seat, young lady." My nose scrunches at that term.

"Rosie, please sit down," Shawna asks, gingerly patting the corners of her crows feet with a tissue. I hate making Shawna cry.

Like the petulant child I am, I opt not to take the open spot on the couch between Meredith and my traitor of an art teacher. Instead, I sit on the floor with my back against the wall. Norah gears up for a fight, but Meredith silences her with a look.

"All I am asking you for here, Rosie, is some explanation because this does not make sense."

"What did he tell you exactly?" my voice is flat and cold, surprising even me. It irks me how quiet he's being.

"All you've wanted for months is to get into that school. Why did we have to hear that you got in from your teacher well after the fact?" Norah barks, filling the room with her entire being.

I focus on a water spot in the corner of the ceiling. I can't bring myself to look at these people. "I don't know if you've noticed, Norah, but lately we've all been preoccupied."

"Again, nah," Norah begins, standing swiftly from her easy chair to tower over the room like the dragon lady she is. "We won't use your mother only when she's convenient. If she's what this is about, we need to get you some help. You're not throwing things away like this."

"Because you know what's best for me, Norah?" I snap back with a venom I didn't know I possessed. With this particular aunt, the best policy was always to take it on the nose and let her have her say and her way, but I'm done playing that game. "Is this because you want me out of here? Sick of having yet another little orphan niece to take care of?"

In all my life, I've never seen Norah express an emotion other than anger or general annoyance, but the blank look of shocked hurt on her face right now is completely unnerving.

"How dare you?" she hisses, her hands balling into fists at her sides. I'm honestly worried she's going to hit me, but when she looks back up, she's crying.

Sorrow and pain sit heavy inside me, and I don't know whether to cry or throw up. I choose a third option instead, a Rosie classic. I decide to run.

"I don't need this." I storm out of the room, ignoring the calls from my aunts.

I'm out the door without a plan. The pie shop doesn't call me with its siren song; all my friends are getting on my nerves. The air puffs in and out in my mouth in angry clouds, my shoes meeting the asphalt of the middle of the road in powerful blows. It's too cold to walk around town aimlessly all night, and if I go to any of my regular hiding places, my aunts will find me. I dig around in the bottom of my bag, unsure what I want. Then my hand brushes a card. I know, of course, what it is instantly. The business card that Kyle gave me screams in my hand, but I can't fight the temptation.

The bus ride to New Shiloh is quiet this time of night. A few passengers and flickering fluorescent lights are the only companions. I don't know why I'm doing this. I can't even chalk it up to a morbid curiosity because I don't feel curious. I'm simply unbridled rage in lipstick and jeans, which probably is not the correct energy to bring, but that's all I have.

He lives in a nice apartment building. The street is clean and quiet, and the brick exterior is welcoming with its sleek black lobby. He's thirty-four years old and lives in an apartment in New Shiloh. Aren't adults supposed to have houses? The elevator ride takes forever with its annoying music. The doors open and close twice before I step into the hall of his floor. I'm starting to feel like this is a mistake.

Outside his threshold is a mat that says, "If you don't have cookies, go away," I hate it. I hate him. Before I can let myself over think it, I knock hard three times. The sound and the vibration reverberate through my body. Avoiding the urge to flee, I grip the door frame like an anchor and wait. When the door opens, seeing him makes me far angrier than I expected. He looks painfully average, from his casual t-shirt and gray sweatpants down to his bare feet and up to the glasses and stubble on his jaw.

"Your doormat is stupid!" I exclaim.

He swallows hard, the lump moving up and down his throat. "I'll get rid of it."

"You seriously live here? Twenty minutes away?" I mumble through a clenched jaw.

His hands mimic mine, balanced on the door frame from the inside. We're like two sides of a mirror. "Would you like to come in and talk about this?" he asks.

"No!" I exclaim, but he doesn't even flinch.

"Rosie?"

"Fine!" I duck under his arm and walk into his apartment. Pale, soothing gray paint covers the walls. His furniture is all shades of gray, black, and many metals. Books I'm sure that Bella has read line his shelves. It's clean and bright. Like everything else about him, it's absurdly normal.

"You never heard of color?" I snap, waving around at the surroundings.

"Gray is color," he says, smooth and even, sitting in one of the charcoal armchairs. He motions for me to sit on the couch, and as petty as my spirit is, I sit down.

"Twenty minutes away?" I snarl the second my legs meet the cushion.

"Only for the last three months," he says, rubbing his palms on his knees. "My family moved to Oregon for my dad's work my junior year, and I stayed there for school. My job transferred me out here a few months ago."

I flop against the back of the couch a few times. It's too plush. It doesn't give any delicious sound I had hoped to match my rage.

"Decided it was a bad idea to go back to Harpersgrove?" I ask, suddenly interested in the motorcycle magazines on his coffee table, anything to avoid eye contact.

He shrugs his shoulders up to his ears, a little color flooding his cheeks. "A place like Harpersgrove has a long memory. I needed somewhere new." He makes a lot of sense, and I hate him for it.

"Did you know about me?" I blurt out after a few moments of insufferable silence. It's the question that has plagued me all my life. Did he know I existed? Or did he choose to stay away from me my whole life? In reality, I know that neither answer will make me feel any better.

He mulls it over, choosing his words wisely before he speaks. His expression tells me everything and nothing all at once. He never breaks eye contact as he whispers, "I did."

I should cry. I should throw things. I should feel—something. But I don't. I never do. An eerie and disturbing calm settles over my entire body. Kyle verified my greatest insecurity, and that's because he did. No one wants Rosie Peters, least of all her parents.

"Why?" I hear myself say without any ownership of the word.

He sucks his lower lip into his mouth, raking his teeth against the delicate flesh. "I don't want it to sound like an excuse, but it will come across that way. I was a kid, Rosie, the same age you are now. What would you have done if you were in my shoes and on the other side of the country?"

"That's not a fair question, and you know it," I growl deep in my chest. "But I'll answer it anyway. First of all, I haven't been stupid enough to get knocked up. But even if I had, I can guarantee that I wouldn't have abandoned my child to hate herself for her entire life because no one ever wants her. Do you have any idea what you've done to me?"

It's too thick, too much, too unfair. I know I can't speak to these scenarios because I've only ever been the result, not through it myself, but I can't stop.

"I don't know what to do here, Rosie," he says, emotion catching his words. I watch his throat work against itself, trying to swallow the tears. "I don't know how to make any of this better."

And like that, the rage subsides, and the numbness returns like a shock to my system that would kill a lesser human.

I—

Feel—

Nothing.

"You can't do anything. I don't want you to do anything. You should have stayed away. Don't kid yourself into ever thinking you showed up at my mother's funeral or the pie shop that day for me. You did it for you and your curiosities; you needed to see some remnant of that girl you claimed to have loved and destroyed half your life ago, and I was all that's left to see."

"That's not true," he quietly sobs. If I were a better girl, a better daughter, I would comfort him somehow, but I'm not, so I don't. I rub my hands on my knees before I stand up. I have to get out of here. I don't belong in his everyday, gray-painted life.

"You can believe that if it makes you feel better, but you were only a teenager for a couple of years after I was born. What excuse do you make for the rest of my life?"

"I thought you were better off without me," he whispers, his sight locked on the floor.

I lean down to catch his gaze, forcing him to see me. My being is cold and dead when he stares back at me. "Sure you did," I say simply before leaving him in his living room. The sound of him crying as I walk away echoes in my ears in a way that I know will haunt me.

CHAPTER TEN

One long bus ride later, and I'm back walking the streets of my hometown. I'm a homeless orphan with nowhere to go. My friends are mad at me, the aunts are mad at me, and somehow my pie shop seems tainted. While walking through the main square, Rust's Drugstore's soft, glowing light draws me in.

Goldie's mom and mine were pregnant at the same time, the stains on the wholesome image of Harpersgrove, Maryland. Not that teen pregnancies weren't always around, but by the time we were born, it was less socially acceptable to force girls into marriage and make them drop out of school. Surely, Pop will take pity on me and let me waste a few hours with him.

But when I approach, I see it's not Pop. It's Goldie's grandmother, Nana. I hesitate. I don't know if she's the right person for me to see right now. Her gray hair streaked with the blonde she shares with her daughter and granddaughter piles high on her head. Rusts never cut their hair. Nana is what I call a Toll House Cookie grandma. She's every after school special wrapped up in a warm hug. Her glasses perch on the end of her nose, and she watches me with kind acceptance as the door swings closed behind me.

"Hiya honey!" she exclaims, slamming the cash drawer shut. "You haven't come by here this late at night in quite a while. How are you doing?"

She wraps her arms around my shoulders and pulls me into a spine-crushing hug, surrounding me with her honey-scented perfume. I interlock my fingers behind her back and hold on for dear life. She makes no move or effort to let go of me or ask what's wrong. She strokes her fingers against the back of my neck and waits. When I am ready to pull away, she holds on a moment longer. "Want to tell me what that was about?" She tucks my hair behind my ears and pinches my cheeks.

Since I'm full of unfair moments tonight, I blurt out the first thing that comes to mind, "Why could your daughter do it and my mom couldn't? Why could she be Goldie's mom, even without her dad around, and my mom couldn't keep it together for me? Why could she do it and my mom couldn't?"

"Rose," Nana begins, "your mom's struggles aren't your fault, and the fact that she couldn't stick around had nothing to do with you. That was all about her."

"But why is it always me, Nana?" I demand, slamming my fist down into my thigh. I want to feel something. "My dad abandoned me, and my mom did too, and then she went and died. Why doesn't anyone want me?"

Her face screws into a twisted configuration, revealing a deep set line in her forehead. "That's not true, Rosie, you know that."

My eyes roll back enough it hurts. "The aunts took me because they had to. It doesn't count."

"They most certainly did not have to. You could have easily gone into the foster care system, but I didn't mean them. What about us? We love you. What about your friends? They love you. Parents aren't everything."

"Says the woman who's the most perfect parent in the world," I groan. I'd kill for Nana to be my grandmother.

She scoffs at me as she pinches my cheek again. "That's what you think?" She reaches into the icebox behind the counter and grabs two soda bottles. She beckoned me to follow her back out front, and we sat on the steps.

The clear skies illuminate Main Street, a blessing since two of the four street lights are burnt out. She knocks the tops of the glass bottles off on the step and hands me one. She's effortlessly cool.

"I remember vividly the day that Lori told us she was pregnant with Goldie. I slapped her." Choking on the bubbles of my drink as they fizz up the back of my nose, I try to hold onto my composure, but my mouth won't close.

"Yes, yes, I know, not my finest moment. Our eldest daughter was simple and always stayed in her lane, but Lori has always been my challenge. When she told us she was pregnant, it was like she was throwing all our hopes and dreams for her in our face. I got angry and I slapped her. Lori declared that she hated us and was going to take her baby far away. All this is to say that perfection is an illusion. It took years, a decade, for us to trust each other again. The outward face of any family would never stand up to the scrutiny of a deep dive into their lives. You can't covet what other people have, Rosie. All it does is diminish the good in your life, and there's a lot of good there, kiddo."

"I worry that I'm destined to be stuck here forever," I wish I could take the words back as soon as I say them.

A sweet smile brushes across Nana's face. "Well, here isn't all that bad. There are far worse places I could have ended up. But that doesn't apply to you, does it? Goldie said you got into that design school up in New York."

Again, with the school. Does everyone in this town know?

"I'm not going," I say with sharp finality. The merry-go-round of telling this story over and over is making me ill.

I expect her to be like everyone else, either call me an idiot or yell at me about throwing my life away, but Nana does what she always does: subverts expectations. "I'm sure you have your reasons for saying that, but make sure they're yours. They can't be about your mom, aunts, or friends. I've seen the clothes you've made and the love you've put into them. You have an amazing talent, and I'd hate to see you deny yourself that because someone else said you should. Rosie, anyone could make clothes, but you could create fashion."

She lets me spend the rest of the night putting the lipsticks in alphabetical order by shade name. No one will ever be able to find anything, and it makes me giddily happy. It also means I walked into school the next morning with no sleep and in yesterday's clothes. I'm full of crabbiness and caffeine to match the dark circles under my tired eyes. I hope for an easy day where everyone leaves me alone, but fate is never that kind. The first face I see barrelling toward me like a bat out of hell is Elle, her face pinched, angry, and determined.

"What the hell, Rosie?!" she shrieks as she gets close. Her voice garners the attention of Lucy Wilcox's minion, Sawyer Blake, who giggles and snaps a picture of me. High school mean girls are the worst kind of humans.

"Where have you been? Your aunts were calling everyone panicked last night because they couldn't find you," she exclaims. "We were worried. Where were you?"

"Here, there, and everywhere, sister," I say, slamming my locker shut. I have neither the patience nor the will to entertain anyone else's emotions.

"What does that mean? What is going on with you?" I open my mouth to retort, but she doesn't give me a chance. "And don't say your mom. Your behavior is not about your mom but about you. I'm your friend, and I'm worried about you."

"Well, knock it off and worry about yourself, okay? I'm fine." It's a lie of the highest order, but I can't take everyone staring. "Aren't you and your boyfriend going to schools on opposite sides of the country in a few months? That deserves more of your attention than me." It's a low blow, especially since I know how much that subject bothers her, but I need everyone to stop pushing me for a while, and I will use heavy artillery when necessary.

She stops dead in her tracks, and I have to double back to her. I can see the tears that brim the corners of her eyes, yet I don't feel the tiniest bit of remorse.

"I don't know what's going on with you or who this person is that you're pretending to be, but I don't like her. Why don't you let me know when she goes away and Rosie comes back? Because I don't think I can be friends with this person." She turns on her heel and hurries down the hall away from me, surely so I won't see her cry. First, I lost Blanche and Beau; now, I have lost Elle. I think about how many more friends I can send screaming from my life.

When Joshua showed up at the pie shop later that night, I was less chipper than normal when I saw him. "What's the matter with you?" he asks, sitting at the counter and digging into one of the covered pies. He should probably start paying for those.

I shrug. I'm not all that interested in talking about it.

"I had a fight with a few of my friends."

"About the school thing?" he asks. Am I that transparent? I shrug again. "Well, I wouldn't worry too much. You know you're making the right call. My parents are putting me up in a nice apartment in the fall, and you can come to stay there with me anytime you need to get away from—this." He waves his hand around the room with an edge of disgust, but he doesn't stop eating the pie.

"You'd let me come stay with you?" I ask, linking my pinky finger with his. He flashes me that smile that makes my heart stop, and I forget every terrible thing that's going on. He's magical.

"Of course, baby, I love you," he says, letting go of his fork and reaching up to brush my cheek.

I suddenly feel incredibly off balance, desperately needing something to anchor me. "Listen, we haven't had this conversation, and it's probably silly at this point, but am I your girlfriend?"

His entire body freezes with his focus centered on his pie. "Why do you have to do that?" he grumbles, pushing the plate away from him and putting physical distance between us.

"Do what?"

"We're having a moment. I tell you I love you, and that's not enough for you. Why am I and what I have to offer not enough?" Joshua shouts, pushing to his feet and pacing the floor in front of me.

"I didn't say it wasn't enough." I can feel my face blanching and my stomach falling to the base of my torso.

Suddenly, he's on me, burying one hand in my hair, tugging at the roots to the point it hurts, and his other hand is at my waist, pulling me flush against his body. He slams his mouth against mine, possessing me in a way that lets on no edge of kindness. It's possessive and raw, and I am completely overwhelmed. When he releases my lips, he settles his forehead against mine, holding me right where he wants.

"You are mine, and I love you, but I am not tied to any labels. That's not the kind of guy I am, and you won't change that. Don't ruin what we have by trying; don't be stupid. You know my feelings for you, and I need that to be enough."

"Why?" I can't help but ask.

"I'm not doing this right now, Rosie. I love you, and I want to make a life with you. If that's not enough, tell me now."

I don't know why, but my panicked lizard brain starts screaming at me to do anything. I must not to let him go. Grab on with both hands for dear life, and don't let him go.

"It's enough. You're enough. I'm sorry, I won't ask about the girlfriend thing again."

I expect him to soften like he has before, but he doesn't. "This is Blanche putting all these bull shit ideas into your head, isn't it?"

"What? No, I'm not even talking to Blanche," I admit, and realize it's true. We've barely swapped eye contact, let alone pleasantries.

That's the thing that brings the slightest spark in him, and I am hungry for more of it. He reaches up and runs his hand through my hair, gripping it as the crown. "That's my girl. Maybe all your friends here have a bad influence on you. You could do better, you know." And without any real reason, I believe him.

I fist my hands in his shirt and silently beg him to kiss me again. Every time I see him, I can't shake the desperate feeling that he's always one foot out the door, and I will do whatever I can to keep him.

I'm grateful the house is quiet when I roll in after midnight. Walking on silent eggshells around my aunts has gotten old fast, and I don't want to do it anymore. I'm heading down the hallway toward my bedroom when the soft glow of the refrigerator light illuminates the house. "Come in here a second," a disjointed voice calls out to me, but it's not Norah or Meredith. It's Shawna. Quiet, simple, sugary-sweet Shawna. She pulls out a carton of milk and clicks on the light over the oven to keep us illuminated. She pours two glasses and hands me a chocolate chip cookie. Shawna's coping mechanism with stress or sadness is neurotic baking.

"You're not going to yell at me, are you?" I ask, trying to bring some levity to her uncharacteristically solemn demeanor.

She shakes her head. "No. No more yelling. It's exhausting, and so are you, young lady," she says angrily.

"Shawna," I begin, but she's having none of it.

"No more talking either," she says as she starts unloading things from the pantry. When she pulls out a pie dish, I realize what's happening. She shifts slightly to the side, making room for me. "Make me a crust, please." I open my mouth to inquire about what kind, but she's having none of it.

"Quiet. Only pie."

I set to work beside my aunt in rhythmic silence. The pressing of dough makes sense to me. The foundation for something wondrous is born from the humble beginnings of flour, butter, and salt. Once the crust forms into the dish and edged in a beautiful pattern, she takes it away from me and puts a bowl in its place. The bowl is full of blackberries because, of course, it is. I usually leave the seeds in, and my mother is always in my head, saying that they deserve love, too.

But I don't want them to stand out anymore. I want them to blend in and be everyday fruits. No fuss. No attention. normal. After bringing the berries and sugar to a boil in a saucepan, I push the mixture through a sieve, removing every tiny seed. I can feel her watching me.

"Holly always left the seeds in when she used those," Shawna finally says, breaking her own rule.

"Can you not?" I ask, returning the mixture to the heat.

"I have to Rose. We haven't discussed it."

I inhale deeply, slowly adding cornstarch to the pan, absorbing the sweet, sugary aroma. "I thought we weren't talking."

"No, lovely, you aren't talking, but I am." She puts down the utensils in her hand with an unpleasant clang and turns to face me. "You and I have never clicked, Rosie. I know you don't like me that much." I open my mouth to protest because it's not true, but she stands her ground. "Don't argue with me right now. I want you to listen for once in your life."

I've never heard her like this. It's unsettling and upsetting.

"I probably didn't try hard enough to meet you on your level. I always wanted to pull you to mine, and that was most likely a mistake and unfair, but I loved you. I've loved you every moment of your life, but you never could give it back."

"Shawna, I do love you," I murmur, barely audible.

"It wasn't your responsibility to meet us like that. We were your parents, and you were our child. I don't know if we did a good job of addressing what was happening." I don't like her calling herself my parent; my orphan identity feels so much truer. "You've created a false narrative in your head that you lived with your mother much more than you did."

"Excuse me?" I ask, taking a moment to catch my breath by pouring the berry mixture into the crust.

Shawna rubs the palms of her hands together, her attention turning toward the doorway. I can't tell if she's hoping the other aunts will show up and stop her or not. "We weren't blind, Rosie. We raised Holly. We knew her better than anyone."

How I wish she'd stop using her name.

"You were two when the drugs began. It started small, and you were both living with us. That way, we could keep a close eye on you both. She moved out when things started to get bad, but we kept you here. She flitted in and out, but you were here with us."

"Why did you let her around at all if she was that bad? Seems like you would have fought to keep me away from her," I said, smoothing the mixture in the pie until it was flat and shiny like a skating rink.

"She was your mom, and she loved you. She was always sober when you were with her, and when she slipped, we made her leave. I'm sure we made a thousand wrong choices, Rosie, but we have always loved you."

"Nobody loves their burdens, Shawna. They're responsible for them."

"Do you intend to use that as a crutch for the rest of your life?" she asked coldly, flicking on the sink.

"Excuse me?"

The woman who turns to face me is not the Aunt Shawna I know. This woman is icy, drained, and devoid of the soft and squishy emotions I've known so well. "When will you stop pushing the button that no one loves you when it's clearly not true? You use it as a crutch to ify any bad decision you make."

"I do not do that."

"Then why aren't we all sitting around in Parsons sweatshirts planning a theme for your dorm?"

"It is a completely separate issue, and you know it. This is unfair, Shawna," I shout, no longer caring who might wake up.

"No, what's unfair is you continually trying to throw your life away because you won't admit you deserve better. And then leaning on things like the death of your mother to excuse those actions because you don't think anyone will call you out on it, but I love you too much for that."

"You are completely out of pocket right now, Shawna, and you need to back off. I meant it. This is something for me to figure out on my own," I warn, moving toward my room. I need to get away before I say something I can't take back.

She doesn't let me get more than five steps away before saying, "I sincerely doubt that you are making this decision on your own."

"What does that mean?" I bark, my tongue suddenly too big for my mouth.

She is empty when she looks up at me. "You're your mother's daughter, Rosie. I can see it in you as well as I did her. You think I don't realize there's some boy mixed up in this?"

I can't tell who I'm more offended for: My mom? Kyle? Joshua? Myself? It seems to be a blow at everyone. "You don't know what you're talking about, Shawna. This is an ugly face you're showing."

"That's not a denial," she says simply.

"I'm going to bed."

I'm under the surface of the black water. Its inky darkness swirls in and out of my fingers. The screams have turned to a call, a call far away. And it sounds like my name.

Tradition stands for me to hold a tasting of new creations once a month at the pie shop. I've concocted a few new pies over the previous weeks that are worthy of trying. The girls then taste them and pick a favorite or two, and they get added to the menu for the next few weeks as specials. Rinse and repeat month after month. Historically, it's been my favorite day, and yet now, nothing could interest me less. Putting the finishing touches on the two pies I've made, nothing special. In fact, I cheated and tweaked two existing recipes because I didn't feel inspired. The shop is in a hustle as the entire crew rushes to close. Everyone shows up for pie tasting.

The loud rumble of the dishwasher drowns out most of my friends' laughs and chatter, and I'm glad for it. Their merriment annoys me in a way that never stops pinching. Bella's head sticks up cautiously through the window, revealing not much more than her eyes. "Hey, Rosie, can I help you at all."

"I'll be out in a minute, Bella," I clip, cleaning an imaginary mess on the counter; anything to keep from looking at her.

"O—okay, I wanted to see if I could help you," she says, and I can feel her lingering. "I wanted to help you." Before I snap at her again, she's gone back through the window, and I can feel my skin vibrating with a rage that has no audience or target.

It's going to be a long night.

After we lock the doors and the closing work finished, I know I can't avoid them any longer. I scoop my hands under the two pies and enter the dining room. Across the counter from me are my five clos-est friends sitting in a row on the neon-colored stools. The silence is deafening. I lay the two pies before them, and Nixie chuckles, "Only two? Was it a slow month?"

"If you don't want it, I'll take it back," I bite. Being here is a mistake. I need some distance from everyone for a while.

"Rose, take a deep breath and start again," Goldie chastises as she passes plates down the line. "Now, why don't you tell us what we have here?"

Even though my initial instinct is to snap, I opt instead to take the breath she suggested. These are my friends. "Okay," I say, forcing the tension between my shoulders to relax. "Option one is a blackberry cream with a spicy chili whip, and option two is blackberry peach pie with a gingerbread crust, which was kind of a risk."

"Risk can be good," Blanche whispers, soft enough that she's barely heard. *Was that comment for me?*

"Big blackberry kick, huh, Rosie?" Nixie asks, slicing into the black-berries and peaches.

I consider letting it go or shrugging it off, but my soul compels me to say, "They were my mom's favorite." For a moment, everyone is silent. Then the plates begin to shuffle, and everyone takes their help-ings. What's left unspoken is a toast to my mom, but I feel it.

"The gingerbread has to be a no from me," Blanche says after the pies disappear. "It's weird, sorry."

"No, no, that's why we do this," I say, beginning to gather the plates. This was a level of normal I didn't know I needed. The other pie seemed to be a hit, so one blackberry special was on the menu.

"I have some news," Elle announces when there's a lull. The room falls silent, and everyone turns. "I have accepted the offer to UCLA! I am California-bound, ladies!" The eruption pulls me out of the happy moment of normalcy and back into my black cloud, not for Elle. I'm delighted for Elle. I know this will put everyone's attention back on me and that I'm not going to Parsons.

My smile is weak compared to the squawking and squealing of the group, but it's all I have right now. "Has Finn decided where he's going?" I hear Blanche ask when I turn my back. It's better for everyone not to see my sour face—college this and college that. Enough already. Plus, was wrong about what I said to Elle in the hall at school.

Elle's silent for a long moment before she says, "Yeah, he's going to Texas A&M." Suddenly, everyone is less cheery. "But I don't want to talk about that right now. I want to relish in the glory of UCLA."

"As well you should," I say, feeling the need to add something to the conversation. "Is your mom freaking out about you going that far?"

"Surprisingly, she's on board." The idea of Elle's mother pleased about anything not involving herself is enough to settle the room into a hush. "I know, trust me! Shocked me too, but she's thrilled."

I'm about to add something more when someone outside the window catches my attention. Joshua looks at me before scanning the room and trying to walk, or should I say run, away. Blanche is too fast, of course, and catches him before he can. She sprints to the door with her long runner legs and throws it open. "McDonald, get in here."

I don't know why he listens, but that authoritative tone she uses to keep her seven brothers in line must have some mystical powers because, with a groan, he stomps around her and into the shop.

Considering how often he's been here with me, I find how uncomfortable he looks unsettling. He keeps pushing his hair out of his eyes and moving his hands around in the pockets of his gray leather jacket. Blanche clasps her hand onto his shoulder. I watch him wince and swear I feel the same pain myself.

"Okay then," Blanche says in her cheery way, which makes me want to tackle her. "Do you all know Rosie's boyfriend, Josh?" If looks could kill, the daggers that Joshua throws me would drop me to my knees. His nostrils flare, like I'm in serious trouble.

"I, um, I never said that he was my boyfriend," I say meekly, but that doesn't seem to calm Joshua down. Blanche doesn't seem angry but fiercely disappointed and determined.

"We're hanging out, right?" It feels like the correct answer, but I still can't read anything on his face, and it's terrifying.

"Yeah," he says finally, wiggling his shoulder away from Blanche's grasp. "Not everyone has to label things the way you do, Summers."

Unfazed as always, Blanche's whole demeanor grows cold as she narrows in on me.

"Hanging out, huh? Well, if you're hanging out with her, she's coming to your party on Friday, right?"

"What the fuck is your problem?" Joshua mumbles under his breath, and it's like a punch in my gut. He'd have a good reason for not asking me to go if he's having a party. He prefers having me all to himself. I know this.

Blanche doesn't back down a beat, which seems to tick him off more. He snaps the collar of his jacket up by his ears like a James Dean wannabe.

"Bring her if you want to bring her," he sneers to Blanche on his way out. He never even looks back at me, and I can take the acidic feeling of fear that burns at the back of my throat. The black water keeps screaming: YOU'RE NEVER GOING TO SEE HIM AGAIN!

All I want to do is race after him, leap into his arms, and tell him I understand, but my body stands frozen. Blanche is on me at lightning speed when the door clinks closed, "You have got to be kidding with that guy, Rosie!"

"Why are you against me being happy?" I murmur, pressing my fingers into the counter.

"This is you happy?" Goldie chimes in, incapable of staying in her lane.

"That guy doesn't give a shit about you!" Blanche yells, pointing at the door like Joshua is still there. "Your entire face went white the second I said he was your boyfriend because you knew it would make him mad."

"You can never mind your own business! I have everything under control. It is my life." I should cry, but instead I'm screaming.

"You don't have anything under control. You're scaring me," Nixie cries, tears streaming down her face.

"Jesus Christ, of course, Nixie is going to get hysterical. This isn't even about you!

"Don't yell at her!" Elle snaps back. Everyone against Rosie, what a surprise.

"None of you have any idea of what I'm going through," I hiss, and instantly, I see everyone turn on their defenses. "And I don't want to hear that your mom is dead, Blanche. Or that your dad left, Elle. Or that your boyfriend has a disability, Bella. Or that you're not going to college, Goldie."

"Who do you think you're talking to right now?" Bella demands, rounding the corner to get in my face. "You think we'd be your friends if we sat by while you threw your life away and said, 'Oh well, that's her journey.' Absolutely not!"

"Get out of my face, Bella," I breathe, but no air will enter my lungs.

"Why won't you listen to Blanche? He is not a good guy for you. Why are you willing to throw everything away on him," she screams, and a little drop of her spit gets on my cheek, sending me over the edge. Before I know what I'm doing, my hands are in the middle of her chest, and I push her away.

Goldie rounded the counter before I had a second to think of what I'd done. She grips my upper arm and drags me into the kitchen, pushing with the force of her weight through the door, which slaps back and forth on its hinge once we're inside.

"Who are you? Because I don't know this person, and I don't freaking like her."

"Stop being dramatic," I bark back, pacing the floor I've walked a thousand times. But I hate it here right now, and I hate her for making me feel that way.

"Rosie, you need to step back and look at what's happening here."

In the vein of people hurting people, I go for blood with my favorite person.

"I know what's happening here. My so-called best friend doesn't care what I want; she needs me to pursue a life she will never have. Face it, Goldie, you're going to spend the rest of your life right here in Harspergrove working at your grandparent's store like your mom, and you can't stand it, and now you're pushing your crap onto me."

I've known Goldie my entire life, and I can't remember ever seeing her shell crack until now. She blinks so quickly that I don't notice the tears until one runs fat and angry down her cheek. She chews hard on her bottom lip and starts fingering through her hair at her scalp like she's lost something inside it.

"You know what? Screw you, Rosie. I'm done with this." It should sting more than it does, but I don't feel it. I don't feel anything.

As Goldie clears the way, Blanche is quick to take her place. I'm in no mood. She doesn't say anything at first; she pulls her phone out of her pocket and taps on the screen. My phone dings a moment later.

"That's where your boyfriend's party is on Friday. See how he treats you in front of his friends, or don't. Honestly, I don't care anymore."

I hear them all leave out the front door, and Bella hits the lights, leaving me in the dull haze of the kitchen. All alone, abandoned, the way I always am—the way it's supposed to be.

CHAPTER ELEVEN

For the next three days, I won't leave my bed. I figure I've stacked up enough bereavement days unused that the aunts can't use them against me for skipping school. As far as the pie shop goes, I'm about ready to quit anyway, so a few days of distance and perspective can't hurt. I don't care about pie, and that feeling chips at my inky black heart.

Shawna keeps trying to feed me, but I'm not interested. I'm fatigued. I've had no showers, no clean clothes, lots of sleep. Sleeping without black water is somehow even more lonely. The rational side of me knows I should feel bad about what happened. They all deserve apologies, especially Bella and Goldie, but—I. Don't. Care.

Friday is the only thing to pull me out of my slump. I'm terrified. Joshua hasn't texted me once since the debacle at the shop. I'm frightened that I've screwed it up, and I have to see him.

I go through my regular motions and get ready. My shower is hot enough to sting. I curl my hair, and do my makeup in that simple, understated way that I know Joshua prefers. I opted for the white sweater and mom jeans, which I know Joshua likes. Everything about tonight is doing what Joshua likes. The aunts are all sitting in the kitchen around the table when I grab my purse to leave. "I'm taking the car," I announce.

Norah opens her mouth to protest, but Meredith puts her hand over sister's arm. "Be safe," she says. I can't tell if they're exhausted with me or if they trust me, but it doesn't matter as long as I can leave. Should I read more into it? Probably, but again, I don't care.

My quick trip to Kyle's apartment aside, I haven't been to neighboring New Shiloh in years. My mother and I went through this way when I was a little girl. Most of her short-lived jobs were here. But we never went to the more affluent side of town, where the big houses and swimming pools sit too close together. It was easy to know which one was Joshua's. Inside, strangers crash into each other like sardines in a can, and I'm instantly uncomfortable. Being here with a group of friends like armor would give me anxiety, but alone is much, much worse.

I see Blanche and Elle standing with Elle's boyfriend in the corner of the room. Why are they here? They hate Joshua. The people who have always been my safe haven are now like poison. I need to find Joshua. I shift in and out of people, bobbing and weaving my way through, looking for that blonde hair and ever-present leather jacket. When I find him, he's in the living room, in front of the fireplace, a circle of girls around him. He's the bell of the ball. The girls laugh at some of the stories he tells, and he seems at ease. Not the introverted late-night Joshua that I have come to know. I thought he hated other people. He doesn't sense me until I'm almost right next to him. When he sees me, a blanching panic falls over him, and he jumps away from the girls as if they burned him.

"Hey," he says like he's not sure I'm there.

I try my best not to notice his discomfort and ignore the sour feeling in my stomach.

"You seem surprised to see me," I respond with too much sunshine.

The swarm of girls has all become a little too interested, but I try not to take it too personally because he's always prided himself on keeping me private.

"Well, when Blanche came in without you, I figured you decided not to come."

If I didn't know better, he sounded disappointed.

I start tucking my hair behind my ears in a rapid succession that borders on mania. "Oh, yeah, I decided to come alone."

"Who the eff are you?" Behind me, with a red cup in hand, Joshua's twin sister, Mallory, watches me with all the judgment a person can muster. Her shiny baby doll dress reminds me of cellophane. She flicks her big blonde curls away from her face, popping her hip to the side, indicating she's waiting for an answer. "Are you deaf?"

"Rosie." I squeak.

"Retract the fangs, Mal," Joshua says with flat affect. He weaves between us and motions with his head for me to follow him. I can feel her eyes on my back like an archer. The back of his hand brushes mine, and I reach to grab it, but he puts it in his pocket instead. I guess he didn't notice me.

He leads me up the stairs and through other party-goers. Their focus on me does not go unnoticed. The stranger that doesn't belong. I can't help but wonder if this is more Mallory's party than Joshua's. Everything I've learned about him says he would hate a gathering like this as much as I do. I relax when we reach a quiet and private room.

The sounds of the party fall away as he turns the lock on the door. He's on me before my brain has a chance to catch up. He scoops one arm under my butt and lifts me off the ground. He urges me to wrap my legs around his waist and kisses me until I forget my name.

"God, I've missed you," he murmurs into my mouth when he comes up for air. My chest rises and falls beneath his chin, and his mouth finds its way to the space above my heart and then up to my neck. I wonder if he can feel the fluttering. His fingers dig into my behind and the nape of my neck to the point of bruising. He tosses me back onto the bed, and his weight is on top of me, all around me. He pushes my head to the side and starts to work some witchcraft on my neck, making my eyes cross.

"Mmm, I love you. I want to stay right here with you all night. You look so beautiful."

Every insecurity melts away under the feeling of his fingers. There's some beauty in being desperately craved and wanted that I need in equal measure. I work my hands up to the sides of his face and ease his lips off of me.

"Hey, hey, relax for a second. Talk to me. I haven't seen you in a couple of days."

A groan resonates deep in his throat as he lets his full weight fall against me, his face in the crook of my neck. "I have an intense need to express myself physically. You look so good, baby."

A tingle in my chest wants to push back and have a long talk. But Joshua makes it so I don't always have to think, and I need that. I dig my hands deep into his hair and tug him back to me. He smiles against my mouth, and it gives me a thrill that eggs me on further. His fingers start inching up my ribs under my shirt, and I let my brain turn off. I want to feel by not feeling anything.

"Well, this is cozy," I hear from the other side of the room. I nearly launch out of my skin. Mallory stands there, twirling a bobby pin in her fingers. She must have used it on the lock.

"You are a fucking cancer, Mallory," Joshua says, shamelessly staying in position on top of me.

"For which there is no remission," she responds flatly. "Why don't you crawl off your girlfriend and come back downstairs. I want to stop pretending to care about your freak friends."

He doesn't say a word to me as he pushes himself off my body and flips his sister off while walking out of the room. I'm not sure how to proceed from here. I find myself fixated on a crack in the paint of his bedroom ceiling. It's an odd imperfection that doesn't seem to match the otherwise pristine nature of the house.

"Are you going to lay there all night?" Mallory says, and I have to face that she's still in the room.

"Nope. I was getting ready to go back to the party."

She's gawking at me like I'm a sideshow attraction. "You and my brother, huh?" It's one of those questions that doesn't sound like a question.

I'm unsure of how to respond. Joshua is keen on privacy, but this is his sister. Surely, the same rules don't apply to her.

"Yeah, it's new—but yeah."

She pops the gum in her mouth as she stares unblinking. It's unnerving.

"Interesting."

That word does not sound positive, but I will show her no fear. I square my shoulders and smile brightly. She looks me up and down, her eyes sharp and catlike. "Well, if you're Joshie's girlfriend, you must be coming to dinner when our parents return next weekend, right?"

My deer-in-the-headlights expression amuses her.

"Oh, I don't know—."

"Nonsense," she says dispassionately, reaching forward to straighten the hem of my shirt. "If you're dating Josh, my parents would like to meet you. My boyfriend and my big sister and her husband are coming. It's Friday at seven. We'll see you here."

She leaves me then, standing awkwardly in Joshua's room by myself. His walls are a soft, muted blue. A few posters of expensive cars are on the walls, and scattered pictures are in frames on the dresser. Honestly, it looks like a furniture store display more than it does a teenager's bedroom, but I guess not everyone is as sentimental as I am. I hunt for some trinket to tell me his secrets, some little totem to let me in. I love him, but I'd be lying if I said it didn't make me uneasy how little I knew. I rest my fingers on the carved handles of the top drawer of his dresser and wonder when exactly curiosity turns to snooping. Looking back, I decide it's worth the risk and pull the drawer toward me. I'm disappointed to find mostly underwear, but I sweep my hands through to be sure when I hit something soft. I pull back a small, brown teddy bear with a blue bow tied around his neck. I smile brightly, tuck the bear into his hiding spot, and close the drawer. Joshua keeps a childhood teddy bear, which warms me enough to endure a little more time at the party. For him, I can do that.

I follow Joshua around the party for a few more hours, trying and failing to get to know some of his friends. All eyes were on me when I walked in, but now they're avoiding me like I'm Medusa. They're all too invested in their little conversations to see me approach. The easiest thing to do would be to go to Elle and Blanche and be with my friends, but I know that's not an option. They barely seem to pay me any mind, which hurts more than I care to admit. Every time I glance in their direction, I hope I catch someone's attention, but they are always laughing or talking with someone else and having a great time—without me.

When I finally had enough to overflow my social battery for decades, I found Joshua and told him I was leaving. He barely turns his attention away from the girl he's speaking to before I go. It's okay. I know how overstimulated he gets in big group settings, and I get the real him when it's the two of us. That's enough. I see his sister when I'm leaving, and she smiles and nods, reminding me to be back for dinner. I will be. I'm too invested in it all now not to.

My hopes that Blanche or Elle might follow me to my car are dashed after I sit for five minutes and nothing. I have never wanted and not wanted something more than for them to come running after me.

It's well after midnight when I crawl through my bedroom window. Slipping into bed, all my attention focuses on the faded glow-in-the-dark stars and planets on the ceiling, and for the first time, I hate them. Irrational anger swells through my body, and I get to my feet on the bed and start picking at the stars. The years have hardened them against the pale paint, and the scratching of my fingernails across them stings, but I can't stop. When they're nothing but gooey, sticky clumps on my comforter, I curl up on the blankets and drift away. I'm spent.

The next few days pass like the ones before. The aunts float in from time to time. Norah to yell, Shawna with food, Meredith to sit on the edge of my bed in silence rubbing my leg. My phone is dead somewhere in my bag, not that anyone would reach out. I finally rise when I'm supposed to go to dinner with Joshua and his family. I have to make some sense of myself before meeting his family. It's the only thing that could get me out of bed.

Everyone watches me like a dangerous predator when I head into the kitchen for coffee. For some reason, I decided to wear my mother's funeral dress to dinner with Joshua and his family, which was a good idea. It was the only thing that spoke to me, and I'm trying hard not to read into it.

"You're up," Meredith remarks from the dining room table.

"Glad to see your eyes are working."

"I will smack the sass right off you, young lady," Norah says from the other side of her paper.

"Calm down." I can feel the rage boiling inside her, but Shawna calms her as usual.

"You missed school again today," Meredith asks, pretending to move her cereal around her bowl.

"Well, it is after five—that's a pretty safe observation there, Mere." I can feel the radiating heat coming off of Norah like a supernova, but I don't care. "I'm going out to dinner. Don't wait up for me."

I grab my purse and leave.

"At least she's out of bed," I hear Shawna reassure the others. I never stop moving.

The ride to New Shiloh is easy and quiet. I keep the radio off, preferring the static noise in my head. What do I even talk about with people like Joshua's family? They have money and status; I'm sure they're on boards and committees for foundations and charities. What if I embarrass myself? What if I embarrass Joshua? I have to make this work; it's the one thing in my life right now that's functioning, and I'll hold it tight until they pry it from my cold, dead hands.

There were four other cars parked in the driveway when I arrived. I sit still for a moment, trying to remember any facts about world politics I may have ever learned. All I seem to come up with is the rhyme about Columbus in 1492, and I don't think that will aid me. In the middle of my desperate scan, a banging sounds outside my passenger window, making me yelp. Joshua scrambles to open the passenger side and slides into the car with me. He looks so unnatural in his sport coat, khakis, and tie.

"Why the fuck haven't you been answering your fucking phone?" he hisses once the door slams.

Surprised at the first words I've heard from him in a week, I blink back. "I—um, I forgot to charge it."

"Look," he says, frantically running his hand through his perfectly parted hair and then panicking as he tries to return it to its previous state. "You know I love you, and because I do, you cannot come inside right now."

The gurgling sound of the black water replaces the static sound in my head.

"Listen to me, my parents are small-minded shitty people who don't like anyone, and I have to spare you from that. I tried to come by the pie shop and see you, but you were never there, and you wouldn't answer your damn phone."

"But—but your sister invited me," is all I can say.

"My sister is a shrew who doesn't think anyone else should be happy and throws pain around like candy—"

Before he can say more, there's a tap on my driver's side window. Mallory smiles back through the window. "Do not open it," Joshua commands, but I roll it down anyway.

"Now, what are you two doing sitting out here in the driveway?" she asks, her tone horrifyingly chipper.

"You are a malignant tumor, Mallory," Joshua hisses, white-knuckling my dashboard like he's fighting the urge to hit something.

She grins, cold and icy.

"Save the compliments, sweetheart; I might cry," she says, pushing away from my window. I realize I've been holding my breath. Before she leaves, she calls back, "By the way, Mother already saw her. She has to come in now."

Expletives fly from Joshua's mouth that I try not to take personally.

"Okay, this is how this is going to go. I need you to be mute. I need you to smile, look stupid, and giggle at my dad's jokes. My older sister will be in there. Do what she does; she's a vapid airhead. I'll speak for you, and we'll get through this. Then we can come back and make out in your car." Then he frowns, "God, did you have to wear that hoop in your lip? You look like a junkie."

My head is spinning, but I start nodding for some reason. It hurt, but I have to do this. I can play dumb if that's what he needs from me. When we leave the car, I reach for his hand to steady myself, but he shrugs away and puts them in his pockets. A tall blonde woman in a pink suit with a blinding white smile opens the door. She's the fakest-looking person I've ever seen.

"Well," she says. "Isn't this a surprise? Josh never brings anyone to family dinner."

"Mother, this is Rosaline Peters," he says, moving past his mother and into the house without me.

Smile and nod, Rosie.

I stick out my hand and grin wide. She eyes me curiously before folding my hand into the crook of her elbow.

"Pleasure to have you, darling." Even her voice is artificial.

In the dining room with the ridiculously high ceiling sits a family of plastic people around the oblong table. On one side sits Mallory next to a clean-cut guy with square shoulders who looks almost as uncomfortable as me. Next to them is a blonde girl slightly older than Mallory in a suit like her mother's, but in tangerine instead of pink. Beside her is a man locked on his cell phone, ignoring everything else in the room. I assume he's her husband. At one head of the table is Joshua's mother, and at the other is a bald older man in a crisp black suit with a sour look. "It appears my son has finally brought a date to family dinner," he says dryly.

"Hardly, Father, this is my friend, Rosaline," Joshua snickers. The "friend" snub stings, and I don't know why he insists on using my full name.

"Your *friend* Joshie?" Mallory questions, complete with air quotes from the other side of the table. The rage radiates off him, but thankfully, his older sister takes up the conversation.

"Mommy," she starts, "Paisley rolled over this afternoon. I have a video if you'd like to see it." She pulls her phone out of her purse when her mother stops her.

"Later, Annabeth, having your phone at the table is rude." A staff of three enters, their arms lined with plates. They sit a bowl of soup in front of me, and Joshua leans over and whispers in my ear, "Use the spoon on the outside, sit up straight, and for the love of god, don't spill or slurp." I'm pretty sure I'm not feral, but I've never been this nervous about eating anything in my life.

Course by course, the food comes and goes, and to my inner glee, I don't spill a bit. My back is aching from sitting perfectly straight, and my face hurts from my airhead smile, but it's all going okay. Joshua and his father seem to carry most of the conversation about sports and business, things I honestly couldn't contribute to anyway, but, weirdly, none of the women seem to pipe up. Mallory's boyfriend and Annabeth's husband chime in occasionally, but all the girls eat or push their food around. It's very Stepford-esque.

It's when dessert comes that the conversation turns to me. And I wish we could go back to sports. "Rosaline, tell us a little about yourself," Mr. McDonald asks, taking a bite of his crème brûlée.

I lick my lips a few times before I speak. Joshua had told me not to talk, but staying silent seemed rude. "Well, most people call me Rosie," I begin and instantly feel Joshua's hand grip my thigh. What is so bad about my name? "I'm a senior at Harpersgrove, and I work at the pie shop in town."

"Yes, it has some punny name, doesn't it? We love the pie from there," Mrs. McDonald chimes in, and Joshua's grip tightens.

"I make the pies there."

"That's amazing, honey, isn't that amazing?" she says to Joshua. He offers only a sharp nod.

"And what about your parents, Rosie," Mr. McDonald says, and the bitter way he says my nickname makes me think there might be something to Joshua's actions.

I stutter internally at how to answer. Everyone in Harpersgrove knows about my life. I've never had to explain it to other people. "My three great aunts raised me."

Mr. McDonald's forehead crinkles. "And why is that?"

"Um, well," I begin and place my hand over Joshua's, but he instantly pulls away. He's staring absently at his plate, willing the moment to end. "My parents were teenagers, and my mother decided when I was young that it would serve me better if my aunts raised me."

"And why did your teen mother decide such a thing?" Mrs. McDonald says coolly.

"Because she was a drug addict, and Rosie's black father wasn't around," Mallory chimes in from across the table, a cruel grin on her face.

"Excuse me?" Mr. McDonald says, settling his fork against his plate.

"Oh yeah, I heard all about it. Rosie's mom was a heroin addict who died from a drug overdose a few weeks ago, and she met her black father for the very first time at her mom's funeral." For some reason, I find myself more defensive of Kyle than Holly. Her attention shifts to me, and that cruel energy returns to her perfectly formed face. "It's fascinating. If you hand a twenty to anyone in your podunk town, they'll tell you everything you want to hear."

"Joshua Alexander," Mr. McDonald begins, "I don't know what kind of cute joke you're trying to play by dating this person, but it's not funny. It's unfair to build up the hopes of lesser people."

I turn to Joshua, hoping he'll say something to my defense, anything, but he doesn't. Instead, he says, "Dad, I'm not dating her. I befriended her because she was tragic, and she needed me. You raised me to look out for the less fortunate, and that's all this is. I am not dating her, and Mallory invited her here. I didn't."

My heart beats in my ears, and my head feels light. I lift my napkin and lay it on my plate before pushing my chair away from the table. I need to get out of this room. It's like a vacuum.

"Mr. and Mrs. McDonald, thank you for a lovely evening, but I should be going."

Joshua doesn't even flinch. I don't look at Mallory—I won't give her satisfaction. I'm almost out of the house when a warmth spreads through my body, and a little voice tells me I do not deserve what happened. For the first time ever, I listen to it.

"For the record, I got into one of the best design schools in the country. I did that all on my own. I even made this dress I'm wearing. I have a steady job and make my own money, which I can pretty much guarantee that none of your children can say. And yes, my mother was a user, and my father wasn't around. But people who know me, see me, and care about me raised me, and my mom cared enough to let them. We don't have the money you do, but after sitting with this family for an hour, you could put no price tag on it to trade." I turn on my heel. I don't want to hear what they have to say or what they do. I need to get out.

At my car Joshua catches up with me. "What was that?" he demands, like *he's* angry.

"I told you to sit there and shut up like Annabeth, and it would have all been fine."

"I'm sorry I have to explain this to you, but let me say it slowly. I. Am. Not. Annabeth." My face pinches like I'm seeing him for the first time. "What happened in there, Joshua?"

"I told you—you shouldn't be here," he says by way of explanation.

"You wouldn't even call me your girlfriend in front of your parents. Why?"

"Fuck, why do you have to define everything all the time, Rosie? I am never enough for you. You have to push and push," he yells as he paces in a circle in front of me.

"What does that even mean? You called me a charity case to your family, but I'm the problem here? And all that shit your sister said; you let her!"

"You should have told me your dad was black," he retorts, and it's like he slapped me.

"Are you fucking serious? Jesus Christ, what am I doing here?!" I started breathing heavier and fishing in my purse for my keys.

I get in the car and lock the doors, gripping my steering. Joshua is at my side, pulling on the handle.

"Baby, get out of the car and talk to me for a second." He keeps pulling and pulling and bangs harder on the window when I start the engine. "Rosie, I love you, get out of the fucking car." Go, Rosie. Go!

That little voice inside me says, and again, I listen. He yells after me until I can't see him anymore.

I should go home, face the aunts, face everything, even if it's for a second. But I can't yet. I can't face them. I need a place that brings me comfort, even though it hasn't recently. I need something that works. Still, no feeling of ease arrives when I approach the shop; it's the complete opposite. I don't want to see them, and they definitely don't want to see me, but I've put it off long enough. I'll go hold up in the kitchen and make pies, and everything will be fine and semi-normal. For a moment, my head will be above the water.

The jingle of the door's bell sounds like a banshee's shriek. My eyes stay locked on the black and white checker of the floor, and I try not to think about the people inside.

"Hey, Rose," Bella's voice rings out slightly too loud and chipper.

"What are you doing here?" Goldie asks as she steps into my path in her skin-tight jeans and black t-shirt. Her long blonde hair swings back and forth like a pendulum at her back.

"I work here," I say simply, trying to step around her, but she blocks my path.

"What is your problem?"

She thinks about it and runs her tongue back and forth over her back teeth. "You know what? Fine, go ahead."

I place my hand flat on the kitchen door, and when I push it open, my brain starts to glitch. Standing in my kitchen, using my equipment to make my pies, is Allisin. When she sees me, she stops dead, a bowl of berries tucked under her arm. I caught her mid-dance—there's no dancing in my kitchen.

"H—hi, Rosie," she mutters, gripping the bowl like it's her lifeline.

"What the hell is going on?" I ask no one in particular, but Goldie is the one to answer.

"You disappeared for over a week. Did you think we were not going to have pie while you figured your crap out?"

And this is the thing: it's not the death of my mother. It's not the mess with Joshua. It's this, the loss of my home, the theft of it, that finally makes me cry for the first time since before all this began. They replaced me. In an instance, I disappeared. They don't need me, nobody needs me. I'm a waste, a speck, a nothing. I grip the counter, a sob ripping through me, my knees buckling. My tear-stained face and entire body shakes. I know people must be staring; I look like a psychopath, but I can't stop. I can't stop when I hear my name, I can't stop when I feel fingers on my body, but when a hand slaps my face—that gives me pause.

I blink through the curtain of tears and hiccup against the sobs. Beattie is on her knees in front of me. Blanche, Goldie, Bella, and Allisin stood behind her with mixed looks of shock and concern.

"Look at me!" Beattie shouts, gripping my face with both hands. "Get up." She grips me by the arms and pulls me to my feet, her arm around my shoulder, lugging me to the office.

She slams the door behind us as my breathing starts to settle.

"Sit down," she snaps, and I know better than to argue. She sits across from me after pulling a chair up to my knees on the couch. "Okay, I have stayed silent long enough. We will talk about this and what is going on with you."

Laying my head back against the top of the couch, I find myself exhausted again. I can't keep doing this.

"I don't want to talk about it anymore, Beattie."

"Anymore? You don't want to talk about it *anymore*? Honey, you haven't talked about it at all." I raise my head to look at her; her stance defensive. Her elbows rested on her knees, hands folded under her chin. Her glasses have fallen down the bridge of her nose right to where the tiny silver hoop glints in her nostril. "I have stood back because I am not your mom, and your aunts are all fine women who have done a great job raising you, but Rosie, it is enough. It's enough already."

"I am sick of this, Beattie. If I wanted to talk about it, I would." My body shuts off the tears and switches instantly to anger.

She stares at me for a few moments past comfort before she speaks again. "You mentally broke down in the middle of my restaurant, Rosaline. You are far beyond the scope of not talking about it."

The rage boils higher and higher until it explodes atop my head. "Then I shouldn't be here." Suddenly, the room feels too small. Harpersgrove seems too small. I've been suffocating long enough. "You guys had no problem replacing me, and I see now that's for the best. I won't do this anymore."

"What are you saying exactly, Rosie? " Her face is like stone, completely impassive. She doesn't care; why should I?

"I quit, Beattie." I leave her there, sitting still as a statue, staring at the place I'd vacated. It's like I was never there.

All I can hear is the clicking of my heels against the floor and the distant sound of Goldie calling after me as I flee the shop. I don't belong here anymore. I get back to the car and I realize I have nowhere else to go. I can't go home and face the aunts. I gave up the pie shop and can't see Joshua. I'm orphaned over and over again, spiraling further into the nothingness of my life. There's no limit to the pit.

I start aimlessly driving. My phone keeps buzzing in my purse, full of messages like, "Stop being stupid!" and "Get back here; I want to talk about this!" from Joshua, and I don't have the strength. He needs to calm down. I don't know how to feel about him right now. How can someone declare they love you so much in private and then act like they barely know you around other people?

My first thought of clarity is to go to the cemetery and scream at my mother's headstone, but that feels crazier than cathartic, and before I know it, I've switched gears. In what feels like the blink of an eye, I'm standing on an overly cheery mat, pounding on a door. The tears return the moment I knock. Kyle opens the door in a pair of flannel pants and a t-shirt.

"Rosie? Are you okay?"

I blurt the first thought that comes to mind. "Did you hold her hand?" His head cocks to the side, trying to read me, but the floodgates have burst open. "Did you put your arm around her? Did you tell people about her? Were you proud she was your girlfriend? Did you love her out loud?!" I'm screaming by the end, smacking my open palm into the door frame.

He beckons me in, but I can't move. I hug my arms around my body for comfort, but it doesn't come.

"Did you?" I demand.

"I did. I loved Holly very much," he can get out before a sob claims his voice. His jaw begins to quiver, and tears line his lower eyelids.

It takes everything in me to stay on my feet. My head sways back and forth in a heavy shake.

"How could you leave? Leave and never come back? She needed you. I needed you."

The reality of it shook me because it was honest. It was real. In so many ways, I still feel like the little girl sitting on a coin-operated horse waiting for one of her parents to come get her.

"Please come inside," he begs me, not attempting to shield the emotion in his voice. "Please, give me a few minutes. I want to show you something. Please." I'm too exhausted to fight him.

He leaves me in the gray scale living room, telling me he has to get something to show me. My head settles back against the back of the couch, and I notice a rip in the seams of the cushion. There's something comforting about the fact that even Kyle has cracks in his life. When he returns, he places a photo album in my lap. I recoil my hands back like it's a bomb.

"This could give you a few answers to your questions," he says. I noticed he's also changed out of pajamas and into jeans. I open the album cover, and its loud cracks break the silence between us. The contents catch my breath. Picture after picture is of my mother and father. They start in middle school with my mother's white blonde side ponytail and my father's braces fixing crooked teeth. They're down by the river and at birthday parties. As the years pass, there are fewer awkward side hugs and more of my mother on Kyle's back. A photo of his arms wrapped around her stomach, another with their foreheads pressed together, and some with kisses. Then there's the picture I remember, the only clue I ever had to my father's identity. My mom was in her cheerleading uniform, and Kyle was in his football one.

"I've seen this one before," I mutter, running my finger over the edge of the picture.

His head snaps up in surprise. "You've seen me before?" he asks.

Their happy faces mock me. I wish I could flash myself back in time and scream and warn them about all the pain they're going to cause each other and me. They shouldn't have had me. Everyone would have been better off, and my mom would still be alive. She and Kyle could've stayed together and had some real kids. That's the better ending to this story.

"She kept it in her underwear drawer. I was able to sneak a look at it." I know there aren't many more after the shot. It makes sense. I would have come soon after that, and that's when Kyle disappeared.

"Do your parents hate me?" I hear myself asking.

"No!" he exclaims, and it pulls my focus. I stare up at him from under my eyelashes and wait. I don't need him to sugarcoat. He runs a hand across his hair. "They don't know you, not a thing about you. To them, you're not a person. You're an obstacle to my life."

I don't know why because it's what I expected, but anger begins to seep out of every pore in my body. "And what about you?" I demand, slamming the album shut. "What do you know about me? Am I some obstacle? You never showed up! Never!"

He swallows hard, once, twice, three times. "If you need me to apologize for that every day for the rest of my life, I will do it on my knees.

I should have been here for you. I should have been your father or at least connected with you somehow. You deserved to have a father."

My stomach flips, and fresh tears fall as I jump off the couch. "Stop it," I hiss through gritted teeth. "Stop.".

"You deserve to know every day that people love you. I loved you. I have always loved you. You are my daughter, and I'm sorry."

"Shut up, Kyle!" I shout, dragging my fingers through my hair. Why doesn't he understand? Nobody loves me, even the people who say they do. My mom abandoned me, the aunts were stuck with me, my friends bolted at the first sign of trouble, and the boy I loved wouldn't even tell his parents he was dating me. I am an unlovable piece of garbage. I am worthless. "Shut up, Kyle! It's too late for this."

"Why? Why does it have to be too late?" he pleads, placing his hands on my shoulders. "Why can't this be our chance? What if this happened so we—" he stops himself.

I smack his hands away, shouting, "Are you seriously suggesting that my mother died so you could try to weasel into my life for the first time after seventeen years? Are you high?"

"I didn't mean it that way. Of course, I want Holly to be here still—"

"Don't call her that!" I scream, stomping my foot on the ground. I hope his neighbors hear and make a complaint. "I don't want to hear her name. stop!"

"I'm sorry. I'm sorry for everything, but I love you. You are my daughter. You have my eyes, for God's sake. I want to know you," he says, stepping toward me.

No. I can't.

"It's too late. You're too late. I'm already gone."

"What does that mean, Rosie?" he calls behind me, and I head to the door. He's close on my heels.

"Leave me alone, Kyle," I sob, reaching for the door, but he holds it shut. That's when I get angry again. "You don't get to do this. You are a pathetic thirty-something single man who looks at me like some second chance to have a kid without any of the work, but I'm not a plaything, and I don't want anything to do with you."

He releases his hand. Pain pinches his entire face like I'd struck him with my fist, but I don't care if it means I get to leave.

I don't remember getting back in the car or heading towards town. All I can feel is this devastating black hole in the middle of my body, an all-consuming hopelessness—orphaned again and again. No one wants me. It's always a lie. At the first test of any relationship, everyone cuts and runs. I'm not worth sticking around for. I'm not worth anything. Only when I cross the bridge that connects New Shiloh to Harpersgrove does my brain awaken again.

It would be easy.

It would be over.

The intrusive thoughts echo at full volume through, and the screeching of my tires and my brain as I pull over on the sleepy bridge that connects the two towns. I don't bother turning the car or its lights off. It doesn't matter, and water's better black. I step out onto the bridge, running my hands across the cold steel of the railing. I lean over the side. The creek that runs below is shallow but fast-moving. It hasn't rained much recently.

It'll get the job done.

My lower lip quivers as I turn to the sky full of stars. I don't believe my mother is there. I've always thought that this is it. Once you're gone, you're gone. The thought doesn't scare me anymore. Being gone sounds like the greatest freedom. For a moment, a smile splits my face. A sudden calm rushes over me, and it's like I'm a bird. I could spread my wings and fly away. I would fix everything for everyone. The aunts would have their lives back, and Beattie already has a replacement for me at the pie shop. My friends might be sad for a minute, but it wouldn't last. Their lives are about to start. And Kyle—he could release himself from all the guilt of having me as his daughter. I close my eyes, stretch out my arms, and take in the feeling of the air on my face.

I'm a bird.

I'm a bird.

I'm a bird.

"Whoa!" I hear someone scream from behind me and nearly fall over the side of the bridge right there. I turn my head to see Beau on his bike speeding toward me. He's in his uniform from the movie theater and huffs and puffs to get to me as fast as possible. "Whoa, Friend, what are you doing?"

I shake my head, looking back out over the opaque water. "Go away, Beau, pretend you didn't see me."

"I can't do that, Rosie. What are you doing?" he demands, and I hear his bike hit the ground.

"Nothing, Beau, I'm not doing anything." I allow myself a glance at him. "Are you wearing contacts?" I ask. It looks like he's lost weight, and his arms are more defined. It feels like I'm losing the Beau I knew in a whole different way. Nothing stays like it was.

"Yeah," he says, confused, rocking back on his heels, trying to figure out what to do. "I would love to talk to you more about that, but right now, I'd like to focus on getting you away from the side of the bridge."

I shake my head, back on my task. I can hear the water rushing beneath me, calling me home. "It's too much, Beau. This will be better."

"How can you say that? There's only one Rosie in the world. You are irreplaceable."

Calm settles over me as a smile comes to my face. "It's okay, Beau. You don't have to do this. I know you hate me."

"Rosie, I don't hate you. I'm disappointed and mad. It's not the same thing. Haven't you ever fought with a friend before?"

Sure, but not all at the same time.

"That's not true. Everyone hates me, Beau. I can't do it anymore."

"Friend, I need you to get away from the railing. We can talk about this. I don't care if you ever go to college, or if you ever wear your normal clothes again, or if you're angry every day for the rest of your life. You can yell, kick, and scream every day with me until we're old and gray."

I peek over my shoulder. Tears stream down his cheeks, but passively, like he's unaware that he's even doing it.

"Why?" I ask.

"Because I would rather have a friendship with you for the rest of my life where we scream and fight to the point that we hate each other than have to go to your grave and yell at you alone. Rosie, I'll come after you if you go over that edge. You're not going to give me any choice."

I slam my palm over and over into the steel of the bridge. I wish for a second that I didn't care, but hurting Beau would hurt me, even if I wasn't around to see it.

"Do you always have to be so God damn difficult?"

I can hear his smile. "Yes," he declares with absolute finality. I hear his feet shuffle toward me. He places his strong hand on my shoulder and holds me there.

"Come on, Rosie, it's time to come back." He's right about being finished with the anger, hurt, and hatred, but then reality hits me.

"I don't know how," I sob, increasing my grip on the steel railing. Beau's arm reaches out to wrap around my waist. The tension leaves his body when he has a secure hold on me.

"Lean back and let me help you." It seems easy and rational, yet I'm still torn. Every ounce of hurt that I've caused and endured is still there, festering and waiting for me. It's too hard to face. But I lean back anyway. Beau cradles me like a child, and I can breathe again.

He doesn't speak as he loads me into the passenger seat of my car, and after placing his bike in the trunk, he claims the driver's seat. The ride to my house is quick. He leaves me in the car, and I'm too tired to argue. The next thing I register is my door opening, and Meredith's concerned face fills the space. She scans my body like I'm some broken and fragile thing, but she must know that's only inside. Her hands are on my cheeks, rubbing my skin with her thumbs. The feelings start to bubble up again.

"I'm sorry," I breathe through my sobs.

Meredith shakes her head, kissing the space between my brows saying, "You have nothing to be sorry for, Rose. We're going to take care of you."

She moves back, and Norah takes her place. My aunt extended her arms to me. I tried to protest, but she shook her head. "Shut up and come here."

I nod and roll into her, wrapping my arms and legs around her. I know I'm too old for this. But her carrying me like a baby is what I need. I tighten my grip around her neck, and a sob rolls through me. She presses her lips against my temple and gently shushes me, but I continue to cry into her collarbone. In my bedroom, Shawna is finishing wrapping my bed in fresh sheets, the stains of tears on her cheeks. Norah places me on the bed, and Shawna wraps me up in the sheets, murmuring, "Snug as a bug in a rug," like she did when I was a girl.

"I'm so sorry," I sob.

Shawna shakes her head, and peppers kisses across my forehead. "No, my sweet girl, there's no need for that right now. You sleep, and we'll figure out everything in the morning."

She starts to pull away from me, but panic swells inside, and I grab her by the wrist. She smiles softly and lays beside me on the bed, wrapping her arm around my middle.

"Go to sleep now, Rosie. It's okay."

When I wake, it's to the morning sunshine slicing through the slats of my blinds, warming my face. The weight and warmth of Shawna have left me, and I'm alone in the bed. I roll over onto my back, and my lip quivers at the outline of where the stars used to be. I've ruined everything.

"Good, you're up," Norah says from the other side of the room. She's perched uncomfortably in my sewing chair, her face puffy from a restless sleep. "I worried I'd have to wake you soon."

"Wake me up for what?" I ask, rubbing the sleep away.

She doesn't say anything at first; she watches me with wonder, as though she's seeing me for the first time. "We'll talk about that in a little bit. Why don't you go ahead and shower and get dressed, then come meet us for some breakfast, okay?"

To call Norah's demeanor unsettling would be inaccurate. I have never seen her this calm. It's like a horror movie. After showering and changing clothes, I head out to the kitchen. I stop in my tracks. Mr. Cooper and Beattie sit at the table with the aunts.

"Good morning, sweetheart," Meredith says with a smile, pulling out the chair beside her. I want to escape.

"Sit down, nugget," Beattie urges, and I know it's not a request. Shawna's already up making me a plate. I'm not hungry, but I know I'll eat it.

I remember the first intervention we had for my mother. I couldn't attend, but I was in a back room and heard everything. The shock and anger that came out when she saw the aunts and the few friends she had left is a vivid memory, but I don't feel that way. I'm uneasy and sad—and tired, very tired. My eggs and toast turn to ashy cardboard in my mouth, and I know it has nothing to do with Shawna's cooking.

"What's going on?" I ask with a full mouth. I get the feeling that forgiving bad manners is the least of my worries.

"I talked to Beau last night. He was pretty distraught," Mr. Cooper says, putting down his "World's Best Grandma" mug. The heavy lump of food pushes itself painfully down my throat.

"I wasn't going to do anything," I blurt out. "I swear, I wasn't going to. I felt confused for a second." The hush in the room is deafening. Norah's keeping up the wall with her back, her face twisted into an anguish I don't recognize. Shawna's taking slow, even breaths and, as always, remains stoic. Beattie's eyes are glassy. I turn to Meredith, who is gripping my hand like it's saving her life.

"Mere, I swear I wasn't going to do anything. I wouldn't do that to you."

She nods her head slowly, refusing to blink out her tears. "I hear you, baby, I hear you."

There's a knock at the door. Norah is out of the room in a flash but doesn't return alone. Behind her is Kyle Roosevelt. Judging by his wrinkled shirt and dark circles, I doubt he's slept since I saw him last. Meredith looks as confused as I am, but Norah answers our unspoken questions. "I thought he should be here too."

He takes the seat across from me and we stare at each other in complete silence.

"You told me you were already gone," he says, his voice wobbling. "And that scared the hell out of me."

"I wasn't going to do anything," I sob.

"I believe you," he says, reaching across the table for my hand. For once, I choose not to put up a fight and let him take it. "But we're going to get you some help anyway."

CHAPTER TWELVE

According to the pamphlet in her lobby, Cheryl Tibbons is a therapist specializing in teen trauma. Meredith and Kyle drove me alone to the office in New Shiloh. I've never really understood people that go to therapy. Deal with your problems or swallow them. But I guess I don't have much room to talk after leaning over the railing of a bridge.

The office is comfortably sterile. Its beige walls, taupe couches, and paintings of ambiguous waves appear meant to comfort, but make me want to punch something. On the small table in front of me lay various tools. A small Zen garden, many squishy stress balls, play dough, and a slinky. Some people fidget. I take the Play-Doh.

Cheryl Tibbons is about forty-five years old with long, perfect braids and smooth dark skin. She wears way too much turquoise jewelry and a bohemian, flowy skirt. I dislike her instantly.

"Do I have to call you Dr. Tibbons?" I hiss, sinking down in my chair like an angry little girl.

Her soft smile never falters. "You can call me Cheryl, Cheryl Tibbons, or Miss Tibbons if it suits you." Cheryl Tibbons seems like the most annoying option. I know it's all I'll ever use.

She sets her glasses into place on the bridge of her nose and flips open the cover of her tablet. "Rosie, what brings you here today?"

I need to calm down and lower some of my defenses. I know therapy is to help me. "I had a momentary lapse of judgment last night and freaked out my family."

She nods slowly, tapping on her screen. "Tell me about it."

I launch into the story about standing at the ledge and Beau pulling me back, and she nods, crossing and uncrossing her legs and watching me with a vested interest. "Okay," she says, setting her tablet outside. "Now, tell me about how you got there."

"You mean in my car?"

Her smile is soft and gentle, and I try to ignore that it's also patronizing. "No, Rosie, I don't mean in your car. What I'd like you to tell me, in whatever way feels right to you, is how you got to the point that you ended up on the bridge."

"I don't know what you want."

"I spoke to your Aunt Meredith on the phone this morning. Could you tell me anything you'd like about your mother?"

"I don't have anything to say about her," I state, squishing the play dough between my fingers.

"No problem, no pressure. Tell me about anything you'd like." I go the next hour telling her, in great detail, how to make a pie—everything from preheating the oven to the best way to slice and serve it. All the while, she sits there, smiling and nodding, occasionally taking notes. When the timer beside her goes off, she closes her tablet and folds her hands on top of it.

"Okay, that was a great start. We'll pick it up again in a few days."

"What are you talking about?" I demand, my mouth open and ready to catch flies.

Her smile is soft and understanding that I have to resist the urge to fight her. "Rome wasn't built in a day, Rosie. We have a lot more to do."

Too stunned to speak, I shuffle out of her office, stewing with annoyance. Kyle and Meredith are sitting on the same couch, each reading an outdated version of Highlights magazine. "How long do I have to do this?" I mumble to Meredith, doing my best to ignore Kyle.

She takes a deep breath, and I notice the darkness clouding the undersides of her eyes, and I'm instantly guilty. It's because of me, after all. "Until everyone's confident that you don't need to anymore."

My pouts go unnoticed in the backseat of Kyle's car on our ride back to Harpersgrove. I huff and harumph, hoping someone will say something, but neither does.

I wasn't going to do this.

I'm ready for a nap and private whining session when Kyle stops in front of Hap-PIE-ly.

"Why?" I groan, kicking my feet against the back of Meredith's seat.

"Beattie asked me to drop you off here after your appointment," she says, unlocking the door. I immediately lock mine again.

"I can't," I murmur, sucking back the tears that sting. I'm starting to desperately miss the feeling of being dead inside.

One of them hits the unlock button again. "But you can," Meredith says.

Entering the shop feels like a scene from a movie. All the heads turn, and the room falls silent. Goosebumps flood my skin and remain no matter how hard I try to rub them away. Bella works behind the counter, and Blanche and Goldie work on the floor. Beattie is sitting on the far stool and pats the one beside it. I had hoped we'd talk in the privacy of her office but leave it to Beattie to air everything out in the open. When I sit, Beattie raises her eyebrows at Bella, who puts a piece of pie in front of me. Before pulling too far away, she grabs my wrists and squeezes. My breathing hitches. Does she know? Did Beau tell everyone about the bridge? Or is this simply Bella and her big heart, unable to stay mad at me even if I deserve it?

"Beattie," I say.

Beattie shakes her head and says, "Pie first. Talk second."

I hate how good it is. The mixture is sweet but not too much to overwhelm the flavor of the berries, and the crust is perfectly flaky.

"She's good."

Beattie runs her thumb around the rim of her plate, scooping up the last bit of pie filling. "She is good. You're better, but she'll learn."

"This isn't a 'give me my job back' talk?"

Beattie scoffs and places her hand on my back.

"If you think I took your resignation seriously, you don't know me very well." She pats me on the back again as she gets up from her stool, beckoning me to follow. I look at Blanche across the room for a second, but she breaks away to where she can't see me.

Beattie pushes into the kitchen, and as much as I don't want to, I know it's pointless not to follow. Inside, Allisin is rolling out pie dough on my counter and snaps to attention when we enter. "Hi, Rosie," she says, bright and sunshiny, with a touch of fear behind it.

"Allisin, could you give us a second?" Beattie asks, and she scurries away. I immediately feel lighter when she's out of my space.

"How is this supposed to work? It seems mean to fire her right after she started."

"I'm not going to fire her."

She can sense my dread. "Rosie, when you go to college in the fall, we'll need someone to make the pies. It's not a bad idea to start training her."

"Beattie, I'm not going." *I'm sick of talking about this.*

"Yes, you are. You don't know it yet."

Rage bubbles in my chest. "You are not my mother, Beattie. We are not your kids."

She's unfazed, leaning back against the counter and nodding at me. "You're right, I'm not. I'm going to tell you about something that I don't talk about very much, but I you need to know." She takes a deep breath and stares at the ceiling for an impossibly long moment.

"Rosie, do I strike you at all as the kind of person who would ever name my pie shop Hap-PIE-ly Ever After?"

"I don't understand."

She continues as if I hadn't spoken, like I'm not even there.

"I hate it, honestly, but my daughter thought it was clever; I couldn't deny her that."

The revelation knocks me off my feet. Beattie's a mom?

"And when she died, I couldn't bring myself to change it. Even the new shops. Clementine named this place, and I couldn't take that from her."

"Why are you telling me this?" I whisper, tears flooding my vision.

For the first time, she looks up and sees me. She holds me with a fierce and frightening gaze. "Because I understand what unbelievable loss feels like. I understand how one person disappearing from your universe can make it seem impossible to carry on, like you're betraying them if you do. I didn't know your mother, and I know you had a complicated relationship with her, but you don't get to stop living because she's gone. Clementine wouldn't want that for me, and Holly wouldn't want that for you."

My body recoils at my mother's name, and Beattie notices.

"Holly would not want that for you."

"Please stop saying that name," I ask, but it's not a question. It's more of a plea.

"No, your mother's name is Holly, and you can't disassociate from her. Her name was Holly, and she's gone, but you're not. You're right here, Rosie, and you don't have to stop living."

"Allisin," I call out into the void when I swallow enough tears away to speak. Her head peeks inside, but the rest of her stays out in the dining room. She's a little scared of me, not that I haven't given her reason to be. "I have rules for how I run the kitchen. Get in here, you need to learn them." Having a worker bee might not be the worst thing.

When the evening at the shop wraps up, Allisin and I close together after I decide that's an essential job of mine for her to know, too. We walk out together.

"Working with you is cool, you know?" she says

"Why?" I ask, dropping my keys in my purse. The temperature plummeted while we were inside, and I regret not having a jacket.

"Are you kidding? Rosie Peters? Everyone's either afraid of you or wants to be you," she says, shoving her hands in the pockets of her sweater.

"The afraid thing I get, but the other part? You have me confused with someone else."

She laughs, turning down a street in the opposite direction from the way I'm going. She takes deliberate steps backward, smiling at me all the while. "I'm starting to think you might have you confused with someone else." And with that, she turns and disappears into the night. Part of me hates that I don't hate her. In fact, I like her. *Damn it.*

"God, I thought she'd never leave," I hear from beside me as my soul flees my body.

"What are you doing here, Joshua," I hiss, picking up my pace and wishing I had my car. Of course, after last night, I'm surprised I'm allowed to be alone.

"Come on, baby, don't be stupid. I want to talk to you," he says, reaching for my hand, but I don't take it. Even from here, I can sense how good he smells. I would love nothing more than to curl up into him, especially after the day that I've had. It's uncanny how good he is at helping me to forget all the bad. I cross my arms over my chest and start walking faster, as though I can outrun him.

"You should go home."

He cuts me off, and I run into his chest. He envelops me in his arms and links his fingers behind my back. Oh God, he does smell good. After an unsuccessful struggle, I let my forehead hit his chest with a little thump. He laughs. "Now hush for a second," he murmurs into my hair, the warmth of his breath giving me goosebumps. When he's sure I won't run away, he loosens his grip and rubs his hand up and down my back. My heart flutters with familiar warmth, and I would pay to feel this way all the time.

"I'm sorry."

"What are you sorry for?" I ask into his chest.

"My parents are not the most accepting people. I knew that if I told them we were dating, they would pounce on you, and I didn't want them to hurt you."

My brow furrows, and I push back far enough to see his face. He runs his thumbs over my cheekbones, and I fight to focus. "But they did hurt me," I reply.

He sighs deeply and kisses my forehead. The stupid, giddy thrill that runs through my body makes me angry with myself. "Now, imagine how much worse it would have been if they'd known the truth."

"Was your plan to never tell them about us?" I ask, pushing myself a little further away. I need some distance from his warmth.

"Of course not," he says, allowing me the distance but holding onto my hand. "I have a plan." He takes a step toward me, and I don't stop him. "I am completely in love with you, and I know that's all that matters."

"What are you saying, Joshua?" As I settle back into his arms, a strange mixture of calm and dread swims through my veins.

The pressure of his chin on the top of my head feels like he's pushing me into the floor. "Well, once we get set up in our place, and I'm at school, and you're working, and all our ducks are in a row—"

He trails off until I look up at him, recentering my attention on him. He smiles so warmly that it makes me forget everything but this.

"You're going to wear a white dress, and we're going to make this official."

My tongue is suddenly too big for my mouth.

"I need you to spell this out for me."

His hands are back to my face, holding me still. He leans in to kiss me, sucking my lower lip in my mouth, and it makes me breathless. "I'm saying I love you and want you forever." Forever. Stability. Permanence.

"You're making my head swim," I cry, shaking my face from his hands. I can't breathe. "I'm confused."

His hands are on my shoulders, squeezing and holding me still.

"Then don't think, dummy, and listen to what you feel."

And what do I feel—confused and overwhelmed? Absolutely. But what else? I look up at Joshua and let myself linger on his face. It's kind and soft, and I feel that he loves me. It's irrational after what happened, but maybe love isn't rational. Perhaps you have to lean into it. I close my eyes and let myself drift forward to kiss him, and as much as my brain wants to fight it, my soul says it's right.

"I don't want to hide," I whisper against his mouth.

He laughs humorlessly, tapping the side of my face with his fingertips, and leans back to stare at the sky. "Only you, Rosie Peters, would think I'm interested in hiding you in the same breath I tell you I want to marry you."

"Well, no, I—tell me it's going to be different," I ask, gripping his arms.

He smiles sweetly and pulls me to him. "It's going to be everything."

"You're late," Shawna says when I walk through the door a while later. "I was about to come looking for you."

I drop my purse on the floor and head into the kitchen to find her.

"What is late? Do I have a curfew? I have a baking assistant at the shop now. I was showing her the ropes. Took longer than I expected."

I see and understand the hypocrisy of telling Joshua in one breath that I don't want to hide anymore to lying about him to the aunts in the next. In all honesty, it's too much. We need to give each other a moment to breathe. Who knows, I could surprise them one day and come home married. That would be something!

"It's been a long day, Shawna. I'm going to bed."

"Hold up a second," she responds, taking long strides across the kitchen to pull me into her. For someone so small, she is far too strong. "Love you, sweet girl. Sleep well."

I immediately change into pajamas and climb into bed. Today was exhasuting, but I stare wide-eyed at the ceiling. I'm fidgety and can't keep still. And then, a thought pops into my mind and invades and overwhelms my brain until it's all I can think about. I turn on the light and hop out of bed.

Throwing open the chest at the base of my bed, I start sifting through the bolts of fabric, pulling the ones I don't need out and discarding them on the floor. The one color I need is the one I never wear, but I must have some. And sure enough, at the very bottom of the chest lies a single bolt of white fabric. Enough to get the job done.

An all-encompassing calm comes over me. My brain turns off, and muscle memory takes over as I snip and stitch the fabric into something new—something that didn't exist moments before. That's one of the things I love most about this; it's like creating a new life. When I finish, it's the perfect white dress. The dress I'll marry Joshua in. And like that, things make a little more sense to me.

What I foolishly didn't expect the following day was that the aunts would make me go to school. I didn't think I'd ever return, though one can dream. I figured I had more time to milk before they made me. Then Norah woke me up by flipping over my mattress at six o'clock, and I knew the break was over. They're determined to push me back to normalcy whether I like it or not.

Everything is the same but astronomically different at Harpersgrove Senior High School when I arrived only a few moments before the bell. Lucy Wilcox and her team of plastic drones congregate by their cars, laughing over their idiocy. Allisin and her theater friends sat under the big tree by the front entrance. She spots me and waves excitedly, turning the heads of her whole group, and color flushes directly to my skin as I wave back. I've returned to my Rosie uniform of tight black shirt and pleather leggings, but now I'm too exposed. Is Joshua right about it not being me? Of course, I am a very fluid concept right now. On my way in, I try not to look at Elle and Goldie, where they hang out with Goldie's boyfriend, Dubuque, and his friends. I know I need to address what I've done and how I've been, but I'm not ready.

I float through my day and bury my face in my books to seem engaged while my brain is a thousand miles away. I text Joshua several times to help me feel less alone, but he doesn't respond. I shouldn't be surprised since it is a school day. I guess he's a little more responsible than I am. My teachers seem to have little reaction to my recent part-time attendance. I'm not sure if it's because of my mother, an overdue reason for me to crack, or it's because I've always been a low-effort student, and they don't expect much from me this late in my senior year. Either way, I'm grateful. Lunch is a terrifying concept that I'm not prepared for. The idea of being in that cafeteria, avoiding my friends, and sitting by myself sends me into a minor panic attack. I opt to hide in the bathroom instead. It's the lamest thing I could do, but I have no choice. There's no way I'm sitting with Nixie and Goldie. I can't do it.

After lunch, the art room door seems far away, glowing like a gateway to hell. I never wanted Beau to see me like he did. More and more people are starting to see too much of me, and it's overwhelming. The room hushes silent when I enter, much like every room today. Beau is sitting at his new table with someone who isn't me, and it hurts my heart as much as it did the first time. Mr. Cooper doesn't notice me as I sit alone at the table.

I flip open my sketchbook for the first time in too long and savor the smell of the charcoal on paper, and the feelings sting my eyes. For some reason, I remember the white dress hanging in my closet and smile. I'm sure it will be for our legal ceremony—the thing that will belong only to us. I can see us having the big party later, something for everyone else. I'll need a different dress for that. I scribble away furiously at different silhouettes, but not one seems right.

About halfway through class Beau sits down beside me and hands me a pack of Nutter Butter cookies. "Take them and don't be weird Friend," he says before returning to his watercolor ducks.

It's a tiny and probably insignificant note of normalcy to have Beau sitting back beside me in art class with the watercolors, giving me snacks, but I can't help how big it feels. I drop the cookies on the table, hop up to my feet, and throw my arms around his shoulders, squeezing him tight.

"Ohh—you made it weird," he says, and laughter slips from my mouth. He wraps his arms around my waist and stands up, crushing me against him, my feet dangling off the floor.

"Don't make me mad at you like that again, okay?" I silently nod because I want to make him happy and need him on my side, but I haven't changed my mind about school.

"What are these?" he asks, peering over my shoulder at my sketchbook and the pictures of wedding dresses. "I don't remember you putting together anything this grand."

I can't tell him about Joshua and the grand plan. It doesn't feel special if it isn't a secret. Besides, I'm starting to bring everyone back to me, and I don't want to ruin any of that. I flip the cover of the book closed. "Oh, nothing. I felt inspired to try something new."

I take the long way to get to the pie shop after school. Allisin may be my new confidant, but none of my other friends are talking to me. It's not like I've done anything outside of having a mental breakdown in front of them to remedy the situation. I want us to be friends again, but I'm stuck in a spot where I'm unsure how much I did wrong compared to everyone else. It doesn't seem fair that I need to make all the amends. The five of them universally chose to drop me, but I'm the bad guy? Something feels wrong about that. Today, I want to keep my head down and make pie. New pie. Pie that could change the world.

Blanche, Nixie, and Bella are working inside, and to their credit, no one has tried to talk to me. Bella smiles because she can't help herself, but the rest ignore me, and I'm okay with that for now, especially with Blanche. I don't know if we can repair the damage to our friendship. We both said some pretty ugly things to each other. Luckily, she's preoccupied with Mrs. McCullen and her four screaming children. I don't think she even registers me as I slip back into my kitchen.

Allisin has rehearsal for the school musical today, and I'm grateful for the quiet. She's chatty. I wait for the ingredients to speak to me, telling me what to create, but they are silent. Assembling all the necessities for a crust, I plan on floating through it and for something to spark genius. My brain disassociates and drifts away to the ceiling. I mash strawberries, blackberries, and raspberries together in a bowl. I start mixing the gelatin on the stovetop and crush pecans in the food processor because why not? Egg whites whisk in the mixer with sugar, cream of tartar, salt, and vanilla. Blackberry meringue sounds pretty good to me. I'll figure out how the pecans factor in later.

When all is said and done, I've made my odd berry meringue sans pecans; there was no hope for them, a strawberry rhubarb, a chocolate cream and butterscotch chip, and a mac and cheese pie in time for the dinner crowd.

"Hey, Rosie Rose," Bella says, sticking her head through the little window. "Want to have a piece of this mac and cheese with me? We haven't done a family meal in a while." Family meals are usually for everyone, but Bella has always been family enough. I smile and nod.

"We need to include this on the regular menu," Bella says, twirling cheese up in the air around her fork. "But you have to call it Norah's mac and cheese. I know the taste of it anywhere." It's true; this recipe is not mine but my aunt Norah's.

"What are you doing, Bella?" I ask, pushing my plate to the side. She peers up at me over the rim of her glasses. "I was shitty to you, and you have no reason to be nice to me right now."

She pops the bite of pasta into her mouth and chooses her words in the time it takes to swallow. "You were remarkably shitty, that is true. I am not a big believer in grief and pain excusing bad behavior, and if you ever put your hands on me again, I will drop you like a sack of potatoes." We laugh a little at that, but I know she's serious. "And no talking about my boyfriend unless you have something nice to say from now on. You called Conrad disabled like it was the biggest slur you could come up with. It was ugly, and you are not an ugly person."

"That's debatable," I chime in, and she flicks me on the bridge of the nose.

"I wouldn't let anyone else speak about you that way; what makes you think you're allowed?" Classic Bella.

"How are things with Conrad?" I ask. I know the logistics for the two of them have been tricky living in different cities, and none of us know him very well. She considers my question. "I'm truly asking, I promise."

The corner of her mouth peaks slightly, and she pushes her glasses into her hair. "I thought it would be much harder, me being here and him being there. I started having panic attacks the week after we got back together because I thought there was no way that we could make it work. I worried that as he started to pull himself out of his shell, he'd find someone new up there, someone easier."

"You're easy like Sunday morning Hells Bells," I chime in, and she smiles.

"Thank you for that, but it isn't always easy for me. But Conrad has been amazing. We talk all the time, fall asleep on the phone together regularly, and he takes the train down every other weekend to see me. He's planning to rent an apartment in town or New Shiloh for the summer and then take me to school in the fall." The brightness of her smile is refreshing and lightens me as much as it does her.

"That's amazing, Bella, I'm happy for you. I was a little worried about you when you came home after Christmas, but you seem together now."

"Thanks, as my therapist says, 'More than one thing can be true at the same time.'"

"You're in therapy?"

She starts to laugh and nods in agreement. Suddenly, my mood drastically sobers.

"Hells Bells, why are you in therapy?"

She balances her elbows on the steelwork table and takes a deep breath. "That feeling you had, when you worried about me when I came home—it wasn't unified." The back of my throat starts to itch. "Something bad happened when I was up there, and I needed help processing that." I'm almost out of my seat before she adds, "It was nothing involving Conrad, Rosie, I promise."

I wrap my hand around her wrist, pressing my fingers down against her pulse, trying to ground myself and remember that she is fine and alive. "Are you okay? Seriously."

She smiles and, with her free hand, reaches up to tuck a piece of hair behind my ear. "A little better every day."

"And therapy is helping with that?" I ask skeptically, returning to my plate.

"It's amazing," she says with a sure finality. "Is counseling something you're considering?"

"The aunts insisted I go, and, apparently, I keep going. I don't get it. It seems silly to me."

"My experience is limited to only that last couple of months, but I have learned that it only works if you let it. You have to be super open to it and let it help. Unless she thinks you're going to hurt yourself, she can't tell anyone what you talk about, even the aunts. You can tell her anything, and she's there to listen and never judge. It's honestly the most freeing thing I've ever done."

Bella's words stuck with me the rest of the day. What I'm doing on my own isn't working. If Cheryl Tibbons isn't allowed to tell my aunts anything, then there is merit to it.

The tapping starts on the window as I'm wrapping up my cleaning for the night. Everyone else has long gone home. Joshua stands on the other side of the door, smiling at me, and my soul is lighter. "Hey you," he says when I unlock the door before sweeping me into a kiss that makes me forget my name.

"Hey yourself," I respond when I can finally come up for air. "How was your day?"

"That's boring," he says, removing the lid from a pecan pie and digging in with a fork. He shrugs out of his jacket and places it on the counter. "Ask me something interesting."

"Um, I mean, it's interesting to me. I want to hear about your day."

He sighs and his knee knocks into mine. "I know you can do better than that. Come on, dazzle me." My brain goes completely blank and fuzzy. He sighs loudly and turns back to the pie, silent and sulking.

I twist my fingers on the counter, panic creeping up my body. "I made a white dress," I blurt out, instantly wishing to shove the words back in my stupid face. I never had any intention of telling Joshua that.

His entire demeanor shifts. He puts his fork down, turns towards me, and gives me his full attention. It is the high that I crave more than anything in this world. If telling him about my white dress gives me this attention, I will tell him everything I can.

"A white dress, you say? Why would you make a white dress?" he asks, spreading his legs apart and yanking my stool closer . I settle between them.

My chest rises and falls in unsteady beats, and a rosy color spreads up my neck. "I started thinking about our conversation the other night about the future, and I was—I got inspired."

He puts one hand on my hip and, with the other, reaches up to caress my cheek. "Baby, are you telling me you made a wedding dress?" The look on his face is blissfully joyful.

"I did."

He urges my legs around his waist and locks my hands around his neck. He scoops his hands under my butt and lifts me, and carries me across the room. "Where are we going?" I ask, my head swimming with the feeling of being in the air.

He's busy kissing the crook of my neck. Without responding he continues to ease me forward. He finds Beattie's office door like he knows where he's going. Then, I'm on my back on Beattie's couch before I realize it, and my brain sprints at the hyper-speed of an Olympic athlete to catch up.

"Woah, woah sailor! Slow down."

He doesn't seem to hear me as he reaches for the button of my jeans, and I instinctively smack his hand away. He pulls back with a start. "Are you being serious right now?" he demands, pushing against me to get off the couch.

"Why are you so upset?" I ask, pulling my knees up to my chest.

He shakes his head, staring off at some distant corner of the room and replies, "You made a wedding dress Rosie."

"And?"

"Christ, if you're going to act stupid, then this is a bad idea," he says, storming out of the office and back into the shop.

I'm on my feet, following him as fast. "Can you talk to me for a second? I don't understand what's going on?"

"You're acting like a baby, and that is what's going on. We're planning to spend our lives together, you made a fucking wedding dress. I'm willing to go against my parents, abandon my family for you, and you're not even interested in being with me." He grabs his jacket and swings it around his shoulders, shaking his head as the color rises through his face.

That acidic bite of abandonment burns the back of my throat, and my heart rate picks up to the point I can hear it in my ears. "I need a second to think. Can you give me a second?"

He rounds the counter and gets up close but doesn't touch me. His breath is hot on my face. "If you have to think about it, then it means you don't believe in us, and I don't have time for you to be this indecisive."

He turns to leave, and the sound of his shoes stomping onto the ground strikes me in the pit of my stomach. He can't go!

"Okay," I whisper, trying not to cry. "I hear you. You're right."

He turns back slowly, the muscles in his forehead still pinched, and he waits for me to come to him. I feel like a dog with my tail tucked between my legs, but I go. I stand before him with my hands folded in front of me, remorseful and waiting. I'm not sure what I'm supposed to do. He digs his hands into my hair and tugs my head back. "I need you not to be stupid. You know how much I love you."

I take that in like oxygen. I need Joshua to love me. This time, when he takes me back to Beattie's office and reaches for the button of my jeans, I don't stop him.

CHAPTER THIRTEEN

The ceiling of Beattie's office looks different after. The sound of my breathing is different after. The couch's texture, the room's temperature, and the feeling of my skin are all different. Joshua doesn't seem affected in the slightest way, though. When he is done, Joshua gets dressed, kisses me on the forehead, and tells me he'll text me later. Then he's gone. I can't stop staring at the ceiling. I thought it would feel something—special. I expected the teen movie fantasy with hearts and flowers, but it's dingy ceiling tiles and a scratchy old couch.

Eventually, I pull myself up and put my clothes back on. For some reason, I rearranged the couch cushions as though Beattie would somehow figure it out. I clean up the kitchen like I would any regular night, only this time in dead silence; no soundtrack seems quite right. The walk home from the pie shop is slow and cold. The ever-present Christmas lights make me more angry than usual, but they don't matter. The aunts are all asleep when I get home, and I'm grateful because there's no mask I could put on right now that would fool any of them. I crawl into bed, fully clothed, and stare up at where the stars used to be. I miss them. And for the first time in many years, I say aloud, "I wish my mom were here."

The next few days revolve around me doing my best not to dwell on what happened with Joshua. When my brain inevitably drifts there, I say to myself repeatedly, "He loves me. He loves me. He loves me." Eventually, it numbs my brain enough that I can function.

"Are you okay?" Allisin asks me as we roll out the dough in the shop one afternoon. I thought her company would annoy me, but I find her a loving presence. "You haven't moved your rolling pin in like five minutes."

"Yeah," I laugh, returning to my dough. I'm working on an apple pie while she creates a strawberry rhubarb. "A little in my head, I guess."

The silence settles for a moment as we return to our tasks.

"Allisin?" I say when the quiet gets too loud and my thoughts scream. "Have you ever had sex?"

I don't see but hear Allisin's pin hit the floor. When I turn back around, she's gone entirely red. She drops to her knees to grab the pin and starts to babble, "I'm not experienced with boys at all. I—I've never done that."

"Hey," I say, lowering down to her level. I put my hand over hers and squeeze until she looks at me. "It wasn't an accusation or a criticism."

"Have you?" she blurts out, shifting her weight to both knees.

I consider it for a second, telling her, telling someone. The shame of the whole thing is eating me alive, and saying it out loud to a person will make it feel better—then again, it might make it all worse. I force a smile to my face and spring back to my feet.

"Nope," I mutter, picking my bowl of apples to start peeling. "I was curious."

"Can you ask Rosie for an update on that pie," I hear Blanche ask Bella out in the shop. The only two people talking to me right now are Allisin and Bella, and it's starting to get to me. Blanche and Goldie are the two I want to talk to about this. Goldie could help me make sense of it.

"I ruined everything with my friends," I say.

Allisin picks up her bowl of berries and joins me at the table. "What happened exactly? I thought it would be rude and gossipy to ask," she says as she slowly stirs sugar into her concoction.

There aren't many people I've ever trusted without knowing them. I usually make everyone earn everything, but I decided to take a leap of faith with Allisin. I told her my whole story, including my mom's history, finding out about Kyle, my apprehension around Parsons, and everything about Joshua, especially how he makes my head spin.

"Wow, that's a lot."

"Tell me about it," I groan before shutting the oven door with our pies inside. "And now I don't know how to fix things, or do I even want everything fixed? Do I even know what I want?"

"Tell me again why you don't want to go to Parsons. It sounds like an amazing opportunity," Allisin says as she starts wiping down the counter, she's much more attentive to continuous cleanliness than I am.

This question seems to be the hardest to answer because there's no good answer. I have no definitive reason why I won't go, but every time it comes up, my stomach drops to my feet, and my heart races.

"It's not so much that I don't want to. I don't know if I get to be happy," I say before I can think too hard about it. "Sometimes it seems like I've used up all my opportunities for happiness already."

"Everybody deserves to be happy, Rosie, and I don't think running out of chances is possible. It's not pie," she knocks me on the shoulder with a smile and returns to cleaning.

As the day ends, I tell Allisin to go ahead and go home. Surprisingly, I enjoy her company, but I'm ready for some time alone. Blanche is the only person left out in the shop, and I can feel her presence through the wall. I take a deep breath and head out with my plastic wrap to cover the pies. I start to work, catching glimpses of Blanche from the corner of my eye. Someone has to talk first, and I guess it's fair that it's me.

"Hey," I say under my breath. Blanche glances up at me and nods, not a single word uttered. I suppose I only deserve her silence. "Can we talk?"

Her body freezes for a moment before returning to what she was doing. "I don't think so, Rosie," she says as she flips the stools onto the counter.

"I screwed up, and I said some things I shouldn't have. I'm sorry."

She flips the last stool, and her hands linger on its legs. "I think you're sorry for the consequences, but I don't think you're sorry for what you said. And I definitely don't think you're ready to face everything you're avoiding."

"Can't you cut me the tiniest bit of slack on all that? My mom is dead."

"Stop!" She snaps, throwing her rag down on the table. She turns to face me full-on, her expression wild and angry. "Do you even hear yourself? Do those words even mean anything to you? Jesus Christ, Rosie, one second it's that she was some loser you didn't even know, and the next it's that her death is the most devastating thing to happen to you. And funny how it seems the latter of those two extremes only comes up when someone challenges your bullshit lately."

"That's not fair!" I shout back.

She rushes me, her long and lanky frame towering over me.

"You don't get to talk about fair! You are done talking about what's fair!" I can see the tears that are forming, but the way the moisture in her mouth is misting my face, I only see red. "You want to have a conversation with me, Rosie? I am totally on board with that. But as long as you're hiding whatever is really going on with you behind your mother's death, I am not interested in hearing another word out of your mouth. If it's not honest and earnest apologies to everyone you've been treating poorly, then stay silent for everyone's sake." With that, she brushes past me. She could blow me over with a breath if she wanted to. "You finish closing. I'm out of here."

It feels like I'm drowning, like a cinder block tied to my feet, sinking me to the bottom of the black water. The pressure crushes from all sides, and I know it's hopeless. There is no other side; there is no rescue or reprieve. This abyss is where I am now. I finish closing the shop in a daze, my body moving independently from my brain to complete everything. I lock the door and start my mindless wander down the quiet streets of the center of town. By ten o'clock, everything is dead here. The lights are on inside the drugstore and I'm inside before I know it. Goldie's mom, Lori, and her grandma, Nana, are counting money at the counter.

"Hey, Rosie," Lori says. Of course, she knows it's me. Who else would be here this late?

"Hi guys," I say, coming around the counter to sit between the two on the footstool between them. Instinctively, I rest my head against Nana's leg and wonder if I shouldn't. She's Goldie's grandmother, and Goldie hates me. But Nana brushes her hand across my hair and tucks it behind my ear.

"What's wrong, buttercup?" Nana asks as she returns her cash drawer to the register.

"Not much, everyone hates me," I say honestly, bouncing my head against Nana's knee.

"Well, at least you aren't being dramatic," Lori laughs, finishing her drawer as well.

"I'm sure Goldie's told you that everyone's mad at me and that I'm a terrible person."

"You seem to overestimate how much my daughter talks to me," Lori says, plopping beside me on the floor. "But you two have been thick as thieves all your lives. Whatever's going on, I'm sure you'll get past it."

"I'll leave you girls to talk a bit," Nana says, grabbing her bag from under the counter. She leans down and kisses me on the forehead, and it takes everything in me not to wrap my arms around her and hold her. "Keep your chin up, sweetheart. Brighter days are coming."

When Nana has left, Lori grabs another footstool and two soda bottles and sits beside me. "Okay, kid, spill."

Lori is an interesting person. She and my mom were pregnant at the same time, but their lives took very different paths. I've never been brave enough to ask her all the questions I've wanted, but I'm beat now, and answers would be better than wondering. "You were a teen mom too."

She swallows hard.

"And Goldie's dad left you, like my dad left my mom," I keep talking, knowing neither of us needs these things spelled out. They're universal facts.

"Indeed he did," she says, wrapping her arms around her legs.

I watch the bubbles twirl inside my bottle, and I wish I could sink into the dark liquid and live there. There's safety there. "But you didn't become a drug addict and abandon your kid and then die."

Lori puts her bottle down and swivels around to face me, balancing her hands on my knees. "You didn't know her very well. That's why you're angry. You've been piecing things together and never had a clear picture. You can't get any more pieces directly from her anymore, and that would make me angry, too." She sighed and reached up to tie back her long blonde hair, which was nowhere near as long as her daughter's but still impressive.

"And in answer to your previous statement, comparing my situation to your mother's is a little overly simplistic. Yeah, we were both teen moms, but the similarities kind of stop there. Your grandparents were gone. My parents were unhappy about it, but they were right there, and they've been there the whole time. Your mom had your aunts; they're amazing, but it's different. Your dad's parents took him away as soon as your mom got pregnant. Goldie's father has his struggles, but he was present until she was five, and she still sees him semi-regularly. That makes a difference. And at the bottom of it all, your mom and I are completely different people. She did her best with what she had at the time."

"It wasn't good enough," I murmur, my jaw tight.

"No, it wasn't. I don't mean to sound like I'm making excuses; she made her own choices. And those ramifications don't disappear because she's gone."

"But?" I ask, a small smile coming to my lips.

Lori smiles back. "But," she begins, nudging me on the shoulder. "More than one thing can be true at the same time." She repeats the exact words that Bella repeated from Cheryl Tibbons, "Your mom loved you most and with everything she had, and it's okay if that still wasn't enough and not all you deserve."

My exhausted head settles back against the wall. "With every day that goes by, I don't know what's real anymore. I only lived with her for a little while. How many good things I made up like fairy tales."

"Tell me a good thing. Tell me a Holly story."

"Don't call her that." I still can't take it. Lori sits silently and waits. My mind starts to drift through the murky black water of memories with my mom. My brain settles in one place. "We used to go to the YMCA in New Shiloh. We'd take clothes from the lost and found and have fashion shows in the locker room. She'd bring this big bag of safety pins and fit the clothes to me so I could strut around."

"Is that where you found the love of making them?"

"I guess. I always linked it to her giving the sewing machine, but you're right. She was stylish and cool. I wanted that, too."

"That's beautiful, Rosie. That would make her very happy," Lori says, squeezing my knee.

"I'm furious at her, Lori. I can't see past the mad."

Lori takes a deep breath, gathering her words. "Do you ever think that she was trying to do her best by you?"

"I don't understand."

"When you're a mom, you want to do everything possible to make the best life for your kid. Your mom knew she couldn't give you what you deserved." Lori pauses, caught between saying more and letting it lie. "I saw her a few weeks before she left."

"What?"

"She came in here, she was sober—"

"Then she was mean, huh?"

Lori chuckles knowingly. "She was curt and mumbling about something I couldn't understand. She put a Coke can on the counter, looked up at me, and said, 'Is this all it's ever going to be, Lori?'" Her question took me off guard. When I didn't say anything, her eyes started to brim with tears, and she continued, "I don't want this to be it for her, too.'"

"How could you not tell me this, Lori?"

She was fiddling with the hem of her sleeve, anything to look elsewhere but at me.

"Because I always thought Holly would come back and tell you herself. Then she died, and it didn't seem like the right time or place to tell you."

"You thought it was the wrong time to tell me that my abandonment, like the cornerstone of my life, might have been a selfless act on her part?" The rage bubbling inside me feels like it's splitting me at my seams. "Jesus, Lori, is that why she left me?"

"I swear, Rosie, that's all I know about it. That was the last time I saw her. I know she loved you. I never thought you believed she left because of you."

"Of course, she left because of me! But I don't know if it was to get away from me or if she was trying to save me."

She reaches out to me, but I recoil like she's a hot poker. I can feel the limits of the dark water creeping upon me, and I'm drowning before it reaches me. I have to get out of here. I spring to my feet and hustle to the door. Lori's calling after me, but I can't hear her. She has no idea what floodgate she's opened.

It's all I can think about until I sit across from Cheryl Tibbons in her burnt orange sundress and oversized black sweater. She looks like a Jack-o'lantern. The sound of her pencil eraser bouncing against her notebook. She's not using the tablet today. I wonder if it's a day-to-day choice or if she's doing it to see if I notice. My mind spirals in the silence and before the darkness settles my way back in, I practically shout, "I've always thought my mom left me because she didn't want to be a mom anymore."

Cheryl Tibbons' eyes widen as she sets the notebook aside. What's even the point of it? "How does that make you feel?"

"Can you not therapist me? That's like what a TV shrink would say," I grumble into my hands. This whole therapy thing is a mistake.

"Well, it's the first real thing you've said. I'm trying to learn where your head's at." Cheryl Tibbons responds, her cool demeanor makes me want to smack her.

I flop back against the headrest of the over-plush armchair I'm sitting in and try to count the bumps in the popcorn ceiling.

"How could it not be that? She left without a note, no explanation, nothing. One day she was here, and the next she was gone. I'd get these secondhand reports from my aunts when they had to bail her out of trouble, but she never contacted me. I'm her daughter. She left me. How could that not be? She didn't want to be a mother anymore."

"Your aunts did give me some baseline information, as I told you last time. I am aware of your mother's lifestyle. Is it possible that your mom left not because she didn't want to be your mother but because she knew she couldn't be the mother you deserved?"

It's like she threw up Lori's words right back to me, and they sting as bad in her smooth, melodic voice.

"Fine, then give up custody so the aunts could raise me. They were doing it anyway, but she dropped off the face of the planet. I didn't deserve anything from her?"

"I could give you excuses and explanations all day, but what do you think?"

"Gah! Can't you give me the answers?" I hiss back to her.

Cheryl Tibbons' mouth stretches into a broad smile. "It doesn't quite work that way."

It's another forty-five minutes of her poking and prodding at me like I'm a Thanksgiving turkey. By the time I leave the appointment, I'm as confused as when I walked in, but I'm ten times as emotionally exhausted. Kyle awaits me in the car when I exit the office building. Some sports podcast is blaring about Michael Jordan and the historic Bulls through his car speakers. He turns the volume down but not off, which is deeply vexing.

"How'd it go?" he asked once I was in the car and clicked into my seat belt.

"I want to punch you in the face," I mumble.

At our first meeting, he would have folded like a cheap suit if I'd said that to him, but today, he stares forward and pulls into traffic. "Well, we can put that on the calendar if needed." I chuckle; it feels like the first smile in days and makes my face feel alien.

"But seriously, how was it? You don't have to tell me any particulars. I want to know you're okay."

What is okay? Honestly, can I define it? Have I ever been okay a day in my life? I don't want to say that, though. I don't want to place more fear and worry than everyone already has. Instead, I say, "Yeah, I'm fine. We talked about Mom mostly."

"I'm sure that's a rough subject."

Kyle trying to act like a father makes me itchy. I'm under-parented, and I don't know what to do with him. He's like a weird toy gifted to me with expectations to play with it. But it has a clown face, and I don't want it.

"Choppy waters, but don't worry, we haven't talked about you."

"You can, you know," Kyle says, changing lanes and heading to the highway. It makes my heartbeat speed up. I can't tuck and roll out of the car on the highway. "You can talk to her about me, and you can talk to me about me. I hope I've made it clear that I'm an open book to you."

"You have to stop trying this hard, Kyle. I don't know what I want or need you to be, and I have too many other things to put you on top of the pile. Okay?"

"That's fair."

Kyle drops me at the pie shop even though I know he'd rather take me home. Joshua is at the door when we arrive. The shop is open. He never comes by when it's open.

"Who is that?" Joshua snaps at me as Kyle pulls away with a wave.

"Well, hello to you too?" I giggle, trying to break the tension, but Joshua's stone face never changes. "That was Kyle, my father." That term still feels sour on my tongue. "He took me to an appointment."

"An appointment for what?"

"Therapy," I answer honestly.

"You don't need therapy."

The little hairs on my neck prickle up, but I shake them off. "Oh yeah, I know, my aunts are insisting for now. Because of my mom."

That makes him visibly relax. He reaches behind him and extends his extra helmet to me. "I want to take you somewhere." It doesn't sound like a question. I glance up through the shop window, and Goldie and Blanche stare at me. I swear they're willing me inside. And the truth is that I want to go to them. I want to go in there, put my head in Goldie's lap, and hold Blanche's hand. I want to be around them. I want to be with them.

But I take the helmet instead.

I focus on the feeling of the cold air whipping against my face and the smell of Joshua's leather jacket next to my cheek. It's not hard to distract myself from the empty feeling inside me at walking away from my friends again when the white noise of being on a motorcycle surrounds me. Every once in a while, when we slow down a bit, Joshua reaches for my hands around his waist, and it helps to silence the butterflies enough for me not to demand him to turn around.

The darkness settles as I realize how long we've been on the road. I want to ask where we're going, but my mind tells me it might be better to stay silent. We drive and drive until I can feel salt on my face.

"Are we at the ocean?" I shout over the rushing wind, but if he hears me, he doesn't answer. A short time later, we pulled up to an old beach house secluded from neighbors. "Where are we, Joshua?" I ask when he finally cuts the engine

He dismounts and takes off his helmet, shaking his hair free. "It's my dad's place. In the summer, he uses it for clients and entertainment."

"Why are we here?" I ask, rubbing my hands together in a futile attempt to warm myself after the long drive. My stomach twists, knowing that I'm as far away as I am without any of my responsible adults knowing.

He pulls me into him, locking his arms around my waist. "I know that things have been insane for you, and we have been kind of out of sync for a bit. I wanted to allow you to get away for a little while without everyone breathing down your neck. I wanted us to get the opportunity to be for a little bit." He kisses my forehead. "You know? Remind you why you love me?"

My brow furrows. "I didn't forget."

One corner of his mouth turns up as he squeezes me tighter. "It's like you're slipping away, and I can't let you. I love you too much, Rosie."

"I love you too, Joshua," and my heart skips a beat in a way I can't define. I pull back enough to create a little distance and take my phone out of my pocket. "Let me call my aunts so they know where I am."

He snatches it out of my hand.

"Now, the point of this was to get away from everything. I need to hold onto your phone while we're here."

"I need to let them know I'm okay. Shawna will have a heart attack if I don't come home at all." I reach for the phone again, but he pulls it further away.

"I'll send a text to Shawna then," he says with a grin. "What's your pass code?"

I stay quiet for a moment too long, and Joshua's eyebrows raised to his hairline, waiting. "Zero-one-three-zero," I finally say when my stomach falls to my shoes. "My mom's birthday."

He's stopped listening. He taps the screen for a few seconds and then powers it down. He grins again before putting my phone in his pocket and grabbing my hand. "Now, I'll hold onto this until it's time to go home. Let me show you around."

Somehow, the house is even colder inside than outside. Joshua immediately starts a fire in the massive fireplace in the main room. "My dad turns off all the utilities until the spring. We'll camp out here." The soft glow of the flames makes his hair look golden. I want to touch it. He flops down on the couch and opens his arms to me. "Come here, let me warm you up."

He smells like firewood and comfort. He has this power about him. All the pain in my life goes away for a second, and I can breathe. I live for those few seconds. It's some kind of dark magic he wields over me and reminds me why I need him. His fingers brush the underside of my shirt, and the blissful nothingness is gone. I reach around and grab his hand.

"Not tonight, Joshua. We're both tired, and I want to be, like you said."

He stares down at me, but his expression lacks its normal depth. He sighs and pulls himself away from me and off the couch. "Yeah, yeah, you're probably right. This wasn't the best idea. It's a long ride back, but we should go home."

The black water floods my organs, suffocating me from the inside out. *He's going to leave you*, it echoes in my chest *Like everyone leaves you*. Joshua isn't perfect, but he's become my peace. I would give anything to hold onto that.

"No, no, I'm sorry. You're right. This is why we're here, to be together." I get up, legs shaky, and walk up behind him, wrapping myself around him. "Please, I want to," I bite my bottom lip to keep from trembling. He turns around, places his hands on my cheeks, and kisses me. He walks back toward the couch, and I let him lead me there, but I am a million miles away.

I awake to the strong dichotomy of warm sun on my face and a chill down my spine and through my limbs. I'm lying naked on the couch in the living room. I reach behind me and wrap myself up in a scratchy handmade afghan constructed of crocheted granny squares in the same blue color as the walls. I hear sounds coming from the other side of the house and wander to investigate. Since I woke up without him, I can only assume that's where Joshua is. I find him in the kitchen, hard at work at the stove in only a pair of gray sweatpants sitting low on his hips. I pull the blanket a little tighter around me. He gives me one of those smiles that made me fall for him in the first place.

"Hey sunshine," he says, flipping a pancake over. "Sorry if I woke you. I was planning on bringing this to you in bed or "on couch" I guess." He leans down to kiss me softly on the lips. "How'd you sleep?"

"Pretty good, actually," my voice breaks like I haven't spoken in days. I spot coffee and practically throw myself at it. "Do you want a cup?" I ask as I search for mugs. He agrees, and I pour one for both of us. For a moment, everything feels deliciously regular and adult—making breakfast in the kitchen in comfortable silence while sipping coffee. The pancakes are delicious. I doubt there's anything Joshua doesn't do well.

"What's the plan for today?" I ask, rinsing off our dishes.

"Plan? No plan. be, remember?" He leads me back to the couch by my shoulders. He opens the lid on the coffee table and pulls out an old beat-up board game. "Ready to get your ass kicked?"

It turns out there is something Joshua isn't great at, and that thing is in Monopoly. We spend the day playing two complete games, and I smoke him in both. We eat snacks and laugh and talk. We talk so much, and it's everything I need. It's like he's come back to me.

"Tell me more about this white dress you made," he says when we finally switch to Clue to give him a fighting chance against me.

My cheeks flush a deep pink as I take my roll. "Oh, come on, don't embarrass me. I felt inspired in the moment."

"Mmm, I wish I could see you in it. Hell, if you'd brought it with you, we could have taken care of things this weekend."

My gaze flashes up to him like he's crazy. "What? Like, we could have gotten married this weekend?"

"Yeah! I'm in a hurry to start forever with you. Can't blame me for that, can you?" He rubs the pad of his thumb over my knuckles.

"Why do you love me?" I blurt out before I have the time to think about it. He immediately takes back his hand. "I guess I've never understood why anyone would like me, let alone love me. I wondering if you could tell me why you do."

He studies my face like he's trying to memorize me. "When I saw you dancing like a crazy person in the shop that first night, you were more alive than I've ever been. I had to know you. You ended up being even more than I expected. You're a reason to wake up, Rosie."

"Thank you for being with me." I move around the coffee table and sit on his lap, burying my face in his neck. "I don't think I'd be surviving this whole thing with my mom, dad, friends, and school if you weren't with me."

"I support you and what you want to do fully. Forget everyone else, Rosie. It's you and me." And that sounds like a beautiful plan.

We spent the night and the next day much the same—board games, food, and cuddling. He doesn't try anything else, and I'm grateful. I love being with him and making him happy, but being with him physically is too overwhelming. I love him for not taking me further than I can handle.

After we've cleaned everything up and returned the house to the way we found it, we climb back on the bike to head home. It's incredible how much more at ease I find myself on the ride back than on the ride to the beach. I'm comfortable and steady. I could sleep pressed up against his back. He drops me off in front of the pie shop and kisses me like it matters before returning my phone and speeding away. I decide not to turn it on yet. I'd rather walk home in silence like I'm the only person in the world. I don't want to let everything back in. Upon approaching my house, I noticed a curious number of cars parked out front, far more than there should be.

I open the front door to an entire task force set up in my family living room: the aunts, Kyle, Beattie, Beau, Mr. Cooper, and all my friends. Everyone's in there.

"What's going on?" I ask when no one seems to notice me after a few seconds. The room falls silent, like the air sucked into an explosion before everything erupts.

"'I left town for the weekend. See you Sunday'?!" Shawna reads off her phone.

"Do you have any idea what you've put us through?" Norah shouts.

"I started calling morgues! Are you insane?" Goldie yells.

"Why didn't you call? We were worried about you!" Nixie cries.

"We raised you better than this! What were you thinking?" Meredith shrieks.

Then suddenly, a high-pitched whistle sounds through the room. Kyle has his fingers in his mouth. His eyes are fiery, and his chest puffs in and out. "Everyone, take a breath! I know this has been a terrible two days for us, but everyone screaming isn't going to fix anything."

Slowly, almost everyone in the room sits down—except for Norah, who never sits if she can help it. Kyle turns all his attention to me, and his face betrayed a deep sadness.

"Rosie, where have you been?"

It takes everything in me not to run. I'm far closer to the door than anyone else in the room. They'd never catch me. I could find Joshua, and we could go back to the beach and never return. I could be happy with him for the rest of my life. I don't know why I stay.

"I went to the beach," I mutter, wringing my fingers together, my knuckles cracking as I do.

"The beach?" Norah says, flabbergasted and annoyed. She pushes off the wall, but Kyle raises a hand to stop her.

"Why did you go to the beach?" he asks, keeping his voice calm and even. "It's not even warm yet, Rosie." Dark circles puff his lower lids, giving away a severe lack of sleep.

I should tell them the truth. I'm going to marry Joshua. They're going to find out all about him sooner or later. My nerves don't meet my intentions, though, and I can't bring myself to discuss Joshua with them.

"It felt like a good place to go. It was nice."

Blanche is incapable of sitting quietly and exclaims, "Horse shit Rosie! You were with Josh, weren't you?"

"Oh, you're talking to me now?" I hiss back.

"Who is Josh?" the aunts and Kyle all say simultaneously.

Blanche waits for me to answer, allowing me to own up to what I've been doing. But since I can't, she does.

"Josh is a guy who goes to my school. He's scum, but for some reason, Rosie has been seeing him. He doesn't like her the way she is—that's a big part of all the changes—and he's why she's not going to Parsons."

"How is the first we're hearing about this," Meredith demands. "Answer me, Rosaline."

"I am not a baby. I don't need your permission to have a boyfriend. And he's not the reason I don't want to go to Parsons. *I* don't want to go. At least he respects me enough to make my own decisions."

"This isn't your decision," Beau chimes in, getting up from the couch. "This is a sad and emotionally vulnerable grief decision. You, real Rosie, would never even consider throwing it away."

"And if some guy is telling you it's okay to do that, then he's not right for you," Elle adds.

"He loves me," I murmur with tears forming at the corners of my eyes. "He wants to marry me. He loves me."

The rush of quiet that speeds through the room is deeply unsettling. It's a glitch in the matrix, and everyone has to reset. The first person to break is Blanche—no real surprise there. She strides toward me and grabs me hard by my upper arm.

"You're coming with me," she announces. No question. No request. She doesn't wait for anyone to argue, encourage her, or give permission. I wish I had it in me to struggle, but I'm all out of fight. She drags me to her car and throws me inside.

After we've been on the road for a few minutes, I ask, "Are you going to talk to me, or is this a silent kidnapping?" She doesn't answer. I wipe the tears away from my face and wait. I'm clearly at her mercy now.

We drive into New Shiloh and to a townhouse neighborhood I've never visited. "Where are we?" I ask when she parks the car and gets out silently. She's still not talking.

We enter a house without knocking, and that's when I get it. It's Blanche's house.

"Blanche, what are we doing?" I ask again. Still no answer. Past the open front door is a sea of unbridled chaos. Wars don't have this much carnage. Toys cover every inch of the floor with a shoes, clothing, and a backpack. A constant high-pitched scream from somewhere in the distance is probably some kind of demon trying to warn me away.

"Martin! Wilson! Get down here and pick up your shoes; don't make me tell you again!" Blanche bellows out into the void. She throws her jacket onto a pile of them on a bench, and I follow suit. "Shiloh, Anthony, and Tyler, I know I don't see your toys in this living room! We talked about this!" She reaches into the refrigerator, pulls out a five-pound package of ground beef, and thrusts it into my hands. "Brown this," she commands and moves back to her brothers. "Brian and Thomas! Am I completely running this place alone?"

She hands me a lot of meat. I've somehow found two massive pans to start on the stovetop. At least the crackling of cooking food is something to ground me. The sound of footsteps barrelling up the stairs from the basement and down the stairs from the upper floor sounds like a stampede.

"Two seconds at home, and you're already yelling?" a skinny, dark-haired boy with glasses about our age says as he rounds the stairs.

"Well, Thomas, if you were keeping some sanity amongst the inmates when I wasn't here, I wouldn't have to yell, would I?" Blanche replies.

Thomas pulls out one of the folding chairs around the massive dining room table and says, "It wasn't my shift to watch them. It was Brian's turn."

"It was Brian's turn to do what?" an identical boy answers back as he comes up from the basement with a small rosy-cheeked child on his hip. Upon seeing Blanche, the little one reaches out his arms to her and squeals, "Mama!"

Blanche is not amused.

She moves to her little brother and boops him on the nose. "Shiloh, my love, if I had to tell you again that I'm not your mom, I'm going to take you to the mall and leave you there."

Shiloh considers this a moment and then pouts out his lower lip. "Mama…"

She chuckles to herself and takes him from Brian's arms. "And another bites the dust," she says to herself.

In moments, the kitchen is full of a sea of black-haired boys of different ages. Of course, I knew Blanche had seven brothers, but seeing them all together in a tiny room was very claustrophobic. "Who's that?" a chunkier brother around middle school age asks with a pointed finger at me. All eight heads turn in my direction.

"Summers Children, meet my friend Rosie. Rosie, these are Thomas, Brian, Martin, Wilson, Anthony, Tyler, and Shiloh," she says, pointing to each of them as though I'm going to remember which name belongs to which eerily similar face. I hope there's no test later. Of course, I can only focus on her calling me her friend. Is that still what I am to her? The feeling of hope that rises inside me is overwhelming and frankly depressing.

"The one that makes the pie?" one of the little ones asks.

Blanche smiles and says, "The one that makes the pie."

Dinner with a family of eight is something to behold. After browning five total pounds of ground beef and adding three jars of spaghetti sauce, we cook two and a half boxes of noodles and slice up three loaves of bread. Blanche and I work together in silence, but the tension there before has settled to a simmer. The two older boys, Brian and Thomas, hold a wrestling match in the living room amongst the small people, and while I keep waiting for her to scream, Blanche lets them go at it. Pick your battles, I guess. Everyone makes their plates before going to the table to eat.

"Bri, Tom," Blanche begins, setting down her fork. She doesn't look at me, but I can feel every ounce of her energy radiating in my direction. "You know Josh MacDonald, that goes to our school."

Both stop eating momentarily to look at their sister. "Yeah, everyone knows him," Thomas responds, and Brian chuckles. I hate not being in on a joke. Now Blanche does look at me, her dark eyes bearing into me. "What do you think of him."

"Littles!" Brian exclaims. "Earmuffs!" The three youngest put down their forks and begrudgingly covered their ears with their hands. If I weren't on edge, it would be adorable.

"He's a piece of shit," Thomas says, twirling more noodles around his fork.

"Yeah, he's an ass," Brian agrees, looking over at me.

"How is he with girls?" Blanche continues. I don't know what the point of this is.

"Like I said, he's an ass."

"He feels entitled to them. He always has three or four girlfriends at a time—" Thomas begins, but I've had enough.

"What are you doing?" I bark at Blanche. "What's the point of this?"

"If you won't listen to me, I hope you'll listen to a neutral third party. You're talking about marrying the guy Rosie, and we know him. "

"Wait, you think you're going to marry Josh MacDonald?" Thomas laughs, and I would like to smack two members of the Summers family. My cheeks flush with anger and embarrassment. "Brian, didn't he say the same thing to Sarah?"

"Who's Sarah?" I hear myself saying before I even thought it through.

"She's a girl in our grade. She's been all about him since we were freshmen," Brian answers. He seems to be the sweeter of the twins. I like Brian.

"Well, she's not dating him. I'm dating him!" I snap, getting up from the table. The littles have dropped their earmuffs. "I'm going home."

Blanche is hot on my heels as I grab my jacket and beeline it out the door. I don't think I have enough money in my account to rideshare home, and the walk would be way too far. I could call Kyle to pick me up. I must have a lifetime of guilt collateral to cash in on.

"Something has to open your eyes eventually! Do I have to tie you to a chair before you come to your senses?" Blanche is screaming at me. I flip around, ready to yell back but stop dead when I see the tears streaming down her face.

"Why are you crying?"

"Because you're breaking my fucking heart! You have no idea how hard it is to watch you do this. You've got your fingers in your ears running into the damn fire, and you won't let any of us save you!" A few of her neighbors flip on their lights, but I don't care. We can have this out here.

"I love him, Blanche. I know him. Why can't you accept that I know him better than you?" I shout back, angry tears of my own forming.

"Rosie, are you kidding? You've known him for a few weeks, only in the little bubble he allows you to see him. I've grown up with him. Since kindergarten, I've seen the person he is, and he's trash. I love you, you fantastic moron. I love you and the other girls more than I've ever loved any friends. You're the sisters I never had. Why don't you see this? You're drowning, Rosie and I'm trying to pull you out of the water. We're all trying to pull you out. Please, let us."

The ground slips from beneath me. The delicate border I've built between me and black water is cracking.

"I *like* the water," I hiss, my vision blinded by anger. "Maybe the water is the first place I've felt safe my whole life. If he's the water, then maybe I've finally found the thing that will work for me, and if it's him, then I choose him."

Her big brown eyes hold me with their sadness. It's the first time I've ever seen Blanche rendered speechless. I need to get out here. The earth is salted. I can't keep standing here. For now, I'll walk.

I only get about a block away before the headlights of Blanche's minivan light up behind me. It rolls to a stop beside me, and I'm ready to give her round two. When I swivel around to start yelling, I see Brian in the driver's seat.

"Please let me drive you home," he says.

The trip back to Harpersgrove is mostly quiet. Brian doesn't seem to have the impulse to fill every space like his sister does. "She does care about you, you know?" he says when we're a few minutes from the shop. "All we hear about is you and the other girls from the shop. You mean the world to her. She's not big on letting people in."

"I love her too," I respond, and it's the truth. I do love her like she's my sister. "I guess I've always understood families to be the people who support you."

Brian chuckles. What could be funny right now?

"I'm not going to pretend to know you or have any idea what's going on between you and Blanche. From what I can gather, that was her supporting you. You saw us in there; it was chaos and yelling, and sometimes we're mean to each other, but I would lay down in traffic for any of them, and so would Blanche. It seems like Blanche and the rest of your friends are pushing back because they know you aren't acting like yourself. Families aren't the people who will always agree with you and tell you you're right. They'll get in your face and scream at you because they know you'll forgive them anyway. They're the people who will let you hate them if it means you do the thing that's good for you. That's a family, Rosie, and Blanche is your family."

Brian leaves me outside the pie shop, more confused than ever. My head is swimming, and I want to sleep. But reality isn't that kind, and Joshua is waiting for me outside the shop.

"Who the hell was that?" he screams as soon as I'm out of the car. I'm too exhausted for this.

"Go away," I mutter, fumbling for my keys. I need to catch a few hours of sleep on Beattie's couch before I completely lose my mind.

"Excuse me, what did you say to me?" he demands, grabbing me by the shoulder and flipping me around. "You get out of some random guy's car and think you can tell me to go away?"

I grind my teeth together hard enough to shatter them.

"It was Blanche's little brother. He was driving me home from dinner at her house." I'm lost in the blubbering of tears, but he seems unfazed.

"Oh, you're friends with Blanche again? I guess how I feel doesn't mean shit to you." He slams his fist into the wall beside my head and stalks back toward his bike. That same sickening feeling settles in my stomach and burns the back of my throat. He is on my brain and in the blood in my veins.

"I picked you," I cry before he's entirely out of earshot. He stops suddenly but doesn't turn back. "Blanche made me choose, and I picked you."

The sobs engulf me, and the exhaustion takes out my knees, but I'm in his arms before I hit the ground. He pulls me up, and he kisses me like I'm on life support. I can't get out. I don't want out. I want him.

He kisses my temple and murmurs, "I love you," into my skin. We go back to Beattie's office, and he expresses his love for me in the best way he can—and I let him.

CHAPTER FOURTEEN

He leaves me before dawn to go home and get ready for school, but I know I'm not going myself. What's the point? I'm floating on an island here, waiting to die or waiting to live. I don't know. I'm lost in limbo. I force myself back into my clothes even though I lack energy. I can't stand the idea of Beattie coming in here to find me naked. As I pull my hair back, the office door flies open, and Beattie stands there boiling. She doesn't speak to me but starts tapping away on her phone.

"What are you doing?" I ask.

"Well," she snaps before shoving her phone into her pocket. "You ran out again last night, and no one knew where you were. Then Blanche told us her brother dropped you off here, but you never made it home. I'm telling your aunts they can stop calling hospitals."

"I'm sorry, Beattie," I whisper.

"For what? Be specific." She's mad. I don't think I've ever seen her this infuriated.

"For whatever gets me out of this room faster."

It's crueler than I intended, but I can't take this anymore. The pie shop is my safe place, but I can't be here anymore. Everyone keeps taking things from me.

"I don't recognize you, Rosaline. I saw you that day when you came here and asked me for a job. I saw you—bright-eyed and full of creativity and life. Honey, you seem soulless now. Where did that girl go? Where is she? Because we want her back, we're fighting for her."

Now Beattie's crying. I break everything I touch.

The last ounces of warmth flee my body. The emotions are gone. There are no more tears to cry, nothing to yell or scream. There's only fatigue, and it is consuming.

"That girl died with Holly," I say, and my mother's name feels like poison on my tongue. I brush past her, and she lets me. The people in my life seem skilled at dropping bombs and then letting me scatter.

The air is cold, and I'm grateful. I breathe in frosty gulps until I can feel it in my toes. I want to feel SOMETHING. A car horn beeping beside me pulls me out of the moment. Kyle is sitting there staring at me. He seems to have aged ten years since I've known him. I'm a cancer. I wait for him to roll down the window, but he leans across, opens the door, and waits. I should walk away—I don't want any more family "love" right now. I get in the passenger seat and slam us inside with all the fury I can muster. We sit there watching the windshield fog with our breath for a while.

"I'm trying hard to understand you, Rosie," he finally says.

"I never asked you to Kyle. I never asked for you, but you showed up and kept pushing your way in. I don't want any of this."

"You're my daughter. If that makes you uncomfortable and you don't want to be related, fine, but it's a fact, and I'm not going anywhere." He squeezes hard on the steering wheel, and emotion claims him.

"You want to be around? Fine. I clearly can't stop you, but you have to stop trying to act like you're my dad. You're a stranger, and I'm one to you. Do you want to be my friend? We can work on that, but I don't need a father. I've done fine without you."

"Rosie, I would argue that you've never needed anything more," he says, turning over the ignition and starting the car. "Regardless, I've built up a whole bunch of vacation days that I've decided to take. Get used to my face."

"Where are we going?" I ask as he backs out of the parking spot.

"You're coming home with me for a few days. Your aunts know all about it. Shawna even packed you a bag."

"I don't want to come home with you," I squeal, dramatically trying to open the door.

"With all due respect, what you want hasn't been good for you. We're trying something else." He rambles on about the "parenting pod" that he and my aunts have created, and now I feel like a science experiment. Once again, my life isn't in my own hands.

Kyle's apartment is as gray as I remembered it. I flop my bag down on his couch and pull my phone out of my pocket to text Joshua when Kyle takes it out of my hand.

"I'll be holding onto that," he says, shoving it in the desk drawer before locking it. "You've lost phone privileges for a bit."

"Are you shitting me? Give me back my phone that doesn't belong to you!" I shriek, standing dumbfounded in the middle of the room.

He sits in his spinning desk chair and looks quite proud of himself. "This is true, but the owner of the phone, your dear Aunt Meredith, said that I could take it. It's mine for now."

I flop on the couch, gripping my fingernails into the scratchy fabric. "Well what, I'm your prisoner? Do I not even get to go to school?"

He sighs deeply, running his hand over his fuzzy hair. "Today? No, you will see Cheryl Tibbons today and discuss what went on this weekend. It's okay if you don't want to talk to the pod, but you must talk to someone about it. I will drive you to school tomorrow and pick you up after."

"What about my job?" I demand.

"Beattie's giving you a break for a few days while you decompress and reassess."

I want to spit in his perfect old man face.

"Well, I have a boyfriend. What about him?"

"Trust me, Rosie, no one has forgotten about your boyfriend." The way his voice drops sends a chill through me. "You told us you planned to marry someone no one knew existed. Did you think that was going to fly—that Shawna was going to start planning a bridal shower for you?"

"Don't make fun of me," I murmur, trying to keep the tears inside.

"I'm not making fun of you, Rosie. I'm worried. I'm worried in a way that I didn't know existed. I worry about you constantly, and yeah, I will be right on top of you for a bit because that's something I can control. I'm terrified for you."

"You're terrified that someone loves me? That sounds like you're projecting Kyle." The room with its gray walls is getting progressively smaller by the minute.

"Does he, Rosie? Does he love you?"

I explode. "Is that concept impossible for everyone to understand? Is it unbelievable that someone might love me? What is so unlovable about me to you people?"

He raises his hands to try and calm me. "No one is saying you're unlovable, Rosie, quite the opposite. We all love you so much, and after talking to Blanche about this guy, we all have some valid concerns."

"Of course, this is Blanche! She seems hell-bent on making sure he and I aren't together. She's jealous! He rejected her and she still wants him, and she hates that he wants me! Why hasn't anyone considered that?"

"Come on, you know your friend, she loves you. She'd never pick a guy over you."

"But she expects me to pick her over a guy. How is that love? How is that what friendship is?" I feel like I'm insane. My brain is on fire, sparking and shutting down at once.

"I don't think that's it. Blanche is trying to protect you. You're not safe with this guy."

"That's bullshit! None of you know me as well as you think you do! He loves me, Kyle. Let me be happy. Please."

He leans forward, elbows on his knees, and over-enunciates every word, "You. Are. Not. Happy. I've only known you briefly, and it is as plain as the nose on your face that you're miserable."

I can't take being in the room anymore and run off to the only place of refuge, the bathroom. For some reason, Kyle's side-by-side matching mint green hand towels make me want to throw things. Everything about him is too perfect, in its right angles and straight edges. I pull one of the towels halfway down—take that perfection.

Whenever I'm getting closer to independence, the people in my life dig their claws in and pull me back. The fact that I can't text Joshua right now turns my stomach. He gets upset when he can't get in contact with me. It's not like we have any mutual friends check in on with. Except Blanche, but I don't see that happening. He will worry about me, but does my family care about that? Of course not! They want to shove me in a little box and control me.

I turn on the shower and crank up the heat. It's the only way I can think to quiet the pulsing rage in my veins. As I'm taking off my clothes, I spot a set of bruises on my inner thighs shaped like finger-prints. At first, it sets sour in my core, but then I trace the purple out-lines with my fingers. I try to see them differently—the way I want to believe he intended at the beach house. He is desperate to be near me, to possess me, to claim me. He wants me completely. He accepts me, and I need him, and if he needs me to do this, to keep doing this, I will do that for him. I have to.

The shower has its intended effect. The edge of my anger has sub-sided, at least for now. Driving in Kyle's car to Cheryl Tibbons' office is especially frosty. Knowing I can't tap away on my phone to distract myself makes me even more antsy. Kyle barely stops the car before I get out.

"Don't come in," I command before slamming it behind me.

Cheryl Tibbons waits for me by the reception desk. "Come on back, Rosie," she says calmly and soothingly, which I know she means as comforting, but my level of irritation is too high.

I take my now claimed seat in the pale yellow armchair across from her weathered dark brown wicker rocking chair and grumble, "Nothing matches in here."

"Does that bother you?" Cheryl Tibbons looks up from over her glasses as she gets comfortable in her seat.

"No," I snap and instantly feel bad. She hasn't done anything wrong. "I wish you'd make a choice and stick with a theme."

"Interesting," she says, tapping away on her tablet.

"What do you mean by that? What's interesting?"

She smiles. "Rosie, I don't mean anything; I'm intrigued to learn more about you. In the first two minutes of this session, you've ex-pressed more emotion than in any of our others, and I'm happy about that."

I don't believe her. There's some psych mumbo jumbo going on here that I'm not thrilled about. She folds her hands on her tablet and says, "Rosie, your dad gave me a little insight into why he wanted you to return in such a short period of time. Do you want to tell me about anything that happened this weekend?"

I heard her, but I felt far away. Then I remembered something Bella told me.

"You're not allowed to tell them anything I tell you, right?"

Her face never wavers. "Unless I honestly believe you are a threat to yourself or someone else, no, I will not share anything with anyone you don't want me to."

I look straight on at her and say, "I lost my virginity recently."

Saying the words aloud feels like the black water is fleeing my lungs and out of my mouth. I can breathe a little better finally. Cheryl Tibbons sets her tablet aside. She leans forward and steeples her fingers under her chin. And then she waits.

"My boyfriend, Joshua, wanted to express to me how much he loves me and it's beautiful. He wanted me to see how much he cared about me and thought a physical expression was the best way. And then he did it again and again because he wants me to know how special I am, and he—" my voice fades off when I run out of words because she's still staring.

"Okay, Rosie," she begins, and now I understand how that soothing voice can affect me. "I hear you tell me what Joshua thought, felt, and needed. Rosie, what do you think? What do you feel? What do you need?"

I think of Bella. She told me to let go and be honest with Cheryl Tibbons, saying that what I told her wouldn't leave the room. "I don't think I wanted to do it at first. It scared me." I silently sob as I hold her kind eyes, completely lacking any judgment.

"I'm sure you were. It sounds scary. Do you want to tell me about it, that fear?" I don't know what she means, but she can tell me. "Fear can be a few different things. In some ways, it's the brain trying to protect you." She lifts her hand and starts counting off things with her fingers. "That fear can serve some need that your body or current situation requires. It can be a trauma response. The lizard, primal part of your brain, controls it, and you have no say over it. That fear is trying to protect you. If you can, I want you to tell me about it. Where did you feel it in your body?"

I take myself back to the first night it happened in the shop. Joshua wanted to have sex, and when I didn't, he was going to leave.

"When I was hesitant, he was going to leave, and I felt my stomach twist and flip, and I started to sweat on the back of my neck."

"Now, if you can, I want you to focus on how that felt in those parts of your body. What happened then?"

"I couldn't take that feeling, and he told me that if I loved him I would do this for him. And then I did."

Cheryl Tibbons sucks her lower lip into her mouth before she speaks again. "Rosie, the first thing I want to say is that I am very sorry you were put in a situation where you had to feel that way. I also want to ensure you know that consent should be given enthusiastically, and if it has to be coerced in any way, it's not consent."

It's like she isn't speaking English anymore but pure gibberish.

"You're not trying to say that Joshua raped me, are you?" The words are like poison as they come out of my mouth. "That's absurd! He loves me! I—I was scared."

"Okay, okay," she says, raising her hands to calm me. "We don't have to talk about that right now if you don't want to. Rosie, you are the boss here."

The black water fills my body again, sitting heavy like a weight on my chest. That makes my ears perk up like a far too eager chihuahua.

"Kyle is making me stay with him," I hiss, completely switching gears. I can't talk about Joshua anymore. The thought of him and that night hurts my brain.

"Kyle is your father, right?" she asks, reading in her seat.

"I mean, he got my mom pregnant."

"Can we expand on that? That's an interesting way to describe him."

"I never met Kyle before my mom died. Suddenly, after seventeen years of not even knowing his name, he wants to be Super Dad."

"How does he do that?" she asks.

"He—he's always there. He brought me to my first appointment here. He's spending all this time with my aunts, and now he's got me staying with him and wants to watch my every move. It's not normal! I don't know him. How am I even supposed to know that he's my father."

"Do you believe he isn't?" she asks with a tiny smirk.

I let out a huff that rustles the hair in my eyes. "No, Kyle is my father. I was mad." Her smirk grows. She knows. "I—I don't have parents. I never have and I don't know what to do with this."

She settles forward in her seat again. "Your father was never around, starting when your mom was pregnant, until very recently. Your mother had personal struggles, and even when she was here with you, she wasn't present. Parents are very much in your business when they're doing it right. They're messy and intrusive and drive you crazy. Do you have anyone like that currently in your life?"

"My Aunt Norah," I say before I realize I'm speaking. That's the definition of her.

"You have more insight into what it's like to have a parent than you realized. "What about a super nurturing presence?"

I look up at her. "My Aunt Shawna."

"How about somebody who's always in your corner to level out the other two?"

Now it's my turn to smile. "Aunt Meredith."

"Sounds to me like you grew up with three parents already."

Is she right?

Kyle is waiting for me in the car as promised after my appointment. The ride back to his apartment is as icy as the ride there, but I can feel myself slightly defrosting.

"Go put your stuff down, and then you can help me make dinner," Kyle says, throwing his keys on the kitchen counter.

"Oh, might I have that honor?"

"Don't be a smart ass, come help me."

Since I met him, Kyle's walked on eggshells around me. There's something nice about him treating me like another person. I don't think I like it.

I drop my purse on a nearby chair and go to the sink to wash my hands. No sooner do I finish than Kyle slides me a bowl of potatoes.

"Wash and peel, and don't slice off your fingers."

"I run the kitchen in a pie shop. I've used a vegetable peeler before," I grumble. I'm no novice. Of course, my attention is now laser-focused as I will not give my father the satisfaction of cutting myself. Every once in a while, I catch sight of Kyle zipping around his kitchen. He's working with some kind of pork and root vegetables. He's at ease and comfortable. It's like a ballet. He knows what he's doing.

"Where did you learn to cook?" I ask.

"Oh, my mom had all the talent of a French chef. She taught me."

His parents. Technically, my grandparents. Am I allowed to ask questions about them?

"You said she had the talent. Does that mean she's not alive anymore?"

I see his face tense for only a moment. "No, my mother is still alive. I honestly am not sure how I'm supposed to talk about them to you. If you want to know anything, ask away. I will answer."

There's only one question that comes immediately to mind. "Do your parents ever talk about me or think about me? Miss me?" I sound more pathetic than I wish it did, but if Kyle notices, he doesn't let on. He sits his knife down beside the meat and turns to face me.

"No bullshit?" he asks.

"No bullshit."

His tongue darts out of his mouth, wetting his lips. "My parents like to pretend you don't exist because it's more than they're prepared to deal with," he says. "And they suck for it."

I let out a snort at the last part, and he noticeably relaxed.

"Do you have a picture of them? I keep envisioning witches from old fairy tales, and that's probably not fair." Or is it?

He digs his phone out of his pocket and taps around before handing it to me. His parents are in matching snowflake sweaters, laughing at the person taking the picture. His mother's hair is black and streaked with gray around her face. His father's is tight and curly against his head. They both have soft wrinkles at their eyes and mouths, most likely formed by years of laughing and smiling. Laughing and smiling when, all the while, they KNEW they had a grandchild on the other side of the country and chose to ignore her.

"Do you have siblings?" I ask.

He reaches forward and swipes a couple of times on the screen until he gets to a picture of two women with the same face, laughing like their parents. "Those are my younger, twin sisters. They turned thirty-one recently."

"And do they have kids?" I ask, pushing the phone away. I don't want to see it anymore.

"They each have two. I guess you have cousins."

"Are your parents good grandparents to them?" I ask. The pain on Kyle's face hurts my feelings. I should have stopped at the snowflake sweaters. "You don't have to answer that. It's not a fair question." I return to my potatoes, but he takes the peeler from my hand.

"Listen," he begins beside my ear. "I love my parents, I do, but I will never forgive them when it comes to you. You were an innocent baby, but they held it against you as much as they did your mom. It wasn't fair. It wasn't fair because after two weeks of silent treatment toward me, they acted like it never happened. I was never the bad guy. Your mom was always the villain to them, and it wasn't okay. Holly and I made you when we were teenagers, but you should have been loved and celebrated. They wanted you to go away, and I let it happen. It was easier for me to be far away. It was easier to keep the peace. I will never be able to make up for that. I'll never get to apologize to your mom for that, and I will carry it for the rest of my life. But I can promise you one thing: I will take every day of my life to keep trying to make it up to you."

Oh, he got real. He got too real.

"What do you want me to do with these potatoes when I finish peeling?"

"Dealer's choice."

Mashed it is.

We eat in silence at Kyle's small dining room table. I will admit Kyle can cook. It's one of the best meals I've had in years, but I would NEVER let Shawna know that. We don't exchange a word until we're doing dishes.

"Do you think I could have my phone back?" I ask, hoping to play a little on whatever emotional buttons we've pushed today.

Kyle never looks up from the sink as he says, "I promised your aunts that I wouldn't. You need a cleanse."

"Says the millennial," I mumble under my breath, and I'm relieved to hear him chuckle.

"All right, that's fair," he says. "I'll make you a deal. You can have it for ten minutes, and then I'm taking it back."

It's not much of a compromise, but some phone is better than no phone—every muscle in my body tenses at the lack of contact I've had with Joshua lately. Kyle goes to his desk and brings me my phone, and it's like reuniting with a long-lost friend. It might take me longer than ten minutes to go through Joshua's worried messages and voicemails. I boot the little machine to life and wait anxiously for the messages to appear.

But they don't.

Not a single one.

I turn the phone back off and hand it back to Kyle. "That's not ten minutes," he says, looking confused.

"Yeah, I don't need it." I can't process my feelings about the fact that I don't have a hundred messages from Joshua waiting for me. I should be relieved that he isn't angry, but I'm not. I also wonder if he is furious and punishing me with silence, or worse, that he doesn't care that much at all. I know that's ridiculous because he loves me, but fear pools in my stomach.

"Want to watch a movie?" Kyle asks after putting my phone back in his desk drawer.

"Yes," I say definitively. "A movie sounds perfect." Sitting with my stranger/father for an awkward evening sounds like the perfect distraction.

As promised, Kyle drops me off at school the next few days and sits in the parking lot throughout the day. I catch glimpses of his car from the windows of my various classrooms. Every parental protective instinct he hasn't had the chance to use is coming up tenfold. At the end of the day, I climb into the passenger seat, and he drives me to the pie shop. I've finally earned my position back after a few days of full-life detox at Kyle's.

"Doesn't this seem a little unnecessary to you? I haven't made a jailbreak yet, have I?"

"I like this life as a personal valet. I think it's time for a career change," he says, leaning back in his seat to relax.

"You're an idiot."

"But I'm your idiot. I'll be here when you finish." There's something comforting about the fact that I know it's true.

"Am I insane, or are we out of sugar?" Allisin asks while we're busy baking in the kitchen.

That can't be possible. The three things we always have in infinite supply are sugar, butter, and flour. What is a pie shop without sugar? I move bowls and bags of all sorts, certain I'm missing some hidden, secret sweetness. Alas, I am not. "Sorry. I'll have Bella order some emergency stuff to be here tomorrow," I mutter, disappointed with myself. I never expected my own crap to interfere with the glory of pie. It's a low point, for sure.

"No worries, happens to the best of us, but what will we do in the meantime? I need to make a cherry pie, or Mr. Johnson might revolt," Allisin says, running her rolling pin back and forth over a clump of dough.

A loud, exasperated breath rumbles through my body. "I'll be right back."

I hustle into the dining room, alert Bella to our crisis, and then out into the parking lot. "Where are you going?" Kyle shouts out his open car window. I guess this is the great escape he worried about.

"Relax, dude. I need to get some sugar," I holler back. It's too chilly to stop and talk.

The bells jingle inside Rust Drugstore, alerting everyone to my arrival. Everyone in this case is Goldie standing behind the counter in her employee polo and long blonde braid to the base of her spine. We haven't spoken more than two words since my blow-up at the pie shop. She watches me like a shoplifter while I hustle to grab three pounds of sugar.

"Will that be all, ma'am?" she asks when I lay them on the counter.

"Ma'am? Really?"

She looks up at me from under her unnaturally long black eyelashes. "Really," she responds.

"Look, I know I haven't been my ideal self recently, but you're my best friend, Goldie," I say, clutching my wallet like it's my lifeline. If I don't give her the money, we can stay frozen in this transaction forever.

"And you're my best friend, Rose," she says, shoving the sugar into a brown paper bag.

"Then can we stop this? Please?"

"What kind of friend would I be if I did that? A good friend can't sit idly by while you destroy your life and pretend it's okay. You don't think it's hard for me to be without you. I miss you all the time, but you're not you right now. I will hold this line until you are again because I love you that much."

In a daze, I leave a crumbled twenty on the counter and don't wait for change. I head back to the shop to work with Allisin in tense but peaceful silence until the end of my shift. I like this aspect of her. She reads me well; unlike my other friends, she gives me what I need.

Kyle takes me back to his house when the work day is over, and we eat chicken salad on top of a regular salad at his small dining room table on his gray plates with gray place mats.

"We need to introduce some color into your life," I remark, shaking my head.

"Gray is a color," he responds with a crinkled brow, making me laugh. Is this a favorite line of his?

We do the dishes and watch another movie together, and it's such a regular family thing I want to cry. This is what it could have been like having a traditional family. Everything always revolved around keeping me from ending up like my mom. There was something intriguing about simply hanging out with a father. It's beautiful and sad at the same time.

Kyle insists that I take his bed instead of sleeping on the couch. It's weird to put him out, but that couch is uncomfortable. I don't fight him too hard. I lay in the middle of his massive mattress, wide awake at two in the morning, unable to sleep. What I can do, though, is snoop. It's probably not right to go through his things, and he has been very forthcoming with me, but I still feel like I know little about him.

The neatly pressed clothes hang in his closet, evenly spaced, like a serial killer's might be. I'm much more interested in the boxes on the floor. I glance at the closed door to be sure he can't see and open one. After all, I'm only looking for a little more insight into my father. The first box contains old baseball cards—typical boy. The second box is a fully stocked sewing kit, which comes as much more of a surprise. Box after box gives me little glimpses into my dad, and it feels nice to know more. The last box lays tucked in the far corner, weathered and covered in flowers. It's the oldest of them all. I crawl on my hands and knees to grab it and sit cross-legged on his gray carpet to investigate it. I take off the lid and can't process what I see inside.

It's me.

Baby pictures, school pictures, and a hand turkey I made in kindergarten for Thanksgiving. The newspaper clipping about me in the pie shop, a third-grade report card, and a pressed flower I'd put in a small frame in middle school. It's my life reduced to a shoebox. How does he have all this?

Before I know what's happening, I'm on my feet, my fingers clutching the box. I throw open Kyle's bedroom door, the handle ricocheting off the wall and awakening Kyle with a start.

"What the hell is this?" I can hear myself scream.

Still lost in sleep, Kyle can only stare at me. "What is what?" he asks.

I can't help it. I turn the box over and dump the contents into his lap. "What is *this*, Kyle?"

He tries to collect himself. "You weren't supposed to find that," he says as though it's some kind of answer.

"This is my whole life, Kyle! How did you get all this?"

He runs his thumb across my face in my eighth-grade school picture and says, "Your Aunt, Meredith, has been sending me things since you were born."

The world falls out from under me as memories of the aunts telling me not to ask about my father come screaming into my mind. He was a no-go subject because he wasn't a part of my life, but Meredith made sure he could be from afar all this time.

"I thought you didn't know anything about me? You said you never saw me until the funeral. But this is every milestone and important event in my life. Is that one of my baby teeth?!" I shriek, pointing to a little plastic container on the floor.

"Meredith knew the situation, but she wanted me to have something of you because you're the best kid."

I put my hands on my knees and bent to his eye level. My entire body vibrates with hurt and rage. "For a second, for one second, I thought you and I were developing something here. I started to think that I had a real family with you and with the aunts. But you've all been lying to me my entire life. How could I ever trust you again after this? You could've been my dad this whole time, but you chose not to."

Tears blur my vision as I rise back to my full height and head for the door. There's no time to get dressed. I have to get out of here.

"Honey, please, give me a minute to explain."

"Don't dare say that. I'm not your honey, I'm not your sweetheart, I'm not your daughter, and that's YOUR fault. You could've had me if you wanted to, but you chose to be a "normal'" teenager instead, with a "normal" life that didn't include me. Well, I hope it was worth it, Kyle, enjoy your God damned shoebox because it's all you'll ever have of me."

I'm down the hall in my tennis shoes with no socks or coat before he catches up.

"Let me take you home, please," he cries, throwing a sweater over my shoulders and my purse on my arm.

"Get away from me! I'll take the bus! I don't want to see you anymore!" I'm screaming in the hallway of Kyle's building in the middle of the night, and to his neighbors, I'm a random teenage girl stumbling out of his apartment at two in the morning.

One of the units' doors opens to reveal a middle-aged woman in a nightgown. "Mr. Roosevelt? Is everything alright?" she asks, her attention glued on me.

"Yes, Mrs. Hernandez, everything's fine. My daughter and I are having a little disagreement."

"I told you that you don't get to call me that," I hiss as I stomp toward the elevator. "It's over now!" I shout for a final time as the elevator closes.

The feeling of betrayal sits sick in my stomach the entire bus ride back to Harpersgrove. I don't know where to go now. I can't stay with Kyle, but how can I return to the aunts? They always dissuaded me from asking questions about my father, and the whole time, they were feeding him information about me. I didn't know him, but he got to have me. How can I ever trust them again? The answer is simple. I can't. I'm tired of being around people who lie to me and put me last. I'm tired of waiting. I want my life to start on my terms, and I'm taking it. I don't think I'll survive if I don't do it right this minute.

Kyle's itchy cardigan barely blocks the cold, late-night air, but I don't mind. I burst into my house like a bat out of hell. I hope I wake them up. I hope they hear me.

They do, of course. As I'm rummaging through my closet, all three aunts fill my doorway.

"Rosie? Are you okay?" The grand betrayer, Meredith, dares to ask me.

"No, no, I'm not," I cry, my voice breaking.

"What's wrong with you?" Norah demands.

I find the dress I'm looking for tucked away near the back of the closet and pull it from its hanger. "Don't worry, I'm not staying," I say as I zip past the aunts to my bathroom.

I change into the dress and pull Kyle's sweater back over it. Even in my distress, I know it's too cold to go without it.

"Sweetheart, you're supposed to be at Kyle's," Shawna says when I finally emerge.

"Yeah, I guess you guys were pretty excited to have someone to pawn me off on finally," I hiss, pushing through them, and they let me.

"That's not what's going on, and you know it. We needed to shake you out of whatever's been going on with you, and Kyle is your father," Norah bites back, hot on my heels.

"But to send me to a complete stranger? Why would you send me to someone who knows nothing about me? Why Meredith?" I ask her directly, looking as cold and dead on the outside as I feel on the inside.

Her face softens in this omniscient way that makes me want to scream. "By the way you're talking, I sense you already know."

"My whole life! All three of you! 'Your father made his choice. He's not part of your life. Don't ask questions.' And the entire time, you were sending him everything he could ever need to know about me. Why did you punish me but reward him? WHY?!"

All three stare back at me, turning paler by the moment. I don't care what they have to say. Nothing would fix this anyway.

"I don't want to see or speak to any of you again," I announce as I grab my keys and fly out of the house in a white dress I made for one occasion. Only one person cares, and I'm ready to be with him.

CHAPTER FIFTEEN

Pulling up to Joshua's house, I pant like I've run a marathon. I pull the rearview mirror around to take in my appearance. My hair falls frizzy and haggard from my messy bun, and my face is puffy and red from crying. I'm wearing an oversized gray cardigan and tennis shoes with the dress I made to get married in, and it's a beautiful dress. It's a bell skirt that brushes my knees with a high neck and lace around the waist. I don't see the dream I'd imagined with the added accessories, but Joshua loves me enough that he'll understand.

I pull my phone out of my purse and call him. The first three calls roll to voicemail, but he picks up on the fourth. "Do you have any idea what time it is?" he barks through a sleepy fog.

"I need you to come outside," I sob into the receiver as my resolve evaporates. Hearing Joshua's voice is like a warm and comforting hug, even if he sounds cross.

"Come outside where?" he asks, his voice on the edge of panic. I see the curtain in an upstairs window flutter. "Why are you at my house?" he demands

"Can you come out here, please?"

He huffs after a long moment of silence. "Do not move or come any closer to the front door."

Sadness and fear pool deep in my stomach as he clicks off the call, but everything will be okay once I see him. Once I can place my hands on Joshua and hold him, I will be okay again. I know it.

A moment later, Joshua comes full force through the front door, his mouth set in a thin line. "What the hell is going on, Rosie?"

I pull off the cardigan and throw it on the hood of my car. Seeing me in this dress that I made to marry him, he'll understand. "I don't want to wait anymore. Let's go."

"What are you talking about? It's the middle of the night, and you show up in a wedding dress, crying at my house. Do you know how fucking crazy you look?"

"I don't want to pause my life anymore. What are we waiting for anyway? We love each other, and we're getting married anyway. Why are we waiting?"

He's looking at me like he's never seen me before, and I can feel the gripping cold of the black, icy water soaring through my veins.

"What is wrong with you? Do I need to call an ambulance to come and get you?"

"What?" is all I'm able to muster.

"Rosie, we're teenagers. Clearly, we're not getting married. You knew that. You knew it was all a fantasy. talk."

"No, I didn't! No, it's not! You love me and said you would marry me, take care of me, and make sure no one hurt me anymore. We'll move in together when you go to college, and we'll be each other's family."

"It's been a few weeks, Rosie. We are not in love with each other like that. We're not getting married. We're not living together. I'm going to college and living in a dorm. We can't tie each other down right now. You exaggerated everything in this relationship, and I'm worried about your mental state."

I don't think I'm breathing. I've left my body, and I'm floating outside of myself.

"What are you talking about? You told me all these things."

"Don't be stupid, Rosie. You knew what we were from day one, and I let you take it too far."

He turns and starts to walk away, and black water begins pulling me down into its depths, and for the first time, I don't want it to. I want my white dress, my happily ever after, and every promise he made me.

I run after him and grab him by his forearm. Touching him fixes everything. "Wait, wait. I don't understand what's going on, Joshua. What's happening?"

He wrenches his arm away from me like I'm filthy. "That's enough, Rosie! You're embarrassing yourself now." With that, he opens the door and, before he closes it on me, adds, "My name is Josh. No one calls me Joshua."

I don't know him at all.

My jaw quivers, and my eyes ache with the pain of unshed tears. I gulp for air like a drowning victim and sink to the ground, muddying my beautiful dress. The dress that I thought held a promise but was, in fact, a lie. Every inch of my body hurts, from my hair to my teeth to my fingernails. *Is this what dying feels like?* With a shaking hand, I pick up my phone and dial before I know what I'm doing.

"I need you," I say

I don't know how much time passes before the headlights of Blanche's minivan come into view. However long it is, I haven't moved from my spot in the grass, and now I'm cold, wet, and shivering, but I can barely feel it. Oh God, I want to feel it!

Blanche and her brother Brian jump out of the car, and even in my state, I can sense their worry. Blanche looks at me, and her eyes brim with tears. She crouches down to my level with a grim, but loving look on her face as Brian moves my car. Blanche removes her jacket and wraps it around my shoulders, taking in my dress.

"Are you with me?" she asks.

She places her hands on my cheeks and squeezes, and I am right about touch. It wasn't Joshua's that fixed anything. I don't answer, but I start to cry, and that's enough for her. She helps me to my feet, and we get into the back of her car as Brian drives. She pulls me onto her lap like I'm a child, and I sob into the crook of her neck, all the while she holds me to her as hard as she can. I don't have to explain what happened. Blanche already knows.

I don't remember ending up in my bed at the house on my faded black sheets, staring up at where my stars used to be. I miss them so much. I can hear Blanche and Brian talking to my aunts in the kitchen, but I don't hear Kyle, which also makes me sad. I hate myself for it because I want to hate him. I should hate him, but I don't. I pull my blanket up to my chin, steady my breathing, and I start to float. I'm ready. I'm ready to float away on the surface of cold black water and never return; sleep takes me there.

"Rosie," a hand jostles my shoulder to awaken me. It takes all my strength to open my eyes enough to see Shawna staring back at me. "It's after dinner time, honey. You slept all day. You must get up and eat something or drink some water." I flip onto my other side and drift away on the water again. It's like years of insomnia have been building up to this moment to get all my sleep at once.

"Hey, Rosie, you have to drink some water. It's been over a day."

Bella is at my bedside with a straw in a water bottle. She runs her hand across my forehead to smooth my hair away, and for a moment, I loathe her for it. I don't want any kindness. I don't deserve any love.

I lift my head above the haze of the black water as much as my weak body will let me and take three long gulps from the straw, solely because I don't think she'll leave if I refuse. The hopeful look in Bella's face makes me sad for her. She doesn't realize yet that I live here now. I plan to stay in this bed for at least a hundred years.

"Do you want to maybe get up for a little bit and get something to eat?"

I stare at her blankly before answering her by shutting myself down again as the blackness claims me once more.

"Rosie, sweetie, you had a little accident. You need to let me change the sheets," I can hear Shawna saying as she forces me awake, my body catapulting out of the sweet nothingness. I smell the sticky, sour stench of urine, but embarrassment escapes me. I'm too tired. I shake my head and close my eyes again, and I can hear Shawna's dismay as she tries to keep me awake, but it's no use. The water has pulled me back down, and I'm floating blissfully in its vastness.

I weave in and out of consciousness as Shawna returns with Norah to lift me out of the bed and change my sheets and clothes. I whimper against Norah's chest, and I want to kick her and scream, but I can't summon the energy to cry. I'm like a boneless rag doll as Shawna gets me out of my muddy white wedding dress and into sweatpants and a t-shirt, but I won't let her take it. I clutch the dress to my body like a security blanket as Norah tucks me back in and kisses my forehead.

And it goes on like that for what feels like eons. People tiptoe their way into my bedroom to force food and water down my throat and try to get me out of bed. Meredith even brushes my teeth the way you would a dog's at one point. I know they're worried. I hear the whispers about taking me to the hospital, but even that doesn't rouse me.

The calm stillness of the black water that I associate with rest and sleep is too enticing to give up. I don't know if I could if I wanted to. I'm not even sure how much it has to do with Joshua. It's also my mom and my dad, and at the end of it all, it's me. The messed up bird nest of knots that makes up Rosaline Peters isn't worth it anymore.

"Rosie, can you wake up for me for a moment," a voice calls through the void. I let one eye crack open enough to see Cheryl Tibbons sitting in a chair beside my bed. I shoot straight into a sitting position for the first time in what must be days, and my head spins.

"What are you doing here?" I croak.

"I'm sure you understand your family's concern." I don't answer. "They called me to come check on you. Do you want to tell me what's going on, Rosie?"

I blink slowly and deliberately, answering her with every ounce of honesty left in my body, "No."

Her head nods slowly, her soft, comforting gaze locked on me like a laser beam. "Rosie, can you tell me about the dress you're clutching so hard?"

My finger runs along the stitching on the seam up the side of the dress, and it reminds me that it's real. It's all real.

"I didn't imagine this, Cheryl Tibbons," I murmur, my fingernail picking free a loose thread. "I didn't make it all up."

She makes no move to touch me, and I'm grateful.

"I know you didn't, Rosie." Then I drift back to sleep.

Kyle hasn't come. I'm sure it's my fault. I pushed too far and too hard. Now he's not coming back. I'm scorched earth anyway. He's better off without me. They all are and Joshua confirmed it for me. I keep drifting away.

"Sit up," Goldie's voice barks out to me in my depths. Like with Cheryl Tibbons, I allow only one eye to open. Goldie sits in that same chair beside my bed with a bowl of soup in her lap.

"Oh good, you're alive," she says dryly. "I'm fully prepared to feed you like you're a toddler, but you'll choke in the position you're in. Sit up."

I stare at her for a long moment and make no effort to move.

"Dude," Goldie mutters when I haven't moved, coming closer to my face. "I took off work from both jobs today to do this. I've got all the time in the world, but the second this soup gets cold enough, I'm waterboarding you with it."

The thing about Goldie, one of the things I usually love the most, is that she never makes an idle threat. I take a deep breath and roll onto my back, slouching on my elbows. Goldie scrapes the spoon on the edge of the bowl to remove the excess from the bottom and extends it to my mouth. Tomato basil usually is my favorite, but now it tastes like sludge. I do end up eating the entire bowl. It's better than wearing it. Goldie doesn't say a word the whole time. Scrape and feed, scrape and feed. After I eat, Goldie leaves—no time for chit-chat—and it's fine by me.

Back to the blackness I go.

I don't know how much time has passed. A week? A year? A hundred years? When you sleep nonstop, you lose track of the passing days. I don't care about missing school or work. I don't care about anything. The only thing that matters anymore is floating while trying not to drown.

"Enough!" Goldie shouts as she opens my shades and sunlight pours into the room. Footsteps scurry around my bed like I'm a sacrifice to some higher power. I wake to Blanche, Goldie, Bella, Elle, and Nixie standing on all sides of me. "It's time to get out of this bed."

I growl, flipping over to my side, gripping the dress closer, and sinking into my mattress.

"Go away."

"No," Goldie shouts, her arms crossed defiantly over her chest. "No more, Rosie. No more pity party. No more throwing yourself to the ground because you have some twisted idea that you deserve it. No more punishing yourself. It's over."

I stare at my best friend, my soul sister since birth, and I hate her.

"I am not getting out of this bed," I growl through my teeth.

The five of them trade looks amongst themselves, and it feels like I'm on the outside of a joke. "We'll see about that," Blanche announces. Then suddenly, it turns into a free-for-all of hands on my limbs and torso. My unused voice finds itself as I start screaming for them to let me go, but no one listens. I thrash like a boated marlin as they lift me off the bed, and we head toward my bathroom. Elle throws on the light and starts the shower. I start screaming louder, pulling every profanity I can remember from my back pocket. The water stings as Goldie and Blanche step into the tub with me, Blanche at my feet and Goldie at my head.

"Stop fighting us! Let us help you!" Nixie cries as she kneels beside the tub, ading the water temperature to make it more comfortable as though I can feel it.

"If you don't let me go right now, I will never forgive you," I scream into Goldie's perfect face, her hair dripping with water.

"I can take it!" she screams back. "I can take anything you've got—lay it on me!"

"I can take it too. Let me take some of it," Bella cries from beside my bathroom sink, her hand over her mouth as she softly sobs. Elle has her hand on Bella's shoulder, tears streaming down her cheeks. "Me too," she whispers when our eyes lock.

"We can take it, Rosie, let us take it," Blanche murmurs as she and Goldie shift down to their knees.

My weight settles into Goldie's chest, and I grab her arm as if I'm afraid she'll run away. An alien sob rips from my throat as the pain finds a valve to escape. Nixie places her hand on my hip and says, "Let us take it from you."

I let go of the white dress and let it hit the bathtub floor, the mud rinsing from it and swirling down the drain.

"I thought he loved me," I scream to the ceiling. "He told me he loved me. He told me he would marry me, and then he looked at me like I was crazy. I'm not crazy. I didn't make it up like he said. I didn't throw it out of proportion. He told me I was everything, and that's why I slept with him even though I didn't want to! Because he told me he loved me that much, and now I know I'll never be clean of it. He marked me with it, and I'm filthy. I'm so filthy!"

I'm gasping for air by the time my rant is over. It feels like I'm dying.

Blanche reaches through the stream of water and clasps my face in her hands as a steady river runs down her nose to say, "You didn't do a single thing wrong. I need you to hear me, Rosie. You didn't do anything wrong. He is the monster here who took advantage of you when you were vulnerable, and I'm so sorry. I'm sorry we couldn't protect you from it, but you are not dirty or broken or bad. You have to hear me. You must wake up and hear me." And I do.

The girls strip me of my clothes and wash me clean while I sob into the chest or shoulder of whichever one is holding me at the moment. They shampoo and condition my hair, scrub my face, and clean every inch of my body with such kindness and caring that it nearly breaks whatever resolve I have left. For the most part, Goldie stays behind me and hugs my shoulders, occasionally kissing me on the head.

A simple truth dawns on me while they're caring for me that I had never considered before. True love isn't always what we read in story books as little girls. It's not the boy with empty promises he never intends to keep. It's the people who will drag you to the shower, kicking and screaming and refusing to let you go even when you tell them you hate them. It's the people who tell you, "I can take it," when you're in agony and you can barely keep living.

True love is my friends, this family I've created. I can't believe I ever doubted it.

Somehow, the six of us fit on my little twin-sized bed, crammed together like cozy sardines. I'm nestled between Goldie's legs while she brushes my wet hair.

"I don't get how I got this far into it with him. I'm not a crazy person to let someone treat me like that."

Blanche puts her hand on my knee. "Rose, you didn't do anything wrong. This situation is all on him."

It doesn't seem that way to me. "I feel stupid. How could I not see this?"

"You ever heard the story about the frog and boiling water?" Bella asks from the foot of my bed.

"Oh, is it time for life lessons with fables?" Elle asks with a smile.

"Yes," Bella responds before turning to me. "If you throw a frog into a pot of boiling water, it will jump out immediately because it knows it's too hot. But if you put it in a pot of cool water and slowly heat it, the frog will be on fire before it even knows the water's warm."

"All of this to say what, Confucius?" Nixie asks.

"All of this to say, if Joshua had been a total jerk right from the start, you would never have gotten involved with him. Instead, he was overly affectionate and told you everything you wanted to hear, making you fall in love with him. Then he started to change, right?" I nod. "You were in too deep with him before you could ever realize anything was wrong."

Blanche squeezes my hand. "He took advantage of your hurt and sadness, and it is not your fault."

"Tell us about the dress, Rosie," Goldie says as the brush's bristles scratch against my scalp. I retrieved the soaked garment from the shower floor and held it in my lap. Even though I now know it was all bullshit, I can't seem to let it go.

My finger traces the delicate lace neckline, and my face flushes with embarrassment. It's beyond humiliating now.

"He told me we were going to move in together after graduation and that we were going to get married right away. I made this so we wouldn't have to wait longer than we had to. God, I'm an idiot!" I crumble up the dress and throw it to the ground.

"It's a beautiful dress, Rosie." Bella picks it up, spreading it across hers and Elle's legs. "You did a great job on it."

"Not that that's any surprise," Elle adds, dubbing a finger along the trim. "Making clothes and pies, these are her superpowers."

"Yeah, speaking of that, are we still getting prom dresses?" Blanche asks. "Because otherwise, I have shopping that I don't want to do."

Elle's face pinches. "Ew, yeah, me too. I'd much rather be one of the first to receive a Rosie Peters design. It'll be worth a lot of money someday."

"We could sell them online after she's famous," Nixie grins.

"You guys still want me to make you dresses?" The hope that flickers in my body warms a part of my soul that has been utterly freezing for weeks.

Elle picks up my ruined wedding dress and smiles. "If you could make something this beautiful because of that douche canoe, I can't wait to see what you'd make for us."

I smile despite myself and nod a few times, sniffing away tears. "Yeah, I'd like to do that." And it feels good to mean it.

The moment I dread comes, and the girls eventually have to leave. That puts me alone in the house with the aunts, and I have yet to forget the fact that they've been lying to me my whole life about my father. Considering I haven't eaten any food voluntarily in days, I head to the kitchen to eat until my stomach explodes. When I emerge from my bedroom, the aunts sit around the table eating dinner and look at me like a ghost. It seems like a crossroads position. I could make a plate and hide away from them again, or I could face it. I choose the latter. I sit at the head of the table between Norah and Shawna, across from Meredith. I make a point to look at only my mashed potatoes. I shovel the food like a wild animal into my mouth, barely pausing to chew before painfully swallowing. I'm detached from my body, as if I'm going through the motions.

I stay glued to my plate as I open my mouth to speak. "I'm going to tell you this once, and then I never want you to bring it up again," I begin, mimicking Norah's words that she'd used to me as a child. "Your father isn't around and doesn't want to be a part of your life. The hell with him. We're not going to give him another thought." I look up and lock my gaze with hers. Her fork hovers over her plate, frozen.

"Do you remember saying that to me?"

She lays her utensil down beside her plate. "I do."

Then I turn my attention to Meredith. "And do you remember telling me you didn't know much about him or where he was? Do you remember that?" She doesn't speak, but she doesn't deny it either. I look over to Shawna, whose crestfallen face resembles a child in trouble with a parent instead of the other way around. "And I guess you were in on this, too?"

"Rosie," Meredith begins, but I have no interest in giving her a chance to explain. There's not an explanation in the world that could ify their deception.

"My whole life, my WHOLE life, the three of you made me believe that my father had no interest in me, and all the while, you were sending him updates on me. What is wrong with you?" I bark, slamming my fist down on the table.

"We were protecting you," Norah declares with a set jaw. I can tell she's stuck between yelling at me for an outburst and eating crow for her mistakes.

"Come on. What were you protecting me from? I understand he didn't want to meet or know me in person, but you've been feeding him information for almost two decades. What did anyone gain from letting him know me but not letting me know him?"

"It's complicated, Rosie—" Meredith begins, but I won't have any part of it.

"Stop with your 'It's complicated,' Meredith. Everything is always complicated. You guys betrayed me. How can I ever be okay with that?" I ask, tears brimming, but I kept myself in check.

"If that's how you feel," Norah says, her voice cold and even.

"And what? Did you bar him from the house? He hasn't been here, has he?" I demand, returning to the shoveling of my food.

The aunts all trade a nervous look that immediately kills my appetite. "Kyle flew back to Oregon earlier this week," Meredith says calmly, her hands folded on the table.

The panic on my face must be evident because Shawna quickly chimes in, "But it was a planned trip. He isn't running away."

It should make me feel better, but it doesn't. I'm suddenly overwhelmed with the knowledge that I want him around. Even though he lied to me and never wanted to be here, I want him now. I want my father. I can't escape the terror that floods me at the idea that he might not come back.

I pick up my plate and take it back to the kitchen. Shawna tries to get up with me, but Norah stops her, and that's smart. In my current state, I'm capable of saying anything to them, and as mad as I am, I still wouldn't want to do that to Shawna.

"You have an appointment with your therapist in the morning," Meredith calls out as I go to my room. That's good because she's the only one I want to talk to.

My mother told me once that clothing choices had strong ties to our identities. It was important to dress for where you wanted to go, not where everyone assumed you should be. Even in her lowest points, she was always stylish. I found myself in awe of her. I've lost a little bit in that area of my life since she died. It's like she took that part of me with her. I stare into my closet, now divided between my before-her-death and after-her-death clothes. On one side, a sea of black that's comforting in its familiarity but also reminds me too much of the cold back water that I'm in no hurry to return to. On the other, all the new clothes. They look much more like 90s sitcoms than the others. Neither feels right on its own, but to combine them might be the solution. I take a pair of loose-fitting jeans, an old, tight black shirt, and a pair of red Keds. I leave my hair down and wavy and abandon the white powder makeup. I like my skin the way it is. I throw on some mascara, my classic red lip, and a thick red headband. The person staring back at me is a stranger, but she looks like someone I could become friends with.

Cheryl Tibbons is wearing a fitted white dress today, which is quite the departure from her flowy bohemian style. I guess we're both exploring different avenues of fashion.

"You look a little better than the last time I saw you," she says with a smile as we sit down together.

I fiddle with my hands in my lap. "Well, that wouldn't be hard to do, would it?"

She smiles a soft and knowing grin before flipping open the cover of her tablet. "Where would you like to start today?" I unload the whole story on her because that's what she's here for. I started back to meeting Joshua for the first time, up to our accelerated love affair, to making my wedding dress, and to him breaking my heart. All the while, Cheryl Tibbons nods along and listens.

"I don't know how I could be this blind. I swear to you, I didn't blow anything out of proportion or make any of it up like Joshua said I did."

My head drops into my hands. I feel crazier every time I go through this, even with myself.

"Are you familiar with the term gaslighting Rosie?" I shake my head. "It is a form of manipulation where someone gets you to doubt your sanity. They warp and twist things you know happened a certain way to make you feel as if you're wrong or crazy."

An acidic taste burns at the back of my throat as the icy chill of the black water pools at my feet.

"There's also a concept called love-bombing that I'd like to discuss if you're up to it for a second." She waits for some kind of response from me, but I can feel the black water invading my periphery. My only option is to nod. I want to know and don't all at the same time.

"Now, at the beginning of relationships, everyone wants to make a good impression. People are usually on their best behavior and trying hard to put their best foot forward. The difference between infatuation and love bombing can be difficult to spot, especially when living in real-time. I want to make sure you know that. When someone pushes love too fast, claiming that marriage was coming immediately after only a few weeks of knowing each other—" embarrassment fills every fiber of my body at this statement. "—or claiming that they are your soulmate right away—those proclamations can mask some other malicious intent. Often, that person wants some form of control, and if they bombard you with love early on, they can more easily attain that control. Now, combine love-bombing with gaslighting, and it's not surprising to me that you feel a little crazy, but I promise you, you're not."

What she's saying to me should be reassuring. She's validating every feeling I'm having and yet I can't loosen the grip that the black water has on me right now.

"I feel incredibly stupid. I thought that Joshua loved me, and I loved him, but how could that have even been possible? I knew him only briefly before he told me he loved me. You can't love someone that fast. I should have known that."

"Why? Why should you have known that? Your mother recently died, Rosie. Your father popped up for the first time in your life. There was pressure from the people around you to discuss things you didn't want to, and then someone came into your world and said everything you wanted to hear at the time. It's completely understandable that you believed what he was telling you. At that point, you had no reason to doubt him. Abusers have a way of finding emotionally vulnerable people, and that is not your fault.

My spine stiffens. "Abuser? He never hit me," I shriek, my entire body twisting and rejecting the notion.

"There are many types of abuse that never involve that kind of violence, and if you don't want me to use that term, that's completely fine. I won't. But I'm wondering if you might indulge me for a moment. If at any point you want to stop, we stop. Okay?"

I take a deep breath and nod. I don't want to do this, but I know I must.

"Did Joshua ever express a negative opinion over the clothes you would wear or even tell you what you should or shouldn't wear?"

I can't help but remember the look on his face when he first saw me in my usual black clothes.

"Did he ever try to put a wedge between you and your friends or your family?"

He did everything he could to keep me from my friends, especially Blanche.

"Did he ever weaponize his attention? Punish you with silence or threaten to cut you off from him if you were doing something he didn't like?"

Every emotion chokes me as every box checks itself off.

"Did he ever manipulate you into doing anything that made you uncomfortable—something you didn't want to do?"

"I didn't want to sleep with him." The tears fell free over the edge of my lids, "I really didn't."

Her face is as soft and comforting as ever. She nods and says, "I know you didn't, Rosie. None of this is your fault, and I'm sorry."

A sob rips from my throat as reality fills in all the cracks. Surprisingly, the black water doesn't suffocate me like I thought it would at the acknowledgment. It rushes from my body like a broken dam. Cheryl Tibbons keeps talking, and I listen my best, but the lethargy is weighing down every limb. We plan to meet again in a few days. She doesn't feel comfortable letting me go a whole week after this "breakthrough," as she calls it, and I agree. She hasn't led me wrong yet.

I should go home. I'm going back to school tomorrow and should take the time to prepare for it, but I can't face the aunts yet. I'm not ready to forgive or to pretend. As I usually do, I make my way to the pie shop. It hasn't held the needed comfort as of late. Now, the relief and utter joy that fills me when it comes into view practically has me galloping to the front door. The smell of sugar and butter wraps me up like a warm hug. Bella sat behind the counter and smiled when she looked up from her book.

"Hey, it's good to see you," she says.

The door to the kitchen swings open, and Allisin comes skipping out with the biggest smile stretched across her face. Running into me full force with the biggest hug, practically scooping me off the floor, she shouts, "Oh my god! You're here! I've missed you so much. Are you feeling better? Pneumonia is the worst! I'm so sorry." I glance over her shoulder at Bella, who nods and mouths, "Go with it." I appreciate my friends not airing my business in public.

"Yeah, yeah, I'm feeling a lot better. I'm sorry I left you here to hold down the fort alone." Allisin wraps her arm over my shoulders, and I instinctively put mine around her back. I'm not big on letting new friends into my circle, but Allisin was too easy to love.

"Pssh, don't even worry about that. It was kind of fun figuring out how to fly solo. Could only do it because I learned from the master, of course," she says. I'm only slightly panicked when I see that she's moved some things, but I know I can move them back without offending her.

"We've been moving blueberry pies like nobody's business the last few days, but I've already made two. We should be good for a little bit. Do you want to do an inventory and see what we need?" she asks, her words going a mile a minute. Her energy level is bananas; I'm only catching every third word.

"I came here with one specific task if that's okay. I promise tomorrow I'll be back full force and normal."

She places her hands on my wrists and smiles brightly. "Whatever you need, Rosie, we're a team." I like the sound of that.

There's only one pie I'm interested in making today. It's a twist on a classic, something in my head I call a *You Were Right, and I Was Wrong, and I'm Sorry I Didn't Listen to You in the First Place Apple Pie*. The title needs a little work, but the sentiment is there. I go to work making a classic crust, a rhythmic demonstration in muscle memory as I mash together cubed cold butter and flour into a dough. I lose myself in the sound of my black rolling pin covered in roses, a Christmas gift from

Shawna. I feel bad for ignoring Allisin, who's back to talking a mile a minute, but I have a job to do. I set aside the crust and peeled apples into the shapes of roses. It's a bit extra, but this is an apology pie. It's time to pull out all the bells and whistles. I combine all the spices and sugar and start to make caramel on the stove—all the things I know she loves. It gets wrapped up in a beautiful pie and placed in the oven, where I watch it through the window, turning from simple ingredients to a finished product. It's my favorite kind of magic.

The pie is truly majestic with its scalloped edges. The apple roses have baked through perfectly, and the caramel has formed the ideal crust on the top. It's my masterpiece. I hope she likes it. Once the pie is cooled, I wrap it in one of our pink boxes and tie it with twine. I'm probably going overboard, but this is worth over-the-top preparation. I hop in my car and head to New Shiloh. I approach the front door, knock with all the confidence of your garden variety chicken, and wait with my knees, knocking for any answer. The man on the other side of the opening door has me checking to see if I have the right house. "Can I help you?" he asks, shrugging himself into his jacket, clearly on the way out.

"Oh, sorry, I must have the wrong house. I was looking for Blanche?" I question, taking a tentative step back.

"You have the right house. I'm her dad. Blanche!" he calls out into the house before brushing past me. "You have a guest, and I'm heading out."

"Of course you are," she calls back dryly as she walks down the stairs. "Hey, what are you doing here?"

I lift the pie box, "Can we talk?"

The pie disappears in a matter of seconds. I should have expected as much in a house with seven boys—the mere mention of food brought on a swarm. Luckily, Blanche can snag a piece for herself. Her little sounds with each bite tell me all my choices are correct. It fills me with a unique type of joy.

"I know you didn't come here to bring me pie—one of your finest, I might add."

"I owe you a big apology, bigger than a pie." She leans back in her seat and waits. "You were right about Joshua; I was cruel to you. You didn't deserve that. I've been a rotten friend since my mother died, and I'm sorry."

"The week after my mom died, I punched Thomas in the face. I broke his nose."

My eyes grow to the size of saucers.

"You did what?!"

She chuckles to herself, her smile flushing her cheeks, illuminating the freckles she inherited from her father. "Oh yeah. I was an insufferable little shit. I yelled at everyone, and my grades dropped at school. My dad didn't know what to do with me." She sighs deeply, recalling the memories with a touch of shame. "Look, I understand not being the best version of yourself when someone you love dies."

While heartwarming, the guilt still overwhelms me. "But I was awful to you. You knew Joshua better than me, and I wouldn't listen."

"Look, Josh was telling you what you thought you wanted to hear while the rest of us were saying what you needed to hear—which wasn't desirable to you. Again, I can understand the appeal of that. Grief can be crippling. You took comfort in the one person who let you be without repercussions. That's not your fault. He's a snake, and trusting him with your heart is not a failure on your part."

"You don't have to be nice about this? You can make me work a little harder for forgiveness," I say, pushing my crumbs around my plate.

She thinks it over, tapping her index finger against her chin.

"I'll make you a deal. You make my prom dress first, and we'll call it even." We shake on it, and things feel a little more okay.

At home, the house is quiet. If there's one lesson I've learned through all this, you can't avoid things or people. You have to face them eventually. Norah and Meredith sit in the living room watching television while Shawna cleans the kitchen.

"I'm home," I declare before making a bee line to my bedroom. No one tries to stop me, and, for only a moment, it makes me sad. I strip out of my clothes and into something comfortable and remove my makeup before crawling into my bed.

When the lights are off, I lay back and stare at the ceiling, and all the emotions that I've suppressed bubble up and over. New glow-in-the-dark stars and moons are there—a little gesture from the aunts that means a lot. For the first time in a while, I drift to sleep without the black water anywhere in sight.

CHAPTER SEVENTEEN

Goldie whispers, "I wish I could have my profile lit like Barbara Stanwyck in her movies." She leans across for more popcorn in the middle of *Double Indemnity*. Nixie joined us for this adventure but bailed after the end of *The Lady Eve*. She isn't built for old movie marathons like me and Goldie.

"That would be lovely, but if we're wishing for things, I wish they'd reupholster these seats already." The itchy red fabric has given me at least three rashes over my lifetime, and chunks of stuffing are missing from every cushion. Two separate springs are poking into my legs, and it's maddening. I've asked Beau many times if the owners would let us fund raise to fix them, but he says that The Representative is an institution and must remain as it is.

"I said you should bring something to sit on," Goldie says, motioning to her Orioles seat cushion. "I'm a pro at this theater."

The marathon lets out a little after one in the morning, and we join Beau at the concession stand before heading out. He's sweeping a massive pile of popcorn off the burgundy carpet. "That's a tragedy," Goldie laments, motioning to the lost food. The girl loves her movie snacks.

Beau looks up with heated cheeks before immediately looking back at the floor. "Yeah, Mrs. Johnson has butterfingers. Did you guys like the movies?" he asks, tugging at the bow tie of his uniform. If I can't have the updated seats, I wish the work uniform could be. Beau deserves that. The tuxedo white shirt, black bow tie, and red vest went out of style in the eighties. I could bribe the owners with a prototype uniform and pie. I make a mental note to come back to this later.

Goldie sighs dramatically and leans her elbows on the counter, balancing her chin on her hands. Beau freezes in place. "Barbara is my favorite Cathy," she says wistfully, and I can't help but roll my eyes. She's such a hopeless romantic. *Wuthering Heights* would be her favorite of the movies we saw tonight.

"And you, Friend?" he asks, glancing at me over the brim of his glasses.

"*Double Indemnity* all the way. Barbara Stanwyck *and* Gary Cooper are chef's kiss, baby," I answer with a laugh, and this all feels so human that, for a moment, I'm fully back in my body, and I've missed it here.

"You've got a lot of Barbara in you, Friend," Beau says, stowing the broom away and wiping down the counter.

Goldie surveys me with thoughtful consideration. She smiles and says, "I can totally see that! You're absolutely a Barbara!" And they don't know it, but it's one of the best compliments I've ever gotten.

Goldie and I part ways at the pie shop. She's off to sleep, and I'm off to create. I'm energized with that new Stanwyck vibe and want to use it. I catch sight of that stupid, coin-operated horse on the porch of the drugstore. Its chipped and faded paint mocks me right along with the soulless eyes. I've had to walk by that horse every day since my mother left me on it—makes me sick to see it. I remember Pop's offer to destroy it, and part of me wishes I had a sledgehammer. Skipping up the steps, I look around and see if there's anything I can smash it with. I run my fingers along the cold, metal surface and use my fingernails to pick away some paint chips. It's a sad little horse. Lifting my leg, I kick into it once, twice, three times, and my breath escapes in gasps. The rage starts to bubble up inside me, and I can feel the black water creep around my feet.

Why won't this thing die? Why can't I destroy it?

I freeze.

Why do I want to destroy it?

It didn't do anything. In fact, I loved it when I was little. I collapse to a sitting position, staring at this mechanical horse with that same plastered expression it always had. I compare it to The Representative and the poor states they are in. Leaving something the way it is because it's always been that way isn't an answer. I know what I want to do.

I run to the pie shop fast enough that the black water can't follow me. In Beattie's office closet, I found all the painting supplies we used to paint the pie mural in the bathroom after opening. I remember locking the shop in my frenzy before I made my way back to the drugstore. Dropping all the painting supplies, I take a moment to look and truly see the horse in front of me. The kids don't ride it anymore. It still works fine. If I put a quarter in right now, it would rock the same way it did on that day when I was eleven, but no one uses it. Not that I can blame them. With its faded paint and jarring expression, I probably wouldn't let my kid on it without a tetanus shot, either. I put my hand on its head and leaned close to whisper, " because you're beaten up doesn't make you worthless."

The horse can't hear me, but I know who I'm actually talking to.

By the time I pack the supplies back into Beattie's closet, the sun peeks over the tops of the buildings. The formally rusted and gray horse is now a happy pale purple and blue, with lashes and a smile. The sense of accomplishment I felt after was borderline ridiculous, but I took an enemy and made it a friend.

I'm about to leave when Beattie's office door opens, and she walks in.

"Do you ever go home?" she exclaims. "Do I need to take away your keys?"

I haven't talked to Beattie much recently, but one of our last conversations still sits heavy with me. I didn't give her a chance to talk about it.

"What was her name? Your daughter? I know you told me before, but I'm having trouble remembering." I ask, sitting in one of the weird blue plastic chairs across from Beattie's desk. I've been unfair to her, and she didn't deserve it.

She watches me curiously, "Clementine," she says, her voice softer than I'm used to from her.

Before I know what I'm saying, I blurt out, "Do you ever hate her for dying?" Her eyes widen and tears flood mine. I slam my hand over my mouth. "I mean—"

"Not hate per se. But sometimes I'm angry with her for dying and leaving me here," she responds. "That's horrible for a mother to say, but it's true. I'm angry at her. I'm angry at God and Clementine's father. I'm angry at the doctors that couldn't save her. I'm angry at everyone where she's concerned."

I bite down so hard on my lower lip that I taste blood. There's a truth inside me that I'm afraid to let out again, but as I feel the black water start to choke me, I choose to let it go. "I hate her more for dying than I do for her leaving or even using drugs."

"Why do you think that is?" she asks. I try to shrug it off like I don't know, but Beattie's having none of it. She waits.

"Death seems to elevate people to sainthood. I don't like it when anyone speaks poorly about her, ever. But her dying doesn't suddenly make her this wonderful mother and person. When she was gone, it was more okay to be angry with her, but now it's not, and I'm so confused and mad all the time."

"Hey," she says, reaching out and taking my hand. Her grip is firm, her silver rings pressing into my skin. "You can be as angry with your mom for as long as you need to be. She hurt you too many times for you not to be."

"I thought she'd get it together someday, at least enough to come back and visit. I keep centering on that last moment with her that I didn't know was our last moment. She walked away from me while I was riding on that stupid horse. The last thing I saw was the back of her head when I was a kid. I didn't have anything profound to say."

"What would you say to her now?" Beattie asks.

"What do mean?"

She shrugs and says, "It's something to think about. I'm not a big hippie-dippy person, but consider writing her a letter and go read it to her."

"Go where? She's dead." Beattie stares. I groan, "You want me to go talk to a gravestone."

"I'm not telling you to do anything, but sometimes it's cathartic to yell at them even if they can't yell back."

"Would you tell me a little bit about Clementine?" A smile spreads across Beattie's face, and it's like she's been waiting years for someone to ask.

I'm thankful to have a project to lose myself in that has nothing to do with my mother, my father, Joshua, or college. Something I can focus my attention and energies on and forget everything else. Sew Cute has become my second home recently, blowing my entire paycheck on fabric for my friends' prom dresses. A pretty periwinkle blue for Elle, a vibrant red for Blanche, gold for Goldie, and a soft sea foam green for Nixie, who is going to our prom with someone from the swim team even though she's only a junior. I've even started sketching something in purple for myself, and I swore I would NEVER go to prom. I guess it's the season of surprises. My look keeps updating, too. Personal style is an ever-evolving organism that one must update or die, but I also know I'd be lying if I said my mother and Joshua hadn't had something to do with it. I've started wearing colors and denim. I even made my first pair of jeans. Everything has my flare, of course, and there's still plenty of black. The black returned on my terms, because I like it now, and less that I feel I have something to prove.

The acceptance letter from Parsons remains pinned to my corkboard, directly across from where I sit at my sewing machine. I can't ignore it much longer, and I have to decide. But there's something still pulling down deep in my soul. I'm suffocating at the bottom of the sea of black water, and I can't seem to find the surface. I'm convinced I deserve to go, but I can't seem to take the plunge.

"I look like an Oscar statue," Goldie whines, standing on a chair in my bedroom in the bodice of her dress. The crew is here for measurements and fittings; one or two are crankier than others.

"If you don't stop moving, I'm going to poke you, and if you get blood on this fabric, I do not have more," I mumble around the straight pins pressed between my lips. "It won't look like this when I'm finished."

At the moment, Goldie's dress is a golden sack. She is tall and curvy which requires more precise tailoring. Blanche is digging through my closet like she lost something, pulling out item after item."

"Rosie Rose, have you been doing anything other than sewing? It's like you have a whole new wardrobe here!" She holds a black and white gingham romper with pressed and pleated rose appliqués on the shoulder. "I need to borrow this."

"You're like eight feet taller than I am," I laugh, helping Goldie shimmy out of her bodice. "When I finish with the dresses, I'll be happy to make you something similar." And it's true, it would bring me joy. I don't know why anyone does drugs when the euphoria of making fashion exists.

"I accept," she says, shoving the garment back into my closet and searching for other things I can replicate.

"Hells Bells," I call to Bella, who's lost in a beat-up paperback copy of Frankenstein on my bed. "I know you're not coming to prom, but I'd be happy to make you something, too if you'd like." Bella's home-schooled, but she deserves a lovely formal gown as well. Besides, I would love to practice making more plus-sized clothes.

Bella closes her finger in the book, shifts her weight to her elbows, and smiles. "There is a beautiful yellow gown hanging up in my closet from a magical night that would put your proms to shame. I am all set, thank you." We've all heard little details about her Christmas celebration in New York, where she fell in love with Conrad. But she's kept the most juicy bits to herself. "But if you're taking orders, I'd like one of those rompers, too."

"Oh my God, we could make them the uniforms for the pie shop!" Goldie exclaims with a clap of her hands.

"Yeah, not like it ever gets cold in Maryland. We could bounce around in those all year," Elle teases, hopping up on the chair for her turn. Elle is more like a runway model with a thin, long frame—more highways and fewer country roads. I've been able to do more with her gown already.

"Stifle all my creative thoughts, why don't you," Goldie giggles, still completely nude from the waist up.

"Golds," Nixie sighs. "Seeing your boobs isn't on my bingo card for today; think you can put a shirt on?"

"No need to be a prude, Nixie Wixie," Goldie laughs as her tank top slips over her head. "Who are you going to our prom with again?"

"One of the guys from the swim team," Nixie replies, applying a copious number of layers of purple polish to her short, chewed nails.

"A guy from the swim team?" I ask around my straight pins. It's not advertised that Nixie's into girls, mainly because she's afraid of her parents finding out, but the five of us know the truth.

Nixie shrugs, closing up the nail polish bottle. "You know Harpersgrove is a relic from the past. Two girls aren't allowed to go to prom together. And we're going as friends anyway."

"Rosie," Goldie begins, switching up the conversation. "I was leaving the drugstore today, and I noticed someone made some changes to the kiddie horse. Do you know anything about that?".

"Well, Pop had given me permission to destroy it, so I decided that also gave me permission to fix it up." It probably didn't, but no one seems mad about it.

"But isn't that the horse—Ouch!" Elle begins, and I accidentally stick her with a pin. Consciously, it was an accident. I don't want to talk about that.

"Have you heard from Kyle?" Bella asks. I shake my head. I haven't heard a word from Kyle since the night I left his house, and I can't fight the feeling that he's never coming back. It bothers me far more than I'm comfortable with.

Thankfully, the conversation goes back to easier topics, like how everyone will do their hair and makeup to go with their dresses, and I can relax. While packing up the last of my pins and hanging Nixie's dress back in the closet, my phone buzzes with a text from my pocket. "Hey baby…" the text reads. It's from Joshua.

I don't tell the girls about the text. I also don't delete it or block his number like I probably should. I don't bring it up at therapy, and I don't tell the aunts or Beau. In my defense, I also don't answer it, but I do read those two words about twenty thousand times. I'm disgusted with myself for it, but a thrill rushes through me at the fact that he reached out. The concept that he still thinks about me twists my stomach in pleasant knots, and I don't understand why. He's a bad guy. I know that. I don't want him anymore. I know that, too. And yet I keep finding my fingers hovering over the keyboard on my phone to message him back before something snaps me back to reality to stop me.

One morning, hard at work at my sewing machine for a few hours before heading to the pie shop, Meredith walks in and sits on my bed. "What's up?" I ask, never taking my focus off the needle. That's how you get pricked.

"I got a call last night from your mom's roommate in Baltimore," the needle catches my finger. "She found someone to take your mom's room and wanted to give us a chance to retrieve any of her things that we want, and I'd like you to come with me."

It's like asking for the eulogy all over again; that cold edge of black water begins to creep in through the door and slosh around my ankles. "I don't know Mere—"

"I get that it's a lot for you," she interrupts, tears rimming her eyes. They look like glass marbles. "Don't do it for you or her. Do it for me. She was my baby, Rosie, like you are. I can't do this by myself." I knew then, and maybe I've always known, that I would do anything for Meredith.

For some reason, in my mind, there were only two options for the kind of place my mother could've been living. Option one could've been an utterly dilapidated crack house—broken windows, hypodermic needles, trash littering the front lawn, and the whole shebang. Option two is a full white picket fence house in the middle of suburbia with a replacement family and a dog.

Never in my wildest dreams did I imagine that she would live on a street in the middle of the city in an apartment. For some reason, this outcome seems even more distressing than the crack house. The street is clean and quiet. All the windows are intact. Parked at the curb next to a tree is a BMW. The question enters my mind like it always has. Why couldn't she live with me if she could live somewhere like this?

My mom's roommate was a woman named Rainbow. She has rainbow dreadlocks, which are a little too on the nose for me. She offers us each a drink and then shows us to Mom's room. I find her unsettling. I expected anyone who lived with my mother to be like her, and while Rainbow may be a drug addict like Mom, she doesn't strike me as the type. Was Mom getting better? That seems highly unlikely, considering how she died. Rainbow opened the bedroom door, and much like the street she lives on, I don't exactly know what I was expecting. Maybe tourniquets all around with needles on the floor and a strung-out boyfriend on the bed waiting for her to come back. But that's not what I find. It's surprisingly neat—bed made, and clothes put away in the dresser and the closet. It feel furious. I suppose I wanted to come here and find out she was a disaster who had to leave me. But no, true to form, Holly Peters was a selfish woman who chose her own independent life over a life with me I should've known better. Meredith must sense my stress because she grabs my arm and reassuringly squeezes it. She tells me we need to look for a minute, and then we can go home. I know she thinks I'll regret it if I don't, but that's not true. I already know everything I need to know about her; simply being here has confirmed it.

"It's a shame, you know," Rainbow says from the hallway. "Holly got her six-month chip a week before it happened. She was doing really good."

"Not good enough," I grumble.

"I get why you'd say that," Rainbow responds. "But I was proud of her." With that, she leaves us, and I somehow feel even worse.

Meredith starts with her dresser, pulling out her clothes to see if there's anything worth keeping, and I flop down on her bed, instantly overwhelmed by her perfume wafting off the sheets. Tears flood my eyes as the scent brings back memories I haven't thought about in years. That smell is my mother.

Okay, fine. It wouldn't hurt to look around.

I go to the closet. If there's one thing my mother and I could agree on, it was fashion. What was her sense of style over the years? Was she still edgy? Has she taken on a more conservative look? Was she sweater sets and strings of pearls girl or still biker jackets and leather pants? After pulling back the white accordion door, I find it's a little mixture of both. Mainly a lot of t-shirts and jeans. There's a box of records that I push to the side. I'll need to take those home with me later. Getting in touch with her musical taste might tell me more about her than words ever could.

Meredith and I go to work, understanding what's left of my mother's life. It's sad to think that one day, we're all reduced to this—boxes and letters, scrunchies and take-out boxes, sweaters, and receipts. Micro archaeological digs for our families to go through and figure out who we were. But can any of this tell me anything about her? I'm a different person than I was on the day she walked away from me. A sob rips through me, and I try my best to swallow it. I don't want Meredith to hear. I want to know my mom. I want to know how she felt on September 11th. I want to know if she cried when Heath Ledger died. Did she watch award shows? Did she eat raw cookie dough? Did she dance in the rain? What did she care about? What did she love? Nothing here is going to tell me those things.

We've nearly sorted everything into boxes to keep and trash bags to throw away when Meredith gasps from the other side of the room.

"What's the matter?" I ask, looking up from the box of records.

She pulls out a shoe box from under the bed. Covered with magazine clippings of purple flowers, one word, Rosie, is on the top. Meredith places it on my lap and rests her hand on my cheek. "I'll give you a minute."

My hands are shaking to the point of convulsion. For this moment, I'm still safe. I can't go back to before, not knowing that this box exists, but how on earth do I go forward and find out what's inside? I must reach deep down and harness some inner strength because I have to know. Ignorance is not a privilege that I have. If I want to know her, this may be my only chance. I lift off the lid and set it aside, finding the box stuffed to the brim with cards.

Each one varies in age and color. Where do I even begin? What is this? I pull out an orange envelope with a turkey card inside. "Happy Turkey Day," the card reads. Many others are the same: birthday cards with simple notes for each year she missed. There are Christmas cards and many postcards detailing what she was doing that day. They mainly seem like notes to me. Updating me on her day, her life, and what was happening then. I could have had conversations with her around the dinner table, but I could only have them now with her through these cards. I wanted something more—something profound. Did I mean as little to her as I always feared?

At the bottom of the box is a longer envelope designed to fit a letter, not a card. I set the box aside and pull the stuffed envelope to my chest. It is the last chance, the last words I will ever read of hers. Questions swirl through my head. Should I open it? Should I let myself pretend it's more than it could be. What if she lets me down again? What if this contains adoption papers for the aunts? What if this reinforces that she never wanted me at all? Is that something I could take?

It's funny; I've always considered myself an insomniac, but I think it is a solid possibility that until this point, I have been sleeping through my entire life. I have drifted through most things, worried about taking a chance because it might hurt me. No one can deny that my mother hurt me. Maybe I've spent this life underachieving to punish her. I don't think I want to do that anymore. It's time to put her to rest.

I flip the envelope over and run my finger across the seal. For a moment, I envision her sitting on this bed, licking the glue, and closing it shut. I dig my finger into the gap and rip it open. Inside are multiple pieces of loose-leaf paper torn straight from a notebook. My hands are still shaking as I unfold it. It's a letter. A letter she wrote to me.

My dearest Rosie,

I'm honestly not sure where you'll be in your life when you read this. I guess that's if you read it at all. I wonder if you're grown or if you're still a child. Did I give this to you myself? Or did one of the aunts give it to you? I hope I get to hand it to you personally.

I've started this letter so many times since the day I left. But, finally, I decided to sit down and write it on this day, the day that you turned 13. The idea that I have a teenager is wild to me, Rosie. And I'm sorry that I'm not there to celebrate with you.

I wish I could tie everything up in a neat little bow for you about why I left. But even at a young age, you can figure out some of it. You were always much smarter than me. But there's one thing I need you to know before I take this any further.

None of this, Rosie, none of this, is your fault.

You are not to blame for me leaving. You are not to blame for my substance use. You, my beautiful girl, are the reason I was born at all. My life's purpose was to bring you into this world. I figured that out the first time I held you. I wish I were a stronger person who could've given you a better life myself, but I'm not. I will never forgive myself if you spend one more day after reading this believing that any of the bad things were your doing. I need you to hear me, and I need you to know that you were never the problem, Rosie. You were always enough. You were worth so much that I knew I needed to leave you.

Thinking about this next part makes me sick to my very core, but I need you to understand. Do you remember that day, Rosie? The day that you watched me use drugs? That day, I knew I'd always be your mother, but I couldn't be your mom. And it's not because I didn't love you. I have more love for you than there are stars in the sky. I wanted nothing more than to be extremely selfish and stay with you. But you deserve better than me. Our aunts are good women, and I knew you'd be safe with them. But I can't tell you what it felt like to leave you that day on the horse in front of the drugstore. I felt like I was dying, Rosie. I know you couldn't see me, but I sobbed the entire time I was walking away from you.

There are some things I need to tell you, things you deserve to know. The main thing I want to say to you is about your father. His name is Kyle Roosevelt. And at 17 years old, he was the love of my life. You saw a picture of him once, one that I kept in my dresser. One of the biggest mistakes we all made was giving you any indication that he didn't want you. After we graduated, he called me. He told me that he was going to come back east. He was going to come back, and we could be a family. I was heartbroken and full of enough fury that I couldn't see beyond myself. Rosie, I'll never forgive myself for it. Your father wanted to be a part of your life. I told him that if he ever showed his face in Harpersgrove again I would take you and leave, and he would never know where we went. I told him that if he ever tried to contact you, I would make sure he could never find you again. The aunts think I don't know they've been in contact with him for years, but I knew. I feel horrible knowing that I denied him the opportunity to be your father. Please don't be angry with him. I gave him no choice.

I want you to have the most beautiful life because you deserve it. You deserve an existence bigger than Harpersgrove, bigger than the whole world. You should have better than anything I could ever give you. I hope that one day we'll reconnect—on your terms and in your way. Because even being a footnote in your story will be worth everything to me.

Don't be afraid to take chances, my beautiful girl. This world is made for little girls with stars in their eyes, and I saw them in yours the day you were born. Live bravely, live dangerously, and live well. Make choices that enhance your life. Surround yourself with people that brighten your light. And don't for a moment ever let anyone make you believe you can't do anything you want. You are the sun, my Rosaline. Know that I am the moon waiting every night to meet you at dawn.

All my love,

Holly

The paper feels like lead in my hands, the weight of it crashing down on me. I leave it on the blanket and wander into the living room in a nearly zombie-like daze, where Rainbow and Meredith share a cup of tea.

"Rainbow, do you have a computer I could borrow?"

Sitting on my mother's bed, holding this long-forgotten letter in my hands, I log onto the student portal on Rainbow's for Parsons. I officially claim my acceptance because I realize an error I've made all these years.

The greatest gift my mother ever gave me wasn't a sewing machine. It was my life. A life that she wanted to be so wonderful for me that she knew she couldn't be a part of it. I will not let her down. I will live fully, I will live dangerously, and I will have the future that she desperately wanted me to have.

CHAPTER EIGHTEEN

I don't let Meredith read the letter. I doubt I'll ever let anyone see it. We packed up Meredith's car with Holly's memories and shut the door on an empty room where my mother didn't live anymore. It's sad how empty it is, but I know it's okay.

"Are you all right?" Meredith asks on the drive home, and I realize I've been staring out the window the whole drive, holding my mother's letter in a vice grip inside my jacket pocket.

"Yeah, that was a lot," I answer, and it's true. "I've decided to go to college at Parsons."

Without a word, Meredith peels off to the side of the road in the middle of a comedically large dust cloud. Her seat belt flew off in a flash, and she reached across and pulled me into her. Her fingers interlock behind my back as she crushes me to her chest. I can feel her sobbing against my temple.

"It terrified me that you weren't going to go."

"Why? I make clothes."

"Oh, honey," she shakes her head, a smile cutting through all other emotions. "You don't make clothes. You take a piece of your soul and turn it into something tangible. You're an artist."

Imposter Syndrome sets in for letting myself even for a moment believe her. But if there's one thing I've learned, it's that the people who love you will lift you up until you believe in yourself. It's the ones who don't that urge you to fall.

A sort of peace comes over my body, and I ask her, "Would you drop me off somewhere?"

I asked Meredith to drop me off at Kyle's apartment. I couldn't wait another second to see him. What if he's not there and never comes back? I have enough money saved to fly to Oregon. I have to see him. I'll burst if I don't. His corny and overly friendly doormat smiles up at me, and I'm already crying. What should I say? How do I even begin to apologize? What I said to him the last time I saw him cut him to his core. Is it finally time for us to stop hurting each other?

Now is not a time to be timid. Live dangerously, Rosie, my mother had written. What could be more dangerous than taking a chance and letting my dad love me?

Be. Barbara. Stanwyck.

I stop for a moment because I'm not Barbara Stanwyck. There will never be another. I'm the first and only Rosie Peters, and that's enough.

My hands shake as I raise them to bang with both palms against the door like a certified crazy person. The door opens, and I'm taken aback by a woman on the other side.

"Can I help you?" she asks with a sweet but questioning smile.

I quickly glance up and check to make sure that I have the right address. This should be Kyle's apartment. "I'm sorry—," I begin, doubling away from her. My face flushed with embarrassment for making this mistake. Maybe this is all a sign that some things aren't in my power to fix. "I was looking for—"

"Rosie?" I hear Kyle call from behind the woman. He steps around her, and she slips back into the apartment. She looks very curious about me. Kyle looks worried. He always looks scared when it comes to me. I need to be brave a few moments longer.

I pull Mom's letter out of my pocket, and my hands shake. My lower lip begins to quiver. "You wanted me!" I sob, falling into his chest. "You wanted me, and she made you stay away."

Kyle never falters. He supports my weight and lifts me up. I think back to the girls telling me that they could carry it. I realize that Kyle can, too.

"Of course I wanted you," he cries into my hair, holding me as tight to him as he can.

"I'm sorry, Dad. I'm sorry," I cry into his chest, holding tight as though I'm worried he'll run away.

"You have nothing to be sorry for, baby, nothing," he says as he takes me inside, and it feels like coming home.

I find out the woman is my Aunt Helena, Kyle's sister. She wanted to meet me and came back from Oregon with my father. While she's busy making tea and snacks in the kitchen, I let Kyle read the letter.

"How do you feel about this?" he asks, handing it back to me. I haven't stopped crying since we came inside.

"It's a lot," I say, parroting what I told Meredith. "I'm probably always going to be a little bit mixed up when it comes to her. The fact that you both wanted me when I've spent my life thinking I was a throwaway is screwing with my world view." I try to make it sound lighthearted.

"I thought she'd run," he admits, a tear running down his cheek. "I hurt her so much, and I figured she'd disappear."

"She probably would have."

"But I also knew when she left. Your aunts told me. I knew then that she wouldn't vanish with you in the middle of the night."

"Then why didn't you come back then," I ask. It's time to fill in all the last blanks. No more wondering. No more secrets.

He looks up at me with sadness, and for the first time, he looks old.

"You were eleven. I know better now that I'm a bit more grown up, and I've watched my sisters with their own kids. I assumed you didn't need me anymore at that point. What good would having me as a father do when you had already grown up so much? I can't believe how wrong I was. We lost so much time."

"We don't have to lose anymore, Dad." I get up from my seat and wrap him up in a hug.

After a few hours of getting to know my aunt, I bring Helena and Dad back to my house to meet the family. When I turn the deadbolt, I hear shushing from inside.

"Surprise!"

My forehead crinkles in confusion as I step in and find everyone I love in one space. There's a congratulations banner, a full buffet of food, and even a few gifts on the counter. Leave it to the Peters sisters to organize a party on short notice. It doesn't take me long to realize that this is in celebration of my college acceptance when I notice everyone is wearing an article of clothing I made. The thoughtfulness is overwhelming. How did I ever doubt them? How did I ever doubt all this? My aunts raised me. My friends love me. My teachers supported me. And my mother and father cared enough to sacrifice their own needs for mine. Of course, nothing is that simple and idyllic, but at this moment, I let it be.

Filling my second plate with spaghetti pie, Norah walks up beside me, running her fingers over the handles on the spoons in the various dishes. Before I can over think it, I set down my plate and grab her by the wrist, tugging her behind me. Norah towers over and could stop me if she wanted to. In the comfortable safety of my bedroom, I let her go. She sat on my bed while I paced the room.

"What's troubling you, kid?" she asks, unable to leave the room in silence.

The boldness I felt only a moment ago evaporated and fled the room much like I had wished I could. I can't look up, but the question burns inside my throat like a hot poker, and it escapes, "Do you like me?"

I hear her weight shift forward on the mattress. I glance up at her from under my eyelashes. Her elbows balance on her knees, and her eyebrows knit close together, revealing deep-set wrinkles between them. In all the years I've known her, she's never changed—the same haircut, tracksuits, t-shirts, and tennis shoes. I wonder if the way I've leaned into my signature style isn't something all my own.

"I love you. You know that."

I sink onto the mattress beside her and say, "I know you love me. I don't doubt that you love me, but do you like me?"

The last part cracks my voice. She's not letting me off the hook, studying my face like she's never seen me.

"Like with my mom," I begin again, trying to explain. "I love her. Even when I hated her, I loved her, but I didn't like her. And I wonder, all the time, if that's how you see me."

I'm crying. I knew I would, but I tried to hide it from her. I try to fight it. I know that Norah is the one I want approval from the most. We always want it from the person who won't give it to us. I knew there was nothing I could do that would be unforgivable to either Shawna or Meredith, but I've always been worried that I'm not enough for Norah.

She sighs and lays back against my bed, staring up at the glow-in-the-dark stars and planets. I join her.

"I never thought I'd live in this house again," she begins. "When I left Harpersgrove, I declared to anyone who would listen that I would never return. There was nothing more humbling than when my husband left me, and I had to come back to live with my two sisters. I mean, Shawna's husband died, and Meredith's at least had the decency to be gay, but mine came home one day and said that I disgusted him, and he couldn't pretend anymore."

I stay frozen, fearful that sudden movements might send her hurdling away. The aunts never talked about their married lives.

"When I moved back in, I closed myself into my room and refused to come out of bed for over a week. I got a job telemarketing because I was too embarrassed to leave the house. My life had absolutely no purpose anymore. Then, one night, the living room filled with the lights from police cars. Two men came to the door to tell us that our brother and his wife were dead, and sitting in the back of the police cruiser was my niece."

I've never heard this story before. We tend to avoid the conversation of my grandparents like it's some kind of secret. Honestly, we avoid most painful conversations.

"And as much as I was in shock and hurt, I thought, 'Here it is, here's what I can do with my life.' I loved your mother so fiercely, and there were plenty of times I forgot she wasn't actually my daughter. She was fun, interesting, super cool, and I loved being with her and then—" she stops herself.

"Then she had me?" I ask, turning my attention back to the ceiling.

"Yes," Norah answers honestly. "Then, the drugs. Rosie, I don't know if you can even imagine the shock and sadness of watching her slip like that. You were such a little thing."

"I think I have some idea."

"I let her down," she cries, sitting up straight on the bed. "I let her down immensely, and I'll never forgive myself." Her broad shoulders shake softly as she cries. "I couldn't make the same mistakes with you. Maybe if I'd been tougher on your mom, she'd still be here. I know I've never been easy on you, but I had to do better for you. You deserved that. Rosie, it's never been that I don't like you. How could I not? You're incredible! I don't like myself for how I failed your mom, and I love and like you too much to repeat my failings."

I gather my thoughts before I roll up to a sitting position beside her.

"You didn't fail her. She was an addict, and some terrible things happened to her in her life. How she dealt with it was the only way she could stand it. You gave her a home, and you gave her a family, and you loved her. You haven't failed me either."

"I don't know," I hear from the doorway, to find Shawna and Meredith holding up the frame. "There was that summer she signed you up for tennis camp. That seems like a failure to me," Meredith jokes.

"You still have the scar on your forehead from getting hit with the racket," Shawna adds as the two sit on either side of us. In unison, my family falls back on my bed. Effortlessly, my hands find theirs.

"Yeah, tennis camp wasn't my finest hour. Lesson definitely learned," Norah laughs, squeezing my fingers.

Out of nowhere, a joyful laugh bubbles up from my diaphragm and out of my mouth. I sense their confusion before the giggle rolls into a roar.

"We are the weirdest family unit I know," I gasp between laughs.

"Not a penis in sight!" Shawna exclaims, saying that we are no good to anyone.

"Then at least we know for sure we did one thing right," Meredith giggles before sitting up. As someone who focuses on all the little details, it's amazing how many I've missed right here in my house. The wrinkles around Meredith's mouth have deepened, no doubt frowning over Mom and me, and Shawna's face looks exhausted. I hate that I've cost her any amount of sleep.

"In all honesty, the three of you really come together to make the perfect parent," I giggle, wiping away a few tears that streamed back into my ears. "Norah's the hard-ass, Shawna's the Tollhouse cookie mom, and Meredith is basically Yoda. You gave me a hell of a childhood. Thank you."

The four of us hold hands like we're summoning something into the room, and I can only hope that Holly is there to see us. "Do you guys realize," Norah says, rubbing her thumb over my knuckles. "When we drop this one off at school, it'll be the first time we haven't had a kid in the house in over twenty years?"

Over the next few days, I read my mom's letter probably a hundred times. I keep coming back to what Beattie had told me. If a letter could tie everything up in a neat little bow for Mom, why couldn't it do the same thing for me? I could write down my jumbled thoughts. It's not perfect, of course. Nothing is. But it'll be enough to help me move on.

I don't want to forget her. She'll always be my mother. And it kills me that she had hoped we would reconcile one day. That wasn't meant to be. The best thing I can do is reconcile with myself—give me enough grace to forgive my mistakes and move forward into the future that my mother made possible. The letter isn't Shakespeare, but it's me.

I don't know what happens after we die. I don't know what I want done with my own body after I go. I do know that don't want to be buried in the ground. Standing at my mother's headstone, I wonder what it feels like for her in there. I know it's a ridiculous question. She can't feel anything. But I wonder if she's hanging around and aware of what's happening. The leaves are back full and bloomed on the trees, cascading a shade over her and my grandparents' headstones. They're all here too soon.

Meredith offered to come with me. Kyle had offered as well. But I knew that I needed to do this by myself. We need to say goodbye, Holly and me. I need to let go, not of her, but of the anger. This is the only way I can think of to do that. The wind starts to kick up, sending the leaves swimming in circles through the air. She would like that. I pull out my letter that's folded, like origami, in the pocket of my jacket. I even used a nice card stock that Bella lent me. For me, this was not an occasion for loose-leaf. I do my best to steady myself.

To my surprise, though, I don't want to cry. I didn't cry at her funeral, and I don't want to cry now. Unlike all the times before, I'm not sad or angry. If anything, I'm calm. It's time for peace. It's time to let go and say goodbye. In my letter, I thank her. I thank her for the life that I am living. I tell her about Parsons, the pie shop, and the girls. I tell her all the little details of my life that she missed. But even when I wrote it, there was no hint of malice. There will always be little feelings of sadness and loss that I have for the things she missed.

But she was right. The woman she was when she left could never have been the mother I needed. Her love for me was unconditional. What she did was selfless, and I love her for that. I told her in the letter about meeting Kyle and that I understood why she fell for him. I thank her once again for telling the truth. I'm sure it was hard for her to let go of that secret. What a gift she gave me to know that he did want me. When I finish reading the letter, I fold it back into its origami shape and place it under a rock next to her headstone. I don't want the caregivers of the cemetery to take it away. I don't know if I'll come back here. I will always carry her with me. Holly Peters was—is—my mother. Regardless of anything else, I love her more than I have words to say.

That night, overwhelmed with emotion, I tried my best to sleep. I fall harder and faster than I have in years, but it's not a restful sleep. I'm conscious, but helpless. I'm back on the lake of black water. I foolishly hoped that it would go away when I let go of at least some of the pain. But the black water is a part of me. It's something I must hold onto whether I like it or not. The blackness feels like an inky spiderweb, grabbing each of my limbs, trying to pull me back under until only my face remains on the surface. And it's when I am ready to finally submit and accept that this is a part of me that I hear my name across the distance in a booming roar. With that single word, the water shakes and suddenly calms. The blackness begins to fade away as though by magic, leaving only a turquoise-blue sea around me. Still in the middle of the dream, I pull myself to my feet and stand on top of the water. The unease is gone. All that's left is—happiness.

My mother is across the lake from me, far enough that I cannot reach her. It's my mother the way I remember her in my most beautiful memories. She's wearing jeans and tennis shoes, a long-sleeved black sweater, and her hair pushed back with a headband. She sparkles as she smiles at me. I want to run to her, but I am cemented in place.

"Hey there, Rosie Rose," she calls out to me, her words reverberating like an echo.

"Is this real?" I call back.

She smiles wider. "It's as real as you want it to be, baby."

"Mom," I begin, happy tears filling my eyes.

She raises her hand to stop me. Her voice is soft and angelic, and she says, "We don't need any more words, Rosie. I can feel everything that I need to know inside my heart. Can't you?"

I place my hand over my heart, instantly knowing what she means. There's a warmth flooding every inch of my body, and it's comforting, like a hug, as if she's wrapped around my entire soul.

"I will always be there, Rosie. I will always be that feeling. You can rest now, baby. You don't need this place anymore."

I awake with a start, tears running down my cheeks, dampening my pillow. I run my fingers through my hair, across my chest, and down my arms. Was it real? Was she really there?

"It's as real as you want it to be," she had said. I still feel the warmth in my heart. I hope that she's right. I hope that's where she'll stay.

My mother may have told me I could rest, but sleep seems impossible. Instead of being on edge, I'm wired, too elated to sleep. I put on comfy clothes and head to the pie shop. No more sneaking through the windows. I honestly wanna work on the prom dresses, but my sewing machine will wake up the aunts, and that's not fair. I can make a pie instead.

Harpersgrove feels different tonight on my walk. This town, with its long memory and complicated people, seems a little more beautiful today. I realize I love it here. I love the fabric and flower shops, the drugstore, and—of course—the pie shop. I love my favorite seat in the art classroom at the high school. I love the front porch swing at Goldie's house and the uncomfortable seats at the movie theater. And I love the sweet, comforting embrace of those well-worn black sheets that have turned heather gray on my bed under a blanket of stick-on glow-in-the-dark stars. My home only has to be special to me. It's the places and the people that make sense, and this town will always matter.

I set to work in my known rhythm in the kitchen. It's a choreographed ballet that brings me comfort. There's no fruit I would rather use than blackberries since this is all about Mom. Strawberries, blueberries, and cherries all have their day, but blackberries will always shine as long as I am around. Holly Peters deserved to shine, and I will do it for her.

When the pie is cooling, I cut myself an oversized slice and slap it on a plate with a scoop of ice cream. I sit on one of the familiar neon stools at the long counter and eat, tasting the joy I have baked. Because isn't that what a pie is, edible joy?

I have one bite when I hear rapping on the glass behind me. I don't know what I expected to see, but Joshua standing there makes me choke. He is as effortlessly beautiful as he has always been. His well-worn leather jacket lays perfectly over his white shirt and jeans. He's like James Dean, lost out of time. He leans against the locked door and smiles that crooked smile at me, waiting for me to approach. I do, of course.

"Hey baby," he says with that sweet smile, his expression softening. "When I didn't hear from you, I got nervous. I figured you'd be here."

I don't say anything. I stand there, staring.

"Are you gonna let me in?"

I don't move a muscle. A nerve twitches in his now tense jaw.

"Come on, Rosie, don't be stupid. You know I love you. I got scared. Haven't you ever felt scared before?"

I'm quiet.

"Will you let me in? Can't we can talk about this?"

I want him to tell me the truth. I want him to tell me that he never loved me. He only wanted to have sex with me. I want him to tell me all these things. I want to tell him that I'm going to college. I want to tell him that I have fixed my friendships and that I have my family. I want to tell him I will survive despite him. I want him to tell me that I know I was a game to him, but that would involve continuing to play, and I'm done.

For me, closure might be an illusion. Life isn't an 80's teen movie where all the conflicts get wrapped up with a nice little bow; where the bad guy has some kind of redemption arc or cosmic retribution. This is the real world, and I no longer want to play this unwinnable game.

No more explanations, no more tears or declarations of false love. I want to move on. It wasn't cowardice that froze me in place the last time I saw him here. I now realize it was peace and self-preservation, and I deserve at least that much.

A soft smile spreads to my lips as I reach up for what I'm sure he thinks is the dead bolt, but in reality is the blinds. They fall shut, and for a moment, I spot a peculiar look on his face. It's an odd mixture of anger, confusion, and even a touch of sadness. The best part is that it's none of my business anymore.

He starts banging on the door, screaming my name, and calling me every horrible thing he can think of. Not too long ago, that would have destroyed me. Now, I go back to my seat and savor the joy of warm pie, sitting on a plate: my blackberry pie, seeds and all.

My mother would be proud.

I now understand that reality is simpler than I ever noticed. My happily ever after was never a boy. It's me and this beautiful life I will lead because I will make it for myself, and that's more than enough.

I am enough.